# MUSINGS

Crawford Washington
Editor

Books recently published by 3 Muses in 2005-7

*Waiting for Better Times*
*Night Wolves*
*Masks*
*Eutopian Essays*
*Tropomorphoses*
*Global Emergency Actions*
*Coyote Redux*
*Carbon Dreams*

Books to be published by Urania Science Press in 2008

*Eutopias*
*Ecologies of Cultures*
*REplacing*

# MUSINGS



## Best Short Stories on the Continent

Crawford Washington
Editor

Calliope Press
Sarasota
2007

**Acknowledgments**: Poetry in "Masks" from various works of A. M. Caratheodory, including *Amphibian Dreams* and *Masks*.

**Photographs**: Spokane bus station 1985 (page 6), Country Club of Virginia 1963 (8), With Merleau-Ponty 1976 (73), Nabokov's birthday 1994 (76), Drug Clinic 1975 (133), Married to Min 1972 (136), Altazor forest cedar 1999 (150), After a marathon 1976 (164), University of Arizona conference 1979 (175), Altazor wildlife tree 1998 (178), Getting the truck ready to leave 1999 (193), Fric and Frac 1986 (199), At the Davenport bar 1984 (206), UA computing center 1973 (210), Chipmunk 2000 (216), Moffitt Cancer center 2005 (229), University ID card 1986 (239), Lecturing 1999 (244), Bulgaria 2002 (256), Russia 1999 (256), The home bus 2003 (258), University lecture hall 2004 (262), Legend wolf 2000 (264), With Pan and Arctic 1984 (266), Examining evidence 2003 (269), Another field trip 2002 (273), At the Roadhouse bar 2004 (275).

This Calliope Press Edition of *Musings*
is Published by
3 Muses Books, Mozart & Reason Wolfe

 Published in the United States by Mozart & Reason Wolfe, Ltd., Wilmington., Delaware

Prepared and produced by Calliope Press, Sarasota
Designed by Rian Garcia Calusa Designs, Cortez

Please address all correspondence for the author, M&RW, Ltd., Calliope Press, Palouse Poets Collective, or Rian Garcia Calusa Designs to:
editor@3musesbooks.com
mozart@reasonwolf.com
design@riangarciacalusa.com

Second Edition
ISBN 798-0-911385-39-7 (paper)
Manufactured in the United States of America

## *Contents*

**Dedicated** respectfully to Benjamin Turnaday. We all miss his lively conversations, wild ideas and enthusiastic hugs.

His auto-obituary from 6 June 2005: "Benjamin Turnaday died in joy last week. It took him a lifetime to learn to be joyful, and for those of you on whom he learned he apologizes and asks that you keep practicing yourselves. His formal education also took way too long, and never was finished, but he kept his attention on the big picture, that is, on the relation of human beings to wild beings and wild places. He asks you to spend time with The Nature Conservancy, the Green Party, and Save the Children Federation, or with the groups of your choice. Converse, create, and make things a little wild."

This book is illustrated with photographs of Benjamin, working and playing, over the past 55 years, by his Friends at the Palouse Poets Collective, Rian Garcia Calusa, and the Eutopian Network.

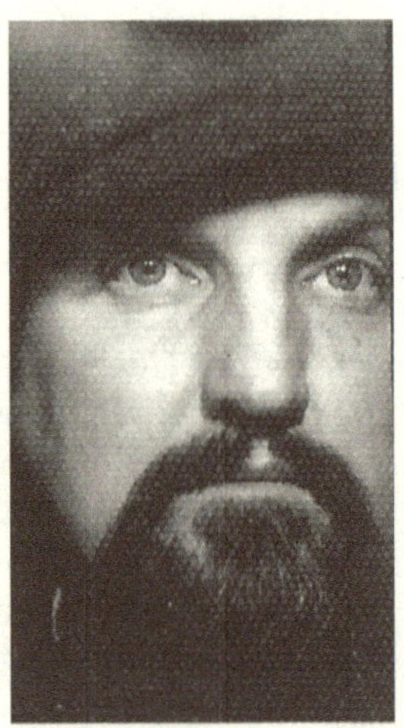

# *The Comedy of War and Uncertainty*

## The Hecathlon

The Month I was the Greatest Athlete in the World
by *Marcus Ryan*

Our hero woke before dawn, dressed quietly and left the house. He jogged down to the South river and undressed. Then dove in. The water was cold, so he swam quickly. Where the river turned the corner he saw Gene, Carl and Mike standing on the dock. When they saw him they starting taking off their sweat suits and stretching—this third-person technique is not working. The hero is me, Des Turner. You're asking, if I am the greatest athlete in the world, why haven't you heard of me? Fair question. Because I am not great at any one event. Most famous athletes are great at one part of one sport, like batting or pitching in baseball, and are forgettable at the other parts. I am very good at many sports, so I invented the dodecathlon and I have the highest number ever recorded for it, 9500. I am going to tell you about it. Meanwhile—

When we were all in the water, we took off upstream. It gradually seemed warmer as we worked to outdo each other. After 20 minutes we turned around and swam back to the dock, racing the last 100 meters. I was fourth. I was always fourth in practice. I simply had trouble competing in imaginary, unwitnessed contests.

I never really thought of being a great athlete. I just enjoyed swimming. But, baseball was my passion, not watching it, but playing it, pitching, fielding, batting, and running the bases. I became very good in our sandlot league. I pitched left or right handed and I batted left or right. In my favorite game of all time, I pitched the opposite to each hitter and hit three home runs, two left and one right. I almost ruined it by deciding to jump over the opponent's bench after the last home run—I didn't quite clear the bench, tripped and the entire team ended up on their backs in the dust. I was embarrassed because I felt clumsy; they were angry because they thought I knocked over the bench on purpose.

I never tried out for our high school team. I always felt it was a step down from the sandlot teams. After a decade of swimming and ball, I became exposed to other sports. Football at the high school, then track, wrestling and basketball. At wrestling it was impossible to pin me. Alas, my weakness was that I was not very good at pinning my opponents.

My father, Wes (short for 'Soyouwes') was good with weapons and targets, which I found odd since he spent the war in a laboratory.

I always wondered if this was how he compensated, but I never dared to ask him. We started out with darts. He kept the darts locked up when we did not play. We found these to be somewhat dull, once we got good at it. Sometimes Evan and I would go outside and put the dartboard on the wood pile. Then we would walk twenty or thirty yards away and throw them as hard as we could. We became quite good at "distance darts" as we called the game.

When we were older, he bought us a bow, which we shared. We made our own targets with bales of hay, which we stacked and pinned paper targets to. We became good at that also. Because we were senseless boys, we also shot at squirrels and people's pets, until we were good at moving targets and had to stop before the neighbors got too suspicious. When we went to camp one year, we took all the medals in archery.

When I was fourteen, we graduated to rifles. Due to neighborhood rules, we had to join a shooting club for that. We all had a natural bent to put small holes into small targets with small-bore weapons. After a year, we all won medals in that also.

Our town had a public swimming pool. It was our practice to go there every day. And after the first year we all had jobs there. Me as a lifeguard assistant. Ryan and Evan as pool assistants, cleaning up messes and topping up the chlorine.

I started diving, also. The board was a wooden board but had good action. I found a short book in the library with some black and white pictures of the basic dives. I became a fair diver, doing a good assortment of twisting and somersaulting dives. One day when I was practicing, the women's coach asked for help with girl's water ballet. At first all they wanted was someone to dive through a circle of kicking legs, which I could do. Then I started doing one and a half and two and a half somersaults. I also became accomplished at changing into a swimsuit in a car, since the places we performed usually had only one locker room.

As I worked with the girls, I started to think of new ways to add dives to their routines, so that sometimes I would dive a long shallow dive when they were at the end of the pool, then come up between them, do a few kicks, and swim back underwater to the one-meter board, jump out of the water, half twist to catch the end of the board and swing myself back up for the conclusion.

I became not only intimately acquainted with the girls, from missing the dives or losing my suit or accidently pulling down one of their suits, but I almost liked one of them.

I practiced every kind of new dive, learning or inventing twisting dives that I could work into the water ballet routines.

The first time I saw Joe Benson, he was on the diving board. He had been doing simple warm-ups, front dives tuck, then pike, then layout, Then half twists from each position. I said do something hard. He ignored me. I started diving, trying some of my best somersaults and twisting dives to show off. After a while, he walked out slowly, stepped high, came off the board into a reverse somersault, but landed back on the board and did an easy one and a half somersaults forward into the water. I envisioned myself doing that.

I asked him to teach me. He said, maybe, in his offhand way. It took me a year to do that backward-forward dive. By then, we acted as a team. I had abandoned the water ballet, so that we could give exhibitions at various pools around the state. We also worked up a comedy routine, where he would be trying a world-class dive and I would run out afterwards and miss the first bounce and careen off the side of the board and land flailing in the water. I also developed many double-bouncing dives, such as a seven and a half somersault off the three-meter board. Then a five and a half somersault off the one-meter. Of course, I should accurately say that these dives entered around the last half somersault, often becoming seven and a quarter or seven and three-quarters, much to my pain and chagrin.

When Joe left to work in Florida, diving at some theme park there, I wanted to go, but my parents refused to allow it. So, I started diving for the local team, the Sharks. Shortly afterwards I won the local, regional and state titles. My required dives always seemed weak and uninspired, but the complex optional dives made up for it. On occasion, there was no posted degree of difficulty for a dive I did, so the judges would assign one from some similar, easier dive.

It turned out that, in addition to trick diving and formal competition diving, that I was extremely good at swimming the butterfly, mainly because no one else could master the kick. So I became a specialist on our swim team. Our town had another swim team, the Dolphins, who only swam in the summer; we were driven to Staunton to practice in the winter at the small overheated YMCA pool. On our medley relay I swam butterfly, and on the freestyle relay I swam freestyle. Even with freestyle I used the dolphin kick for the first fifteen meters underwater (and then for backstroke and breaststroke, also, when I didn't get disqualified). At first we were only regional champions, then state champions. But in 1964, we won the national AAU National Championship for the 400 medley relay.

Usually, towards the end of every swimming meet I would participate in the diving competition. Oddly enough, I was always tired. Then they switched diving to first in the meets and I would be tired for the swimming events. The coach, knowing this, would always say, "Des, I need you to get third place for the team points". Once I decided that I could get the state record in 100 butterfly, so I went out fast, very fast, faster than I ever had, but I faded in the last few meters and ended up third, only much more tired than my usual third place.

In diving I had no such restrictions by the coach, who didn't pay much attention—he assumed I would get first or second in the meets and counted on it. One year I skipped the state championship and went to a national meet at Kelly pool in Philadelphia. I was third. I should have done better, but I was nervous and uneven. Two years later I started at the state level again, getting third the first year, second the second years and first place for the third year in Richmond. That year the Olympic coach, Dick Smith, came to watch me and offered me a chance to come to a demonstration and workshop of his in Phoenix. He brought one diver from his "stable." She was excellent in required dives but uninspired in optionals. The coach said I would never go farther without a coach and that I would never make the Olympics without his help. I foolishly said I was happy with my current coach, myself. He told me some story about courts, judges, lawyers, and clients who represented themselves. I wasn't in court, although I suppose I was being judged. I was sure that my parents would never let me go anyway since I was being groomed to be a chemist like my father and had a long academic schedule to keep. I could hear the echoes of my mother's voice, saying, "Dekaeayough (not Deskai or the preferred Des), focus on your career."

After 1960 there was a new resident in Waynesboro, Gunther Hess. He claimed to have been on the German fencing team, whose responsibility was to train Hitler and some of his officers in this gentlemanly and warriorly sport. Although I seem to remember in its earlier manifestation in Germany it resulted in many, many scars on the faces of the gentlemen. In any case, he organized a fencing team after school. Me and four others, including two from the local military academy, came daily and learned and practiced.

I bought a foil from the proceeds of my paper route or life guard activities—the money went into one account, so I didn't pay much attention to the exact source. We learned the basic stance, movements, and positions. It soon sorted out that three of us were far better than the others. Dirk Woolworth, a slight kid with a scar on his face, who fought with great finesse left-handed, Chris Stone, a hulking beefy military-academy guy who fought with right-handed strength and resoluteness rather than skill or finesse, and me, who was ambidextrous and planned my bouts according to the opponents weaknesses or strengths.

Because there was no state level competitions, the best would go to the national meet. My first duel was with Chris. He threatened to slice me to pieces. If we had to fight with tongues, he would have won. I watched his approach. As he tried to stab downward—his height was an advantage—I swung sideways and scored on his chest. The next time I tried that, he stabbed downward, ripping the rubber point off and cutting the back of my hand. I was too excited to feel the pain, but I had to get it bandaged right away. I was asked if I wanted to stop. I thought that was unnecessary. But, I was distracted and he scored the next point quickly. So, I took a break and asked Rich if I could borrow his foil for the rest of the match. I was reluctant to use mine left-handed, although I had practiced with it. So, I switched to left-handed. That confused Chris and I scored running away, literally, as he thought he could race in for a quick point. When I took my mask off, there was a bright scratch on the left side of my arm from another of his strong misses. I watched him take off his jacket. I noticed that he had a new foil with a pistol-grip handle.

I offered Rich my foil for our match. He declined with a smile. I smiled too, knowing that he thought being left-handed gave him an advantage. I had always fought against him right-handed, so I decided to use my own foil in my left hand for this match. It would also give my right hand a rest. We were evenly matched and each scored two points quite rapidly. For the final point, we went back and forth down the strip (the *piste*) three times. I had been studying his movements for weakness. When he lunged again I leaned far over the strip, almost leaning horizontally and scored. The judge immediately called a foul, which I argued against it for a few minutes to no avail. My feet had not left the strip, although he claimed one foot was off the strip. The point continued. Neither of us could get an advantage. Fencing rarely lasted more than a few attacks and ripostes. Then he touched my armpit and received a score although I thought it missed the target area by several inches. Again, I could not prevail against the judge and lost the match.

Although Rich was supposed to go to Detroit by dint of his victory in our local championships, Gunther decided that I was the best candidate, an assessment that I agreed with. My ability to switch to right or left. My subtlety and patience. Humility. Openness.

So, I went with him to the nationals. I had never been in an electrified competition before. Although I preferred the idea to the unreliability of human judgment, I kept getting tangled up. My first match went quite badly. I only scored once. The second match was very close. After losing the first two points I came back to take the next two. I was getting used to my electronic leash. The last point I simply tried too hard to win, instead of waiting for an opening. I had lost both of my matches. Gunther won both of his. I watched him and compared his style with mine. Although I was more acrobatic and athletic, and perhaps more graceful in the long reaches, he was perfectly poised and perfectly precise. We won our division team title in Detroit. I could not decide whether to feel great or miserable, or both.

The next year I went to college. Despite a scholarship from Columbia, I went to Penn State so I could be on the gymnastics team. Their chemistry program was rated highly but was surrounded by the uninspired humanity and social courses that guarded it with their mass. I sat in class, but my heart only started beating in the afternoon.

Trampoline was my specialty. Actually, I was most graceful when I was in the air, and I was incomparable in that medium. I never became good at strength moves, on rings or high bar, but I became serviceable on the floor exercise, parallel bars and pommel horse.

We practiced with the harness for difficult moves, the coach screaming at us the entire time that we were animals. Yes, I thought, trained animals that would rather be sleeping or rutting. Many of the jokes were about the hardness of the anatomy of female gymnasts, but when the others went on dates, I practiced. Motorcycles were the choice of transportation, but I could not afford a bicycle, much less.

The next year we won the national championship. I only performed on the trampoline. I never got to do my floor exercise routine.

The following year I dropped out. I spent the year running and writing, working as a gardener and trying to get published—even I was shocked by the subversion that the humanities forced on me. The first ten-dollar payment I used to open my account was the most I ever had in it. I finally spent it for groceries.

When I went back to school at Sewanee, *The* University of *The*

South, I ran track and practiced with the football team, although that team was never formal and we never played real games. I enjoyed being quarterback. Although I was never accurate with a pass, I was very difficult to catch. Most of our plays ended with me running or handing off the ball.

I ran at nights. It seemed so much faster, After my youngest brother died in an accident, I ran faster and more often. Running was my only form of expression.

I dropped out of school. I got a job and saved up for another school. Every time I went to school I dropped out after a summer school or a semester. Every time I dropped out of school, I got a good job as a chemist in a lab. As the jobs got better, I ran less and took classes only part-time.

Then I got a job at a university in eastern Washington state. I started playing racquetball and tennis with a group of other engineers. Then I started running again. And, when I lost weight and got my air back, I started swimming and diving.

Some of the guys were in the ROTC and they had to meet certain standards of fitness. So, I started running with them. One day we were running on the golf course. We were passed by three Kenyans, whom the university had imported to help the track team. So, we sped up. The others dropped off after a six hundred yards. I got close, but could get no closer. Then, they pulled away after three or four miles. I nodded and wondered what it would take to become that fast.

I started going longer distances. I ran between the two towns, from Moscow to Pullman and back. That was 17 miles round-trip. One day I was running towards the stadium in Moscow. There was a hundred yard dash ready to start. I accelerated. Just as I was parallel to the start the gun went off. They sprinted, I sprinted. But, the road I was on went up hill. The seconds slowed down. They gained on me but I accelerated with a final burst. If I didn't finish before the fastest of them, then it was a tie. I slowed down, went around the campus and ran back to Pullman.

One day, after Gil and I had played a fast, violent game of racquetball, I asked him if he was good at any other sports. He said no. After running with Jaromil one day, I asked him if he was good at any other sports. He said no. I didn't think more about for a while.

I was playing handball with Greg, when we got on the topic. He had been a baseball player, wrestler, and a runner, an odd combination that I could understand. He even said that he had been an auto racer in Tucson one year—I wanted to hear more about that. I suggested a friendly competition. That we go running next time, around the university track, maybe time ourselves for the mile or

5000 meters. We did. We were closely matched.

I decided to take a master class in swimming, mostly so I would have to swim, but also I was curious about new stroke techniques. I practiced with the women's team sometimes (there did not seem to be a men's team). I was good, usually second or third in the mile, but I was still excellent at butterfly. One day the women's coach, Michelle, matched me up with the best on the women's team and suggested that we race. We started dead equal. When I sped up, she sped up. When I accelerated she did. When I put everything into it, she kept pace. I suspect that she was trying to leave me behind also. But, we were too equal. She was 20; I was 50 something. Our fingertips touched on every overwater stroke. The video of the race looked like a perfect water ballet. We touched at the same time.

Her name was Nancy. After the race I asked her if she was good at any other sports. She said track, tennis and bowling. I asked if she wanted to run or bowl together. She said yes. The next day, I won the run. The following day, she beat me badly at bowling. The week after that, she humiliated me at tennis, which I had never played for more than 20 minutes—at least I felt I should be humiliated. I suggested billiards or pool, but she said it was more likely I would win at that. I suggested that we keep in touch, but she said she had a boyfriend her own age. That was okay with me. My girlfriend was older than I was, but we had grown up with the same music. What would Nancy and I ever talk about or listen to when not being physical? On the other hand, two finely-tuned athletic bodies . . . never mind.

During on of my biweekly games with Greg, a youngster barely into his 30s, I asked if he had ever really tried some other sports, such as fencing or gymnastics. He said no, but he was playing pool regularly and was taking a class in judo. So, after work, we started playing pool. Once in a while we went over to the gym to the wrestling area and tried to throw each other. It was very instructive. I started taking my own class in Tai Chi.

One day, after discussing how to rob banks or defraud insurance companies to get rich, I suggested that we try to initiate a different kind of contest. A much more formal contest, where we each would choose five or six sports—not events in a single sport, but different sports—and then compete in one event in each of them. He thought it was a great idea. I suggested that we think about which sports and then think about a scoring system.

I talked to Nancy the next day at swimming practice. She was not enthusiastic—must be the age difference or sex difference—but she said she would think about it.

I went home to my girlfriend Tina and asked her if she wanted to participate. She said only if she could choose finger sports, like typing or tiddlywinks. Later, I thought of one sport she would be really good at, but she pointed out that it was an art, not a sport. I bowed my head respectfully and agreed.

The next swim practice I talked to Nancy again, after the interminable kicking and stroking exercises. She said she had thought about and was 'mildly excited, whatever.' Also, she had an idea of how to score it. The best way might to be to take percentages of current world records in each event in each sport. I asked if it might be better to use an absolute system, maybe set the scores to records for one year, like 1976 or 1992. We both agreed to look at the scoring systems.

I made up some arbitrary rules. For instance, it had to be individual sports, not team sports like football or baseball (well, there goes my strength). It had to be a human body sport, which let out horseback riding or auto racing (there goes one of Greg's strengths).

On a Friday in February, I met with Greg, Nancy, and Jaromil to have the first contest, running. Since Jaromil had pulled a muscle on the track the week before, he said he would be the judge for this contest, and take notes, and participate in any subsequent contests with us, if any of us lived. We decided to call this a dodecathlon, and treat it as two separate competitions of 12 events each. Of course we could have gone to 18 events or 24 or 100, but who would have known those names. There would be 12 events in 12 days, and each athlete chooses six in common with the others and then 6 of her own. Points are scored against world records, set at 1000 points. By the time we finished talking, it was too late to run. And, we had some more figuring to do anyway.

**The events**

So, we met at Karl Marx pizza restaurant early on Monday evening. We decided to each choose six events, then we would compete in all the events. There were only three of us this time. Nancy thought that might be six too many, especially since we decided to only have one event per day (after work or school). Greg thought that it might be unmanageable if we ever had four or more people. Nancy wrote down the list; the number indicated the order of events to be played. We decided to do it alphabetically to avoid any favoritism. We also decided that each event should be scored at a maximum of 1000 points, thus equalizing each event, so that one sport was not considered to be harder than the others (although I believed that some sports, such as gymnastics, were far harder than others, such as tennis, and should be given more points—perhaps on a degree of difficulty basis. No one else agreed). The maximum for all twelve would be 12,000 points. Greg pointed out that we could use some team sports, such as baseball or basketball, if we chose just one individual aspect of the team sport, such as throwing or hitting, but we decided to keep to individual sports. There were, of course, sports that we did not choose to play, such as pole vault, hurdles, skydiving, or skiing. Perhaps in the championships next year someone would select those sports.

We hired three judges from the computer science department, Jaromil, Neil, and Phil, and two from athletics, Rex the track coach and Hamud the racquetball instructor. They would rotate so that each sport would have at least three judges or timers simultaneously.

Des's List

15. Swimming (100 meters butterfly) Monday 4/4
6. Diving (six required and five optional dives) Saturday 3/26
7. Fencing (best of three matches) Sunday 3/27
9. Gymnastics (trampoline or floor exercise) Tuesday 3/29
13. Running (10,000 meters) Saturday 4/2
14. Shooting (25 shots, 10 targets) Sunday 4/3

Nancy's (she could have chose swimming, but I went first in choosing. Doubtless she thought she had a chance to knock me off in my best sport. The sports that she chose with balls might be a problem for me, though).

4. Bowling (three games) Thursday 3/24
3. Billiards (three games) Wednesday 3/23
2. Bicycling (10,000 meters) Tuesday 3/22
8. Golf (36 holes) Monday 3/28
16. Table tennis Tuesday 4/5
1. Archery (25 arrows, 10 targets) Monday 3/21

Greg's (he very cleverly chose sports that should eliminate Nancy and could also give me a hard time).

5. Boxing (6 minutes or 3 rounds) Friday 3/25
10. Judo (6 minutes) Wednesday 3/30
18. Weight-lifting (3 attempts, snatch and c&j) Thursday 4/7
11. Racquetball (3 games to 21 each) Thursday 3/31
17. Tennis (three games) Wednesday 4/6
12. Rowing 1-person (30-minute course) Friday 4/1

We decided to have the events be alphabetical, depending on the special requirements, such as a track. We decided to start the competition on Monday March 21st; temperatures would be moderate; the universities were in session, but we would also have spring break for nine days, which would reduce the competition for the equipment and playing areas.

*Round One. Archery Monday*
Archery went first. We decided to skip ranking rounds for each sport, since there was only three of us, and go straight to modified Olympics rounds. Neither would we have elimination or semi-final rounds for any sport. Nor seeding competitions. To make sure that each sport was equally weighted, each sport had a perfect score of 1000 possible points. This meant for archery, we would have to each shoot 50 arrows. Five ends of ten arrows each, with alternating ends. The target would be at 70 meters. There would be a maximum time of 40 seconds per arrow.

The bows could not be crossbows or footbows (where the arrow was drawn with both hands), but they could be longbows or modern compound bows.

Hamud agreed to be the judge, since he taught the sport every third semester at Idaho. Rex, Neil and Phil were each assigned to one of us as a scorer.

Hamud explained the scoring, "The scoring system is based on a 10-ring target. Each section of the target is worth from one to 10 points, with 10 being the best. Arrows on the dividing lines are given the higher score and deflections score where they land. Arrows that bounce off the target or pass through are also counted. The target face is set 70 meters (229 feet, 8 inches) from the shooting line and the center gold of the target is set 130 centimeters (4 feet, 3 inches) above the ground. The target is usually made of paper and has a diameter of 122 centimeters (4 feet). The target is divided into five colored rings and each ring is divided in half. The width of each color zone is 12.2 (4.8 inches) centimeters and the width of each scoring zone—half of a color zone—is 6.1 (2.4 inches) centimeters.

"The rings and the corresponding point values are as follows (from innermost to outermost): Gold inner (10 points), Gold outer (9 points), Red inner (8 points), Red outer (7 points), Blue inner (6 points), Blue outer  (5 points), Black inner (4 points), Black outer (3 points), White inner (2 points), and White outer (1 point).

"Ties are to broken with a "sudden death" overtime, where each archer shoots one arrow and the highest score wins. If tied, a second arrow is shot for highest score. If still tied, a single closest-to-the-center arrow determines the winner. Nancy, you won the draw and will go fist. Are you ready?"

She nodded and stepped to the mark. It was a sunny day with a small breeze from the west. The field, below the book store at Washington State University (Wazoo to all of us), was laid out east-west. We would rotate after every round of ten; that was figured to equalize and weather changes also.

Nancy shot first, using a modern blue bow. Her first shot was low, a blue outer ring. She made a small adjustment to her bow sight and her next shot went inner gold for ten points. Her next eight shots clustered the red circles for a total of 77.

Greg went next. His first shot barely touched the straw butt. He improved steadily. His bow was the most complex, being a compound bow. He worked back to a 58.

I was adjusting my old yew bow, which I had made five years earlier in Idaho. I knew I should be using a modern bow, but I had used this one for practicing in the woods and was comfortable with it. The modern bows had more accuracy and power. My first shot was an inner blue and then I marched steadily into the gold, but then just as steadily out to blue again for a 75.

We sat around and talked for a while on break. None of us was sure about how long a time bows had been used for hunting (30,000 years?), but we agreed that bows were used for warfare in Mesopotamia 5,000 years ago. Although archery was made obsolete by guns, the French made it into a sport, and now technology had refined it in many ways.

We repeated series for another ten arrows. Greg went first; his worst shot was an inner white ring but his best was a bull's eye. We had a judgmental decision on his third shot. The arrow head split the line between inner and outer blue; the judge ruled that it was outer blue, even though the shaft seemed to have rotated toward the inner circle. We had a short discussion about how the lines were divided. He improved his score to 74. I went second and scored my best at 80. Nancy finished with 79. She was still the leader overall.

For the third end, I went first. My first shot I held for a long time (38 seconds) before releasing, waiting for the wind and the moment. It hit the gold outer, high rather than low. I made the next shots evenly getting a gold inner and several gold outers, ending up with 76. I felt just right.

Nancy went next. She held too long on her first and technically, it should not have counted, but the judge asked us if we would allow it; Greg and I nodded, not wanting to have technicalities dominate the first event. The shot was a gold outer ring. Her next two were blue inner rings. Her next two shots were gold inner and gold outer. Her final shots were off a little and she ended with 73 points.

Greg improved again, landing mostly in the red rings; his score was 75.

For the next round Nancy shot first. She got her best score at 80. Greg continued to improve again, adding two points to his score. And, the first three arrows I shot were in the gold center. I could not keep it up, but got my best score of the day at 87.

Greg went first for the last end, but he started badly; he recovered enough for a decent score of 76. I went next and shot well, but could not get a good grouping in the center. Nancy closed the end with another 79. We totalled the scores.

| *Name* | *End 1* | *End 2* | *End 3* | *End 4* | *End 5* | *Total* |
|---|---|---|---|---|---|---|
| Greg | 58 | 74 | 75 | 77 | 76 | 360 x 2 = 720 |
| Nancy | 77 | 79 | 74 | 80 | 79 | 389 x 2 = 778 |
| Des | 75 | 80 | 81 | 87 | 83 | 406 x 2 = 812 |

I had won. Nancy was gracious, saying that she might have to start using her old bow. Greg gave me the finger, with a smile though. We talked to the judge and scorers, thanking them, but also arranging to meet the next day for the cycling event. Nancy suggested that the next time we try field archery, rather than a range competition. It sounded intriguing, since the targets would be a different distances, and half of them would be unknown to the shooters.

That night I had a small Cuba libre with dinner, which was left-over lasagna. Tina was too tired to cook and we had leftovers from the weekend. I asked her if she wanted to come and observe. She said she preferred to spend her vacation traveling, but she might observe over the weekend, if I could remember what sport that was. I suggested that we devote the evening to art.

*Round Two. Bicycling Tuesday*

For cycling, Nancy's choice sport, we decided to forgo the complicated Olympic event and stick with a triathlon approach. We set out a course going from Pullman to Moscow on the old upper highway, around Moscow, and back on Highway 8 (approximately 25 miles or 40 kilometers). This was a classic race on a pre-determined course between two cities, although it combined mild elements of cross-country mountain biking, especially the gravel road, but no obstacles or mud holes. No outside assistance would be allowed. A car would follow, but there would be no lead car, team car, or director car. There would be no time trial or individual pursuit.

There were no rules on the bicycles, either. Greg had a hybrid mountain bike with 27 speeds (three sprockets, good grief). I had my old 1975 white, ten-speed Raleigh, with new tires, brakes and everything freshly adjusted. Nancy had some new contraption with five-spoke carbon-fiber "mag" wheels. It looked like it had 18 gears. There were no rules on clothes either. Nancy had long, tight-fitting lycra shorts and yellow lycra jersey. I thought her shoes matched the top. I nodded in appreciation, but she ignored me. So, Greg wouldn't be jealous, I nodded in appreciation of his outfit, which was jeans and t-shirt, with hard leather shoes. He ignored me. I must seem ancient. I had track shorts under a sweat suit; I had clipped the legs above my running shoes. We all had helmets. Nancy's was black and yellow, Greg's red, and mine black (my roller-blading helmet in fact), so we were color coded. Nancy and Greg had gloves; I didn't worry about that since I had new foam and rubber near the bars and levers.

Greg's wife Lacy agreed to follow the racers in their car, an older Audi. She had a first-aid kit in case of injuries. If any of us got in trouble, her role was only to pick up the pieces.

Hamud started the race. He, Jaromil and Phil had stop watches and would time us with those. I suspected they would play poker or something while we were out of sight. Nancy started out with a lead. Greg was doing well. My legs felt unused and took a mile or two to get the knots out. Then I started catching up to Greg and Nancy. The first half of the race went along the old Moscow-Pullman highway, which wound around fields and boundaries and moved up and down in the hills. It was not paved, so there was an uncomfortable disadvantage to being behind.

I began to feel more comfortable as we rode. I noticed that I caught up a little going uphill. That was going to be a problem going back to Pullman—it was all downhill, flowing along with Paradise Creek, which wasn't flowing at the moment because there was not enough sewage from Moscow. Since the first half was on gravel roads, Greg did better, as expected and pulled into a lead. About three quarters of the way, I passed Nancy. I knew that she would have the advantage on the pavement.

Greg pulled away as we came down by the athletic field and turned east towards the east side of town; we would be circling the town on another highway, Mountainview road, then the new bypass. This was the part of the race that I was uncertain about. Traffic could be a problem, although at 9:40 in the morning, the rush hour traffic of sixty cars should be settled at their destinations, north towards the highway.

I tried to keep within sight of Greg. Nancy was much further back. Fortunately there was not much car traffic. When I caught up to Greg again, near the new Safeway, he pulled away strongly. That was discouraging. I noticed Nancy seemed to be off her bike, doing something to the chain. That was encouraging.

I decided to try Greg again. As he pulled away, I kept up with him. A green ford station wagon passed us. After a mile, he slowed a little. I pulled ahead as we turned from Mountainview road to the north edge of town. Going down the steep hill towards 95, he pulled ahead again. I was content to coast.

We turned north on Main street, then by the Rosauer's supermarket, we turned southwest onto the bypass. I stayed a few meters behind, as we turned west on Highway 8, breezing by another grocery store, fast food row, the bowling alley, by the south side of the blimp hanger, for foosball and backitball, named after an alumnus who donated almost a tenth as much money as the students did from the student funds, and by the new university mall—the one to which the university essentially donated its valuable land so that merchants might be disposed to hire three or four students for minimum wage at Christmas time. Although I rarely agreed with anything the university did, I enjoyed living next to it, just for convenience to the library and gym. Now the highway followed the creek between rolling hills. We were back in Washington state again, by the old drive-in theater, now a building supply store.

Going up the next hill I passed Greg again. He sped up and we peddled side by side for a little while. He pulled ahead again and I kept off his left shoulder. I peeked behind and saw Nancy, who looked like she was closing on us. Traffic was light, but the breakdown lane was wide enough. The trucks hit us their forced air, but, on the other hand, it might have pushed us a little faster.

Nancy was only a few hundred meters behind. Greg was picking up speed as was I. Near the Water Power company, I decided to sprint, before Nancy overtook us. We were only three miles or so from the finish line, on campus by the administration building. I passed Greg and kept sprinting so he could not pass me. I kept thinking I could be going faster if I had another gear or two. Just at the entrance to Pullman, Nancy passed me. We started up the hill towards campus. I shifted and kept sprinting. As we went up the hill I gradually overhauled and passed her. My legs felt like hot rubber. She was sprinting. But, it was uphill—my specialty. As I got near the admin building, the stoplight turned red. I saw Phil, Jaromil and Hamud on the other side, waiting at the line

I turned right on red, and after the first car, which was turning left, I raced between cars and sprinted the final 50 meters. As I looked back, Nancy remounted her bike and started on the green light. Greg was in sight behind her, but could not overtake her. That was how we finished. I expected Nancy to protest the stoplight move, but she only shook her head.

We headed to the admin lawn and flopped down with the bikes. I felt energized and surprised. I had won the first two events. I had a vision of winning every single one. That was interrupted by Greg, who started talking about tomorrow's contest (or 'agony,' in Greek).

I didn't feel like eating at home, since Tina was working late, so I suggested eating out. Nancy said yea, but I ought to pay. Greg said he couldn't because of Lacy, but I pointed out that she was just parking the car. We all went to back to Moscow for a pizza at Karl Marx. Jaromil gave us the scores, which he had converted from the times: Des—891, Nancy—885, Greg—857.

Nancy suggested that we needed the quantitative calculations for each round, but Jaromil was able to explain his formula for bicycle racing, that related time and distance.

"What about age?" I asked.

"Sex?" "Weight?" Nancy and Greg suggested simultaneously.

"I don't think we should factor those in with ball or equipment events," Jaromil answered. "With boxing, judo, wrestling, or weight-lifting, absolutely, maybe tennis, but not running or swimming, where weight can be a disadvantage."

"Sex?" Nancy repeated.

"No thanks, not now. I had a good morning with—" Jaromil paused reflectively.

"Wrestling?" I asked, trying to remember if we were going to do that.

"No, thanks, did that, too—look, pizza!" Jaromil pointed. He seemed to be as food-oriented as ever.

*Round Three: Billiards Wednesday*

"Ah, billiards, the tragedy of my freshman year at school," Greg announced, "when I dropped out to be a professional, a one-eyed one at that." Greg went on to describe the game, "The game of billiards can be played by two or more people. Three balls are used: a 'plain' white, a 'spot' white and a red ball. Billiards is a game of pots, in-offs, cannons, and positional play. Points are awarded for scoring strokes and forfeits from opponents fouls. The winner is the player who has scored the most points at the end of an agreed period of time—"

"I thought we were playing Eight-ball?" Nancy interrupted.

"I was getting to that," Greg protested.

I tuned them both out and looked at the hall. I remembered that this used to be a furniture store next to an old hotel, now torn down and replaced by the new bypass. I walked over and inspected a few of the tables for wear on the felt.

Greg was just getting into the rules, holding a small white book at shoulder level, "These general rules apply to all pocket billiard games, unless specifically noted to the contrary in individual game rules. To facilitate the use and understanding of these general rules, terms that may require definition—"

"Did you ever see *The Hustler*?" I asked.

Nancy giggled. Greg sighed, and finished, "All games described in these rules are designed for tables, balls and equipment meeting the standards prescribed in the BCA Equipment Specifications. That's okay?"

"We agreed already," Nancy nodded.

"Who invented billiards?" I asked, always curious about the origins of games, as well as who played them for fun, money, or as death sports (I was thinking of the Aztecs).

"The French, of course," Nancy answered.

"You have French ancestors, I'll bet," I suggested, just as Greg was trying to educate us.

"Possibly the Chinese, with carved ivory balls. But, maybe the Arabs, who had a game called pall-mall, which was brought back by the Crusaders, as a booby-prize. The first modern table was built for Louis the Eleventh ..." Greg tried to educate us.

I was looking at the customers. There was one old man, smoke-yellowed fingers, playing a very careful game in the corner. I finally selected a table near the center. I asked Jaromil, who was here as the judge, if that table would do. He agreed and went over to reserve it. I noticed he also ordered a slice of pizza, French fries and a coke for himself.

Nancy was responding to something Greg had said, "You mean Eight-ball is a form of American billiards, which we will be playing and not the Classical Billiards or Snooker?"

"Exactly," Greg smiled, "Classical, or carom, Billiards is played on a table with no pockets. American Billiards is pocket billiards."

I noticed that the old man was playing on the only table in the room without pockets. Hmmm. I decided to watch him for a while. He only kept two balls on the table.

Jaromil came over with a tray of balls and three cubes of chalk. Greg immediately looked at the balls and nodded. I went to the wall to pick out a cue. When I came back, Greg was screwing his cue together. Nancy was watching, having put hers together already. I wondered if I was going to be in trouble. I went back and tried out a straighter cue from the racks.

Nancy and Greg were shooting balls to the edge of the table, trying to approach the cushion without touching it. I suggested that they play first.

Jaromil said yes, and pronounced that the tournament had officially begun. Nancy was elected to be starting player, since she had seemingly won the preliminary tests. Greg set the balls in the triangle, then removed it. Nancy put the cue ball behind the starting line. Her strike was rapid and hard—it was a good break. The balls scattered obligingly. The 14 went into the north corner pocket. She would be shooting for striped balls (numbered from 9 to 15). Of course, regardless, the black ball would have to be sunk to win.

Jaromil reminded us that after the break, we had to call the ball and the pocket for each shot. He needlessly reminded us that the cue ball had to hit one of our balls first, and that we did not have to call ricochet shots or number of cushions hit.

Nancy put in the 9, but then missed a long straight shot on the 12.

Greg took over, quickly pocketing the 1 in the south side. But, after a power shot on the 3, he hit the 8 and it bounced off the table.

As he picked it up, Jaromil reminded us that that meant he lost the game. Greg protested weakly, saying that he had not sunk the 8 ball. This inspired Jaromil to go over the rules again, noting that the game would be lost if the black ball went into an uncalled pocket, or if the cue ball jumped the table while trying to pocket the black ball. Greg nodded glumly and the first game went to Nancy 8 to 1.

In the next round, I played Nancy. After her break, and a pocketed 4, she sank the 6, but missed the 7. I quickly sank the 9 and 15 with straight shots. But, then Jaromil called a foul on the 15, so I put it back on the table on the Spot. He claimed that the cue ball struck the 3 ball first and that was not a legal object ball. I nodded, thinking to myself that that was why we had a judge, to observe and correct any irregularities. Nancy took over, but missed a difficult ricochet off the 2 ball.

I touched the 14 into the north side pocket. Called the 10 into the corner, and also got the 12 after bouncing off two cushions. I felt good, but then missed an easy shot on the 15. Nancy banked the 7, then missed the 2 again, which just hung on the lip of the corner pocket, defying gravity.

Then we entered the frustrating period of play, where there seemed to be no good shots. She played her last one by putting the cue ball against the north rail, where it would be impossible for me to use wisely. Suddenly, she pocked the 5 and 1. Only the 8 remained. She missed and I pocketed the 11, but I left the cue ball in a position to her advantage. She took the advantage and won the game, 8 to 5.

"Uhuh," I thought, things were not going to plan.

But, then the second round went to Greg, as he beat both of us, 8-6 and 8-7. And Nancy beat me, 8-6.

At the beginning of the third round I beat Greg 8-5. I started far ahead, but could not sink the 8 ball safely for many shots. He almost caught me, before I finally got it. Greg beat Nancy 8-5 and Nancy beat me 8-4—talk about your busted hierarchy.

Now it was time to switch to straight pool for the final series of three games. In this game the objective was to sink the balls in numerical order, again calling the ball and pocket.

In the first one I broke, but nothing went in. Nancy started with the 1 ball, which was conveniently sitting by a corner pocket. She could not get to the 2 and moved the cue ball to the other side of the table. I sent the ball to the center, separated from the 2 by the 9 ball. She tried to get to the 2 and moved it to an unprotected spot. I sank it, then the 3 and 4, before missing.

Surprisingly I won 8-5. Then she beat Greg 8-7. That was a good close game.

In the second round of straight, they both beat me again, but Greg beat Nancy.

I was not going to win, but I was wondering if I should try to be the spoiler for Greg or Nancy. I decided not.

I beat Nancy 9-6, then Greg beat me 9-6. For the last game, even Jaromil stopped practicing on the next table. Greg broke, but was unable to get the 1 ball. Nancy got the 1 by ricocheting it off the 6 and 8. Then she missed the 2 ball. Greg was able to drop it in the southeast corner pocket, using the ladies helper (I mean the "rest" cue). Then he ran 3, 4, and 5 with straight shots by clever placement of the cue ball each time. They exchanged singles for three turns. Then Greg ran the 12, 13, and 14. Despite Nancy's late run, Greg won the game 8-7.

Greg won the series. Nancy was second. I alas was third, quite a fall from my previous two first places.

| | *8-ball* | *8-2* | *8-3* | *s-1* | *s-2* | *s-3* | *Total* |
|---|---|---|---|---|---|---|---|
| Nancy | 8 | 6 | 5 | 8 | 6 | 7 | = 143x4.5=644 |
| Greg | 2 | 8 | 8 | 7 | 9 | 8 | |
| | | | | | | | |
| Nancy | 8 | 8 | 8 | 5 | 8 | 6 | |
| Des | 5 | 6 | 7 | 8 | 7 | 9 | =124x4.5 =605 |
| | | | | | | | |
| Greg | 8 | 8 | 5 | 7 | 9 | 9 | =168x 4.5=756 |
| Des | 7 | 7 | 8 | 8 | 6 | 6 | |

We went down the street to the New Hong Kong restaurant and made Greg pay for dinner. I had sweet and sour shrimp, my favorite since I first ate there in 1973. The decor had not changed sine 1973 either. It was quiet, only one couple at the bar having, of all things in a Chinese restaurant, chocolate milk shakes. We talked about our names, after Nancy asked what 'Des' was short for and I replied, "'Dekaeayough,' a Cayuga name."

"What's it mean?" she asked.

"Got me," I answered. "Dad never said. I don't even know if he still speaks the language."

"Not your mother?"

"No, she's part English and Greek."

"Greek! That's my name, I mean my ancestry," Greg exclaimed. "Gregorios. I think it means 'from the earth' or something. And your name," he said, pointing at Nancy, "means the garden I think. What does Nancy mean"

"No one ever asked," Nancy said, "I think it's a place name. Hey, here comes the food."

*Round Four: Bowling Thursday*
Rather than use the public lanes in Moscow or Pullman, we decided to use the University of Idaho lanes, especially since two of us were students there, and knew those lanes offered the least crowding.

We met Jaromil and Phil in the main lounge by the giant vandal statue (and what a perfect metaphor for American industrial civilization, a metallic image who accumulated wealth through theft rather than through invention or creation) and all went downstairs together.

I was putting this sport into historical perspective, "—in ancient Egypt, and from there to Rome, Germany and the Netherlands, where it was played at religious festivals. Recently, less than 200 years ago, the number of pins was raised from 9 to 10. The player—"

"Yes, Greg interrupted, "gets to knock down the ten pins by rolling a ball at them. If he cannot get all ten the first time, he gets a second chance. Each ball is worth one point, but there are bonus points for knocking them over in one or two tries, that is, strikes or spares. Then—"

"The ball is a standards size and weight, made of plastic and fiberglass," continued Nancy. "Don't forget that the bonus points exceed the normal points. So, who's keeping track of scoring?"

"I am," Jaromil answered. "Or rather, Rex, Hamud, and Phil will keep track of scoring for each of you. I will be the judge. Now, who is paying?"

Nancy nodded. We had divided the payments so that we each ended up paying one third of everything that required payments. Our efforts to get merchants to donate free time for us did not seem to be going well, even with the new neat logo for the Dodecathlon Universal League (DUL) on our stationery.

We picked out shoes and put them on. I was shocked that neither Nancy nor Greg had their own personal professional bowling shoes or balls.

We bowled a few practice rounds. I remembered how to bowl, but had not played for over ten years. I hoped the memories were adequate. I noticed a grim set to Nancy's jaw. The first four sports had been chosen by her and she had not won one of them yet.

For this sport, we decided to roll for position. Nancy won the roll with a strike and elected to go first. She rolled a strike in Frame 1. Greg and I exchanged that look of the knowing doomed. Greg went next and got a spare. I went third and knocked over 9 on the first roll, then picked up the last for a spare. Nancy got two more strikes in a row, before missing three and settling for a spare. Greg picked up two more spares and an open frame (missing one of two on the last throw). My first I fouled by sliding across the foul line. Although I got nine balls on my next throw, the foul was bad news.

I watched Nancy's footwork. Her first three steps seemed small, and even her fourth step did not have a deep slide. Greg used similar steps. My own steps were too long. I thought they were graceful and flowing, especially the slide, but I was not curving the ball like they were. So, I decided to modify my approach. I worried less about style and more about wrist action and aim. When I changed I got three strikes in a row, a kind of beginner's luck perhaps..

Nancy seemed to alternate between strikes and spares. Greg had mostly spares, with a few strikes. I had two open frames, plus the foul. Nancy won the first game 263 to 230 to 180.

Nancy won the second game also, 240 to 224 to 190.

Nancy won the third game 250 to 228 to 224, with Greg third.

To round off the points, we played a fourth game to only four frames (for the 1000-point limit). I won that 85 to 80 to 78, too little too late. I probably would have lost had it gone a whole ten frames.

We sat around and talked while the scorecards were completed and signed. The other two congratulated me on picking up quickly. Greg and I complimented Nancy on her dominance. Phil brought us a few sodas. As we were drinking them, Greg went over and played a few games of electronic speed driving.

| | Game 1 | 2 | 3 | 4 | Total |
|---|---|---|---|---|---|
| Nancy | 263 | 240 | 250 | 78 | 831 |
| Greg | 230 | 224 | 224 | 80 | 758 |
| Des | 180 | 198 | 228 | 85 | 691 |

*Round Five: Boxing Friday*

"I respect tradition as much as anyone," Hamud was saying, "but some sports are barbaric, and some scoring systems are just silly."

"You mean tennis?" Nancy asked innocently.

"No, I mean the sport that you, girl, are so keen to donate your teeth and ears to," Hamud paused, "boxing. I want to ask you to reconsider. Will you?"

Nancy looked at the ring, then her feet, then Hamud's eyes: "I would, if it were bare-knuckle and if Greg weighed over 300, but," and she pointed to a mound of equipment, "with all of this safety equipment, what could go wrong?"

"You can still end up with a broken nose or bloody kidney," Hamud sighed, with his last argument.

"Besides," Greg offered, "she is expecting us not to hit her.

And I do weigh over 200, so anything I do from pushing to glaring, is going to be a problem for you, punky."

"Ms. Punky to you. Don't count your goose-eggs until they're laid."

"Hamud," I asked, "if you think the sport barbaric, why do you coach it?"

"It's a long story. Not here," he paused. "I also coach judo and wrestling . . . maybe it's just—"

"Yes?"

"Never mind. Anyway, for this historic event, I have come up with some new rules and a new scoring system. Let's go over them, eh?

"The rules for scoring, in order of priority, are: First, for a knockdown. If one fighter knocks another down legitimately, that is, with a punch, that fighter gets a 10-point bonus. In the old system the round was scored 10-8 in favor of the boxer delivering the knockdown. But, there were problems with, on some occasions, a fighter being 'out on his, or her, if you insist, feet.' But, then the fighter remains standing and rebounds. So, for example, Ward should not have been given a 10-8 round against Gatti."

"Who?" three of us asked at the same time.

"Never mind, no, do mind. You ought to read up on the sport. I thought you had boxed, Greg?"

"I did, in college. I know Des did some, also."

"Uh, okay. Second priority, staggering. If one fighter clearly staggers his, uh, or her, opponent he gets a 3-point bonus, instead of winning a 10-9 round. A 'staggering' is a momentary loss of physical equilibrium caused by a power punch or series of punches. This is the equivalent to noticing a fighter has been visibly hurt by an opponent's punch. If the number of staggers is even or none occurred, move on to rule #3.

Thirdly, I mean third, clean effective punching. Each unblocked punch to the body is rated at 1-point; punches to the arms or gloves, or head, are considered countered and not counted. This replaces the 10-9 round scoring. And finally, fourthly, fourth, aggressiveness. The more aggressive fighter gets a 5-point bonus per round. By—"

"What about grace and speed, style?" Nancy said.

"What about unpimpled face, hair-style, and cleanliness?" Hamud responded, "save it for skating."

Nancy wrinkled her face.

"All those things are counted under aggression. It would be too complex to give points for graceful back-peddling, since that results in fewer points for the opponent. Same with 'heart' or courage. Too difficult to count. The fighter who takes the initiative, who dictates the pace of the fight, gets points. No points are added for adherence to the rules, but points are rapidly deducted if you don't adhere. For instance, 5 points are deducted for a head butt or hit below the waist. Same for biting and kicking."

"Awww," Nancy moaned dramatically, "my advantages, all stripped away."

Hamud smiled and continued: "—Now, I had suggested and you have agreed to Olympic round, that is, four 2-minute rounds. Did any of you want twelve 3-minute rounds?"

"Not to start, I think" I answered.

"Des, you might as well say it. I can see it building up. When and where did boxing start?"

"Maybe 686 BC, or 668, maybe, in Greece. The boxers, or pugilists from the Greek word for—" I could see eyes rolling into the backs of heads so I cut it short, "wrapped their hands with leather thongs to protect them, and they boxed nude."

"I think 668 is right. Did you know that later, in Rome, the leather was reinforced with lead balls? I imagine there were more, faster knockouts."

"Are we following the Marquis of Queensberry rules?" I asked.

"Yes, in terms of the ring size, gloves, and mandatory counts, but weights are a problem. Normally, you would never fight each other. Nancy looks like a Junior Flyweight—"

"Hey, I weigh 120—oppss!"

When we were finished laughing, Hamud corrected himself: "Okay, featherweight. Des, you're a middle weight, Greg a heavyweight or super heavyweight—"

"What's the difference?" Greg asked.

"Super is over 201 pounds."

"And I weigh 203," Greg nodded.

"Yes, but you carry it well," Nancy flirted. "How tall are you?"

"Six-two. That means I don't need to worry about illegal head shots from you, ha, ha."

"Oh, that reminds me. A few more considerations and rules," Hamud started, "unlike professional boxing you will not be fighting bare-chested," he paused smiling at Nancy, who inhaled deeply (and since I saw her wrapped in nylon at the pool every day I knew she had attractive breasts), "and you will have full protective equipment, especially helmets. Now, what else?"

"Betting?" Greg asked.

"Not allowed. Oh, speaking of head shots, no punching of the back of the head, neck, or back."

"Why?

"I think it had to do with appearing cowardly, hitting a

retreating opponent. Besides it's dangerous, more dangerous I mean. Now, we will have four judges, one for each side of the ring: Jaromil, Phil, Neil, and Chuck. I will be the referee, in the ring with you. Dr. Mixon has agreed to attend; he will be bringing duct tape and carved wooden replacement teeth. He is from the WSU student health. You may each have one trainer. I will see you tomorrow at 2:00."

"Will this be sanctioned by the IBF or WBO or WBA or—"

"No, Greg," Nancy answered, "but we could start our own, the MAWUBA."

"MAWUBA?"

"Men and Women's Universal Boxing Association," Nancy announced.

"Why not BAA?" Hamud suggested, "Boxing Association of America."

"How about PAD?" I offered, "Punishment after Dollars."

"BYE," Hamud left the track.

We stood around talking for a few minutes, while the lunch-hour people ran around the indoor track. Nancy decided to go running now. Greg and I went next door to play some racquetball, if we could find an open court. We had already decided to play the racquetball round here at Wazoo, with their newer glass courts.

The next day, we met at 11:00 to get dressed and warm up. I was still concerned about fighting Nancy. We had sparred a little and I didn't see how she would survive. Maybe if she had been 6'1" and 200 pounds. The ring had been set up in the martial arts room. It was not elevated, but it had the posts and three ropes. The padding seemed a little to thick to me, but didn't have any seams like the judo pads.

Nancy and Greg would go first, then after an hour break, Nancy and me, and after another hour, Greg and I. Hamud's schedule was that Greg and I would warm up for each other. He was still concerned about weight differences.

Fight Number 1. At the bell, Greg walked to the center, stretched out his right arm, and held Nancy away. All she could reach was his arms. Demonstration over, Nancy backed away quickly, then circled and closed more quickly. She got in several shots to Greg's right side, before he recovered and danced back. They danced for a while, she avoiding his reach and he trying to land a punch.

Then he did, on the crown of her head—a fair punch—and she fell backwards. We all raced forwards. The referee pushed Greg away and started to count. Nancy got up before four and bounced up and down to show she was ready and willing. Greg had a problem since the best opportunities were to her head. He tried to hit her upper chest and stomach, but had to crouch. The round was over.

The next round was more of a complicated dance. Nancy trying to pursue a large target and Greg trying to attack a small, rapidly-moving target. They each scored a few hits. I suspected Greg was pulling punches and trying to just score coups on the body.

In the third round Nancy moved back after the first close, and pulled her jersey, saying "Look, I'm triple wrapped and padded; you can't really hurt me that much!"

Greg nodded and approached her. She had both arms up, but he got in a good hard jab to her right shoulder. She spun but kept her balance. I could see one of the judges clicking the point with a counter in his right hand. Nancy came back with a flurry of shots, mostly spent on his arms and gloves but she got two or three to his side, and one to his hip. Greg shrugged it off and she made motions of apology. I think one judge subtracted a few points from his left-hand counter for the foul. Greg counted coup several more times to her forehead, and the round ended without death or dismemberment.

I watched the judges meet and add up their scores, discussing differences and counts. After 5 minutes, Hamud made the announcement.

"The Winner, by a score of 59 to 37, Greg Soros over Nancy Deschardin. Congratulations to you both for a clean and, uhmmm, interesting fight."

Boxing always had way too few points anyway, making it hard to determine a winner in many cases. Not any longer. Nancy went back to the locker room. I went to Hamud and mentioned that I thought we were going to fight four rounds.

He shook his head, "For you guys maybe, but not with the girl, ahh, lady."

Fight Number 2. Round 1. At the bell I started moving counterclockwise, then stopped. I remembered that I wanted to save any surprises for Greg. I stopped and waited for Nancy to close. She started with a manic flurry of punches that mostly caught my arms and gloves. I backed up. I knew she was tired; it was after 3:30. And, I knew she was trying to cow me. We were more evenly matched in size; I did not have as much of a height or weight advantage—only 40 pounds, rather than 80 pounds. We were also evenly matched at swimming and probably other sports where grace and technique counted more.

She stunned me with a good hit to the stomach. I bent over and backed away. Too much thinking. She followed landing two shots on my shoulder. I hit back with two taps on her forehead.

Then, I hunched over and connected to her sides with a few roundhouses. Unfortunately, that left my head open and she hit me twice on the forehead. We both backed up and moved warily. Her face looked beet-red from effort. When she closed again. I snaked in a fist over her guard on the open chest and she went down. She rolled over right away and arched her back, gasping. I waited as Hamud started to count. I figured I was ahead on points now. She was up by 5 and circling. We exchanged a few more taps on gloves before the round ended.

Round 2. I came out with a flurry of light hits, mostly to her gloves and arms. And a few to the air, when she ducked. She started ducking more now, making a hard target.

Round 3. I could see she was tired. She still moved well, and fast, but she threw fewer punches. Even when she charged she aimed several times before attempting a punch. She caught me with a good one to the left side of my chest.

At the bell she collapsed into the corner. I went over and Helen, her "trainer" gave her a cold towel. I asked her if she was okay and she gave me the thumb's up sign, but using the middle finger. I blew her a kiss.

After the usual counting and conferring, Hamud made the announcement: "The Winner, by decision, and a score of 65 to 52, Des Turner over Nancy Deschardin. Congratulations to you both for a clean and entertaining fight."

I hugged her but she punched me below the belt, As I bent over she tagged the back of my head.

"Okay, okay, sorry," I said.

"No. It was a good fight, there just has to be a way to make up the weight difference. Maybe you guys should have a hand tied behind you back or have to wear a 90-pound pack or fight on your knees or something."

I nodded and waved as she left. Then I sat down heavily and started to breathe to relax.

Fight Number 3. Now I was in Nancy's position, as Greg was four inches taller and forty pounds heavier, numbers that mattered little on a racquetball court or track. We went through the introductory ceremonies and the bell. Unlike Nancy I did not come out fast. Neither did Greg. We circled each other like super heavyweights, slowed by our weight but knowing the power it added when we would punch. We tested each other with glove touches. Greg swung hard once but I backed out of range. Of all the things we had played through the years, hitting each other was not one of them. I knew he had boxed in school and I had worked out on punching bags for years. But, the bag had never hit back.

I decided to take the plunge and moved in, circling counterclockwise.

Round 2. I felt confident. I knew I could hit Greg regularly and he had trouble pinning me down in the corners. As I switched to a series of right jabs, I was staggered by a fist from nowhere. I put my head down and covered up near the ropes. He was landing hammers on my ribs. I moved along the ropes, almost tripping. When he paused I lifted a good punch out of the air. He didn't blink. I could not match him for strength. I attacked him, landing a few good strikes to the body. Then the round was over.

Round 3. My head hurt. My body felt numb. My arms and legs, however, felt good and powerful. So I danced into the round. I danced in to score and danced out to avoid his punches. I thought, maybe imagined, that he looked confused. Then he caught me in a corner. I covered up and caught most of his punches, but I could not strike back. I pushed him out on the arms, so I could get room. As I started to attack the round ended. I was sure I had outscored him this round.

Round 4. Everything was numb, now, even the headache. I danced in and tried to knock him down. That didn't work. I had to spend equal effort avoiding his swings. Every once and a while he swung a roundhouse, that exposed his ribs, but all I did was tag him. When I covered my head and chest he made some good hits to my stomach. Fortunately it was the strongest muscle in my body. I decided to try the ropa-dopa strategy and let him hit my stomach for a while, but then I realized he was scoring each time, so I went back to circling him and scoring strikes to his right side. He was vulnerable to my lefts, so I slowed down with the right hand, except for an occasional jab to keep him honest. He was very slow, now and could not fend off my attacks.. I was still attacking at the final bell.

As I collapsed in my corner, I saw him collapse in his. We nodded to each other between gulps of water. I probed a tooth that seemed loose.

We watched the judges quietly and then Hamud as he got in the ring and made the announcement: "The Winner, by decision, and a score of 78 to 76, Des Turner over Greg Soros. Congratulations to you both for a clean and exhausting fight."

We met and the ring and he collapsed against me. "I didn't know you were tired too," I said.

Greg replied, "Under the old system, I think I would have won, for the stagger and the domination—"

"Hey, I didn't go backwards," I responded a little archly. Then we walked out into the hall. "The ceiling is too low in that room. I should think you could hit it jumping in martial arts."

| | *Score* | *Calculation* | *Total* |
|---|---|---|---|
| Greg | 59 | 59+10 x 10=690 | 725 |
| Nancy | 37 | 37x10=370 | |
| | | | |
| Nancy | 52 | 52x10=520 | 445 |
| Des | 65 | 65+10x10=750 | |
| | | | |
| Des | 78 | 78+10x10=880 | 815 |
| Greg | 76 | 76x10=760 | |

Greg muttered, "So, you're the MAWUBA champion, ma-ma-wuba! Your treat, and I need a steak for my eye."

We went to the Nobby Inn with Nancy and Hamud. I did pay. Greg and Nancy got steaks. I had a Caesar salad.

*Round Six: Diving Saturday*

"You know," I was lecturing Tina, "Fancy diving goes as far back as the 17th century in connection with the great gymnastic movement in Germany and Sweden. In the summertime, the gymnasts moved their equipment to the beach to practice, and acrobatics that ended up in the water became a part of their activities. So, springboard diving is more related to gymnastics than to swimming, although since they both conclude in water, they have naturally become linked."

"Yes, you are very graceful in the air. Are you ahead in this new Greek-numbered megasport?" She asked sweetly.

"I am ahead, but I expect to be trounced in tennis and some of the other ball sports. If—" I paused. She was making a Chicken Voulevent for dinner and was shaping a pastry chicken out of filo dough. Pelleprat's recipe, I knew. At least we ate well. She had just gotten a raise at the University was now making more money than I was, a fact that had improved her mood significantly.

"Yes?" she wondered. I grabbed her from behind and let my hands go a roving. She dusted me with flour. Then .... ah, well, then. Then.

"Then again, there is no platform available at either university. I suggest that we keep to the one-meter board, although I would prefer the three-meter board." I finished making the arrangements with Michelle, the coach of the women's swim team (and Nancy's coach).

"For insurance reasons, and insurance has gotten bitchy about diving boards, I agree we keep to the one-meter. However, you can go through a whole series on the three-meter, as long as we have the judges. You know Nancy used to dive a long time ago, but I haven't seen her practice here. Of course, I haven't seen you practice either."

I raised my eyebrows, "I go through a set of dives a few nights a week, but only when Mike is lifeguard—no one else allows me to practice," I shrugged.

"See," she said. "Insurance. It sucks. And these same stupid companies insure people who build houses on primary sand dunes and active volcanoes; they insure automobile racers, sky-divers, ohhh," she fumed.

I was thinking about what dives I would do. After 1904, Olympic diving started to change in leaps and bounds—literally—and is still developing. In the early days there were only 14 platform and 20 springboard dives. Now, there were officially 63 dives on the 1-meter springboard, 67 dives on 3-meter springboard and 85 dives on platform. Of course, I had over 80 dives on the 1-meter and almost as many on 3-meter, and over 100 on platform. Many of them had no official degrees of difficulty, and I had to guess that they were similar to the recognized dives. Difficulty had changed dramatically from a dangerous double somersault from the platform, in 1904, to an easy performance of a reverse three and a half somersaults in 1984. I would be doing that dive off the 3-meter. I wondered whether anyone would ever do more difficult dives that I did. Was there a peak? Someone made the statement 25 years ago that difficulty had peaked then.

Michelle was talking about the judges: "—don't have a panel of seven experts who can score each dive considering four phases of the performance: the approach, takeoff, technique and grace during flight, and the water entry. We can get three educated judges, so we won't throw out the highest and lowest scores. Do you know any names?"

"No, just you. Who scores in the meets?"

"We never have diving." she answered.

"Have you given Nancy and Greg the information about the six compulsory dives and the five optional dives?" I asked.

"Yes," she said sweetly (I was surrounded by people behaving sweetly to me, as if I was retarded). "And I told them each dive is scored on a 10-point basis. We need to have three judges. There are thirty points maximum per dive, which is multiplied by the degree of difficulty, which has a maximum of 3.3. As, you know, degree of difficulty ranges from 1.2 for a simple forward tuck off a 1-meter springboard, to 3.0 for a reverse 3 1/2 somersault with a half twist off a 3-meter springboard."

"Yes," I murmured, "I'll be doing both of those dives. See you tomorrow at 2:00 then." I had analyzed my weaknesses and decided on a program that would minimize them. It would mean doing lower degree of difficulties, but I could go wild on the 3-meter, when it didn't count.

When I got there, Nancy was already in the water trolling along so beautifully lazy and fetching. Greg and I came out together. He was not happy doing this; he confessed it would be his weakest effort. We were introduced to the judges, Michelle, Bill Williams, whom I had seen on occasion, and Martha Kirsten, whom I had never met. Our team, in the form of Phil and Neil had come along also, just to witness this part of the contest. I had asked Neil to keep score on paper, just for comparison.

It was decided that we alternate for the first six compulsory dives, then have a half hour rest before the optionals. Michelle decided on a rotation led by Greg and concluded by me. Greg started by doing a decent front dive tuck; his weight allowed him to get really good height. His height made the dive look more dramatic also. Nancy did her front dive pike, And, I did mine layout, using the new straight as a board layout without the back arch that I had always used in the water ballet. I was ahead, whooppeee.

Greg did a reverse dive pike, barely making it. Nancy did her back dive layout. I also did a back dive layout, with a deep arch and straightening by swing my arms straight over my ears to punch into the water—no splash at all. I noticed on television that Olympic divers did not use this particular arm motion. I thought it looked better than their arm motion, and it had the effect of straightening the dive well.

Greg did a really good tuck back dive. It was dramatic partly because no one did it that way anymore. Nancy did a very good inward pike. I did a very good inward dive layout, which looked higher and more difficult than it was. I remember I had first added to my repertoire at the State Championship, almost missing it, but still winning the gold metal; now it was one of the easiest I did.

Greg did his inward dive pike, reaching down too fast, but getting vertical at the end. Nancy was slow on her reverse dive pike and lost points from the unfinished rotation. I did mine pike also, because I could get higher and it looked good when I brought the toes up to touch the vertical fingers.

The twist dives were completed by Greg and Nancy doing the same half twist layout. I did one and a half twists, which one of the judges questioned. Michelle talked to him, doubtless pointing out that we had submitted the dive list to them several days before, with the approved difficulties. He seemed uncomfortable, but shrugged and held his card up as a 7. I had to remind myself not to frown or glare. I though about floating in air.

Greg performed a single somersault tuck, making some splash. It was hard to land blind and feet down. I still had a few dives that entered feet-first, but like most I had converted to headfirst dives.

Nancy did a one and a half somersault tuck. And, for mine, I did a one and a half somersault layout, almost over-rotating since I had gotten so much height, but pulling it under the water.

And, it was time to rest. I went over to Greg and congratulating him on doing so well.

We kept to the same rotation for the final dives. I calculated that Nancy was far enough behind and Greg was out of the running, unless they came up with something awesome. I was quite happy since I did my best dives with a comfortable lead. In fact, I remembered that the week after the state championship, I was close behind Ben at the last dive and flubbed it. In fact it seemed that the only time I ever won was when I had an insurmountable lead. At the nationals I had the lead after the first dive but dropped almost a place with each dive, finishing eighth.

Greg started with a one and a half, and actually went over a little; he was happy, since in practice he had trouble rotating all the way (he said). Nancy did the same dive almost perfectly. I tried a more difficult dive, a flying reverse half twist with two and a half somersaults tuck. It was perfect, if I don't say so myself. The problem judge signaled for a meeting with Michelle before he held up his card. I suppose they talked about the fact that there was no formal degree of difficulty for that dive, so Michelle had assigned it a 3.0 and I was happy enough with that. He gave me another 7. I put a gymnast's smile on my face and walked to wash off.

Greg did a reverse somersault, coming too close to the board and landing on his knees. I think he got 3s. Nancy did a back one and a half, coming up a little short on her extension. I did a back one and a half with one and a half twists.

Greg did a back somersault tuck, going in with little splash. I noticed he had learned the new style of tucking with the legs apart. I always thought that was cheating. It may have looked okay to the judges on the side, but from the front or back it looked a little froggy. I kept everything pressed close together, even though I might not have been able to rotate at the highest speed possible. Considering some of my dives, I think I rotated about as fast as anyone. Nancy did a reverse somersault tuck. She was really graceful. I reminded myself to ask her where she had learned to dive. I cranked out a forward three and a half somersaults tuck. When I hit with my hands, I was still in a tuck, so I extended my legs and back straight as I entered the water, praying that it looked like I was straight the entire time. The problem judge questioned that, also and dropped me to a 6.

Greg did an inward somersault, landing flat-footed but extended. Nancy did an inward one and a half, with a perfect entry. I did a flying inward one and a half somersault with a flying end, also.

It looked really good when it worked because minimal time was spent in the tuck; it seemed that most of the dive was layout.

For his final dive Greg did a forward somersault with a half twist at the end, with his best entry. Nancy did a one and a half somersault with a full twist. It was good but she was a little wild with her arms and a little uncertain on the entry. I noticed that the "problem judge" gave her an 8. For my last dive I did a reverse double with one full twist, but I did half the twist first, then one and a half somersault and before I finished the other half somersault, I added the other half of the twist, whipping my arms down to my sides. This let me see the water so I could point my toes. I extended my toes so far my calf cramped as I entered the water. When I came up, Michele was conferring with "Mr. Notes-unread" judge.

I went over and blew water at Greg and Nancy. I felt so good. I reminded them that I had asked to do a series on the 3-meter for points (that did not count). Then I went over and talked to the judges about the 3-meter dives, just to make sure there was agreement. For instance, I knew my front five and a half somersaults would also raise questions about degree of difficulty.

The dives themselves did not quite go as well as the 1-meter, partly because I was tired and partly because it was hard to adjust so quickly to the change in height. I only made one awkward mistake. On the back double somersault layout, I went slightly too far and my suit went halfway up my lower intestine. It took me a minute under water to pull it out. When I got out I saw Tina in the balcony. It figured; she always was there to see my worst effort.

| | *Required* | *Optional* | *Calculation* | *Total* |
|---|---|---|---|---|
| Nancy | 191 | 278 | 469x1.2 | 563 |
| Greg | 170 | 229 | 399x1.2 | 479 |
| Des | 287 | 421 | 708x1.2 | 858 |

I won. It was my best sport. In the air I was godlike, in the water I was a fish, but on the land I was an arthritic wolf, no good at the sprint but good for the distance. Nancy claimed second, Greg was happy with third.

Nancy wanted to eat at the new Motel by the mall but Greg and I overruled her and we went to Sweet Ed's at the other mall. Tina met Nancy for the first time; I could read her body language, poised to respond to the threat of a younger woman. I ignored both. I loved that place; Ed and I had graduated together, and I had been eating his food once a week ever since. Milk shakes. Nancy said she would win next time and we would go the motel, Best Worstern. Tina fiddled with my hair during the conversation.

*Round Seven. Fencing Sunday*
We had decided on the foil, for basic reasons: No one had any Épée or sabres locally. I still had my foil from high school and Hamud was able to find a few more at Wazoo. We had reserved a room in the new gym for this contest. I was telling Hamud and the rest, "The foil has a flexible, rectangular blade, about 35 inches in length, and weighing less than a pound. Points are scored with the tip of the blade and must land within the torso of the body; no head or arm contact. You've had a month to plan for this. Have any of you ever used this before?"

"Yes," said Nancy and Greg at the same time, Nancy adding, "No contact on the legs or neck either. Are you going to introduce this sport?"

I figured that she was humoring me, but I had spent part of the past week familiarizing them with the positions and techniques of the sport. Greg had done a little fencing also in high school. "Well, at the time of Ramses III, a bas-relief shows fencers wearing masks and holding button-tipped weapons. After that, Romans used swords, Japanese sabres, Turkish scimitars, and Spaniards rapiers. The French, Nancy please note, first used the foil in the 1600s. The foil was used in the first modern Olympic games."

Hamud said, "I have the uniforms. The vests are not lamé, so the judges will score points. I will be the head judge, and Jaromil and Phil will be assistant judges. Only hits on the target area, the torso will be scored. The "off target" hits do not count in the scoring, but they do stop the fencing action temporarily."

I was thinking about my last match with the sabre, which I had won by scoring my point on my opponent's big toe.

"—you know defense must be effected exclusively with the guard and the blade, used either separately or together. You may hold the handle in any way you wish and you may also alter the position of your hand on the handle during a bout. The weapon must be used without your hand leaving the hilt. Obviously, I hope, it may *not* transformed into a throwing weapon. Understood?"

I still had the scars on the back of my right hand from Chris's vicious overhead assault once, long ago.

Hamud was continuing, "—maximum length of the grip in foil is 20 cm. Nothing, not part of the handle or your thumb, can extend beyond the surface of the guard. Okay. Let me look at the weapons."

"I will be the referee again. Phil and Neil will be the floor judges at each end of the piste, you know the long mat that you have to stay on. Rex and Jaromil will be the timers, who also record each touch, as signaled by me, the referee. As you remember, I hope, each bout is 9 minutes long, in 3-minute segments, divided by 1 minute of rest. The winner is the first to score 15 points, or if the time expires, the leader. If the score is tied after 9 minutes, then there is a 1-minute sudden death. Take a few minutes to warm up. The piste is 10 meters long and 1.5 meters wide; the last two meters at each end is marked with tape, so that you know when you are at the end. Remember, if both feet leave the piste, a touch is awarded to your opponent."

There was a small audience, with Tina, Lacy, Mars (I think Nancy said he was from Germany—I had asked her to ask him if he wanted to participate), and Michelle, the swim coach.

Nancy and I had the first match. Hamud introduced us, and we gave a salute to each other, before we put on our masks. The referee blew his whistle and the timers started keeping time. Nancy lunged first, but I parried with a quinte and riposted straight to her middle. Hamud signaled a point. We walked back to the middle to the on guard position, the back arm bent upward and the weapon hand held out to the opponent. We were both fencing right handed. It occurred to me that she had a slight tactical advantage, being smaller and presenting a smaller target.

I stepped forward to attack, but she stepped back at the same speed. So I attacked faster and lunged, throwing my back arm down; lunged again, stretching out. She backed up and kept backing off the mat. Hamud signaled another point for me.

Nancy, well her mask, looked thoughtful coming back to the center. We started again. She remembered the fleche, the running attack, but I was able to parry as I was stepping back covering more distance than she did. I attacked to her prime, but she parried with a prime and reached my chest, the tierce, with her riposte. She did learn, rats.

I won the first segment. I won the bout 15 to 7.

Greg and I fought next. I won that bout 15 to 11.

Nancy and Greg fought to 12-9 after 15 minutes, with Greg the winner. Because I won the second bout against each, there would not be a third bout. Then Nancy reminded Jaromil that we had decided to always have the third bout, even in tennis, to keep the point count even. So, we went to the third.

| | *1* | *2* | *3* | *Calc* | *Total* |
|---|---|---|---|---|---|
| Nancy | 7 | 6 | 8 | | |
| Des | 15 | 15 | 15 | 88x11.1 | 977 |
| | | | | | |
| Des | 15 | 15 | 13 | | |
| Greg | 11 | 8 | 12 | 68x11.1 | 755 |
| | | | | | |
| Greg | 12 | 11 | 14 | | |
| Nancy | 9 | 15 | 8 | 53x11.1 | 589 |

*Round Eight: Golf Monday*

"You mean you've never played golf?" Tina asked me two weeks ago.

"Of course, I've played golf in the original form, hitting small stones with a wooden stick towards a specific point, like a tree. But, I only got to the clubs and ball invention last week on a miniature golf course. What on earth will I do with a choice of eight clubs?" I wondered.

"You know, I mean remember, that I used to play golf at Whitman College," she offered, "so I could teach you the basics of the equipment and the course."

"Thanks," I said appreciatively, "but remember, I've been running on that course five times a week for the past ten years."

So, for the first time, since we went bicycling together five years ago, we went out on the university golf course and engaged in a sport together.

I was saying, "I never really consider golf, bowling, billiards, or car-racing for that matter as being real sports. Any activity you can engage in with a drink in your hand cannot be a real sport."

"Many golfers are great athletes," Tina said in a measured tone. "You would do well ..." she trailed off.

And, I got the message. So, I held my tongue, since I needed her help.

"My philosophy is to listen, then, maybe to evaluate your swing flaws, and let you fix it. My goal is to encourage you to reach your goals, and to have as much fun as possible." She was so formal.

After a week and a half, I almost felt ready for today.

"Welcome to the Common and Modern Golf Club of St. Potatoes," Jaromil greeted us, referencing the Royal and Ancient Golf Club of St. Andrews, the founders of the first rules of the game. We had reserved the course at the University of Idaho, in Moscow for Round 8 of the Dodecathlon.

Jaromil continued, "You can rent what you need from the office, if you don't already have it. We have the course from now until dusk. Those of you who were here yesterday had a chance to familiarize yourselves with the course. Others of you already used it. As you know, the course is 18 holes through a nice natural environment—"

"Natural?" I burst out automatically. "It's quite unnatural, this is at best a short-grass prairie—"

"I know, I'm aware of your views on ecology, Des," Jaromil interrupted back, "but for the purpose of describing the course design, it is called natural, with natural obstacles, even though the fairway, teeing ground, and putting green are made of an exotic grass. The course is a Par 70, with 18 holes. We will—yes?"

"Is this going to be stroke play?" Nancy asked.

"Yes, I was getting to that. Please let me finish, please," Jaromil begged. "It will be stroke play for 36 holes, which will be played in two rounds, both today, with an hour between rounds."

"Can we use a cart?" Nancy asked.

"I was getting to that, please. You may use up to 14 clubs and 14 balls. You may use a caddy or cart to transport them."

"Hey, is that standard?" Nancy asked.

"It is the rule we will use. You may also wear gloves, or a glove. Golf shoes are optional; you may also wear running shoes, track shoes or soccer shoes if you want."

"Any rules on golf bags?" I asked, planning on using my old leather postal bag for my three whole clubs.

"No. I will be the rougheree, I mean, referee," Jaromil smiled.

"Maybe the reeferee? Are we allowed to laugh or make noise?" Greg asked.

"No. According to the rules in "The Golf Whisperer" there can be no loud noise of any kind. Furthermore, no spectators—"

"You're kidding, right," Greg and I chorused at the same time.

"Yes, I was kidding, but please do not bring more than two guests each. Do not bring guns or any other weapons that make noise—just kidding, really, seriously. Any disputes will be resolved by the Rules of God, I mean, Golf. For instance, a player or caddie must not take any action to influence the position or the movement of a ball except in accordance with the Rules. The penalty is disqualification of the player.

"Now, just to remind you, the goal of the game is to drive the ball from the tee to the hole in as few strokes as possible; the ball must drop into the hole. This is a stroke-play tournament. You will keep your own score, and compare them to par for the course. In order to have this add up to 1000 points, every shot will nominally be worth 6 points; shots under par are added in at 10 point each and shots over par are subtracted at 8 points each. Any questions."

"Why those numbers?" I asked.

"Nancy can explain this better," Jaromil suggested.

So, we discussed it briefly. We all knew who would win (Nancy); this was just for the purpose of equalizing the different scoring systems of the sports.

We walked over to the club house to pick out our equipment. As we were assembling our various accoutrements, the golf pro, Blake, came up to introduce the course, "This golf course is a challenging par 72. Originally designed by Francis L. James as a nine hole golf course in 1933, it was redesigned and expanded by Bob Bolduck in 1968. The front nine of U of I golf course is a par 37 with three par fives. It plays at 3117 total yards from the middle tees, 3344 yards from the back tees—"

"We'll just be playing the back tees," Nancy interrupted.

"Okay, then the back nine is a par 35 with only one par five, but it's equally challenging because of two long par-three holes. The back tees' make a sum of 3293, Only three greens, all on the front nine, are two-tiered. Some greens play faster than others. Playing surfaces vary a great deal throughout the day, depending on the local weather conditions. You may be surprised by the rolling hills, some quite steep—lots of tough side-hill lies. But, it's a fun course. I hope you enjoy it."

Greg was thinking out loud, "If we hit the first ball 6636 yards, then get it in a hole at 1 yard, can we birdie the whole course? At par, it averages 92 yards per stroke. I suppose that's irrelevant, considering the greens—"

"Thank you, Blake," Jaromil said. "We appreciate it."

"Remember," Blake reminded us, "we have the NAIA tournament tomorrow."

I shrugged. I was sure we would be through by dawn.

We had paid our fees of $10 each. Nancy had rented a power cart for $12.50, Greg a pull-cart, and me a set of clubs for $6.

We walked out to the first tee. I looked ahead. It was straight with a few pines uphill. Jaromil felt it was important to announce the hole and so he did, "Hole 1 is a par 4 dog-leg left with a pond wrapping around the left front left side of the green. It plays at 386 yards, from the back tee, that is. Nancy, ladies first."

Nancy teed off first, with a 3-wood and drove the ball about 200 yards straight down the fairway. I went next, with my yellow ball and 1-wood. Although my ball went a few dozen yards further, it was close to the rough on the east side. Greg's ball went just under 200 yards. I noticed that we all used different grips, from my baseball to Nancy's interlocking grip. Nancy got on the green on her second shot, using a 9-iron. I managed to get almost as close, but in a sand trap. Greg was at the left front edge of the green, a good place. Nancy looked in her notes for the ball speed for the first green; then she putted it in. It looked so easy. Greg missed, going past the hole, but only went a foot or two past. I used my 8-iron, having decided not to carry a wedge in my bag. I was sure I would be missing the traps. Bad plan, in retrospect. I barely got on the green. Greg tapped his in. I had to putt mine 14 feet, but I made it. Nancy was ahead by 1. Greg asked if she could carry his bag in her cart. Neither of us had carts. I was so used to running on the course, so I could not imagine driving.

Hole 2 was a short par three only 156 yards from the back tee. Nancy hit straight at the flag stick, hitting the green as it sloped slightly left. I followed with a 200-yarder that went behind the trees. I was wondering if I should have carried more clubs. Greg drove a modest 120-yards to below the green. Nancy missed the putt. I had to declare my shot unplayable and take a one-stroke penalty. I dropped a new ball next to a tree. Normally I would have tried to play out, but the count probably would have been worse, or the same. Anyway, I got back on the fairway about 10 yards from the hole. Greg's ball almost hit Nancy's, it was so close. Nancy got par.

Hole 3, from the back tee markers, was 390 yards. Nancy drove 220 yards. I drove 230 and Greg 240; all three balls were within spitting distance, Nancy's being furthest left. The green was fairly flat, but was two-tiered. Nancy's next shot was about 15 yards longer because of the uphill approach. I decided to imitate her in all things now, rather than try to beat her with strength. I also went slightly uphill of the hole. Greg went too far uphill I thought. Nancy birdied the Par 4, while I took two to get par. Greg ended up with par also.

Greg decided to tease me, "So, are you going to shoot your weight?"

"Well," I answered, "I'd prefer to shoot my age."

But Nancy had the last word, "If I shot either of your IQs, I'd be course champion."

I knew the 4th hole; it went straight to the water tower, which I ran along every day to get to the old highway. At 556 yards, it was the longest hole on the course, and a difficult Par 5. And it seemed longer because it was slightly uphill. If at all possible, keep your ball on the left two-thirds of the fairway, I remembered from Tina. I knew every drop and rise in the ground. Nancy did a decent job getting to par. I aimed dead-center at the water tower and swung; the right side was out of bounds towards the highway and the left side sloped downs towards the Hole 3 fairway. My ball landed in the center. Another long shot and two puts and I had a birdie at last. Greg landed at the edge of the rough after his first shot, but was able to play it well, although it was almost a blind shot. He also got a birdie. I saw Nancy raise her eyebrows minutely.

Hole 5 ran down hill into a bowl. It looked like an easy 171 yards. Nancy made the birdie look easy. My shot was long again and the follow-up went into the sand trap on the left. Greg hit the upper slope of the green and made an easy par from there.

Hole 6 was a 491 yard par five. Nancy birdied it with good shots. She told me to slice away, although I was not sure what she meant. The fairway sloped dramatically from right to left. I got to the green in two, but it did not do me any good, as I flailed around and was lucky to get par. The green played a little long because it was uphill. Greg got there in two shots also but got a birdie. I watched as he put the ball uphill from the hole and let a gentle putt roll in for a birdie.

Hole 7 was gently rolling, like a miniature course that had been inflated. And, a miracle of water management, there was a pond in front of it. From the back tee, the hole was 526 yards. Nancy did not try to get over the pond with two shots. She carefully placed the third at the upper edge of the green. But, she needed all five to get to Par. I was able to get past the water hazard on two shots, but I needed three more to get to par, also. Greg got by it in two, and he needed only two to get a birdie.

Jaromil felt compelled to introduce this hole, "This is a 375-yard hole. Your tee shot must be hit far enough to get a look around the sweeping dog-leg to the left, but if you hit too far, you'll end up in the rough or the trees."

"For god's sake, Jaromil, every hole here is a dog leg, either a short front dog leg or a long one. Even 13 is the hind leg of a dog. Stop saying that," I was not happy.

"It's just an expression, Des, don't sweat it. You should be concentrating."

I ignored that, but he was wrong, I should be unconcentrating. What should I do? Be the ball? Be the course? Be the leg?

The approach to Hole 8 was flat, with a few pine trees. Nancy got an easy birdie. I on the other hand flirted with the stream on the right side, but was still able to get a bogie with a maximum of effort. Be the rough, be the bogie. Indeed. Greg got the Par 4 for himself. His second shot made it to the elevated, two-tiered green, but the sloping front half, so he needed the second putt.

Hole 9 looked like an easy finishing hole for the front side, at a modest 293 yards. The fairway traveled uphill from the tee box almost all the way to the two-tiered green, which lay in front of the club house. After our first shots, however, it looked all uphill. Nancy made a good approach shot. She was able to cut the left corner successfully. Many golfers try to cut the slight corner to the left, but the cart path designated the out of bounds line. In fact, we all made par. We took a break and had parts of bottles of water. I had decided to forgo my cola addiction until after the game.

Despite the fact that two large trees threatened to catch the tee shots, all three of us birdied Hole 10. It was a good start for me. I did not feel the need to driver the ball as far as I could. The hole was straight downhill 375 yards away. I noticed that Nancy had used a long iron off the tee, while Greg and I used fairway woods.

Hole 11 went straight uphill 406 yards with two pines. Par four I remembered, then spoke over Jaromil, saying, "another dogleg, left, I know." Jaromil shrugged. No one else mentioned it. In fact, we were very quiet. That has a slight dogleg to the left. Nancy hit her tee shot to the left, to miss the trees. I tried to follow exactly, but ended up in good position anyway. Greg came closer to the trees. When we got to the green, it seemed to slope even more to the front. Now, three pars were recorded. I wondered how often people got in synchrony at this game.

Hole 12 was only slightly shorter at 400 yards. But, the tee sat high above the relatively wide fairway. Nancy was as precise and controlled as ever, but I think Greg and I both swung for world-record drives. Mine certainly had distance, but it went out of bounds. I got it back in easily, but then I was in the trees around the green. Nancy and Greg birdied it, but I made par, with a heroic put.

This hole, 13, had a back dog leg. Crowded with trees at end and was a par 5 for 504 yards. Nancy cut the corner from her tee with a hooking drive. I tried to duplicate it. Greg hit his shot out of bounds. Nancy got an eagle. I got a birdie. Greg recovered to par.

Hole 14 was straight, slightly uphill, and short like Hole 2; it was only 227 yards, but the fairway was lined with trees. Nancy shot well. Greg and I restrained our drives. No one went out of bounds this time. Greg and Nancy got birdies. I got one over par.

To the right of a mown wheat field, Hole 15 had a dog-leg right around a group of large willow trees; other trees elsewhere begged to come into play. From the back tees, there was a good view of the course. Nancy and Greg got birdies, and I had to settle for another over par, all because my put rolled too fast over the hole. I mentally blamed the hole—it should have gone in, in fact, it did go in, it just bounced out immediately.

Hole 16: Open, treeless, waterless, but bounded by a severe drop and a narrow bounds, right and left. The green, 383 yards away, was flat but also dropped off in the back. Nancy and I got birdies, and Greg had to settle for a Par 4.

It seemed that Hole 17 was skyward, uphill, with a few trees on the sides. It seemed longer than its measly 232 yards. Nancy was lucky to get par. Greg was one over and I was two over. My muscles seemed to be ignoring the messages from the brain. I had shot the ball out of bounds on the right side, and my chip back to the green was a blind shot.

From Hole 18, we could see back to the clubhouse. It was a right-sloping fairway. Nancy said, charitably, "Choose the upper fairway. The lower is nearly out of bounds on the right side and the left side has a drop."

Greg nodded. Hole 18 played at 415 yards from the back tees. Nancy drove 180 yards. I followed closely. Greg hit further, but still in good position. Nancy birdied. Greg and I got par. I almost birdied but my ball stopped an inch from the cup. I sighed. I had done better than I thought, but not good enough to get better than third.

| | *1* | *2* | *Calculation* | *Total* |
|---|---|---|---|---|
| Nancy | 68 | 67 | 72+4x2+10x10 | 900 |
| Des | 82 | 81 | 72-10x2x10 | 520 |
| Greg | 74 | 75 | 72-2x2x10 | 680 |

We congratulated Nancy, then told her we had to have burgers at Sweet Ed's. She agreed. It was the least expensive dinner, even with milk shakes all around.

*Round Nine. Gymnastics Tuesday*
The next day was to be mine. I knew that because I had helped Greg and Nancy with their routines. We were at the gym room at the new gym at Idaho. It opened out to the sloping field where I had practiced with the gymnastics club for years. I had good memories of that field, which was useful for learning somersaults, since it sloped just enough to yield extra momentum when learning.

When I had worked at Penn State, with the Litany Nylons, I mean Nittany Lions, it had been called the free exercise, possibly because it was free of objects or apparatus—the gymnast had only his own muscles on a flat surface, and that was once a bare wooden floor. Ah, I was rambling.

Hamud was hamming for the camera, which we had decided to use for the rest of the rounds, "The entire floor area, the entire 40 by 40-foot mat, should be used during the exercise, which consists primarily of tumbling passes performed in different directions. Some elements must be performed during the routine: Acrobatic elements forward and backward and an acrobatic elements sideward or backward take-off with 1/2 turn. There must also be a balance element on one leg or one arm, held for two seconds with a minimum of "B" value, or a static strength move, held for two seconds with a minimum of "B" value. Transitional skills, dance, or gymnastics movements performed in between tumbling and acrobatic passes, should be executed with proper rhythm and harmony. The exercise must be at least 50 seconds long and must not exceed 70 seconds in length."

Hamud," I asked, "are the judges going to concentrate on tumbling primarily, and continue to neglect grace and continuity?" I was expressing my own prejudice here, at the turn gymnastics had taken after the Russian dominance, where stiff wooden figures tumbled dramatically but then moved awkwardly in the seconds between.

"Um, as you know," he started, "neither university has a gymnastics program, none of the judges are really very sophisticated, and you guys are either callow or elderly," he said, winking at me, "so I suspect that we will be emphasizing nontumbling aspects as well."

I did not take offense at his comment. The hardest thing for me to do at my advanced age was to get flexible enough to bend my back or spread my legs in a split. So, that was what I had worked on the most.

He concluded: "During a floor exercise routine, one mat up to 4 inches thick may be placed in one location for a D-skill landing. Another rule: Full difficulty exercise with less than a B-value dismount shall receive a medium deduction. And, finally, you get a bonus for each C or D part over three receiving a 0.1 bonus, up to 0.6 point. Are the judges ready?" he asked, making eye contact with them. "Let's begin, then."

By the draw, Greg went first. He did an cartwheel into a short series of back handsprings, ending with a back salto tuck. He immediately moved about thirty degrees to the left with a cartwheel into a handstand. He lowered his handstand into a planche, but could not hold it. From his knees, he pushed back into another handstand, held it for two seconds, then did a half turn into walkover then another walkover and a front handspring and a half handspring to his hands and another handstand.

Nancy started with a leaping split, then a cartwheel to a back handspring to a salto. She rolled over then arched her back. She smiled in a natural, unforced way, as she moved. That was great. She looked like she was enjoying it, rather than straining.

Now, it was my turn. I started with a hand stand, then went into a forward handspring and two more, each accelerating until I did a one and a half somersault, catching myself on my hands and tumbling, but immediately leaping into a reverse somersault and nailing the landing, which I held for two seconds. When I was younger I might have tried a double or thrown a twist into it. Jumping with my own muscles was the hard part of tumbling, especially after depending on the diving board or the trampoline for the extra push. From the landing of the reverse. I moved left into a half cartwheel into a handstand. Then I brought my legs straight down 90 degrees and brought my nose between my knees. Then I lifted my right arm out and held that for two seconds. I lifted out and into a back walkover, and started a series of back handsprings, with a layout somersault, then a tuck double. I nailed the landing although I had not quite untucked completely. I fell forward into a planche. I pushed up into a handstand. From there I tucked and tumbled, leaping straight up into a swan dive and a half rotation and another tumble, but this one to a swan with a half twist and a roll to standing, then to an almost good split. My dismount was a simple back somersault layout, which I really punched.

| | *Routine* | *Calculation* | *Total* |
|---|---|---|---|
| Des | 8.9 | x100 | 900 |
| Greg | 7.1 | x100 | 710 |
| Nancy | 7.5 | x100 | 790 |

I won, but then that meant I had to pay for dinner. I think we ached too much, all of us, to eat or talk much.

*Round Ten. Judo Wednesday*

Greg and Nancy were matched in the random draw. We were in the new martial arts room at Wazoo. They bowed to each other before moving on to the tatami, which was 10 meters square, including the danger area, and the safety area was another 3 meters on a side. They positioned themselves on their marks according to the color of their outfit (judogi—Nancy was in blue because her name was called as first fighter, judoka, Greg was in white). At the marks they bowed again.

The referee, Hamud, started their fight with "Hajime!"

They circled each other, looking for a hold. Greg grabbed Nancy's left sleeve, but couldn't hold as she moved. She grabbed his sleeves and pulled whichever way he moved. He ran towards her and threw her onto her leg, getting credit for a koka. Greg then threw her and pinned her to the ground for 25 seconds, gaining an "ippon," which won him the match.

Nancy and I fought. I threw her and pinned her for over 20 seconds, but was missing sufficient speed to win immediately. My Waza-ari was worth 7 points.

Greg and I fought. Greg could not use his superior strength, without me using it against him. But, then he was better at this than I was. He got me with a controlled throw. I rolled on my back and was up so fast that I pushed him to his knee. Three points for me. I rushed him, but stopped and the referee blew a penalty, a Shido, for faking an attack. He got 3 points for the penalty. I danced backwards from him, not letting him even get a grip on my sleeves. Then the referee blew another penalty on me, this time for overly defensive conduct. That was ridiculous. Defense was the essence of "the gentle way." I suppose though it was much less exciting than the throws and pins. Greg was awarded 3 more points. The mat judge signaled the referee and they conferred. They changed the penalty to 5 points instead of 3 points.

I was able to throw Greg with a technique that was missing only one of the four elements: landing, control, force, and speed. That gave me a Waza-ari and enough to get me over 0 points again.

I couldn't keep away from Greg, and yet I could not throw him and pin him to the ground. Then I was not careful and he threw me, getting credit for a Waza-ari.

The rest of the match I was able to hold on to his sleeves. The match ended after five minutes, without a definite pin, an Ippon. Greg had the highest score.

| | *GvN* | *NvD* | *GvD* | *Calculation* | *Total* |
|---|---|---|---|---|---|
| Greg | 10 | | 15 | 500+400 | 900 |
| Nancy | 1 | 4 | | 100+200+200 | 500 |
| Des | | 13 | 10 | 415+375 | 790 |

Greg agreed to treat us to dinner at the small vegetarian restaurant on Main Street, there not being a Japanese restaurant in Moscow or Pullman.

*Round Eleven. Racquetball Thursday*

"Racquetball is the wacky cross-product of tennis, handball, and squash. It is played on a standard squash court, but the ball is bigger, bouncier and bluer," I was explaining to Tina.

"Yes, I know. You made me play last year," she sighed.

"I thought you enjoyed it?'

"No, too much running around in a cage."

"Yea, okay, just remember how easy it was to get the ball next time we play tennis, which reminds me, I need to practice that. Can we play soon?" I begged.

"Maybe Saturday, after the vegetable shopping. Okay?"

That was two months ago, and I was remembering when I had free time to play for fun. Today was racquetball.

We met Jaromil, Neil, and Gil at the computing center, under the armpit of the stadium at Wazoo. Since they were ready, we all walked down the stairs to the reserved court, which had a glass back wall and bleachers for observers. The court was an enclosed rectangular room with a flush glass door in the centre of the glass rear wall. In play, all four walls and the floor would be used.

We sat on the bleachers and went over the basic rules. Jaromil was making the formal presentation of them, "Two players, each with a racquet, take turns to hit the ball onto the front wall within the large area defined by the red line at the top of the court ('out of court line') and the red line marking the top of the tin at the bottom of the front wall.

"A rally begins when the server, standing forward of the short line, bounces the ball and strikes it with an under-arm action. For the service to be good, the ball must directly hit the front wall between the 'out of court' line and the tin, and rebound back to land on the floor behind the short line of the serving zone."

I was looking at my racquet, unlike a tennis racquet, with a larger head and a shorter handle, so it was easier to manipulate. It encouraged longer rallying, and improved hand-eye co-ordination skills as the ball bounced around the walls and between the players.

Jaromil was saying, "The receiver stands between the short line and the back wall. If the service is good, the receiver strikes the ball so that it returns to the front wall. On its way to the front wall, the ball may hit the ceiling, back or side walls first, but must not hit an opponent, hit the tin or touch the floor before reaching the front wall. The receiver may chose to strike the service ball 'on the full,' before it strikes any surface.

"A match will consist of three games with each game played to 21 points, with the player having the highest score winning the match. If the score in any game in the second version reaches 20-all, the winner of that game is the player to first reach 22 points. Any questions?"

"What's a tin?" Nancy asked.

"I don't know," Jaromil confessed, "I think it's the upper part of an open court without a ceiling. The only thing I am concerned with now is that you use a standard racket, and goggles for eye protection. You can wear any light clothing such as a t-shirt, shorts and white-soled sports shoes, and I see you are."

We warmed up for five minutes by specific muscle stretching and hitting a few balls. Then Jaro brought out a coin. The player winning the coin toss has the option to either serve or receive at the start of the first game. Nancy won the toss and decided to serve. The second game would begin in reverse order of the first game.

Nancy and I went first. The games was started by the referee calling "time in." She was serving from the service zone—two lines that ran the width of the court—and although her left foot was over the line, it was not completely over it, so there was no "foot-fault" (and of course she was not allowed to start behind the zone and move into it either). She dropped the ball and hit it against the wall on the first bounce up. The server must always begin the service motion in the service zone. She had to drop the ball, allow it to bounce on the ground once, and hit it towards the front wall. The serve must hit the front wall, and may hit one side wall, and must land on the ground between the service zone and the back wall. She was trying to serve fast and low so I could not get to it, but her first serve hit before the rear line of the zone, and she had to serve again.

Her second serve was a floater that landed in the middle of the court; I almost waited too long before returning it. I hit it low, but she had been watching and ran forward quickly to catch it on the first bounce and hit a high return. So, I also hit a high one. On her next high return I hit it at a sharp angle in the corner and it went immediately from the corner to the side wall and the other side wall—it died before she could follow it all the way. It was my serve and my chance to score. Scoring is done the same way as volleyball. Only the server can score points. The server scores one point for winning a rally. The receiver gets a "sideout" for winning a rally and serves the next rally. We were playing our games to 21 rather than the traditional 15.

It was my serve and I tried a fancy high shot. I thought it was perfect, but the referee called a "single fault", saying that the served ball hit the front wall and then the ceiling. I disagreed but had to give up the serve. Other single faults are the long serve, where the served ball hits the front wall and then the back wall before hitting the ground and the short serve, where the served ball hits the front wall and then the ground before passing the service zone; the screen serve, where the server blocks the view of the ball; and, the 3-wall serve, where the served ball hits the front wall and then two side walls before hitting the ground. Two consecutive single faults are a "double fault" and result in the loss of service.

She served again. It was a good serve and it died in the right back corner; I couldn't scrape it up. It was her point and she led 1-0. We returned to our respective positions (we had 10 seconds to do that), and then the score was called. I blasted her next serve, which was low, into the front corner and it was my serve again. I served a high ball that hit the floor, then back wall and moved along the sidewall. She could not reach it and the score was 1-1.

The next couple of points were interesting. First, her goggles started to slip, so she raised her racquet and turned away. It is the server's responsibility to look and be certain the receiver is ready. If the receiver is not ready, the receiver must signal so by raising the racquet above the head or completely turning the back to the server. These are the only two acceptable signals.

She had great vitality, running all over the place. But, I was more efficient. I was able to hit the low shots that rolled out and were impossible to return. I also had a wicked serve that went from the front wall, grazed the side wall, and died before it hit the back wall. Her youth and strength gave her little advantage, though. I won all three games by at least five points each, crafty old fart that I felt.

I was not too tired to play Greg afterwards, but I knew we were evenly matched, from years of playing together. He was able to get most of my good serves. I was able to respond to his, which were mostly low and fast. The first game, we went to twenty each, before he pulled ahead and won at 23-21. The second game I won 21-19. The third promised to be another close one but he won it 21-18.

Nancy had been resting and studying us. Although Greg won the first one with an easy 21-17, she came back and won the second, 21-19. But, Crag responded to her style. The last game, she was red-faced from exertion, Greg was huffing a little bit, but he was able to play with less movement and effort; the ball seemed to come to him no matter where he was.

Greg won the round, but I was a close second.

| | *NvD1* | *NvD2* | *NvD3* | *GvD1* | *GvD2* | *GvD3* | *GvN1* | *GvN2* | *GvN3* | *Total* |
|---|---|---|---|---|---|---|---|---|---|---|
| Greg | | | | 23 | 19 | 21 | 21 | 19 | 21 | 920 |
| Nan | 11 | 15 | 16 | | | | 17 | 21 | 18 | 794 |
| Des | 21 | 21 | 21 | 21 | 21 | 18 | | | | 884 |

No one could think of a good place to eat. Greg suggested McDonald's, but we glared at him until he shrugged. Finally Nancy suggested the new restaurant at the Best Worstern, which had a good salad bar and decent fish. So, we went there.

*Round Twelve. Rowing Friday*

We were five minutes into the rowing. I was breathing well and trying to increase my strokes per minute to beat Greg. As usual, I was daydreaming about the next book review I was going to write. Then, I had a small twinge in my back that reminded me why I was here, in the weight rooms at the Wazoo gym.

Just ten minutes ago Neil had been saying, "Let me give you a few insights into rowing. First of all, rowers are probably the world's best athletes. Rowing looks graceful and sometimes effortless when it is done well. Don't be fooled. Rowers haven't been called the world's most physically fit athletes for nothing. The sport demands endurance, strength, balance, mental discipline, and an ability to continue on when your body—"

"Smells like 'bullshit.' I bet if we put rowers in the water or a ring, they wouldn't hold up much," Greg interrupted.

"—demanding that you stop. Okay, no need to be rude," Neil answered calmly. "This, I mean, because we do not have a water course, we are hosting the rowing here. It will be like single sculling, where the athletes have two oars, one in each hand, but on these machines, which we adjusted just yesterday. Normally, rowers are categorized by sex, age and weight. However, at your request, with such a mix of all three, we will ignore that and have a mixed open-weight, open-age contest."

"You will still be competing in terms of strokes per minute (SPM). The machine will record time, and this will be a thirty-minute race, as well as distance, heartbeats, calories spent, and whatever. At the end of the time, whoever has gone the farthest distance wins. Are there any questions?" Neil asked. "You had a few days to familiarize yourself with the equipment. I'll be the referee. We start at exactly 1:30 p.m. Oh, you can each have a bottle of water by the rower."

Naturally I had read up on this sport, and I suspect Nancy had, also, and I knew that we had all used the machines before, but I also knew Greg had rowed on water.

I had started at a really high stroke rate for the first two minutes, maybe 43-44, but I noticed Greg did also. When he settled into a rate of 35, I dropped back to 32-33 for a while. That was what I was trying to make up now.

I decided to do a power 10, the best strokes I had, but Greg ignored that. He was on his own schedule. Normally, we could not see each other's distances, but Neil had arranged for a display of all three machines, so we could see heart rates also. Although, Nancy was doing well, she was not going to have the longest distance. My only hope was to sprint before Greg started and trust that I would outlast his sprint.

The time accelerated now, as did my day-dreaming. I was actually dreaming that we were on Lake Coeur d'Alene, rowing under the bald eagles' nests. I remembered a few of my canoeing trips there. When I looked at the time, almost 28 minutes had gone by. And Greg was still rowing about 32, so I decided to sprint, raising my rate immediately to 45. I thought I could maintain it. After less than 30 seconds, Greg started sprinting. I was still behind, but I could go no faster. With less than 30 seconds to go, I was able to get up to 47, but dropped off a few.

Greg won. I was a relatively close second. Nancy was a respectable third. We were also acutely aware that Greg had won the last three rounds.

| | *Time* | *Distance* | *Strokes* | *Calculation* | *Total* |
|---|---|---|---|---|---|
| Des | 30.00 | 5.11 | . . . | . . . | 851 |
| Nancy | 30.00 | 4.93 | . . . | . . . | 821 |
| Greg | 30.00 | 5.20 | . . . | . . . | 866 |

I told Greg we had to go to the University Inn as Nancy wanted. I had a Mexican salad, Greg a sirloin steak and Nancy a chicken Caesar salad.

*Round 13. Running (10,000 meters) Saturday*

For round Thirteen, we were back at the track in Moscow, now called the Dan O'Brien Track and Field Complex, in the semi-natural amphitheater behind the giant blimp hanger. It was a cool spring day. I would have preferred a summer day, since I was able to endure heat better than most, especially running, since my running season was at its peak in July.

"Call it the 'Kibbie' dome, not the blimp hanger," Jaromil admonished me.

"How about a compromise," I suggested, "the Kibbles sans Bits dome?"

We were all dressed lightly in nylon tops and shorts. I had finally switched to nylon myself. I wore the black of New Zealand. Greg wore white and Nancy wore a sky blue outfit. We carried our warm-up long sleeves with us.

I knew that Nancy had trained with running sprints for her swimming, but I guessed that she could not hold up to distances. Greg was in good shape and more muscular; I suspect he might have been a threat in the sprints or short distances. I felt comfortable with the distance and my strategy, which was to start fast, roll for a mile or so, then go faster, then glide, and for the last two miles, accelerate. I figured that the two sprint parts would confuse my competitors. Actually, these sprints were a result of my running along the old highway and having to sprint by houses with free-roaming dogs.

The three timers were there, with their university watches. We had asked Jaromil to start us. But, first we stretched and warmed up. I jogged a hundred yards and then walked back. I thought about the course: We would start by doing 100 meters on the track, the straight out the back gate and up the hill on the old highway towards Pullman for about 4800 meters, turn around and return, but continue up the hill above the dome and finish at the gymnasium—that was my idea since the last 100 meters was uphill. It was more of a cross-country race, but I could not stand the thought of running in circles for half an hour or more on a track.

Jaromil signaled that we should line up. Hamud was going to bicycle along behind us to make sure no one cheated (or was attacked by dogs), so he went outside the gate and mounted up. When we lined up, Jaromil blew the whistle immediately, the timers clicked their watches, and we started running. Nancy shot out first. Greg and I loped along slowly for the first 20 meters, then lengthened our strides. We had not talked about strategies with each other, so I was not sure if they were working together or had individual strategies. I might have started a little faster than I would have, running alone. I pulled away from Greg; once we were on the hill I started catching up to Nancy.

I was careful not to sprint—it was just the first hill. I paced myself for a while, breathing a little more deeply now and controlling my breathe. I pulled up to Nancy and then in front. As she speeded up, I did also, to make sure I pulled far enough in front to set a good rhythmic pace. I was remembering running with the Kenyans, who seemed to always to maintain the same pace. When we got to the end of the pavement, I accelerated my pace as much as I thought I could keep for the rest of the race. Nancy and Greg had spread out behind me separated each by 150 meters now.

It was a beautiful, sunny day, with a small breeze. I had run this path so many times before, in the day, evening, and sometimes at night. At the last house, there was only one tiny, yapping dog, who could not escape the fence. Now, there were only wheat fields. I picked up the pace again until I felt the stitch in my side, then kept it there. Greg was closing on Nancy, when I turned my head a moment (the road was curving also). Feeling confident, I was thinking about why distance runners were so short and light. At 5′9″ I was taller by 3 inches than most and outweighed them by 30 pounds (at 163). Greg was four inches taller and 40 pounds heavier. Nancy at 5′4″ was average height for a woman distance runner, but I figured she outweighed the average by 10-15 pounds. From what I could hear of her breathing when I passed her, I did not think she would have much left for a kick at the end.

When Greg got closer to her she accelerated. I think she wanted to catch me about now, but I was in good stride. I was first at the halfway mark and made the loop back to the road. For the first time I could look at my competitors as they approached me. Nancy was 300 meters behind me and 150 ahead of Greg. It looked like she was still pulling away again. I could hear her breathing again as I nodded and passed her. She ignored me, as did Greg. I could not hear his breathing.

Again, I put myself in an imaginary race with the Kenyans. I calculated how much energy I had and picked up the pace again. My lungs were fine, but I could feel a little tension in my calves. Maybe there were too many fast-firing muscles in my legs, as I had heard that sprinters had and distance runners did not, and not enough slow-firing ones. As I reached the pavement again I lengthened my stride to its maximum; it was slightly downhill, now. I knew that I would win. I was running as fast as I ever had, maybe as fast as I could. At the bottom of the hill I sprinted the last 150 meters uphill. When I got near the finish line I aimed myself at a pointed about ten meters past it. I watched Phil with the stop watch to make sure he clicked it off. Then walked over to the edge of the arboretum and walked around, looking back to see if Nancy had reached the bottom of the hill; she had not, but I saw her come over the rise then, and Greg had not come into sight.

I walked around until they both had finished and had cooled down, Nancy had collapsed and was breathing raggedly. Greg came over and punched my arm, but did not speak. When I asked Nancy if she was okay, she managed to say, "next time, rollerblades," and smile. I felt good. I went over to the timers and watched them write down our times. My time was 33 minutes 11 seconds, not a world record by a long shot, but a very good time for off-track, on uneven terrain and various surfaces. Nancy clocked in at 36:35 and Greg at 38:06.

Jaromil was describing how the points would be calculated, "Assigning 1000 points to the current world record ... then we simply take a percentage and multiply for each of you ..."

| | *Time* | *Calculation* | *Total* |
|---|---|---|---|
| Nancy | 36:35.57 | . . . | 761 |
| Des | 33:11.04 | . . . | 836 |
| Greg | 38:06.93 | . . . | 727 |

We agreed to have showers and go to dinner at the pizza place. Jaromil offered to drive in his giant Ford van.

*Round Fourteen. Shooting Sunday*

I shut out the environment, with its constant chatter and choruses of insistent identities. I was able to get my breathing under control, then my vision, and finally my heartbeats. In a pause between beats, I squeezed the trigger. I heard the "plup" through my ear protectors; I saw the bullet travel to the target through my tinted goggles. I saw the hole appear in the "10" circle. That marked the end of the second round and twenty shots. I put the pistol down on the shooter's table. I went over to the telescope. Jaromil was marking my score and motioned to it. I looked through. The last bullet had touched the line of the "9" ring, not as I thought I saw. I shrugged. My envisioning perfect shots had not made them so. I went and sat down for a moment on the bench with Nancy and Greg.

"You guys don't have to wait, you know," I commented.

Nancy replied. "We all seem to be well under the two-hour limit, and, well, I was hoping you would get nervous and miss."

Tina waved to me; she had been watching. Then she left. This was alright because I knew it was not as exciting as ping-pong.

Greg just held up his hand. He had finished first, with a score of 487. This was a free pistol contest from 50 meters. Like all shooting events, the aim was to place as many bullets as possible as close to the center of the target as possible. Jaromil was the referee and spotter. Using the 5.6 millimeter pistol, each competitor had six rounds of ten shots under a two hour limit—the longest pause between shots was fifteen minutes. The maximum score was 600 points, but the total score was to be multiplied by 1.65 (plus ten to the winner) to normalize it to 1000.

I daydreamed for a moment about shooting bullets straight up in the air and seeing how close they landed to me, sometime later. I wondered. Then I had to stop, I placed my hands in front of me and made a finger tent. And relaxed.

After five minutes I moved back to the table. Put on the goggles and ear protectors. I wiped the grip. I loaded a bullet into the gun. I extended my arm and kept the arm at a 45-degree angle. Then I raised it and sighted through the sight. My shoulders were square to the target, but my legs slightly apart, left one forward. At the perfect center of quietness, the trigger squeezed. I did that nine more times. Then it was time to rest again.

This time I did not sit immediately, but did a few push-ups and sit-ups. Shooting tended to stress the muscles in odd ways, with the same movements over and over. I just needed the muscles to do something different for a few minutes.

Each series got slightly better. Most of my shots now were in the "9" or "10" circle. After the fifth round my wrist was tired; my fingers did not seem to fit the buttstock correctly any more. I was eager to get the last round out of the way, but I knew that I had to be patient. Nancy and Greg were sitting a little to my left talking softly. I knew Greg's wife, Lacy, was as inauthentic as Tina. I wondered what they talked about. I suspected she did most of the talking, since Greg was a good listener. Where did that come from?

Before the last round, I unbuttoned the top button of my shirt and tightened the laces of my running shoes. I prepared at the table. My first shot was high, a "7", still in the black, but my worst shot so far. I looked at the clock for the first time. I still had a full hour. I changed hands and sighted with my right arm. I put the gun down and wiped the handle again. I decided not to change now. I inspected the floor for dirt. I inspected the table for grains of powder.

I raised my arm, sighted, and shot. It was a good shot. The last of the series were mostly "10"s, so I was pleased. My total score was 571.

Nancy stood right away, and tucked in her vest; she was wearing grey trousers and a white blouse. I looked at Greg in his jeans and plaid cotton top. I looked at my jeans and my black shirt—the one with front pockets and cigarette pockets in the arms. We all were wearing low running shoes, although Nancy's looked subtlely like track shoes.

I watched Nancy closely. Unlike Greg or me, she had no wasted movements. Every movement seemed precisely programmed, even those that I was sure were superstitious behaviors, as when she pulled her sleeve before raising her shooting arm. Her first shots were "8"s or "9"s and as they seemed to continue, I grew more confident I would win. I moved over and started talking to Greg. We talked about the competition and how it was going. We talked about what sports we might have chosen, and what sports might be fun to try, such as sky-diving or the biathlon. When Nancy sat down, we were quiet.

When I started watching her again, I saw that her concentration was paying off. She was over 500 already. I started watching her carefully. She was shooting like clockwork, one shot every 90 seconds, including time to load. And, I was watching when her last shot holed a "9", making her score more points over mine. Her 579 gave her the win.

| | *Score* | *Adjustment* | *Total* |
|---|---|---|---|
| Nancy | 579 | x1.65+10 | 965 |
| Greg | 487 | x1.65 | 804 |
| Des | 571 | x1.65 | 942 |

She treated us at the Seasons Restaurant in Pullman. I had chosen shooting because I was so good at it. I never guessed that I would lose. I had a small glass of Vouvray and toasted her win. I could tell that she expected to win tomorrow.

*Round Fifteen. Swimming (100 meters butterfly) Monday*

"In the 100-meter butterfly competition, where the swimmer moves like a dolphin, using her body to push herself through the water, there are three turns. And, Des, tumble turns are not permitted," Michelle said.

I was thinking that the stroke was the most tiring, but also the most dramatic. It was almost as fast as the freestyle or crawl. In fact Johnny Weissmuller had been lucky to survive his first encounter with it while he was racing in freestyle, which used to mean you could use any stroke you wanted, although virtually no one uses anything but the Australian crawl now.

We were able to secure the Idaho swimming pool for the afternoon for an hour. That was a class time, but the instructor was going over the videos that day. In addition to the three timers, Jaromil, Phil, and Hamud, we decided to ask the women's swim coach, Michelle, if she would videotape the match. She agreed to do more than that. She wanted to have her assistant videotape the race from underwater, through one of the portholes.

The pool was a 25-meter pool, with eight lanes. We chose lanes 4-5-6 to swim in. Nancy won the draw and chose 5 as her lane. Greg took 4 and I took 6. We agreed to a 5-minute warm-up before the race. Nancy started doing kicking exercises with a kickboard. I dove in and just moved with a very slow crawl, playing between the flutter kick and a dolphin kick just to warm up—and because it was fun. Then I did a few cork-screws, switching between freestyle and backstroke with every other stroke. Greg treaded water for a while, then floated and did a little breast-stroking.

We were called to the start position. We got out of the pool and in back of the blocks. Gil was the starter. The other three were timers. I had reviewed this race so many times. I knew exactly what I needed to do to beat Nancy. As we assumed the start position I noticed she kept her right leg slightly behind. Then I heard the gun. I took off as far as I could reach to the end of the pool; as I entered the water I started the dolphin kick. I stayed under and kicked as long as I could. Then I threw my arms and hands forward and followed them. Without breathing the first few strokes, my body undulated in a perfect wave, pressing with my legs as my arms plunged back into the water. The next time I came up I breathed to the side. I saw Nancy go up just before me, so she had taken an extra stroke, and perhaps she would get tired sooner, although probably not at this distance. When I came up again I angled just towards the outside lane, in case our hands might touch. I had figured she might go out fast, so I pulled back a beat. But she was still across from me.

We turned at the same time, but again I stayed under water a little longer. I ignored her for a moment to concentrate on pushing water with my arms before bringing them overhead. I started breathing on every stroke, alternating sides to keep an eye on her or on Greg who was falling back now.

After the second turn I decided I had to sprint for everything if I was going to win. I increased the stroke count, still pulling and kicking deeply. I felt good; I was fluent with water. I was sweeping forward tremendously, but, I could not open a lead. I pushed so hard I felt like I was flying out of the water, but she was matching me at every stroke. At the final turn, I was tired. I ignored it. How long could the final sprint be? 12 seconds? Halfway; our fingertips touched once, then again. I stopped breathing now and kept my head down for streamlining. She was still matching me smoothly. As I neared the wall, I extended every finger and jerked my head up a few milliseconds before I touched, hoping to key the judge early.

I could not tell who won. I think neither could Nancy. Greg came in 5 seconds later. I splashed at Nancy, who made a farting sound under water. I rested on the edge and watched the timers confer.

We had tied again. This was unbelievable, Unfair. Unscientific. I could not even imagine a tie, even if we tried. The judges were asking us if we wanted to have them rerun the race or declare a victor by some combination of size, sex, age, or coin toss. We both agreed to leave it a tie. I wondered if we had had an electronic sensor plate at the end of the pool if we would have tied. The next time I knew that I would have to choose the mile swim. I needed to have the distance to pull ahead.

| | *Time* | *Calculation* | *Total* |
|---|---|---|---|
| Des | 58.34 | 52.27/58.34x1000 | 896 |
| Nancy | 58.34 | x | 896 |
| Greg | 1:06.33 | x | 788 |

Greg offered to treat to dinner; he chose the new Eric's whataburger Cafe. My only consolation was that Nancy kept shaking her head. We had broken the women's world record—at least the one eight or nine years earlier, although we were far off the current men's (and I was thinking that I still had not beaten Mark Spitz's time, either the world record or his 1991 comeback time, but then I am older than he is). Nancy was doing the calculations herself, using Denis Pankratov's recent Olympic and World record. Greg suggested that we take the next day off, but I begged to keep going. I was afraid I would have trouble with my schedule.

*Round Sixteen. Table Tennis Tuesday*

"Please note, Nancy, this game was not invented by the French," I said, "but by the Brits. It is the smallest game surface used, although the floor area is 14 by 7 meters marked by short blue panels." I paused. A few people had wandered in and sat on the bleachers to one side; I nodded to Tina, who was wearing a long brown cotton skirt and light blue peasant blouse.

Greg and I had never played this game. Neither had Nancy or I. Greg had chosen the sport, so I suspected he was good. Nancy seemed very comfortable with the choice and very confident. When we were warming up, I noticed she used the penholder grip while Greg and I used the orthodox grip.

Greg was inspecting the table, something I had not thought to do. It looked regulation blue, and the net looked tight. We would be playing three 21-point matches, quite similar to racquetball.

Neil was explaining the rules, "After a ball bounces off her side, a player must hit it to the opponent's side of the table. If the opponent cannot return the ball, or plays it after the second bounce a point is won. As you know, the entire top is part of the playing surface, but not the side of the table or the legs. Each player serves five times in a row and then the serve changes. Now, we have this real neat paper scoreboard," He pointed to the scoreboard on the desk of Jaromil, the assistant umpire. "I, as umpire, will be at my desk on the other side, and I will also announce points and call out of bounds balls. Now, I want to inspect your pimples before we start," he smiled.

I held my paddle in front of my face so he could see that it had long pimples. Neil looked at our blades to make sure they were mostly wood and that the covering was legal.

"Des and Greg, you are up first," he said and then took his seat, lining up three yellow celluloid balls on the table.

Greg served a simple straightforward shot and I returned it directly. We bounced it back and forth three times getting the feel of each other's small turns on the ball. Greg snapped a fast one to me and I backed up and returned it. That let him hit another fast one that I returned high. It hit the table but as it began its bounce he slammed it at a steep angle and I could not reach it.

His next serve was sharply undercut, but I had no problem and sent back a fast response, that he could not react fast enough to get. Greg keep serving with the wicked undercut and I had a few problems returning it. I found that if I keep returning fast and straight I could catch him sometimes. Nevertheless he won the first game without my getting too close.

Now that I had lost, I could relax. I started the serve. I used the same severe undercut that Greg had; the ball hit the far end of the table and almost rolled forward. He missed. For the next serve, I used a straight shot, which he hit high; as the ball landed close to me it hit the edge of the table and bounced out and down. I got under it, but my return made an arch like a returning space capsule. Greg slammed at across and I touched it before it went towards the bleachers. I kept ahead of him for the rest and won a close game.

For the third game, we both came out fighting. After his serve, I hit a hard one that he backed up to return. I backed up also and soon we were sending the ball an extra ten feet with each return. I had seen a demonstration game like this once, where the players seemed to be playing tennis, although the table made a much smaller court, and I enjoyed playing this way, although it required more control. I won the point with a net ball that dropped on his side. We fought on. Whenever I got ahead, he would come back and get ahead by a point. When I had 19, he went to 20. It was his serve again. He tried an overhand serve, but I returned it straight and fast. We volleyed a few times, then I hit a fast one that tipped the edge and went down. We were tied at 20. Then tied at 21. I served a high bouncer that he had trouble controlling, then I touched it home sideways and he could not reach around the table quickly enough. He served a straight ball and I returned it quickly and straight. His return missed the table by an inch (or two and a half centimeters, since we were thinking internationally). I had won a squeaker.

We rested for ten minutes. I drank some water. Greg went over and sat next to Lacy. I bounced a ball with the paddle in my left hand. Neil signaled us to approach the table. Nancy and I saluted each other, then the audience and judge. I hated that we thought so much alike; it was like she was my daughter or something (and I tried not to think about the details of that something).

I served left-handed. Nancy had a propensity for twisting her paddle to maximize the spin. Rather than return it with a spin, I always hit it straight. I figured if we went faster I had the advantage, especially if I kept hitting to her backhand. The penholder grip, which looks upside down to us old fogies, was at a disadvantage with backhands and required a tiring quickness on her part. I kept surprising her with the left-handed play and built up a good lead, that she could not overcome in the first game.

She served with a startling overhand that made the ball jump straight up after it hit. I had to hit it right away before it changed its mind. She pulled ahead by two points. I changed to my right hand for my serves, looking to see if Neil called a foul or rule—he didn't. I used the severe undercut and gained back to a tie. That serve was not hard once you got used to it, but it required a fast response before the ball hit the second time. We volleyed for a while and exchanged points. She was very fast and some of the points seemed instantaneous. I kept with my straight hits for a while and won the second game by three points.

I served straight and we suddenly were each fifteen feet—I mean five meters—from the table, sending the ball from orbit to tablefall like an astronautical computer. My computer did not seem to be as good and she stole a few points from me. So, I moved back in, which was harder at first because my reaction times had to accelerate. Pink, pink, pink, volley, volley, volley.

We were tied at 19. She surprised me with a return to my left-hand side. Without thinking I moved my right hand behind my back and tapped the ball back to her side. She was standing, looking at the ball when it became my point. She looked at Neil who shrugged, 'no broken rules.' It was my serve and she came back hard. I lofted it higher than I meant and she slammed it straight at my throat. Her point, and it was tied again. We fought like banshees over the next point, in and out, up and down, around the table, almost under the table, but then she dropped a light one that hit the net and died on my side. I sighed. I tried too hard on the next serve and missed the table. She had won the last game.

We got another ten minute rest. I sat over on the bleachers in front of Tina, who started ruffling my hair. Neil gave the signal to Greg and Nancy, who approached the table. I was ahead so far, but if Greg or Nancy won all three, then they would win.

Nancy served with her top spin. Greg knew better than to try to answer with an undercut. His serves, however, were even more wicked. She answered and had a slight lead. I noticed a pattern: That whoever had played last had momentum into the first game. Nancy almost lost that momentum but eked out a tie-breaker. Tina was still rubbing my head, which was a mistake—I always fell asleep when she did that and I missed the second game. Greg had apparently relaxed too much and Nancy won it too.

Now, it was really exciting. Greg was serving and had just won two points with his serve before Nancy could figure it out. I noticed another pattern with them: When they moved away from the table Nancy would score better; when they were close Greg would score better. There were some odd configurations where Nancy would be three meters from the table and Greg would be hunched over his end. After Greg scored a few with soft bounces Nancy had to stay closer. So, she tried soft touches and won some points that way. It was 20-19 and Nancy was ahead. Greg tied it with a slam, but Nancy went ahead again after some curly volleys, Greg tied it again. He motioned to Neil and stepped back from the table for a 30-second breather. Greg controlled the next two points like a Ninja master, simply and effectively. He won the final game.

Neil called Jam over and they tallied up the scores. The rest of us toweled off and started talking, discussing the best shots.

| *Name* | *Game 1* | *Game 2* | *Game 3* | *Subtotal* | *Total* |
|---|---|---|---|---|---|
| Greg | 21 | 19 | 21 | 61+10 | 143x5=715 |
| Des | 17 | 21 | 23 | 61+20 | |
| | | | | | |
| Des | 21 | 21 | 20 | 62+20 | 163x5=815 |
| Nancy | 15 | 18 | 22 | 55+10 | |
| | | | | | |
| Nancy | 23 | 21 | 21 | 65+20 | 160x5=800 |
| Greg | 21 | 18 | 23 | 62+10 | |

I hugged Greg, decided against hugging Nancy and held out my hand, which she shook formally, as I made a slight bow. I suggested that we eat at the Moscow Hotel, which had good sandwiches and salads, and desserts, at least the cookies and cookie bars. We autopsied the game. I think we were all surprised, not only by the result, but by how good all three of us were. I wondered what the difference would have been had we gone to five games each. I prayed that I would do as well at tennis.

*Round Seventeen. Tennis Wednesday*

Of all our sports to have a big audience, it had to be tennis. I counted 30 people in the stands and I suspected that most of them were Nancy's friends. Tina did not make it, but Greg's wife Lacy had shown up with their daughters

Jaromil was in his element, also, announcing the contest with a celebrity flair and announcer's confident baritone voice, "Tennis is a game played on a rectangular court by two players (singles). The players stand on opposite sides of a net and use a stringed racket to hit a ball back and forth to each other. Each player has only one bounce after it has been hit by their opponent to return the ball over the net, within the boundaries of the court. Should a player fail to do any of these three things, her opponent wins a point," and he swept his arm to include Nancy, warming up with a girlfriend, Gina. Greg and I had already warmed up and were sprawled in front of the bleachers.

"The aim," Jaromil was explaining, "is to win enough points to win a game and enough games to win a set and enough sets to win the match. This match, as part of this first-ever, international contest—"

"International?" Greg stage-whispered to me.

"Yea, Nancy was born in Ontario, eh?" I answered.

"—will be a full three sets, rather than a best of three or best of five sets. The winner of a set, of course, is the first person to win six games," Jaromil paused and lowered his voice.

I noticed that almost everyone was young and female, maybe students or staff. Our referee and judges were all male, except for Marilyn, the women's tennis coach at Wazoo, who was umpire.

"Because this two-player game is a singles match, players will use the narrower singles court," Jaromil was expanding in his low, public, intimate voice, "The game is officially called lawn tennis to distinguish it from court tennis (also known as royal tennis), an older form of the game that is played indoors on a very different kind of a court. Tennis is played on a 23.7 m x 8.2 meter (78 ft x 27 ft) court, which is divided in the middle by a net, such as that each side measures 11.9 meters (39 ft) in length. The player who plays the ball first is the server and the person who returns it is the receiver. The players will swap serve every game and change ends of the court every other game. The right to be server or receiver or the choice of court end is decided by tossing a coin. I have the coin here, a silver dollar. I am now tossing it. Nancy, please call it."

Nancy said "Heads."

And Jaromil answered, "Heads it is. Please choose one of the four following options—"

"Service," Nancy picked immediately.

"Very well," Jaromil sighed, frustrated that he did not have a chance to explain the options. "And, Des, which end of the court do you choose?"

I had already looked to see where the sun was. The court was laid on a north-south axis, and the sky was slightly overcast anyway, so I opened my hand to the south end.

"Very well," Jaromil acknowledged. "Are the umpire, Referee, Score-keeper, ready? Well, let the match begin." Jaromil did not need a microphone or any kind of amplification. He had good lungs. And he was frustrated by not being able to participate in this. I think he had actually approached the athletic department to see if they would sanction it. I was thinking of asking at my Alma mater, Oregon.

Nancy went to the north end. And, we started.

Her first serve was good and strong. In fact, I missed it.

The umpire called "15-love."

Tennis has an unusual scoring system. I remembered asking Hamud why we didn't revise it, like we did for boxing. He had said that we better leave tradition alone on this one; besides, the number of points was fair enough, it was just a silly uneven way of announcing them. 'Love' for instance, is said to come from the French word 'oeuf,' which means egg and is shaped like a zero.

—and suddenly it was 30-love, according to the umpire. I had missed another serve. I put the memories away and assigned control to the muscles and eyes.

I moved a little more to the center, Her next serve came slightly to center and I was able to hit it with a forehand. She returned it to the other side and I hit a nice backhand right back. When her return arrived, I slammed a fast low ball to her far corner, but it hit the net, and I watched it fall onto my side, and I heard the umpire say "40-love." I thought that it should be '45-love' to have any kind of mathematical consistency.

Her next serve, I returned to the opposite corner and she barely caught it. It landed again outside the lines and it was 40-15.

The next point was a hard contest. My return was weak and she slammed it cross court. I got to it and lobbed it back. She could not kill it, and I lobbed it back again. She rushed the net after her return and I lobbed it in back of her. It was high and she hit a smooth ball that I could not reach. The first game was hers.

I noticed that Nancy had been using a two-hand grip on forehands and backhands, ala Monica Seles (I had been reading up on tennis before I started practicing seriously). That gave her more power. I started to think that she might be susceptible to slice shots, if I could manage them.

It was my serve. The serve was my weakest action. I thought that I should have practiced it more. So, she returned my first serve. On my forehand reply, I angled my racquet to slice the ball with an underspin. She had no trouble with that. Since she played to my backhand, I sliced that with an underspin, Ken-Rosewall-style. That made no difference, either. Then she caught me with a dribble over the net and it was love-15.

I tried real power on the next serve. I heard Greg say, "Easily, 50 miles-per-hour, ladies and gentleman." It was funny, but I was sure it was 75 mph at least. Nancy returned to my backhand, and I hit it really strong with a topspin, which she could not reach. It was 15-15.

On the next serve I just made sure it was strong and accurate. Her return was too long and it was 30-15. To my serve, she responded with a drive to my backhand, which I again put a hard overspin on. And again, it got away from her.

I noticed that she stopped playing to my backhand when she could. We exchanged a series of long balls from the ends of the court. I tried rushing the net, but hit the ball too long. It was 30-30.

We exchanged points, and it was 40-40, deuce. This was the exception to the point count. The winner had to win two points in a row, now. She returned my serve to a backhand that I could not reach.

Then suddenly, with another fast low return, she had broken my serve. The air that normally went to my brain, I had to divert to the leg muscles. She won the second game while the brain was on cruise-control, although I did better. I knew the third game was going to be mine, statistically, anyway. So, I served hard and built up a lead. Then I was ahead 5-4, but I could not put it away. She tied it and wore me down psychologically and physically before winning.

We had a ten-minute rest. I needed the momentum to beat Greg, but I didn't have it. Greg and I had played handball, racquetball, baseball, basketball, and every other kind of ball, but not tennis. I knew he was stronger and I would have to watch his serve. But, I figured that I could beat him on the volleys, with finesse and placement. I was partly right, but I lost the first game on his serves, either a vicious top-spin or a vicious slice, or a vicious flat.

For the second game I tried hard flat serves, driving my fastest ones of the day. I won the second game in a reverse of the first.

When Greg scored with an overhand smash in the third game, I responded to his backhand, which seemed weaker. And, I kept responding as he missed. Then he caught me with a drop shot and fast serves. I stormed back and we tied at 4 each. Unfortunately for me it was his serve now. He won and broke my serve to win the game.

After a ten-minute break, Nancy and Greg played. Nancy confused him with lobs and took the first set 6-4. Greg played back with stronger serves and wore her down for the second set, 8-6.

Nancy needed treatment to her thighs after the second set.

During the third, she was able to return his serves with slices. When he got a chance at an overhead smash, he usually got the point. Nancy overcame her tiredness to win on her second match point. He had his first in the final set on the other's serve, but hit a return long. Nancy then broke back for 3-3 and the next few games went with serve. Greg had two match points on Nancy's serve, but missed a chipped backhand return on one, and mis-hit a forehand chip on the other, allowing Nancy to hit a winning forehand. In the next game Nancy broke Greg, and then served out the victory.

"This is a strange way to score this," Marilyn said. "There are some things to note. For instance, in real life, the third game between Des and Nancy would not have been played at all, since she won the first two. Also, look at the first game between Greg and Des. Greg won the game, but Des had more points. I understand how that is possible, but it means that one could win on points, under some circumstance, even if one lost on games. That would be weird."

No," Jaromil said, "because we give the winner ten points extra per win. Look at column 8."

"Seriously, I would multiply the points differently, such as add up her points, 38 and multiply by 25 = 950. (For Des 625 and Greg 825)," she said scribbling like mad on her notepad.

"Why on earth did you pick tennis?" I asked Greg.

He replied with a shrug, "It was something we had never played. It was fun."

| *Player* | *G1* | *G 2* | *G 3* | *T 1* | *T 2* | *T 3* | *Grand Total* |
|---|---|---|---|---|---|---|---|
| Nancy | 6 | 6 | 7 | 31 | 35 | 40 | 106+20=927.5 |
| Des | 2 | 4 | 5 | 27 | 33 | 36 | 96+10 =742 |
| | | | | | | | |
| Des | 4 | 6 | 4 | 34 | 29 | 32 | 95+10+ |
| Greg | 6 | 4 | 6 | 32 | 35 | 34 | 101+20=829.5 |
| | | | | | | | |
| Greg | 4 | 8 | 5 | 31 | 43 | 33 | 106+10 |
| Nancy | 6 | 6 | 7 | 35 | 44 | 40 | 119+20 |

And so it went on like this, as the spectators crowded around Nancy and congratulated her. When we were all ready Nancy took us out to dinner at Alex's Mexican restaurant downtown. I had two mudslides.

*Round 18. Weight-lifting Thursday*

I was not happy. Neither was Nancy. We both knew that Greg would very likely, most probably, win this round. Our only concern was to get as many points as possible. Weightlifting had a kind of primitive purity about it. It is a pure test of muscle and bone against iron and gravity.

"Or between will power and doubt," Nancy added.

"Was I talking out loud?" I asked.

"Yes, mumbling audibly. What's your problem. I thought you were really strong?"

"No, my arms are not big enough," I sighed.

"Boo hoo, want me to help? Never mind. I thought you were the thin graceful type. Good thing he didn't choose arm-wrestling! Wait a minute—you don't lift with your arms, anyway; it's all back and legs."

"Sshhhh! Don't let Greg hear." I said. She was right.

Our situation was somewhat certain and awkward. I had a big lead overall. Nancy and Greg were close overall.

With a whirl of his wrist, Hamud got our attention, "Weightlifting as a sport has been part of the Olympic movement since the first modern Olympic Games in Athens. For our weightlifting competitions there will be two different types of lifts, the Snatch and the Clean & Jerk. Because you have different levels of training, more or less sophisticated techniques, and because you are in different weight classes, we will use a multiplier for the final score. Although commonly seen simply as a test of strength, Weightlifting is a sport which develops many other physical and psychological attributes in its participants, from coordination to confidence."

I was looking at the weights. They were the same that we had been using in the weight room.

"As you know, the order is alphabetical. You get three attempts at each of the two lifts. You have one minute after your name is called to start your lift. After your lift we will have three minutes to set up the loading for the next lift. I am the referee. Jaromil and Neil are the timer and scorer. Gil will be the loader. As you see, we do not have the big time competition scoreboard, lights, or a jury," and he waved at the room.

Greg was first to the platform. His barbells were already set up, a steel bar 2.2 meters long and 28 millimeters in diameter. Greg had started at 90 kilograms (198 pounds). He was wearing a red costume, with the knees and elbows traditionally uncovered. Although he was thick in the shoulders and chest, he did not have the massive thighs and stomach of a weight-lifter. I had seen him lift more on the bench. He adjusted his support belt. Then crouched and spread his arms apart. Inhaled and exhaled. Applied maximum strength to begin the upward movement of the weight. He pulled upward, the "clean," and moved his body under the bar with his arms straight, all in one movement, then locked his arm joints and extended his legs for the final push. He held it for the required seconds.

Hamud signaled a clean lift, no knee-touch or drop.

Greg dropped the bar.

Now it was Nancy's turn. Gil brought out the woman's bar, which was slightly smaller and already set up with the first weights. She started at 40 kilograms. The trainer had put on her wrist and knee bandages. Her costume was gold. Although she filled it nicely, she did not look like a weightlifter, either.

She assumed the starting position, bent knees and straight arms. After controlling her breath, she lifted upwards and got under the weight quickly, so it was above her head and her arms were straight and locked. She rose up, hesitating only for as moment. It was a good lift.

I was telling Greg, "We should have one of those strong-man competitions, too, where they have to twirl a bus or push a tractor up a cliff."

Yea," Greg said wistfully, "my favorite event is the crush your own skull with your hands competition. I haven't seen that recently."

"They moved it to the last event, to make sure the competition lasted longer. Ah, my turn."

Now, it was my turn. I had decided to start at 80 kilograms. When my name was called I went over, settled in, grabbed the weight and lifted. It was a good lift. My heart, however, was beating too rapidly.

We did two more snatches each.

Greg failed at 136. I failed at 132.5; each increment had to be at least 2.5 kg.

Then after a fifteen  minute break, it was time for the clean and jerk portion. Greg went first again, at 130 kilograms. The C&J was slightly easier, although the muscular actions are almost the same, the back and thigh muscles doing the work. The arms were placed closer together. Greg lifted, then got under it easily, straightened his body, then straight-armed the weight, locked his shoulders and brought his feet together.

Nancy also took an easy weight, for her, at 45 kilos. She made it easily.

For my first C&J, I had decided 120 kilos. It was far less than double my weight, so I was sure I could do it, and I did.

Later, when I tried to go to 132.5 I just could not lift it. We were done. It was over. Hamud was explaining: "First add the total weight. Then triple it. Then multiply the total weight by the percentage of body weight to equalize over weight and divide by half. Add the two columns to get the final number. Greg wins."

Our weight totals looked like this.

| *Name* | *Born* | *Wei* | *S 1* | *S 2* | *S 3* | *C&J1* | *C&J2* | *C&J3* | *Total* |
|---|---|---|---|---|---|---|---|---|---|
| Greg | 1970 | 92.3 | 90 | 90 | 92.5 | 130 | 132.5 | ~~136~~ | 949.5 |
| Nan | 1978 | 54.5 | 40 | 42.5 | 45 | 45 | 45 | 47.5 | 592.0 |
| Des | 1946 | 74.1 | 80 | 82.5 | 85 | 120 | 130 | ~~132.5~~ | 942.4 |

There was something funny about the scores; they seemed to high, since we had not come close to any world records. Hamud said he would revise the calculation at home, after reintroducing himself to his family.

Gads, my body hurt. I was afraid to ask anyone else if they hurt as much. Nancy suggested that we skip dinner tonight and meet tomorrow night and go over the scores; spouses and significant others should be invited. I agreed. I offered to pay, but Greg said it was his turn. There was a restaurant in Potlatch that I wanted to try—Tina's parents had recommended it. Greg suggested the new Mexican restaurant in Moscow, the one that replaced the Nobby Inn, as it would be less driving. We agreed to meet there at 4:00 p.m. I went home to sit in a hot bath. Tina offered to let me wash her back—she never refused a bath, even when she was not dirty or tired. I think I fell asleep.

*Round Nineteen Counting Friday*

The restaurant was quiet. Sombreros were hung along the walls. Nancy reminded me that it did not replace the Nobby. It was where the Biscuitroot used to be, which was part of the old dime store that closed in the early 1970s—at least I think that was it. Greg and Lacy ordered Bloody Marys, Nancy and her boyfriend Mars got Tequilas. Tina got a Bloody Mary and I had some coconut/rum drink. As we were guzzling, Greg listed the final scores:

1. Archery (25 arrows, 10 targets), Nancy's chosen, Des wins
2. Bicycling (10,000 meters), Nancy's choice, Des wins
3. Billiards (three games) Nancy's choice, Greg wins
4. Bowling (three games), Nancy's choice, Nancy wins
5. Boxing (6 minutes or 2 rounds), Greg's choice, Des wins
6. Diving (11 dives), Des's choice, Des wins
7. Fencing (best of three matches), Des's choice, Des wins
8. Golf (36 holes) Nancy's choice, Nancy wins
9. Gymnastics (floor exercise), Des's choice, Des wins
10. Judo (6 minutes), Greg's choice, Greg wins
11. Racquetball (3 games to 21 each) Greg's choice, Greg wins
12. Rowing 1-person (3 mile course) Greg's choice, Greg wins
13. Running (5000 meters) Des's choice, Des wins
14. Shooting (25 shots, 10 targets) Des's Choice, Nancy wins
15. Swimming (100 m butterfly) Des's choice, Des-Nancy tie
16. Table tennis, Nancy's Choice, Des wins
17. Tennis (three games) Greg's choice, Nancy wins
18. Weight-lifting (6 lifts) Greg's choice, Greg wins

Jaromil had put it in a table. He was saying, "Had I participated, I would have easily walked off with the weight-lifting and basketball. Look at this table, though."

| Sport/*Name* | *Des* | *Greg* | *Nancy* |
|---|---|---|---|
| Archery | **812** | 720 | 778 |
| Bicycling | **891** | 857 | 885 |
| Billiards | 605 | **756** | 644 |
| Bowling | 691 | 758 | **831** |
| Boxing | **815** | 725 | 445 |
| Diving | **858** | 479 | 563 |
| Fencing | **977** | 755 | 589 |
| Golf | 520 | 680 | **900** |
| Gymnastics | **890** | 710 | 750 |
| Judo | 790 | **900** | 500 |
| Racquetball | 884 | **920** | 794 |
| Rowing | 851 | **866** | 821 |
| Running | **836** | 727 | 761 |
| Shooting | 942 | 804 | **965** |
| Swimming | **896** | 788 | **896** |
| Table Tennis | **815** | 715 | 800 |
| Tennis | 742 | 830 | **928** |
| Weight-lifting | 942 | **950** | 592 |
| | 14,757 | 13,940 | 13,442 |

Jaromil then presented the results in a different way, with points (10-7-5-3) for placements. Des 8 wins, 1 tie; Greg 5 wins; Nancy 4 wins 1 tie (but with Nancy having a higher score than Greg overall).

| Sport/*Name* | *Des* | *Greg* | *Nancy* |
|---|---|---|---|
| Archery | **10** | 5 | 7 |
| Bicycling | **10** | 5 | 7 |
| Billiards | 5 | **10** | 7 |
| Bowling | 5 | 7 | **10** |
| Boxing | **10** | 7 | 5 |
| Diving | **10** | 5 | 7 |
| Fencing | **10** | 7 | 5 |
| Golf | 5 | 7 | **10** |
| Gymnastics | **10** | 5 | 7 |
| Judo | 7 | **10** | 5 |
| Racquetball | 7 | **10** | 5 |
| Rowing | 7 | **10** | 5 |
| Running | **10** | 5 | 7 |
| Shooting | 7 | 5 | **10** |
| Swimming | **9** | 6 | **9** |
| Table Tennis | **10** | 5 | 7 |
| Tennis | 5 | 7 | **10** |
| Weight-lifting | 7 | **10** | 5 |
| | 144 | 126 | 128 |

He had forgotten to present it as a dodecathlon, twelve events between two of us! I kept my mouth shut. We discussed the strange disparities between billiards, which had the lowest winning score and fencing, which had the highest. I pointed out that the discrepancies were unavoidable, since we were matching perfect hits against world records, which were rarely perfect and could always be improved.

Greg noted that we should test swimming times against dolphin times since they were close to perfect. I noticed that his voice was hoarse, he had dark circles under his eyes, and he looked exhausted after two and a half weeks of competing. Nancy looked a little drawn, but otherwise okay. I hoped I did not look as stretched as I felt.

I was surprised that some of us did so well in sports that others chose. Nancy of course had no way of knowing how many years I had been shooting arrows. Greg had no way of knowing that I had boxed before. I had no way of knowing that Nancy was more patient and controlled at shooting targets than I was. Greg had no way of knowing that Nancy could play tennis so well. Nancy had no way of knowing how many years Greg had "wasted" playing eight-ball. Now, we knew, but next time we might choose different sports. Diversity and fun are the essences of this contest. Then, we started talking about a Hecathlon (100 prizes).

## The Five Imperfections

(The Five Cherished Imperfections of Yolande Esperanza de Sieto Vivos)
by Merissa Nieman

**1. Yolande** Esperanza de Sieto Vivos maintained a hacienda on the plateau above the blue Atoyac River, which in its backwaters was shallow with trees and shrubs harboring communities of fat, grunting frogs, but sometimes ran deep, with certain kinds of silvery, inedible fish. Its luminous waters ran through the properties of the three powerful families in the state of Taxoco, one by one. The waters are in fact as blue as the Senorita's Yolande's silk dressing gown from Madrid, a fact reported by Senora's maid, Rosina Zavada de Viva Aquas. The comparison was made as well as by Rosina's middle-aged lover, the ranch foreman, Carlos, who may only have only been repeating Rosina's description, but doing so with a lip-smacking motion that gives the innocent detail a faint and ridiculous hint of scandal. It was also the color of the fresh violets Yolande placed annually in the bronze sconces set on either side of the heavy doors of the family tomb in the Merida cemetery. Also, of the ribbons on neighbor Senora Teresa de Centesquivas de Ramat's straw hat that only recently had flown and snapped in the wind as she stood among the crowds at the Fete of San Cristobal, flirting with the handsome young men selling melon ices and wearing tight satin sashes about their waists.

The river Atoyac in its deep course was also as blue as the walls in Yolande Esperanza de Puig's casa grande, an intensity of color perfectly concordant with sky and ribbons, and laundry bluing, whose application to the walls was said to deter roaches and reduce decay in this, by turn, sultry and dry climate of Ayoquezco.

If true, then the house that Yolande lived in and rarely left, was an exception to the rule, for most of the walls were in some degree crumbling and the house itself seemingly pitched on the edge of ruin. The ceilings, all plastered and painted over with eighteenth century frescos, had not the benefit of the bluing treatment given to the walls, and were in an even more severe state of decay. After each rainy season, great patches of the painted ceiling fell to the crimson Turkish carpets, alarming the Senora's spotted cats, and arrangements would then have to be made with the artisans and plasterers in Oaxaca to restore the cherubs and goddesses. Needless to say, their original Spanish Baroque character was long gone. They were now a collection of Indian babes, rolling their eyes toward the heavens, in which a few exotic birds flew.

Despite the inevitable decline of the house—add to its physical state, the familial and social declensions—which these walls bear witness to, it was still a strong, graceful, and impressive structure, with huge spaces and marble floors and melon-colored stucco walls, of furniture and furnishings in the grand style, built and furnished in a time when the Aqua Caliente elite spoke an affected and bad French, and, outside, of aromatic gardens and groupings of *Euphorbia lactiflua* and mango, and of terra cotta and stone urns planted with rosemary and lemon trees, roses, and high stuccoed walls laced with vines and overhung by bird of paradise and pepper trees.

It had been, by all accounts, in this, Yolande's last year at her beloved hacienda, a terrible year for moths, meaning that moths were for as long as anyone can remember, everywhere. In late last summer a few of the grey-winged ghosts had, according to the Oaxaca university entomologist, first spawned in the acacia leaves draping the sweet unusually high waters of the Atoyac, then, hiding as tiny maggots in the manes of horses pastured in the early spring on the grassy plateaus but having access to the shade and nourishment of the narrow Atoyac valley, had transferred to the riding apparel of humans, thence as pretty caterpillars they relocated to the banquet of human things, they had first eaten the eucalyptus leaves strewn in closets and drawers precisely to deter them; they nested in embroidered hats and molted in the tapestries, they had chewed their way through woolen shawls, dainty underwear, and all the linens. Then, joined by new hatchlings, they dined on silk, boot strings, and even the binding threads of rare books. Only this morning, Yolande, determined to look fine for an extremely rare visit of Senora Ramat, a woman of whom the Senora was extremely suspicious, had unfolded her lime green sweater made in Paris and all the beads came loose at once, falling to the floor in a pretty chaos. She screamed for Rosina, forgetting that Rosina had gone to the market with Carlos. Of course, the indianistas, having nothing splendid save their hand-crafted machetes and big baskets of onions, but everything else already worn and frayed and caked with dirt, were not in the least menaced by the moths. They would see stray specimens occasionally, as though lost, and who, having gained their wings, fluttered sadly through the twilight in a doomed flight, for, it was said, the nectar-loving bats dined on them at night as a first course.

The beads, which had been sewn with silk thread to form an intricate pattern on the bodice of Yolande's sweater, were now scattered to the floor, but remained as an impression in the wool of the sweater. Like so much of my life, inwardly whispered the Senora, thinking of her lovers, and, in particular, of one, Cincoguerras, and of their innocent first meeting in Veracruz.

They were separately passing time in the Cafe Parroquia, drinking the best coffee in the world, which was "as hot, sweet, and strong as love," she in a striped dress and on her honeymoon, he in a green shirt and on his honeymoon. Their casual, lazy, glances about the environs met and then, in that instant of meeting, froze—or, rather, ignited.

"There is no doubt," Cincoguerras said, suddenly at her side and biting her ear, breathing about her the perfume of coffee and fire "I have married the wrong women; it is you I should have. I have known you all my life, and now, at last, too late, we meet."

Then they had walked along Zaragoza Street, passing by the chic cafes, boutiques, souvenir shops and post card stands and found a quiet cafe in which to eat chocolate cakes while, under the table, their legs entwined, producing such electricity and heat that the ceiling sprinklers came on. Laughing, they vowed to meet later along the sea wall, where all the best hotels stood and where, in different hotels, each couple had been spending a languid honeymoon. Conjugal possibilities were suffocated by ennui and disappointment, and by the interminable monotony of an overpopulation of noisy, rich gringo tourists.

Now Yolande stands before the gilded Italianate mirror in her dressing room, a sea of little pearls at her feet. It is nearly thirty years since Cincoguerras, though in this light she might pass for 30 years younger. Her auburn hair is still lush, her face still urbane, and her memories are suffused with anticipation. Yes, yes, what is 30 years but an abstraction, a mountain of seconds you can blow away with a simple, amply-felt, longing. There was Cincoguerras beside her, biting her ear; smelling of tequila and jacaranda flowers. His arms embraced her, oh, she could feel them still about her, hear the crackling of his leather jacket. He was only a young viajero, a traveling salesmen, taking his shrimp weekly from the Isthmus to sell in the marketplace of Oaxaca, and afterwards for only a month, in the Ayoquezco Plaza, and recently married to a very rich, young woman. This crossing of class lines was a miracle of course. Later, he went to the university, and became an ophthalmologist who practiced in Mexico City. When she knew him, he was only a newly-married viajero, though one must admit, a viajero of shrimp cargo rather than, say, corozo nuts, or brooms, or tamarind. Aside from his excellent marriage, there wasn't much to suggest that he would ever be more than a viajero, but it had not mattered ... they were lovers, and that put the whole affair in its own universe. She had not known this other side of Cincoguerras at all, that he had the ambition and discipline to become a medical student and then a surgeon, renowned. For a while, they had corresponded, he writing on the embossed stationery of the big clinic where he worked. It had made her think, from a relatively early age, how deceptive are appearances, and especially one's perception of them.

The Senora's eyes focused narrowly as she bent toward the mirror, suddenly smacking and brushing her earlobe from which a filigreed silver earring dangled. It was a garrapata sinking itself into her white flesh, a tick; of course, she had been out riding in the morning, surveying the limes and mangoes and what was left of her father's and her father's father's cherished agave plantation. No doubt she was covered in a curse of garrapatas, maybe thousands of them, for they bred in the sextillions in the cattle herds of her neighbor Senora Ramat.

Elena Miranda Padilla Ramat—the indianistas said she was a bruja, a woman of magical powers who could put spells on people and animals and who could read the future. This was precisely why Yolande did not trust her, though, at the same time, she did not either wholly concede the existence of such powers. It was certainly superstition, yet how aggrieved she, Yolande, would be to give offense and thus evoke some irritation in Elena Miranda that would in turn produce in her, say, a terrible headache and then—awful to consider—a painful death, such as happened to Senor Ramat following his infidelities. Yolande's only defense against such a terrible plausibility was to become spiritually impregnable; that is to say, she retreated to the stronghold of her own thinking, experience, and training. After all, Yolande had gone out into the world; she had gone swimming in the ocean, so to speak. There is something to be said for having first-hand experience of cities and populations in other places, in other cultural worlds. Though clearly of two minds about Elena Miranda's powers, Yolande had first to remember her own powers, powers generated from knowledge of the world, as it were. She must remember her worldly experience, how she had once enjoyed a little fame in flamenco dancing, had danced in coffee houses in Seville and even appeared as a flamenco dancer in a Mexico City production of Carmen. This she must keep uppermost in her mind: how it felt to carry herself as a professional woman, an artist, and she must not dwell on the fact that it was many years ago —years that were after Cincoguerros —and that her career as a flamenco dancer had been cut short by her responsibilities in Ayoquezco and specifically to her family dying out in this very hacienda. It was not unpleasant for Yolande to recall her professional experience as a dancer of flamenco, which in fact, had began in Merida, and that was because of Roberto, and so what if Roberto and flamenco music existed in the distant past, as Cincoguerras did.

It would always be true, thought Yolande, that I once carried myself with artistic dignity down the streets and into the cafes and onto the small stages of Seville and Barcelona, Oaxaca and Mexico City. Had she not, in fact, studied dance—though briefly—at El Escorial? Yolande simply had no patience for the feelings of uneasy anticipation she had experienced since receiving the note from Elena Ramat. She should have simply made some excuse, I'm afraid I must spend the day in shopping in Oaxaca or I'm off to the ruins at Ixtaltepec, sorry, but the urgent note from Senora Ramat had arrived by courier only the day before, and it had thrown her off her guard. The note had read:

"You are in mortal danger. I'll explain when I see you tomorrow, regards, EMP Ramat"

**2. The hacienda** stood in front of an agave forest; it had once been her father's carefully tended plantation and the source of the family's wealth. Agave for tequila and agave for sisal. The family god was Agave, her father's god, anyway. But, the rest of the family, her mother, her aunts, uncles, and cousins had embraced Catholicism, or, more accurately, the blend of Mayan magic and missionary Catholicism that produced the popular colorful chaotic, resigned structure for life and death, and festivals, in the dying tropics. In the flaming heat of the late afternoon of this July day—on the eve of the bruja's visit—Yolande recalled her own lack of position on the subject of religion; certainly in the burning heat of this July late-afternoon, the sun seemed the devil's smile.

It was not a comforting fact that Rosina and Carlos would remain in Oaxaca until the next day. Only Dona Elpida, the cook, remained at the crumbling family hacienda of her ancestors, and Dona Elpida was half-blind and nearly deaf. Now, she resorted to her keen sense of smell and taste to define the universe, to select a fine onion or a fat garlic for a frijole stew, to determine whether the eggs fallen into the straw had been laid that morning by the chickens or by the pigeons on the roof. Dona Elpida was nearly an onion herself, round and white. It was a tribute to her lasting culinary instincts that she produced such tasty dishes, like her mother had done when Yolande's father, for instance, had been a boy. Like everyone, she had a bit of history about her—she was not all compost for her kitchen heap—she had, when in her early twenties her own cucina in Teotixclan, catering to rough men and rough women, meaning the gringos who came down from the States, pretending to own everything, or who wanted to make movies, or carry away the antiquities, or who thought that Incan gold had been stashed in the lakes, who thought the indianistas lazy and who complained constantly about the heat and the sultry purple evenings when the agave and jojoba flowers exploded their pollen into the atmosphere, creating a kind of perfect hell for asthmatics and allergics.

At a time like this, Yolande concluded, after much thought, the only thing to do was to seek the refuge of crowds. So off to Merida she determined to go.

**3. At the market** square, Yolande made her way through the stalls and crowds that filled the plaza. The vendors and their wares stood under great canvas awnings, their goods ranging from edibles to huaraches, to carnations and fake artifacts. Gladiolas and roses overflowed tables and baskets; beans and squash were piled in abundance. She passed through the commotion with barely a glance toward any of these temptations and marched up the broad steps of the great Cathedral of St. Cristobal.

She passed through the great bronze and oak doors and, entering thus from the hot morning glare and the plaza filled with noisy Indian peasants, touristas, and hawkers, she plunged into the high Spanish Baroque splendor of a twilight sanctum sanctorum lighted by a thousand votives, tapers, candelabra, and a magnificent gold-blazing retablo.

A great flickering of candelabra, candlesticks, sconces of all sizes, some standing as a high as the statuary of saints and martyrs in the resplendent retablo, and higher, into the glittering hemispheric dome loaded with saints and studded with gilt stars. But, this was nothing compared to the thousands of votives placed at the various altars and stalls and shrines of the saints in commemoration of deceased relatives, or expressing the endless hopes of the faithful. Her intention was to say a prayer for her own protection, but she felt intently the hypocrisy of her mission in the sudden light-trembling gloom, not to mention in the sleepy skeptical stare of the five spotted cats—belonging to Father Angostino and thus permitted to come and go as they liked—sleeping in the cool shade on the worn blue velvet cushions in the christening vestibule, sleeping off their breakfast of mice and moles. When she entered, each of the cats observed her indifferently with an open eye, then, sensing no harm near, settled into their naps again. A sleek, creamy, blue-eyed beauty, clearly Siamese, padded across the cool stones of the floor and disappeared into the deep shadows of the sacristy. She thought she heard it purr as it passed her. This cat was Father Angostino's favorite, said by the devout Mayan Catholics to be the incarnation of his ancient, unrequited love for a woman he had once known and never forgotten.

Peacocks also roamed the interior of the cathedral. Peacocks were everywhere. They moved through the stalls of the plaza, too, through the jojoba cacti and the rosemary hedges of the ramshackle Opera House, like foreign dignities acting the part of courtiers in a strange land, that is so say, fully at home in their awkward, self-contained exoticness. Their metallic blues and greens, like that of old Chevrolets and Pontiacs, launched a certain feeling of dignified frivolity as they strutted across the roof the de Diaz hacienda in the morning sun. Certainly they challenged the preeminence of Senor Mariano Jorge Maria Bernardo Fortuny de Diaz y Carbo's machismo, which was now evidencing itself on the promenade beside the cathedral. Yolande saw him in his prideful maleness strutting across the plaza with a bundle of bananas and guavas under his arm. Despite his thyroid eyes and enormous belly, he had long been an enticing subject for her fantasies.

"Senor Bernardo," she called out, running out of the cathedral and down the steps toward his startled "ola!' as he saw, but had not heard her, for, pressed to his ears were the headphones of a walkman carried in a pocket of his sequined satin vest.

He had stopped, but he also frowned. He did not wish his privacy dispelled by anyone on such a fine morning while he, his heart nearly leaping with joy, was listening to Placido Domingo singing Puccini love songs. For Jorge, if nothing else, was a romantic, and a taste for Domingo had developed during cherished days in graduate school at the University of California, Davis. He liked to imagine that his inward voice, that is to say, the quality of his feeling, had all the eloquence and power of the great tenor's.

"Senorita Yolande,' he exclaimed with false heartiness, yet, it must be said, in a voice sonorous, even trembling with musical force, "to what is owed this wonderful apparition, that is, of yourself, so rarely seen beyond the hacienda of your father and of your father's plantation and of his father, and on and on.'

"Senor, my dear Jorge, have I ever asked you a favor before?"

"Yolande, I don't understand." With a sigh he unhooked the earphones from around his neck and stuffed them into his pocket.

In all his life, he had passed not more than three collective hours in Yolande's company, though to be sure, he had heard hours of stories about her, about her great fire as a flamenco dancer, about her passion for the land and the hacienda. Their first meeting had been at his sister's wedding reception, where he had drunk so much liquor he had found the courage to dance with her, and Yolande having studied flamenco in Seville with the famous Pedro Romero de Terreros!— and she had flirted shamelessly with her fan while together they stood beside the big agave in the garden. He remembered having pressed his cigarillo out against the tiles of the balustrade, the heavy perfume of the jacaranda suspended in the humid evening air. The second, ah, it was merely an accidental meeting at the local Cafe Flores; the third, again an accident, lasting merely a moment. And now: He considered it abnormal that she, an unmarried woman of indeterminate age, rode horseback through overgrown and decrepit agave plantations that swarmed with bandits and brujas, and that she put up with the snickering Rosalina and Carlos and the completely bald and deaf Dona Elpida—mon Dios, the woman was an oddity, a mystery—living on in the crumbling splendor of the finest hacienda in all Taxoco without company, without, particularly, male company or, let be said, protection. What did she do all day?

It was said that she did nothing but dream.

But now, Yolande heard something astonishing. She gestured toward Jorge to wait, and then quite suddenly whirled toward the cathedral. From inside, tumbling out into the broad daylight, came the deep, trembling sonorous notes of a cello. A cello in the tropics, in the stupendous heat and violence of sun in the southern hemisphere! At firsts beguiling, exotic, reasonable, the music calmed and excited her, then it possessed her entirely. The tones swept her up and deposited her once again in the Cathedral's twilight. "In your green eyes, I've seen the ocean, and where the ocean meets the sky," the music seemed to say. Covered with goosebumps, yet suffused with a bright warmth, she stepped deeply into the cathedral's glittering darkness. Candle flames danced to the deep vibrations; shadows leapt and flung themselves against the darkness and against the retablo, shimmering in its ornate sheet of gold leaf. The cats had fled, but not the svelte grey Siamese; she lay on a cushion, washing her face, and flicking the end of her tail. The unknown cellist drew the bow across the lowest string, forming notes of unbearable beauty and depth, then leapt to the other strings, plucking, bowing, taking two strings at time with one exquisite, confounding chord after another, producing, in fact, a music that every moment surpassed the previous moment in its unutterable beauty, until, it seemed, the sounds produced were of the gods roaming among their ancient ruins, weeping; sounds beautiful and sad beyond bearing.

As abruptly, however, as it had seemed to begin, the music stopped. The quiet that now filled the cathedral was deeper than night, more still and eternal than a moonless night when even Father Angotino's cats prowled without touching their pads to the stones. At first, almost imperceptibly, and then proceeding to fill the silence and the emptiness like a swoon, longing overwhelmed the cathedral and overtook Yolande's heart. Knowledge of some vaguely remembered, important fact filled her side-by-side with the longing. The feeling swelled like an ancient sea on a night when the moon is a silvery-gold gash in the nacreous tapestry of the cosmos. It was warm and energetic, it seemed to pulse with life and to be possessed of some identity. What a blue-filled void it seemed to leave within her, an intimation of distant memory and desire.

Yolande regained her balance and walked slowly forward, until she reached a filigreed wooden partition from which, it seemed, the music had seemed to come. She carefully stepped around it, moving into a drafty silence. An ornate candelabra with dripping burning tapers before a saint in estofado gilt garments greeted her, the licking lights causing the expression on the elaborate sculpture to seem demented. Nothing beyond the heap of plastic flowers, the burning candles, the painted saint. With her head full of confusing impressions, yet how long she could not say because time had no meaning, she stood there. Then she, Yolande, stepped into the sunlight where, before her, the market spread out upon the plaza with its brilliant color, sounds, odors. Canvas awnings spread over tables displaying mountains of carnations, roses, and bananas as well as landscapes of tropical fruit. Jorge had disappeared, but she did not really notice, nor particularly remember their previous, brief meeting. She walked toward the heaps of flowers and piles of huaraches, rebozos, vegetables, chocolate, the displays of faux majolica and the chattering crowd through which a few peacocks idly strutted, with tears blurring her vision. A thin wavering blue, as though of some huge curtain through which she was about to pass, was what she saw before losing consciousness from the scratch of Madame Eleana Padilla Ramat's false fingernail that had been carefully dipped in a drop of hemlock.

The doctor who attended her was applying some cool mechanism to her upper arm and chatting with one of the nurses whom he called Mina. Though his movements were precise he was, visually at least, focused on a further apparatus attached to the mechanism, his voice—which Yolande apprehended as cello-like —seemed to be recalling—

## The Drug Clinic

by Marcus Ryan

Andrea burst from the building, holding her torn blouse up and screaming for help. Suddenly, Roger lurched out behind her, with a crazed look on his face and a giant hypodermic needle, filled with a leaking yellow substance. He chased her down the main drag, laughing maniacally to punctuate her screams. People's jaws dropped; mothers covered the eyes of their young; men admired the size of the yellow tube. I started to run after them, then decided to go directly to the Mayor's office and explain that the clinic staff was just acting rambunctious again, you know, letting off steam and play-acting for public education. The office door was open, so I went directly in—apparently, I was expected. I sighed and shrugged. Harcourt shook his head, still building up steam for the explosion. As I sat there, letting the green invective flow over me and through the walls, I contemplated how my efforts at academic career planning had led to this circus.

*For the Academic Record*

The semester before, the fall semester, I had barely passed. I had signed up for 64 semester hours. All because of an accident at the bookstore, where I was working part time. I was stocking books for a course on anthropology. The book for the course ANT 311 on Cultural Problems, Wilson's classic on Social problems, was the one I was going to buy for my Abnormal Psychology class. That was odd. I was sure it was also required for SOC209, Social Problems. I went to the computer and did some cross-checking. It was being used for four classes, including one on Education for Social Science.

An idea formed. What if I signed up for courses depending on textbooks? It was a bad idea of course, since I only had to finish 13 hours to graduate in Psychology. And, I had been going to college for seven years already, so I had better start earning money. On the other hand, I didn't have any debts, so what was the hurry. College was great; my girlfriends were great: Irina was here from Poland and in no hurry to graduate and return. We only shared one class once, in computer economics. Emily was in a hurry to teach French. Kate was in a bigger hurry to start earning big dollars as an art historian, a field I was unaware could earn big dollars. Patty was a brilliant student unaffected by any social or political problems, a trait I wished that I had. Hmmm. Now, what was the idea? I was being distracted by the team of memory and desire. I need not describe in detail how attractive each was and how each was special, even as I started thinking ... Hmmmm.

Oh, yes, the idea was to reduce my workload and improve my

grades. By simply not duplicating efforts. An additional benefit was that I would save 75 percent of my textbook costs. I straightened out my trousers and went back to work.

Yet, it did not work out that way. Another idea had formed as I was finishing my work in the bookstore. And, that was the one I decided to realize. I signed up for the last psychology courses I needed, plus a few extra in Communications and Accounting. The following day. I submitted a drop-add for dropping the accounting, and for adding 3 new courses in sociology and one in business ethics. The very next day I dropped biz-eth and added 3 courses in anthropology and one in English literature. And, the fourth day, I dropped Eng-Lit and added 4 courses in Philosophy and Interdisciplinary studies. I now had 64 credit hours, pretty much filling every day Monday to Friday from 8 a.m. to 5 p.m. Of course, I was scheduled to work in the bookstore from 5 to 8 p.m., then the library from 8 to midnight, and the language lab, a position I had just been offered, dubbing French tapes, from midnight to 4 a.m.—actually the language lab I could do at any time just so they were finished by the first class the next day—after midnight was the only large block of time I had left. That left me four solid hours of sleep and 3 hours at various times for catnaps. Saturday mornings in the library still left most of the weekend for romance, or studying a little.

After five weeks I was amazed. It was like being always in high gear. I had a good B average, my love life was hectic but satisfactory, except for Patty's odd lust for parties with physically and emotionally overburdened and mentally unburdened assletes, I mean athletes. The plan was working.

Then one day, during a 3 o'clock gap (accidentally extended by skipping two classes) I was walking Emily back from the French House (where I had climbed the fire escape to sneak in her room for "tutoring" [and oh, I was becoming so educated]), holding hands and hugging, when we ran straight into Kate coming the opposite direction. She wasn't supposed to be on this street! Turned out she had been to the Deer Park for a beer, musing on my unexplained absences, and had to go back to the library to work. I thought we could walk by, but it was not to be. After mutual exchanges of "who is she" and less flattering comparisons, Kate stalked off. Emily slapped me and ran off, crying. I could not help but notice the shape of her breast as she turned and fled.

Unbeknownst to me at the time, Patty had seen the entire tableau and alerted the rumor squads, with the result that Irina refused to even speak with me. When I saw her at the Student Union, she retreated soundlessly, only her very-oh-so-short skirt whispering goodbye. I was going to miss her accent and the phonic changes when she was excited. I was getting depressed. I could barely keep the B average in my classes.

Weeks went by. Mid-terms went by. My academic performance improved, since it was the only play I could perform in. Patty still visited me at odd times in the apartment, but it was only to talk and joke. She always complemented me on my cat-like grace sitting or rising, but she never wanted to stroke the cat-like form it seemed. Her focus on her academic requirements was inspirational. I was tempted to tell her about my special course load just to impress her. But, I couldn't.

It turned out not to matter. I was suddenly ordered to report to the Dean's office. Dean Wordsmith of all names. There were two other men waiting in the office the next morning—and that meant I had to miss at least one class. After the dean introduced himself, he introduced the Assistant Dean and the University President, who said he was just here to observe. The Dean explained that a hand-check of the drop-adds had revealed that I was somehow overloaded. I explained the system and how it worked, why it was good and how it would benefit me. The Assistant Dean explained what changes the university would make in registration, course-load rules, and computer programming to prevent such abuse in the future. I begged to be allowed to finish all the courses. The Dean explained that it was impossible and a bad, unfortunate precedent. The President was trying not to smile, but he did not say anything. I explained that I was doing very well with the schedule and really wanted to finish the semester. The Assistant Dean said that I should just finish the psychology courses and would be dropped from the rest. I shrugged. What more could I say? We parted amicably.

I was depressed. A few days later I was fired from the language labs for falling asleep at night and recording only silence, snorts and moans for the French tapes for French 201. Merde. I wonder if they were French snorts and moans? My grades in the few pathetic psychology courses I had left started to slip. All of a sudden I was a C student. This was ridiculous!

Then my boss at the bookstore, David Snekrank, fired me for refusing to call in a book -return pickup. I told him that I had already done it and refused to call again. When he insisted I call to check, I suggested that the sniveling mama's boy cranksnot do it himself. While he went to arrange my firing, the pick-up driver came and collected the box of books for Harper. I sighed and shrugged at his greeting and timing.

I still had the library job and Helen graciously said I could increase my hours. But, the library seemed cold, especially since Emily and Kate worked there at different hours. I traded jobs with Bruce and started shelving instead of working the circulation desk. Kate actually spoke to me a few times, but seemed dedicated to finishing the semester, the basic unit of time for students, a limited artificial chunk of time in which to study an abbreviated circumscribed chunk of formal knowledge. I really wanted to hug her and apologize, but I knew better than to try.

When I went to the Student health to complain about tiredness, they tested me and told me I had mononucleosis. Great, mono. I was told to go to bed the last few weeks of the semester and stay there until after the holidays. I tried to finish a few classes, but had to take 2 incompletes in Abnormal Behavior 645 and S&P 345. During my strangely reversed days, reversed from the beginning of the semester, I worked enough to pay the rent and wine, but I also used my down time to plan the next semester, which I was going to be forced to take.

Given that the new rules forbid any student from ever having more than 20 hours, I needed a new kind of challenge. So, I chose a very special group of professors and went to discuss a project with them, individually, of course. I met with Bunker in Geography, David in Philosophy. Burton in Anthropology, Kreske in Psychology, Wimput in Sociology (I had taken his excellent course on the Amish), Chiltonberg in History, and Vellstein in Intercultural Communications.

To each I presented my new idea and casually mentioned that I was going to ask another professor about a similar directed study. Each proposal to them was part of my grand plan to write a book on the complex interplay of personal, social and cultural collapses. I would take 3 hours from each and 2 from Vellstein, which was an 863 level course. I was still tired all the time, but as a result of my talents in persuasion, of the academic variety at least, not the romantic kind, I had a 20-hour semester of my own choosing on one large special topic.

Helen gave me better hours at the Library. So I did not need to work until midnight anymore. Once a week we went out for cherry cokes at Howard Johnson's. We drove in her mustang since I did not have a car. One might think I had romantic designs on her. She was nice-looking, even in her late fifties, but I knew her husband from the Theater department. And, it was nice to have a normal friend. I wondered if she pitied me, as a result of what she had heard on various grape-vines and rumor mills (or in my case trumpets and truths). Anyway we always talked about books, and I was hoping that Kate or Irina would get jealous of her white-haired elegance and come back.

I had almost forgotten about my two incompletes from the previous semester, gack, two more papers to finish. I also found out that I was not completely recovered from the mono. So, I worked a little less and concentrated on my magnum opus or magnus offal

I thought. The outline alone was 30 pages long. I had to do more reading. More knowledge. More distilled wisdom. My wisdom tooth hurt.

On a lark, I went to the career day and filled out applications in anticipation of my finally graduating. I was hoping to line up something for September, so I could have the summer off and try to salvage my love life, or at least catch up on sun and sleep. That afternoon, after the career center excitement, I went out and bought a new shirt and fishing vest at the import store on main street.

*Give Me Merciful Rest*

In early April, I was surprised when I was told by the career placement office that I was going to be interviewed for a position as a psychologist at the Home of Merciful Rest in Wilmington.

The Home was located in a brick building facing a tree-lined boulevard, an old parkway, I learned. Dr. Bernard Grotius was waiting for me on the steps, posing like a pint-sized Mephistopheles. He was the resident physician, who had enlarged his private practice to include the state prison, two other rest homes, and the Delaware State Governor's Drug Abuse Council. Understandably, he could only spend one hour a week on the premises. He hired me after a one-hour interview. He wanted me to start right away. His reasoning was impeccable. I was studying to be a psychologist. Didn't I want to work at it before I graduated? I said I would consider it.

He showed me around the premises. There were forty private rooms, for patients with terminal illnesses. Usually, they were women, ranging in age from 19 to 70, with cancer, diabetes, cerebral palsy, and Alzheimer's disease. Half a million people had Alzheimer's; it was responsible for most of the beds in nursing homes. Mostly it affected people in their seventies and eighties. It started with the loss of learned skills and progressed to total shutdown. Sadly, it was not fatal. Its victims could live to advanced ages, as vegetables. What was it caused by? Who knew? He didn't remember any virus name associated with it; just that it might be related to kuru.

There were two full-time nurses, four part-time, and four lay volunteers, who helped with the shopping. An emergency room was on the third floor; it was not necessary for it to be fully equipped, since the state hospital was six blocks down-hill. The first floor had a large meeting room, for relatives. I would have an overnight room, with two beds and a color television, for sleeping over. I immediately moved my suitcase there, since I would not be paid in time to keep up my rent in the house.

My first night, I came down and spent in the Doctor's room and watched a science-fiction movie about a man-eating plant. The color emphasized the green; I wondered if I should try to fix it. I rented a small room six-blocks up the hill. The home was depressing to work in. There were no rewards, as in a hospital. The patients were there to die. It was a warehouse for the terminally ill. It was bleak and badly managed, but the nurses were compassionate. And, it seemed better than having the families destroyed by the costs of dying. It was a state-supported home, that received donations from those who could afford it. From relatives of the patients, that is.

I got used to the schedule. After a while, I altered it so that I wouldn't be there when the families were. Sometimes it was more important to be there at night, or during the early morning. I understood that my job was just to be a listener, basically.

Sometimes I wondered if any of the patients would make better presidents, governors, and senators, than the current crop. Many of them had a better perspective. I was interrupted by one of the volunteers.

"Mrs. Denison refuses to take the chewing gum I bought her." was the complaint.

I took the offered package of gum. Doublemint. "What kind did she ask for?"

"Spearmint." Becky answered contritely.

"This is spearmint." I observed.

"She says it's the wrong kind!"

"Umm, could be," I shrugged. "What kind did she ask for?"

"Wrigley's."

"Tell her we're getting the right kind, immediately, okay. I'll talk to her, later."

"Yes, sir, thank you."

"Oh, Becky, be sure to ask explicitly what brand, when you go shopping. Most people here have little enough to look forward to."

"Yes, sir, I know," Becky replied. She was a sensitive high school girl, who had volunteered to do some of the shopping for the residents.

"And, quit calling me 'sir.' I haven't been knighted, yet," I joked as I went around the corner.

Each resident had an 'allowance' of five dollars a week for personal expenditures. Volunteers from high schools and ladies aid societies actually did the shopping for them. Most of the residents had little necessities that made their time easier; a special deodorant or hair spray, a candy or magazine. Mrs. Denison needed gum.

I poked my head in, "Claire, keep this gum for now. I'll bring the right kind in tonight." I tossed the gum on the bed and left while she was winding up to complain.

She nodded as a went back to the Doctor's lounge.

I watched a green Johnny Carson for a while. When my vision

had become too blurry, I turned it off.

After the third week, Grotius took time out to talk to me.

"That's a handsome beard you're starting," he observed self-consciously, stroking his grey hairs.

"Thank you, uh, yours is quite Dutch," I replied politically.

"Yes, uuhhhmm, have you had any experience with drugs, in your studies, uuhh," he spoke haltingly.

What is he leading to? I screamed silently. "No, haven't had time," I replied. "Health is more interesting and more mysterious," I added thoughtfully, "I want to know how my own mind works."

"Well, You're young, with long hair and a beard. You would be trusted by other young people, of similar constitution. You would understand their problems; you could learn about them fast enough," he observed.

I was gripping the chair arms.

"You see, Dr. Weinstein at Beebe Hospital has just been incapacitated by bleeding ulcers. He is in charge of drug abuse problems at the hospital. I have been asked by the Governor's committee to find someone who can replace him on short notice. The summer season is approaching. Most of the problems increase in the summer there. Are you familiar with Rehoboth Beach, Delaware?" Grotius concluded.

"Yes, well, aren't I needed here?" I asked, flooded with relief.

"You would have a raise, a room at the hospital, and a new title."

I was suddenly depressed. I needed something brighter, but this didn't sound much brighter. Its only attraction was that it was something new.

"Of course, you needn't work hard. I will arrange for medical doctors to be visiting a week at a time. These are specialists from the Wilmington and Philadelphia area who want to help, and who will be provided with accommodations at the shore. You will not prescribe drugs or offer treatment. You would be mostly responsible for preliminary diagnosis and conveying them to the clinic." Grotius smiled grimly, his pointed beard dipping.

What Grotius hadn't told me was that I had to undergo a 30-day training program at Wilmington General, at the methadone clinic there. I started working at the hospital from six to ten in the morning, when dosages were available. I had long arguments with Grotius about the virtues of methadone maintenance, which kept addicts addicted for an indefinite period of time on an artificial narcotic. After reading up on it, I wondered why a negative reinforcement on heroin wouldn't be just as effective. Then a program of heroin reduction.

My opening day at the hospital had been a shock. At seven, the junkies came shuffling in like damned souls approaching the Styx. I watched them congregate around the orange juice for the measured sip and reprieve from hell.

It was my responsibility to interview the souls regularly. I called the name of Marga Roland. No one answered. Confused, I asked the nearest nurse, who smiled tiredly, and pointed out a girl in dirty jeans and peasant blouse. I escorted her into the glass cubicle.

"Are you satisfied with your program?" he asked.

"Yes, it's wonderful," she replied. But her eyes said 'soon you will be like us—you are damned.'

I laughed uneasily. I suddenly remembered that I was not working on my newest and best academic project. And, I was getting tired again very regularly.

*Discovering Mysteries Of The Mind*

When I related the interview to Grotius, he just shrugged it off, "It's a double-bind. They need support and a positive social role, but we can't trust them, because they don't have a positive social role. So, they are cunning children who cannot delay gratification; they challenge us with their cunning—it's a game," Grotius dismissed the problem.

I depended on my reading to keep me a step ahead of the disaster of ignorance. I found out that methadone was first made in Germany in 1944. After the war, it was marketed in America as a synthetic pain-killer named dolophine—after Adolf Hitler. "Dolly" never became a popular street narcotic because of the difficulty of manufacture.

After it was discovered to facilitate the detoxification of heroin addicts, it was dispensed at hospitals in baby bottles. Most of the nurses regarded addicts as children, also. At General Hospital, now, it was offered in paper cups, mixed with equal parts of Tang. The program currently treated fifty-three out-patients. Sometimes a few more, or less.

My responsibilities included helping the nurses monitor daily urine samples, which always created tension and an attendant bodily humor. I learned that heroin, cocaine mixed with quinine, and amphetamines showed with the test, but snorted cocaine did not show. I was also expected to conduct therapy groups for the addicts, but, with the exception of three or four older ones, most considered the groups a form of brain-washing, and avoided them. And, of course, the interviews.

My next interview went more smoothly for both of us. I asked Harper Went if he was being helped by the program.

"This is godsent, godsent," Went answered. "I been messing

around with drugs for fifteen years more or less and for once I can go straight ahead. I can go to bed and I don't have to worry about being arrested; I can get up and not worry about breaking into no house and stealing teevee sets. I feel good. And with meth I can still get tore with a beer with some pills behind it. I can do my thing, man, and I don't look no different'n you, now, do I? Do I?"

"No, you look fine," I answered.

"Shittin' straight," Went emphasized.

"How's the job search going?" I asked. I even felt slightly guilty that I myself had this job. And I knew how frustrating it was to be without.

"Not good. People afraid of me. Like I'm a freak. They don't understand meth—it makes me normal. I'm no threat. Sure I'm a freak, but I feel good about myself. I'm out there trying to find me a place. I applied for many jobs. You think I could get a job here?" Went asked.

"No, sorry, rules say you have to be off the program for a year. You could try—"

"Shit! You want'em all for yourselves."

"The hospital could not employ everyone that came here," I countered weakly.

Went drummed his fingers on the chair, waiting for the interview to conclude. I felt dissatisfied, but couldn't think of anything else to offer.

The weeks carried that same theme, repeated endlessly. Then, I was declared ready to set up the Beach clinic. I drove to Rehoboth Beach for Memorial Day. I stopped and had a milkshake at a little dairy stand. I checked into the room that had been rented in my name in a private home. Mrs. E. M.. Malley, a widow. She rented the top floor of her house; three rooms. I got the key and carried my bag upstairs. She followed me, wheezing. I backed down a stair and offered her my arm.

She waved it off, "I'm all right." She followed him into the room. "I have rules, here. No drinking. No smoking. No consorting."

Each commandment could have been carved in rock for the time it took her to list them.

"All right? All right?" she asked.

"Absolutely," I swore.

The Beebe Hospital was four blocks away. It was four stories and painted yellow. Possibly so people would see it coming. It was on a residential road, but had entrances on three sides. The building was situated on a slight rise. My office was next to the morgue, in the basement. Room 6. It had a desk, single bed, color television.

"Used to be a patient's room, but we don't put anyone down here anymore," the hospital administrator, Nick Thurmond, explained. "We can have someone move the bed out for you."

"Oh, no, I'll move it later. Show me the emergency room."

Thurmond introduced me to the resident staff and the nursing staff. "Watch out," he confided, "the nurses really run this place." Thurmond was a weasel.

Later in his office, Thurmond was explaining the set-up, as he understood it.

"As you know, Dr. Grotus, a fine doctor, fine man, was asked by the Governor, Peterson, a fine governor, to coordinate drug abuse counseling in the state. He made arrangements with this hospital to have its services available to the community. A social worker, that's you, will be in charge-"

"Excuse me," I interrupted, "I was hired as a psychologist."

"No, I'm sorry, I'm looking at the contract here. It says 'social worker.' See?" he waved it at me.

I grunted. I wondered how alert Grotius was with his diagnoses. Probably not very. 'Grotus' Thurmond had called him.

"Now, where was I?" Thurmond was deciding. "The social worker will be in charge of counseling, therapy, and recommending admissions. He will work with the special program doctors, who will—"

"Excuse me, what special doctors?"

"Ah, uhhm, the ones listed here."

"May I see the list?"

"Certainly. These doctors will each be here for one week, on call. Most of them are bringing their families-"

"On vacation?"

"Yes, that was part of the attraction. They are only receiving a stipend of $300.00 for the week."

"Where are they staying?"

"Someone will have to rent a house on the beach for them."

"Have they been contacted, yet? Have dates been arranged?"

Thurmond shrugged, so I continued, "May I have a copy of this list?"

Thurmond nodded. This smelled like a royal fuck-up.

When I got back to my roomlet, a telephone message was pinned to the door, to call Mrs. Carson. Under the note was scrawled, 'I don't take messages. Don't leave this number.' Mrs. Carson was a friend of Grotius's. She and her husband were also more comfortable than most Dupont's, money-wise.

I went down the street to a pay phone and called. She wanted me to come to a party tomorrow night, given for me. I agreed to go.

The Carson summer house was located inside a walled estate, with other summer homes. It was one story, grey stone. I was greeted at the door by Mrs. Carson, a heavy-set blonde woman charging through her twenties and into her fifties.

"Hello, George, we're so happy to have you working on this terrible problem. Bern can't be here tonight. Let's get you a drink and introduce you."

Bern was Grotius, of course. I shook hands with everyone politely. Some of the accents were from Philadelphia. I recognized one from the Main Line, one from Virginia or Maryland. Judging from the number of husbands who were vice-presidents of movie companies, banks, silicon valley companies, this neighborhood had to be the vice-presidential ghetto. I was surprised to see one of the doctors from the hospital, until I learned that it was his wife who was from Greenville (another Dupont VP ghetto).

Some of the women who came and spoke to me later had sons or daughters with drug problems. I was treated to hearing about their problems. Dinner was chicken with stuffed tomatoes. I traded my chicken for two more tomatoes. Prepared by the Carson's cook from the Virgin Islands, Raphael.

I was sitting in a rocking chair on the porch when Mrs. Carson came out to talk.

"You know," she began, "I am on the steering committee for the Lewes Drug Abuse Council. Jim Trip is the head of that. Are you familiar with it?"

"No, I didn't know there was already a Council in place here. What does the Council do, exactly?" I expressed curiosity.

"Well," she wound up, "we intend to have an information center. Downtown. We would like to provide drug—ahh—education materials to the public. There's a lot we could offer . . ." She put her hand on my thigh and continued for some time. I found out that the Council had weekly meetings on Friday in the Conference room of the Beebe Hospital. Tomorrow was Wednesday. By the time Mrs. Carson left, I was curious and frustrated (about the other group, not from the impression of her hand burned on my thigh).

When I left at 2:30 a.m., I was already working out plans for the county. The people on the councils and boards and committees meant well, but had trouble acting. There were three groups that had intentions and plans. Very well, I would unite them.

Wednesday, I arranged for a meeting in city hall. I called the local papers in each city, Seal Beach, Rehoboth Beach, Lewes, and had an announcement entered for Wednesday evening. I called the county sheriff's office, the city police offices, the state police, the hospital board, the council and invited them personally to the meeting. That night I went home and laid out more plans.

"Good afternoon, officers and citizens, ladies and gentlemen. My name is George Walker. Last month I was appointed a psychologist with the state of Delaware and empowered to set up a drug abuse treatment program in the city of Rehoboth Beach, for Sussex County. This program is sponsored by the Governor's Office, the Governor's Committee on the Treatment of Drug Problems, the Department of Mental Health, and the Sussex County Medical Society. According to Dr. Grotius, who has coordinated this effort, the program is geared to first offenders. It is an attempt for rehabilitation and education, in place of punishment and prison.

"Here is how a typical case would work. Any person caught with drugs by the state or city police would be taken to a magistrate, who would determine the seriousness of the offense. Sellers, or pushers, would be handled in the standard way. First offenders, would be taken to the Drug Abuse Clinic at Beebe Hospital, which I am setting up, now, to be interviewed and counseled, and, if necessary, treated by a Clinic Doctor. The Clinic doctors are in the process of being selected from a pool of applicants. Dr. Hotzman of the hospital has generously put two of the twelve psychiatric beds at our disposal. Let me emphasize that the program has been formed to provide a better alternative for young people just 'learning,' shall we say, the serious legal restrictions on drug use. We are going to offer them information and a medical facility.

"I am aware that there are already many fine groups making plans to combat the drug problem. That is why I have asked for this meeting, to find out what your plans are, and to see if I can be of any assistance. Before you tell me of the particulars, I would like to outline my own plan for a comprehensive approach to the problem. Then, perhaps you can help me with it. First of all . . ."

I outlined the general ideas. First, I discussed 'What is.' The habituations of society, and the associated behaviors. Illegal habituations and criminal behaviors. Then I broadly outlined 'What is wanted.' Health, without addictions to nicotine, alcohol, or drugs. Meaningful work and recreation. Vital lives in a loving community and a clean environment. Then I proceeded to 'The Means.' Individual and community responsibility—the Hippocratic oath for everyone. The physical and social resources. Time, to change.

"A three-pronged approach should be tried. Education, Counseling, and Treatment. There should be some public unit dedicated to making information available; perhaps in a storefront in Rehoboth Beach, with another in Lewes. HELP telephone lines."

Everyone knew that Rehoboth was the critical city. It had the beaches and the motels for summer visitors. And, there were plenty of those. Ocean City, Maryland, as well as all the towns inland, were also flooded during the summers. And people flocked to the coast on weekends. North were other beaches. South were more beaches. Lewes was in the center of vacationland. It was also in the center of drug traffic from Florida to points north, Philadelphia and Boston.

"I think that we should present an honest case against drug use, by admitting the good things about drugs, and then—"

"What good things?" a voice demanded.

I recognized Corporal Hall from the state police. "All right. Let's consider the good things. Physically, drugs relieve pain, kill infections, correct maladjustments, and many other good things, too. Socially, drugs, like alcohol, release inhibitions. Mentally, drugs can alter awareness-"

"A fever can do that." I looked up at a comely woman in white, who later introduced herself as Jean Moyer.

"Please, people, contain yourselves, you'll get a chance. Mr. Walker," Vince Harcourt, the mayor, indicated for me to continue. I looked down at my notes, searching for a point of continuation.

"In any case, we can't fool ourselves that drugs don't have good effects. That is why people use them. They make us feel good. What we have to do is complete their education, by telling them of the bad effects: physical dependency, imbalance of the brain's own natural drugs, risks from impurities; socially, insensitivity, paranoia, financial cost, illegality; mentally, habit, delusion, and mental imbalance—" I was going too fast. I forced myself to slow down.

"—and the multitudes of unknowns. We don't know all the effects of most drugs, or even many of the ingredients. So, after putting drugs in perspective, we also need to show them alternate ways to have the same benefits: physical exercise, artistic creation, meditation ..."

I paused and looked around at the faces expecting something from me. I wasn't sure how the next sentences would go over.

"I would like to propose as part of the program that we consider having weekly concerts on the bandstand, that we have races or frisbee contests, and perhaps painting sessions, to raise money, as well as consciousness." The murmuring had been swelling after the first mention of the word 'Concert.' Now it crested.

"You can't mean rock concerts. That would be terrible. We can't have that—" Chief Alfred Purdy's voice broke.

"Why not?" asked a younger man with large eyes and limp hair; the Reverend Melvin Bull would become a valuable ally.

"Please," Vince's voice rose like a break before the wave.

I waited a moment, and then continued, "We can leave that for later consideration. The counseling, which is the second prong, will be coordinated by me. It will include drug counseling, personal, family, and community counseling as well. I am hoping to arrange for a separate place for counseling. I also hope to arrange work opportunities for those who want them. Three or four other, part-time counselors will probably be hired or accepted as volunteers."

I didn't think that now was a good time to mention that many of the other counselors would be reformed users, rejects from other programs, or released prisoners.

"Last, treatment will take place at the hospital Clinic. The physicians in charge will be responsible for emergency and voluntary treatment. A Methadone program will be established for those people trying to conquer a heroin habit. Methadone will be dispensed—"

"We don't have hard drugs here! We don't—"

The angry father was interrupted by Thurmond, who calmed him down with, "Then, we won't need that part of the program."

I could see that Corporal Hall and another state police officer were chuckling over something. I continued, "That's basically all I have to say right now. I am still looking for a summer residence for the physicians to use. I would be grateful for any help. Mayor Harcourt, if you will take over the microphone." I stepped back on the little stage and sat down on his folding chair, between Lt. Gibson of the state police and Jim Trip, the chairman of the Lewes Council on Drug Abuse.

The Mayor was saying, "—a few words on another effort, by Jim Trip. Jim?"

Trip outlined the founding of his council four weeks earlier, in April, by a number of concerned parents. Since then, they had had weekly meetings concerned with area drug problems.

"We have decided that the best way to combat drug problems is to provide as much information as possible. We have written to the American Medical Association in Chicago, requesting a number of their pamphlets, including one titled, 'The Crutch that Cripples: Drug Dependence.' We are negotiating with the city, now," he nodded at me and at the mayor, "for the vacant lot next to the Lewes Hotel for an information center. We would be very pleased to join forces with the state effort, directed by Mr. Walker. It is our understanding that his abilities were to be concentrated on the counseling and treatment end." I suspected the old fox had been a lawyer; he knew something about separating territories.

After Trip concluded his presentation, Lt. Gibson gave a few sentences, indicating that the police would certainly work to cooperate with the Governor's wishes. Thurmond gave a short testimonial for the willingness of the hospital to offer its facilities. Mayor Harcourt closed the talks, expressing the city's desire to be clean and drug-free, to avoid all the horrendous troubles experienced by other cities with their wild youth. I turned the microphone over to the public for questions.

"Who's going to pay for it?" Harcourt leaned over and whispered something to the speaker, who spoke again, "My name is

Jean Moyer, over at Beebe. So, who pays?"

Harcourt gestured to me, so I stood up, but didn't use the microphone, "The state has allocated $200,000, after July first. Our share—the County's share—is about $29,000."

"Who gets it?" she asked.

"The hospital will administrate it," Thurmond answered.

A heavy-set, balding man approached the microphone, "I'd like to know where Mr. Walker got his information that hard drugs were in—"

"Ed!" Harcourt warned.

I confessed, "From your children, basically."

After ten more questions had been answered, the panel broke up and circulated in the audience. I met most of the rest of the state police, including Corporal Moyer, head of the Drug Disposal Unit of the state police; and husband to the nurse.

Mayor Harcourt said to me, "Say, I'm sorry Representative Wynn couldn't be here on such short notice." Then he went over and talked with the group from the VP ghetto, Carson, Hollinsworth, Theiss, Tonemaker, and two others I didn't recognize or remember.

Trip invited me to the Council meeting on Friday. I agreed to come.

That afternoon, I made notes in a journal. I set up a bank account for the Sussex County Drug Abuse Clinics. I wrote letters to the editors of local papers and to the county radio stations, asking for çoverage. I wrote another letter to the city council, asking for permission to have jam sessions on the Beach and Wednesday evening concerts on the Bandstand. Before I finished that letter, I was interrupted by a knock on the door. I hoped it wasn't the old woman with another rule. Instead it was the Reverend Bull from the meeting. With him was a freshly scrubbed young woman with an innocent expression and a toering, sophisticated beehive hairdo—altogether a masterpiece in contrasts.

"Hello, I'm the Reverend Melvin Bull, with the Baptist Mission. This is my wife, lovely wife, Pamela," he stood aside so we could shake hands. I kissed her hand, instead.

She blushed. "Oh, a southerner, I see," Bull observed.

"Well, southern Maui, anyway."

"Are you an African? I didn't think you were that dark," Bull started.

"No, honey, that's in Hawaii," she corrected.

"Really! I don't think we've ever met a native. And we were there on our honeymoon. Are you a native?" Bull asked, hanging on the answer.

"No, unknown composition on both sides."

"You're so brown," she touched his arm. "And your profile—it's so Greek. I love it." she reached to touch my nose, but I stepped back and addressed the reverend.

"I had hoped to talk to you more at the meeting."

"Yes, I wanted to talk to you, too," the reverend became serious. "I think that we can help you. Pamie and I run the Anchor House for the church. We would like you to stop by tomorrow, and see it."

"I've got a meeting at five. Would three be all right?" I asked, looking at Pamela, who had fastened on to her husband's arm, possessively, and was smiling back at him.

"Oh, yes, fine. We'll expect you then." Melvin started to leave the room, but Pamela anchored him there.

"You'll have to come swimming with us. Saturday. We love to swim."

"Oh, yes," Melvin added. "We're like little children in the water."

I started to answer, but was preempted by the widow, who was standing in the doorway. "I hope your not doing any—oh, my, I'm sorry Reverend. I didn't know it was you. Well, I didn't know what to think when two people went up the stairs. And then it was so quiet. Well, you just can't be too careful."

"That's all right, Mrs. Malley, Pamie and I were just leaving. Thank you, Mr. Walker. See you tomorrow."

After everyone left, I packed my bag, and moved into the hospital, room 6 (hoping the bed was still there). Some aggravations were too costly.

Friday, I made final arrangements with Beach Real Estate to rent a four-bedroom house on Bay Avenue, overlooking the water. It was $250 a week. I left a $100 of my own money for deposit. Bad idea but convenient. In the afternoon, I was given a tour of the Anchor House. The Bulls had two young women living with them, Angie and Lisa, who were as freshly scrubbed and innocent-looking as Pamela, but not old enough for beehives.

The reverend was saying, "Call me Mel, that's no bull." And he cackled at his own joke.

I smiled and said, "George."

"Well, George, we—the church—want to do something to stop this pernicious plague. What can we do for you?"

"What did you have in mind?"

"Well, sing-alongs, picnics, things like that."

"That's very nice of you. I'm sure that that would be a help. But that would come later, you realize, as part of fitting back into the community, after rehabilitation or detoxification."

"Hey!" Mel remembered. "We have two extra beds that you—well, you could send people here if they needed someplace to stay. Kind of like an accident pad."

"Ah, a crash pad," I identified. "We could keep that in mind. Aren't you worried about the girls?"

"No, they have their own room. Oh," Mel realized. "Jesus would protect them."

We had some iced tea in the kitchen together, the five of us. They invited me to services on Sunday. I declined saying that I had not decided what services to go to here, as there was no Royal Hawaiian Polynesian church in Delaware. They bought that, and invited me to sing with them Sunday evening. I promised to try to come.

The Lewes Drug Abuse Council held its meetings in the conference room at the hospital. They were all there before me.

Trip introduced me to the steering committee. "Mr. Walker, this is the reverend Hardy Cane, our treasurer. Reverend Cane is with the Rehoboth Beach Presbyterian Church. Rebecca Pope, our secretary. Becky used to teach school."

"Substitute." Becky said.

"Ed Evans, the Principal of Nixon Junior high school, is a member of the steering committee. Dave Bosenkrantz is vice chairman. Dave couldn't come today; he's bank manager of Delaware First, in Lewes. Oh, this is Roger Sims," Trip indicated a thin young man, hopped up on something, adrenaline possibly. "Roger is a student at the university, in Newark."

"Hey, man," Roger acknowledged.

"As we all know, Mr. Walker was hired to head the state's program here."

Everyone murmured cordially. But Roger hungered for this job, for this power—I could sense it.

"Now, this meeting will come to order. Mrs. Pope will read the minutes of last week's meeting. Mrs. Pope, you have the floor." Trip sat.

As Becky read the minutes, I looked at Trip again. Maybe not a lawyer, maybe military. He certainly ran a tight meeting. I enjoyed watching. Why lead where others were competent?

Trip took the lead again. "We have a number of things on the agenda. First is funding. Hardy, what have you got for us?"

The reverend stood, with several sheets of paper. He was short and chubby, with pleasing features. "As you know we are entirely dependent on donations," he nodded at me, "being entirely separate from the state program. This week I received $300 from the Kiwanis, thanks to Mayor Harcourt's recommendation. We have not heard from the Eagles, Elk, Moose, or Odd Fellows. I think we should ask the Masons, also, but we haven't, yet. Uuhhm, we have received a total of $104 from private businesses; Good Medicine was the latest store to donate."

"Should we even be accepting money from stores like that?" Evans asked.

"What's wrong with them?" Roger flashed.

"They sell drug paraphernalia," Evans replied evenly.

"But, not drugs!"

"Let's let the report finish, before any discussion. Hardy?" Trip suggested convincingly.

"Uhhm, where was I?"

"Businesses."

"Businesses. And we have $92 from individuals. Our total operating capital, after expenses, is $418."

"What were the expenses?" Trip asked.

"I'm passing around a report. The first page lists current expenses and cash income. Note the expenses were mostly paper, letters, postage, and printing. On page two are estimated expenses and income, through September 15th. Notice-"

"What is this bake sale listed here?" Becky asked.

Hardy and Jim looked at each other. Jim answered, "Becky, we would like you to coordinate a bake sale for Rehoboth Beach and Lewes. The proceeds would go to-"

"I'm not good at baking, Jim. Let's ask Mrs. Carson. Her servants are good cooks."

"All right, Becky, we'll ask," Jim sighed.

"Are there any corrections or suggestions?" Jim recovered. I raised my hand slightly, "Yes, what about banks and large businesses, Dupont, Yellow Cab, Carson Communications, that rental truck company?"

"We're working on them." Jim answered.

"What about concerts? or cash donations, like, for the United Fund. You know, cans on counters?" Sims offered.

"We should consider everything," Jim admitted reluctantly. "Well, are we in agreement that the treasurer's report be accepted as distributed?" he paused. "Good! Now, next on the agenda, we have the problem of deciding on a program director." Trip glanced at Roger, and announced, "I'd like to recommend Mr. Walker as program director—"

Both Sims and I were surprised. Sims looked at Mrs. Pope, who averted her eyes. I looked questioningly at Trip, sure that Sims was going to be a real problem, now.

"There are a number of advantages to us," Trip justified. "First, he is the choice of the state; he is educated." But not for this, I breathed. "He is being paid by the state, so we shouldn't need to pay him. And he is our contact with the state; this assures us a close working relationship. And finally, he will unify the two largest county programs." Trip sat, satisfied with his promotion. Mrs. Pope rose awkwardly.

"Shouldn't we consider someone local, who knows everyone, who can give a different outlook?" She still would not look at Roger.

"I think we need someone professional," Hardy added.

I was nominated and confirmed as director. By 3 to 1. I asked if I could appoint my own assistant. No one saw any problem with that, so I appointed Roger Sims as Assistant Director. Becky Pope was smiling. Jim Trip was frowning. Roger was trying to do both. I thought that this Brutus had a lean look about him. My impulse to make peace might backfire someday.

Trip took over again. "The next item on the agenda is the information center. That is my bailiwick. Bosenkrantz is sure that the bank will let us use the empty lot between the bank building and the hotel in Rehoboth. But we have to insure it first. He mentioned a minimum of $100,000 liability. According to Harve Mason, that's only $15.00 for the premium. We need to put a stand there. Any ideas?"

"I could build one," Roger offered.

"The state has trailers, used for emergencies—hurricanes—that they move around. We might ask to borrow one." I suggested.

"Good idea. Next item on the agenda. What? Oh—"

"Can we have a resolution on that? An official resolution?" Becky asked.

Trip pronounced, "Let it be resolved that the Chairman and Secretary of the Council are authorized to sign a lease for the lot at 15 Lewes Avenue in the name of the Council. Furthermore, to insure the property for Public Liability at $100,000 with the Farmers Bank being the beneficiary. That do? Now, has anyone had a chance to think about the drop cards, a design, how many? Roger?"

"I have a design." He passed around a sketch of a thick, three-colored triangle.

"What does it stand for?" Evans asked.

"Ultimate reality, the earth, and man." Roger replied, anxious to clarify it.

"Could be man, God, and earth," Hardy suggested.

"Three is a mystical number. Could be sky, sea, and land, too. Let's use it," I agreed.

"All right, let it be resolved that we will adapt this symbol for our logo. What else should we have on it? How many copies should we have printed?"

"I think a 1,000." Roger recommended.

"Let's wait until we get a telephone, before we go with it." I suggested, trying to slow down the commitments.

"What about the letter?" Becky reminded Jim.

"Oh, yes, thank you." He passed around a sample letter asking for donations. "4,000 of these ought to do. Look okay?" Jim asked, as we all scanned it.

"You need a comma, before the 'and' here," I corrected.

Becky marked hers.

"These will be distributed, along with yellow information sheets—you haven't seen those, yet, George—to every household in the Rehoboth Beach-Lewes area. Oh, Hardy, I have some bills for postage and envelopes." Jim handed over the paper to Hardy, who added it to his folder. "Let it be resolved then, that the letters and cards be prepared for distribution." Jim pronounced.

"Wouldn't it be wise to wait for a phone number for those, also?" I questioned.

"Not necessary," Jim responded. "We have a post office box, and Hardy's number."

"Is there any further business? No? The next meeting will be Friday June 12, at 5:00 p.m. Meeting adjourned." I was properly impressed. The council had gone through more business in an hour than the Governor's committee did in a month.

Trip came up to me, "I guess we don't need the phones until you know about the trailer."

I shook hands with him, "No, not before."

"You mentioned that you wanted a place to conduct counseling. It turns out that the Boy Scout House in Lewes is empty for the summer. Jed Walker, head of the Kiwanis, is in charge of it. He's a friend of mine. Want me to put a bid on it for you?" Trip offered.

"Yes, I'd be grateful if you would," I responded.

"No relation, are you," Trip smiled.

"None that I know."

Things fell together fast. I confirmed most of the doctors by phone on Monday. I had eleven doctors for twelve weeks: Paulson, Pool, Baker, Gill, Brown, Montgomery, Martin, McCall, blank, Proctor, LaBine, and Wiklander. Grotius agreed to fill in the blank, himself. The state had two trailers in the county. I got them both by Tuesday. Jim Trip found a truck driver to haul them for the cost of gas. The phones would be installed Wednesday in the trailers and in the Scout House. Two bake sales were set up, one each in Rehoboth Beach and Lewes. For Saturday, at the Rehoboth Center and the Newport Safeway. The Chamber of Commerce gave $100.00 to the

Council, and agreed to try out Wednesday evening concerts at the Bandstand; no beach sessions, however. I interviewed twenty-six applicants for volunteer positions.

*Generators Winding Up*

I called Mrs. Carson to see if she could find volunteers to help me clean up the Scout House to prepare for counseling. The House was a single-story, single-room log cabin about twenty-four by forty-eight feet. Off the front door were a single bath and closet. I took an inventory of furnishings. I set up four areas with chairs and tables. Then swept the floor. I found a hand mower and decided to mow the grass, which had escaped attention since the Scouts left in April. I had been pushing for twenty minutes when someone, an attractive woman, came around the side.

"I'm Patty Theiss," she introduced herself. "Phyllis said you needed help."

"Pleased to meet you. Who is Phyllis?"

"Mrs. Carson."

"Ohhhh." I rounded my lips.

"You must be Dr. Walker," she licked her lips.

"Oh, yes, George Walker, not doctor, though." I corrected.

"Ohh," she rounded her lips.

"Please come in, and we can talk," I licked my lips. And dropped the lawn mower in its path. I followed her up the three wooden stairs, letting my eyes follow her round buttocks as they announced her successful negotiation of the stairs. She turned and smiled at me.

We sat in one of the neat counseling areas talking. She had two children and was divorced. Her parents lived here. So she was renting, just to put her life together, in a familiar place. I was curious to know what life in Rehoboth was like. She told me about high school and marriage, and moving out to Pittsburgh. She offered me a drink at her house.

"There's water here," I commented.

"Don't you want anything stronger?" she asked.

"Are you trying to tempt me with drugs?" I asked, mock-seriously.

"Well, alcohol, then," she retreated.

"Okay," I agreed quickly. I showed her to the door, then turned out the lights. As I groped toward the door in the dark, the tops of my thighs collided with her buttocks. As she turned around, I leaned over slightly and kissed her. I felt an electric discharge between our lips. She messed up my hair and ground against me. We melted down to the floor.

When I was conscious of anything outside of us, I noticed that the door was still open. I pointed my toe and nudged it shut. Enough light was coming in from the street for me to see the outline of her face; her head was crooked in my arm. Her face was attractive, her hair was attractive. I looked down at her small breasts and exquisite thighs. Her generating equipment didn't seem much different than anyone else's, but she sure managed to make more sparks. I kissed her tenderly, then started to get up. It was too late. I was taken by the current, again.

I met with Dr. Paulson, our first volunteer, who had just arrived five days late for his week of vacation on call. Paulson was a pediatrician from Wilmington. He stopped long enough to get the keys to the beach house, check in, and promise to be back. As I saw his plush rump disappear into the station wagon, I suspected that was the last I would see of Paulson. I was right.

I still had two hours before the staff meeting in the conference room. I was tempted to apply to Ms. Theiss for more electric shock therapy. But two hours wasn't enough time. I walked up to the wards, looking for Mrs. Moyer. She wasn't there. I went back to the cafeteria and procured a pre-made, pre-heated cheese sandwich in a plastic wrapper. Hospital cafeteria food may be bad, but at least it tried to be warm. As I was sitting at an overly large table, looking through a handbook on thoracic surgery, one of the doctors approached me.

"You must be Walker." He held out a freckled hand. I looked up to see freckled arms and a freckled face, under a shock of red hair.

"My name is Mark Sullivan. My wife is colored like this, also," he added, tracking my eyes.

"Ghia Mwirragwitch, Dr. Sullivan."

"And may the road rise up to greet thee, Mr. Walker," Sullivan waved. "I thought I might be able to offer my services."

"I would be grateful. Especially since it seems that you might not be so easily lured to the beach. What is your specialty?"

"Psychiatry."

"Oh, you're the one."

"No, that was Weinstein—with the ulcers."

"So sorry."

"No problem, he did not fit very well. Anyway, I noticed from the list that Thurmond passed around that all your specialists are pediatricians, IMs, or EENTs—Ear, eye, nose, throat." he explained.

"Oh, I had hoped that Paulson was an exception."

"No, the rule. Anyway, If I can be of help, please ask me."

"I will," I intended. "Sit down for a minute. Can I get you an artificial sandwich?"

"No, thanks, but I will sit. I'd rather not eat that." Sullivan waved at the yellow and brown cardboard sandwich.

"Tell me how you got here?" I asked. And, we had a good conversation about our histories and experiences in the medical profession.

Thurmond started talking before everyone was seated, but after the second hand had left the 12 (This was the first hospital meeting): "Dr. Grotius has asked me to describe to you the hospitals involvement with the Governor's Drug Abuse program. Dr. Grotius is the physician in charge of the program, and he has arranged for a number of physicians-on-call for the Drug Abuse Clinic."

I sighed with the realization that Grotius was getting the credit for everything in absentia. I went on listening to the weasel.

"—are to work closely with the Clinic physicians and utilize them to the maximum with any drug problem you encounter. The program began June first and is intended to run through September seventh.

"Mr. Walker is a social worker from the Wilmington Medical Center who is to be used specifically for any people with drug problems. He is working closely with the Kiwanis organization in Rehoboth, where they have a special trailer on Rehoboth Avenue. The phones there are manned twenty-four hours a day by lay volunteers. Furthermore, the police have agreed to take obvious drug cases to the emergency room, where they will be screened by Mr. Walker. Are there any questions?"

"Yes, Nurse Sanderson?" Thurmond acknowledged.

"What do we do if the Clinic doctor is not available?" she asked. Everyone, especially the nurses, knew the level of expertise to be expected from the 'specialists.'

"Wait until doctor can be contacted. Mr. Walker is not authorized to prescribe any medicine or treatment for patients. He is expected to refer patients to the Clinic physician, who will eventually prescribe the appropriate treatment."

"May Mr. Walker make informed recommendations?" Nurse Moyer asked.

"Of course. You are to use his expertise whenever possible. But it has limits."

I fooled with my beard for a moment. "I would like some write-up sheets, please; some stationery. Also, is it possible to avail myself of the secretarial pool?" I inquired.

"Of course, see me afterwards," Thurmond admitted.

"If that's all the questions, the meeting is over. Thank you."

"Do we have to keep any special hours for the Clinic?" Mrs. Moyer asked quickly. Thurmond glowered. The form of the meeting had been ruined.

"Ask Walker, he will have the schedule." And he left.

"I'll type one up for you and the staff," I said. "In general, Methadone will be available from eight to ten in the morning only. The Clinic hours will officially be from 4:00 p.m. to 4:00 a.m. and I will be in residence during that time, or at the phone in Rehoboth, on demand. That sound reasonable?"

"Why those times?" she asked.

"Those are the exact times people experience drug overdoses. Just kidding, sorry. Probably ninety percent of our problems will be during those hours, with peaks around 11:00 p.m. and 2:00 a.m."

I went back to the hospital room and spent the night composing rules and procedures. Roughing it out first in the journal.

**Compromising Conditions for Contacts**

A. Keep within sound of phone and sight of trailer at all times. This is your primary responsibility—be there

B. Be able to give attention or help to anyone who asks or needs it.

C. Limit friends to one in Trailer One, the display trailer. Trailer two is set up for counseling and crashing.

D. Use discretion with volume of music; yield gracefully to complaints. Use the area behind the trailers for games (horseshoes, ringolevio, dice)

E. You may eat, read, or sleep on duty. Just be ready to help.

F. Operators have priority on parking and phones, and the authority to enforce the priority.

*Physical Contact*

I. Opening
- A. Extend greetings and invitation to enter
- B. Offer information or help

II. Next
- A. Information
  - 1. What: just facts, no judgments; care, understand
  - 2. How: verbally, nonverbally
- B. Help
  - 1. Referrals: advice, crash pads, lawyers
  - 2. Medical counseling, hospital

III. Then
- A. Observe signs and symptoms
  - 1. Straight
    - a. curious
    - b. sincere concern
    - c. other—bureaucratic, emotional
  - 2. Crooked
    - a. loss of control
    - b. feeling of rejuvenation
    - c. alterations—in image, expression,

time, perception
d. indescribable
B. Observe your own reactions
1. inform
2. determine if you can help
a. take it slow, get facts
b. use intuition, be positive
3. get help if necessary (refer to phone #s)
IV. Specific drug groups; blanket action patterns
A. Alcohol depression
B. Narcotics: heroin, morphine, codeine
1. effects
2. treatment
C. Sedatives and hypnotics
D. Tranquilizers
E. CNS Stimulants
F. Hallucinogens

*Phone Contacts*

I. Opening
A. Identify yourself 'Hello, my name is Feelgood, may I . . .'
B. React to caller
1. If he/she is talking, make listening sounds like 'uh-huh'
2. If he/she is listening
a. Be definite in offering help
'May I help you' or 'Do you want to talk about . . .'
b. Be aware of background noises, comment on them
'Is that the radio?'
'You sound out of breath'
c. Allow silence to continue for minutes if necessary but comment 'I'm still here if you want to . . .'
d. If no response, make a final offer
'Can you speak or make a signal?'
e. Offer the possibility of calling later before hanging up
'I have to hang up, now, but you can call."
3. If he/she becomes aggressive or obscene
a. Listen and reply with unflustered language
b. Try to move conversation to positive exchange
c. Close gracefully
4. If caller is speaking dialect or foreign language be patient let them know you can't understand
5. If caller threatens suicide . . . .

I put away the journal and lay down. The wake up call was coming at 5:00 a.m. I had to open the information center at 6:00 a.m. I wondered, how could I be so naive to get involved in this? This shallow hell of misery. Some people will do anything for food.

"Okay, here are the general procedures to follow when you're on duty. Nothing is strict or firm. Follow your nose and fly by your seat. Everyone else will be," I smiled. "The first sheet lists general suggestions for working in the information center. All the telephones, displays, and handouts are in Trailer One. This is the one closest to the sidewalk. The one with the open door; people are more likely to approach it anyway. Trailer Two is set up with two beds in one half, for crashing. If they are available and you need them, feel free. The other half is set up for counseling; there are four chairs and a table.

"The most important thing for you to remember on duty is that you are here to inform and help people. And the people who come in here for both may not be easy to inform or help. Sincere concern is going to be cleverly disguised as bigotry or anger. As long as you know that, you won't need to be angry or prejudiced in response.

"Each of you has been selected because of important characteristics; you are warm, under the age of eighty, and can talk. Some of you have experienced the pain and pleasure of drugs, in various doses—wake up Roger." I prodded him playfully with my foot. "Let's go over these sheets briefly."

As I read over the handouts on contacts, I evaluated the volunteers as they sat in various stages of consciousness. Molly Hoody was a slim blonde, an army brat. She looked like she was fifteen; she was twenty three. She was also one of the more successful pushers in town. Mary Hostetler was a tall, slim brunette. I didn't know much about her history; she was interested in counseling, and seemed intelligent and knowledgeable. Kevin Murphy was a college student from Claremont; sophomore? His family doctor was one of the visiting specialists. He was short, bowl-legged, and enthusiastic. Jodi Friend was Mrs. Theiss's half-sister; she was a senior in high-school, a large-boned girl of good humor. She was sitting on her boyfriend's lap. Mike Camp had graduated from high school the year before and worked in a Getty gas station this summer. I remembered him with his Mustang. Andrea Marinetti was a heavy-eyed, heavy-bodied Italian girl in gypsy clothes. I recognized her from the methadone program in Wilmington. I also knew that she could never be allowed to work alone. Mike Koestler I recognized. The remaining boy must be Bill Mariner, who had talked to me over the phone, to ask to work. I hoped they all worked out, but knew that the odds were against it.

"—with suicides, don't argue, don't give platitudes. Don't say 'it's wrong,' or 'don't do it,' or 'it can't be that bad.' Get them to talk about it. Be positive about helping. Invite them down. Offer help. If you can get name and address, but don't try too hard.

"On the general guidelines: Remain calm, don't talk too fast. Remain neutral; accept obscenity, pedantry, idiocy without replying in kind; use your own language. Remain objective; don't expect miracles; admit your limitations, give away calls you cannot handle. Remain task-oriented; try to get the caller to the appropriate facility. Don't ask for more than is necessary.

"For special cases, be sympathetic, but avoid judgments. Understand the situation as soon as possible. Is he drunk, is she on acid? Let them talk about the pain or fright, but don't over-react. Follow up on everything: How did your foot swell up and fill the room? What did the chair say next? Be positive if you can. Give the caller all the information you can.

"For referral, we have the phone numbers of two lawyers, Jones Gordon and V. Milo Sanders. There is a psychiatrist at the hospital. We have a Clinic doctor on call—if you can't get the clinic doctor, try the emergency room. The Clinic doctor is supposed to take his beeper to the beach, but—" I shrugged my shoulders, and everyone laughed knowingly. "

"Just a few more things. First, drug testing or disposal. For testing. If you think it's bad, and it's on the street, call Corporal Moyer of the state police. The number is on the board. He has agreed to respect our confidence. All we are worried about is warning people about bad dope. If you don't want to do it, I'll do it. Moyer will also dispose of dope we give him, that others give us, I mean. Chief Purdy of our beloved local police has also—"

"Can we smoke it to get rid of it?" Mary Hostetler asked. Everyone laughed.

"Use your discretion. Purdy will dispose of it, if you ask him. If you dispose of it yourself, or intend to, call him first and leave a message telling him of the intention. If you're busted with someone else's dope, tough luck.

"Now, the facilities. We have a doctor's residence on Bay Avenue. The Clinic has two psychiatric beds for emergencies. For counseling we have Trailer Two and the Scout House on Kent Street and Columbia Avenue. Crash pads: two female beds at the—"

"What's a female bed?" Bill asked unnecessarily.

"If you don't know by now, it's too late for you," Jodi chided.

"It has a hole in the middle," Andrea whispered to him.

"—Anchor house. Two neutral beds in Trailer Two. Later this week, we will have five beds in a house on the King's Highway. This is the official Half-way House. And, I need volunteers for tomorrow, to help clean it up. Volunteers?" I waited a moment, then continued, "Sign up later. We have designated the following businesses as outposts: Rexall Drugs, Owl Boutique, Hotel Lewes, Fantasia, Good Medicine, and Something Else. Most of the people there are willing to help and have experience with drug problems—"

"Especially Josh," Molly giggled.

"The Scout House will also be the planning center for the art poster contests and the Wednesday night concerts. Lastly, and leastly, the Duty Log. That's it next to the phones. Use it. Sign on and off duty—the duty schedule is posted on the wall, there; log all calls; add anything else that might be useful, later; and use 24-hour notation. Any questions? About anything?" I paused.

Bill looked sheepish for a moment, "Can we trade hours?"

"As long as the phones are covered, I don't care."

"Should we record every visitor?"

"Is there a dress code?"

Both questions came at once. I answered them both. "Use your discretion, on both. Roger, did you want to say something about dress code?"

"Pepperland. It's cool."

"Thanks. The schedule's posted. I'll open every morning at 6:00 and stay until 2:00. Then I'll be at Beebe from four to four. Some of you are scheduled with others. Those are the times we think will be heaviest. Everyone ODs at the same time, I hear."

"Do you do drugs?" Molly wondered.

"No, too expensive," I shrugged.

"Did you ever?"

"No, never." I decided to offer them a pure image, a shining example from the fount of purity. Why not? I thought of myself as pure reason.

"What are you doin' here then—get your kicks from telling people what to do?" she demanded.

But, before I could answer, Roger woke up, "You can't know how to help if you haven't done it."

"Why not?" I reasoned. "Lawyers don't have to kill before they defend or prosecute for murder-"

"Boo, boo!"

"Bad example? Okay. Doctors don't have to have appendicitis before they operate. Friends don't have to commit suicide before they talk to someone who wants to."

"But how do you know?" Molly repeated.

"Like Plato's philosopher-king—by listening to others, and by learning. By acquiring the experience second-hand, without making the mistakes."

"We could turn you on without mistake," Roger offered.

"I'll pass. Besides, there are better ways to get high—"

"What?" came a chorus, "Yea, what? What?"

"Going without food, spinning around until you're too dizzy to stand, then lying on the ground watching the world spin—"

"Hiss, hiss." Someone laughed.

I shrugged. "Let's move on to whatever we're moving on to."

Later, I watched the people walking toward the beach. Some of them looked interested as they passed by, but didn't come in. It looked kind of bare in the trailer. The display hadn't been finished. Roger and I had compromised on the design. Instead of resembling a series of triangles that Roger favored, or the circle and square I wanted, it looked like nothing except a giant eye, with writing on it. We decided to emphasize the likeness with a pupil.

I was adding lines to it, when a nine-year old boy came running in, "Are you a doctor?" he asked and went on without noticing me shake my head automatically.

"My brother's under the pier, acting funny. I think he needs someone to—help, I think."

I left the door open and went out with the kid, asking how old his brother was, and if he was doing something funny. Under the pier, we found the ten-year old giggling by himself. I looked at his eyes and sniffed his breath. I found a container of glue under his leg.

"What's wrong with him?" the younger brother asked. "Is he going to—will he be all right?"

"Sure he will. What's your name?"

"I'm not supposed to tell."

I sighed and pocketed the glue.

"What shall I do, now?" Not-supposed-to-tell asked.

"Splash water on him. He'll be all right." I reassured Not-tell. As long as he never has to add more than two digits, I added under my breath.

Two men, one middle-aged with brown shoes and brown socks and one younger with black shoes and a crew-cut, were sitting in the trailer when I got back. I saw their shoes first, as I came up the wooden stairs. They were both sitting, looking at the 'Drugs: Threat or Menace' type of pamphlets that the reverend had ordered.

The older man spoke, "I wanted someone to talk to."

"My name is Walker, can I help you?" I offered, trying to remember my own rules.

Before the man could respond, a young woman ran up the stairs, shouting, "Help, someone fell down on the sidewalk!" I noticed her red and white striped uniform, but didn't recognize it.

"Excuse me," I called back as I followed her down the street.

I immediately saw the form on the sidewalk, plaid shirt and jeans. Now I recognized her uniform. She was from the Chicken Delight fast-food place, looming over the still form. I registered the brown hair and pale skin of a late-teenaged face, as I moved the body onto the grass strip off the sidewalk and checked for a pulse. The girl was still standing by.

"Call for an ambulance, please," I asked her. As she ran inside, I checked for food blockage and started giving mouth-to-mouth, holding the tongue flat. The girl reappeared. The pulse was stronger and breathing regular.

I stopped, and asked the girl, "What's your name?"

"Mary-Anne. Did I do the right thing?"

"Yes, thanks. Mary-Anne, did you see this guy take anything?"

"Yes, that's why I came up to get you. He had a bottle of pills on his table." I felt the hip pockets—nothing.

"Would you check inside, please?" I asked.

She ran back into the restaurant. And came back a moment later, with a vitamin container with one red pill. It was probably a red devil, but I had never seen one before. What else was red? I tried to remember all of the pictures in the Physician's Handbook.

"Did you see him taking pills like these?" About four people were standing around them. I was still kneeling over the boy.

"Yellow."

"I think they were yellow," someone else added. Yellow jackets. Seconal and Nembutal. I tasted the slight alcohol on my own lips, from his. This dude must have been drinking, too. As I looked up, a black squad car, state insignia, pulled up.

"I called them," a portly man announced.

The girl glared at him, as at a roach. I assumed he worked in the restaurant, too.

I addressed the officers, "I'll help you get him in the car. We need to get him to the hospital." One of the officers opened the rear door. The other helped I load the limp body.

He bent over the face and sniffed, "Hey, this man's drunk!"

"We have witnesses saw him taking pills. Let's let the doctor decide, please," I urged. The two officers huddled in conference.

"We're going to take him to the drunk tank."

I got angry. "I want you to take him to the hospital. My name is George Walker. I'm in charge of the Drug Abuse Clinics, that the Governor—"

The second officer interrupted him. "He's ours. And we're taking him in, where he belongs."

"If you're wrong, Officers Bailey and-" I checked the other name plate, "Kolley, then I'll have your hides stretched on the fence," I promised.

"Back off, buddy, or we'll take you in," Bailey pointed. They drove off, lights flashing, and I ran back to the information trailer.

No one was there. The suits had left. I called Grotius, Lt. Gibson, and the Governor. Finally, I reached Roger and begged a ride to Beebe. Roger was here in moments and we raced the jeep to the hospital. The police car had just gotten there, with its unidentified male passenger. I helped Bailey carry the man in.

Bailey apologized, "Hey, We're sorry, we didn't know about the program."

"I'm sorry, too. No harm done," I shrugged, awed at the speed and effectiveness of the Governor's response.

In the emergency room, I asked the duty nurse to call the Clinic doctor. She held on to the phone for a minute and then informed me that there was no answer.

"Damn," I pronounced, watching the emergency room doctor check blood pressure. "Dr. Gianelli, my name is Walker. I'm the Clinic psychologist. I think we should hold this man over for observation in one of the psychiatric beds assigned to the clinic."

Gianelli nodded. I escorted the police out, apologizing for any misunderstanding. When I got back in, Gianelli had finished the examination, and was ordering the patient to be taken to room 218.

"Alcohol and pills?" he asked me.

"Barbiturates, maybe," I nodded.

"He's down pretty deep—comatose."

I nodded.

"Shall we check for ID?" Gianelli asked.

"Good idea." We went through the shirt and jeans, but found only $6.85 and no identification.

"I've got to get back to the center," I resigned. "Thanks."

Rehoboth Beach from Lewes was a fifteen minute drive. Roger and I did not speak on the way back. Jodi was on duty when I came in.

"Heard you had an emergency."

"Thanks for covering. You're not on for over an hour."

"Yea, I was rapping, over at Good Medicine. Bad news travels fast. What happened?"

I told her.

We only had two visitors in the next two hours. Parents who wanted to know how to tell if their children were using drugs. The night clerk at the hotel called up at 10:30, saying that there was some strange behavior on the top floor. Since the fire escape overlooked the lot with the trailers, I went up that way.

In the hall, seated on the grey carpet, was a twenty-year old

Caucasian male, staring at his hands, which were resting awkwardly on the floor. "They're getting larger," he shrilled.

I whispered to the young man and woman standing on either side of the tripper, "Please go back to your room. I'll handle it." I pointed to the information center, "I'm from down there."

They nodded and left. I sat down in a lotus position opposite. I stared at the young man.

"Oh, look, I can see through them—God, the bones!"

"Look!" I commanded.

As the eyes raised slowly to meet mine, I locked into them, and dreamed for both of us, 'running down a spit of rock, and leaping off the low cliff into the ocean, surfacing in a spray of air and water, then weaving in and out of the surface . . .'

"They're beautiful," the young man whispered.

After two hours, I was tired. I knew that the terror of hallucinations was the lack of control, so I was the control. The night-tripper was dozing off. I planted a subliminal message, 'the tripper cannot surface, the water gets darker, lungs labor, and as the last air leaks away, water floods the mind.' His eyes rolled wildly, then he collapsed into an exhausted sleep. I knocked on the door of the couple, but there was no answer. I decided bot to involve doctors or police. I rolled the young man into a comfortable position and left.

Jodi was ready to leave when I got back. Mike had been due half-an hour ago. I decided to stay in his place. For a while. At 1:00, two visitors showed up and wanted to know what the eye meant. I suspected that they were drunk and curious. While I was explaining, the tall one fell asleep in the chair, dropping one shoe on the floor. The other, who finally identified himself as John Tilson, wanted to know why people took drugs.

I was getting blurred by fatigue. "Same reason as alcohol, to feel good."

"But alcohol's legal."

"Yes, it is," I replied, "but not necessarily harmless or nonaddictive."

At 3:30 I woke both of them and closed up. They were irritated at having to leave. I got Mike to drive me back to the hospital in Lewes.

June was an unreal month. I spent most of it in a haze of exhaustion. I set up HELP telephone lines in Newport and Seal Beach, using volunteers attracted by ads in the local papers. The Half-way House opened without flourish. I failed to get one single prisoner released early, to work on the program. One who was released after a maximum sentence, stayed at the house only two days before he got fed up with the amateur dips, who were also staying there and left.

The July fourth weekend was relatively uneventful. Two Thorazine ODs were taken to Beebe. One man sped for several hours in Trailer Two. The Chicken Delight people called with a D&D. I took him home in my Volkswagon. Where Virginia Beach had 186 drug-related arrests, and Ocean City went over 200, Lewes and Rehoboth Beach had 0—goose egg. Luck? Coincidence? Fate? Good Work? Who knew? On the 10th, I copied the duty logs, and bound copies for the Governor's Committee and the Lewes Council. I scanned over them, picking out typical entries.

*06/08* 0020 Terry Row OD to Beebe
0150 Susan visited; Terry okay. Sam Bakeman juiced.
0230 trespasser out by RBPD (no contact)
0345 shift over Murphy out
*06/11* 1604 Mr. B. visited wanted to see some dope
1800 city inspector for electrical
1839 Jack came over Jack left
2153 Alan called going to BB
0630 shift off no activity MD out
*06/13* 1200 shift on Mary here
1438 Samantha your mother called
1500 Jim Tripp came to work for a couple hours
see what it was like.
1620 friendly visitors 'can't believe it's so progressive!'
1810 Gary brought guitar and played.
1844 Judy taking darvon for her teeth
wanted to know if okay was perscription
2025 J.A and C.G. here
not too together
2310 Mike came with hamburgers
2350 Roger "on," really
*06/22* 1030 open for public
1110 visiting nurse from Los Angeles just looking
1343 man in suit visited
1630 shift change french fries
1700 Alan to kent st. for counseling
2030 bad acid trip took to 2 for talk
2245 strange visitors bikers
0330 useless to keep up I off
*06/27* 1100 day shift on Mariner
1150 Tina Williams looking for I bad news
1230 Jim Trip to pick up tools from display
1320 9311 caput telephone people called on other
line coming by

1700 []
1420 drove Davis to hosp. for check.
1500 Social worker from Cleveland
1555 Rev. Bull called for George
2100 Ron bad?
2310 Mrs. Lovatos referred to I for couns.
*06/30* 1015 Koestler in
1100 McCarthy asks questions
2100 no comment
2140 Ralph Gore admitted to hosp.
2230 I back call about methadone
2310 Guy with Mary to see what time it was told him
2317 visit from obvious narc, ex-narc, and cop
2356 stereo too loud—complaint from hotel agree to
turn down
0015 Mary says Ted offered $50 for a fuck could
we use the money NO!
0100 Jack wants to appeal case who is lawyer?
0130 Darvon + wine = nausea
*07/01* 0940 open with I garbage man cometh
1010 Belle from the east with Librium on vacation
walk by shore, swim to relax
1030 Bill here two people want to join clinic live
in Newcastle
1220 I back Rep. Wynn waiting VIP tour
1615 Trip here with Johnson from newspaper
want case studies for art.
1900 Old man came in wanted to smell heroin
didn't have any son was busted for possess.
1930 Middle-aged couple with kids fro Penn, wanted info
good rap
1950 Girl with cut hand driven to hospital by Mike.
2230 Joy Kurney and her scag want test for
powder called Cprl. Moyer
0400 I out

July promised to be a busier month, and August, worse yet. That morning, two people from the HELP telephones in Ocean City came in to see what was what. The Chamber of Commerce had wanted papers signed for insurance. One of the counselors landed in jail and had to be bailed out with more of my salary. More state officials were interested and coming by. Two Correctional Institute personnel had been given the tour.

One quiet evening, I just got tired of sitting and thinking and walked down to the beach. Someone was scheduled in an hour anyway. Hopefully, the world wouldn't fall apart. I started jogging north on the beach, towards Lewes. It was fun. I ran into the small waves, and every once in a while I would be upended and get wet. Before I got all the way I turned around. I had no idea what time it was. When I got tired, I lay on the beach and slept. It was starting to get very cool. Every time I ran, it seemed that the sky was darker and I was running faster. Finally, when I got to the trailer again, I fell asleep on one of the bunks.

In mid-July, I collapsed at work. Dr. Sullivan said he had better examine me. I said that I had gotten up immediately and that I felt okay. He said he was told that I was unconscious for a few minutes. That, I didn't remember.

It didn't make much difference. I kept working. I finally got the approval from the university to extend my incompletes. That seemed so long ago. My project was just hundreds of pages of notes and ideas in 11 folders packed under my bed.

Dr. Sullivan told me that I had cirrhosis of the liver. He asked if I drank. I said I would if I had time. He asked about other things, including mono. I told him that I had it last fall, but it went away. He said it didn't go away at all, just got worse. I was also getting an ulcer. I thought immediately of my predecessor and understood, now. The little aches and pains, especially stomach and abdominal pains, were almost explained.

He ordered me to be confined to my office, next to the morgue—now that was an incentive to recover. The bed was moved back in. I told him I still had to work. Gradually, I resumed a schedule of 6 hours a day and I slept the difference. Patty visited once, that I remember, and broke my fever by increasing my temperature dramatically.

Days and weeks went by. More people, more problems, patient problems, staff problems.

It was 2:20 in the afternoon, and I had to get ready for the meeting at the hospital. As I left the trailer, my peripheral vision tracked a gloved hand descending toward my temple. I bent at the knees to a crouch. The hand missed and I dragged an unbalanced body over me. I grabbed an arm and leg and lifted from my knees. I tossed a large body over the stairs onto the sandy dirt in front of the trailers. I walked down the stairs, locked the free arms behind a dusty black jacket and asked reasonably into a lumpy ear,

"Pardon me, did you want to talk to me?"

"Let me up and I'll break you," the man threatened.

"Common sense is an alien concept to you, isn't it?" I pressed the arms toward the neck so they creaked. "I already have you down. Now what is it?"

"My girl, don't mess with her," he groaned, straining to keep his arms down further on his back.

"Now, I have to guess? Did she have a tattoo on her chest, with your name on it?"

"Bastard! Theiss, Patty Theiss," he grunted, feeling dirt on his tongue. I stepped on the man's buttocks to stand up without any surprises.

"You ought to work that out with her," I suggested.

The black jacket came at my ankles in a hurry. I jumped back, then up on his back again, wunking it into the dirt.

"Oahh, I'm hurt," the jacket complained.

I got in the staff car and drove to the meeting at Beebe. What kind of person was I becoming? Worse, was I liking it?

The meeting was as tightly run as ever. Mrs. Pope read the minutes. Hardy Cane handed out the latest budget sheets. Everyone was thrilled at the $406.40 from the bake sales. The state coughed up $500.00. The American Legion and Rotary Club punched in $50.00 each. Over thirty individuals had donated amounts ranging from two dollars to fifty. The treasury stood at $2152.00.

I was glad, since I submitted expenditures for the Council totaling over $879.00. For the Half-way House rent, telephone and cleaning supplies; for telephone and janitorial for the Bay Avenue doctor's house; for telephones, paint and art supplies for the Scout House Counseling Center.

During my report, I notified them of Roger's arrest and release. And, of my decision to remove him as assistant. The Council affirmed that authority. The Council felt that anyone caught with drugs be discharged. I was relieved, since Roger was making deals left and right, while trying to consolidate authority for himself. The funds were approved, and resolved. The musical programs for Wednesdays were voted to be continued; no one dared call them rock concerts. The Council set its next meeting for the following Friday.

That night, staring at the phones, once called instruments of the devil, Mike and I were surprised by a HaHa visit from the Chicken sisters and Niki. Every week or so, after the 1:00 a.m. closing time, three of the girls from the Chicken Delight would come by with buckets of chicken and cheeseburgers—all ostensibly left over and unsold. I could not think of any more generous reward for working at the devil's instruments than spontaneous gifts from nubile youngsters. They sat around eating and talking of high school, which I barely remembered, having flunked out, and which Mike still thought of from college, and which the girls were just enjoying. Grease had become popular with fast food chains, but cold grease had a punishment all of its own. I ate french fries ceremoniously, knowing that my time on the toilet would come shortly.

There were five regulars on methadone at the clinic. There was a sixth regular, Benny Raider, who hated hospitals and cops, but couldn't afford the scag or the jail sentences. Him I was trying on a heroin reduction program. We both knew where the 'shit was hid' as Benny laughed. The agreement was that I would always parcel it out and he would be responsible for the consequences if he was caught; that commitment let Benny be committed, too. The five regulars had to take their methadone in orange juice between seven and nine in the morning. I had to supervise them. They all tended to come in together. I found out why the second week, when I caught them hoarding the juice. Each one would take the dose under supervision of the nurse, but only pretend to swallow it. Then they would spit it all into a thermos, and sell it to Molly for resale. It was a nice profit for everyone. I never would have guessed if one of them, Peggy Coles, hadn't been angry at being cheated by Molly, and ratted.

That afternoon, I met Patty Theiss in an apartment on Oregon Avenue. It was a two-story redwood; the apartment was on the second floor. When I came in I saw a pile of vegetation on the counter that resembled parsley.

"Oh, shit," I said.

"What's the matter," Patty poked her head around the corner.

"That," I pointed.

"That is parsley. I was dicing it for your lasagna. The grass is in my purse, but you can search me if you want, officer," she flirted.

I sighed deeply and went in and laid down on the bed. It was a studio apartment so I watched her as she sautéed onions and mushrooms.

"It won't be as good as yours," she said.

"Sure it will, I watched you," As she walked overI grabbed her hips and buried my face in her stomach; then levered her into bed.

"50 minutes," she managed to say.

That night was busy. Two more overdoses and a couple freaked by the eye display, which had become more psychedelic; someone had outlined it with different colors of phosphorescent paint. When it was quiet, I went out and looked at the sky. Bill had put a spotlight in the branches of the tree, so it was lighted up dramatically. Then I noticed someone slumped in the phone booth on the sidewalk. I ran over and opened it. The figure straightened out and thrust a knife into one of my ribs. I turned sideways, feeling the blade skid through muscle. I rammed myself backwards, grabbing the collar of my assailant. I pulled the knife and flung it aside, kicking the figure in the back, pushing it into the street. An engine roared, and headlights glared. The car stopped, the figure dived in the open window, rubber squealed as the shape leapt forward. I watched, holding my side, feeling the blood leak between his fingers and the sharp pain of each breath.

Then I ran down the street paralleling the car. I knew it had to turn right in two blocks to get to the highway. When I realized that I could not get to it, I grabbed a garbage can lid as I ran. As the car turned, I threw the lid. I saw the white face in the open window open its mouth before it was eclipsed by the metal lid. The car kept going, untouched. I slowed down and turned back toward the staff car.

Mary Sanders was on duty at the emergency room. I took off my shirt. She probed the wound.

"Are you going to report it?" she asked skeptically.

"Report what?" I responded. "He missed."

"Doper?" she asked.

I shrugged. "Moron. Could you just tape it? I heal fast."

"You might scar, though," she considered, then noticed the other scars. "Tape it is."

I was back at work that evening. Someone had been working on the eye display. The blue of the iris was identified as consciousness. Green rays in the iris as perception. There were yellow, orange, and red lines radiating out, making it look slightly bloodshot; the lines were identified as physical needs (eat, sleep), emotion, and sex. The whole image from a distance did look like an eye. Close-up it had the aspect of a flow chart diagrammed by a mad computer programmer. Classes of drugs were superimposed on categories of reaction (fear, aggression, nervousness, curiosity). A young couple came in and traced some of the connections.

*Vacation Day*

Mary had suggested that I take a vacation day. Normally, I would have worked through. Patty came over when she heard. She was dragging her two boys with her, so we decided to go to the beach, which made the boys cheer. They asked if we could ride in my VW Karmann Ghia. I said sure. They thought it was a real sports car, because it was a convertible, that and the Porsche muffler and engine, which reverberated through the neighborhood. So, we drove three blocks to the beach.

The kids wanted to go swimming right away, so I swam out with them. They had grown up here and could swim like crazy. As I was floating while the boys played shark and attacked me, I saw the reverend Bull run in dragging his lovely and over-coiffed wife. As soon as he hit the water, he shouted, "Jesus, look at me. I am like a child!"

Yet, I had never heard a child say that. His wife came far enough in the water to get the front of her suit wet. Then she waved at me. The bull saw me too and swam over, greeting me with genuine enthusiasm. I liked him too and we hugged formally. I winced at the salt under my bandage. He said, "I am like a child."

And I answered, "It is a good way to be,"

Then he swam around me and played with the boys.

When I saw Patty looking at her watch, I rounded up the boys, except for the bull, and we used the beach showers to rinse off. I put on a shirt and put Denny on my shoulder, and we went shopping—I had wondered what that watch-looking thing meant—time to shop.

We went to Targ's Leathersmith. Patty tried on some leather pants, so I did too. I immediately started sweating, although I suppose that they looked good. Black leather. I was grateful to get them off. She found a pair of yellow plaid bell bottoms that I was too slow to refuse. She bought them, as well as leather pants and a white cotton blouse for herself. Dougy wanted to ride on my shoulders next, so we went across the street to look at pipes and marijuana paraphernalia—what a strange place where one thing was illegal but all the accessories for it were popular. As we went to the curb I tripped and had to catch Dougy before he broke the pavement with his head. He was crying that I did it on purpose.

I raised my eyebrows at Patty, and we walked back to her house and put the boys in their room for a nap. We decided to take a nap, too. She was a voracious napper.

The phone woke us up. It was her sister Deborah, who reminded her that she had agreed to help her move into her new apartment with her boyfriend, Fred. I foolishly offered to help. She tried to get a babysitter for the boys, but they wanted to come and offered to carry boxes. So, we piled in her car and drove to her parents mansion in the gated community of Dollarwort or whatever it was called.

I had not met her parents, the matching green bowling ball people, but I recognized her sister from the drug trade. Ah, how could parents know so little? My heart went out to them, in a way, a small way, anyway.

We loaded the boxes in the rental truck, then we all piled in the back and Sarah, another sister, drove to the apartment at the edge of town, far enough from the beach to be almost affordable.

We went in to reconnoiter first, As we went in, Fred said, "I understand you are really athletic. Do some trick."

I looked at him. I understood him to mean, not fuck him, but do a somersault or something. I looked at the hall, and the open bathroom window over the entry hall.

I ran up the stairs to the landing and dove across the lobby and caught the bathroom window sill. I pulled myself into the window, looked back, and said innocently, "You coming?"

He laughed and raced up the stairs, but did not jump.

It took us an hour to move all the boxes in. Thankfully that was all they wanted. Deborah reminded us that the concert was tonight!

I groaned as I remembered. All I could think of was overdoses and cops. But, Patty thought it was a good idea and begged to go. We got Sara to take the boys home and babysit, for only 50 dollars—the rich *are* different from you and me—they charge more.

We stopped for dinner at the Dairy Princess (no copyright infringement there). We each had a chocolate milkshake and decided to split an order of fries.

We were able to echolocate the concert, with Joe and the Rebels, right away. We followed the sound east to the beach. The band was at the end of the street, overlooking the beach. Maybe there were sixty people sitting and listening. A few kids were in the water. A few people were milling around in back of the band.  I doubted if there was another beach concert within five hundred miles. I was dull and torpid, from the loudness and from the effort of the day.

I had forgotten to mow the grass at the Doctors rental house. It was now over six feet tall. I would have to use a scythe next week, or get Andrea to do it.

I went back to the redwood house alone. Patty wanted to make sure the boys were okay. I collapsed in the bed immediately, taking off my clothes just before I fell asleep.

I was awakened by a movement. Charlotte, Barry's girlfriend stood at the head of the stairs. She dropped her nightgown and walked down slowly. The sun had made patterns on the wall that changed as she moved. I rolled over and closed my eyes. I felt her get into bed and the slight touch of fingertips on my back. Then I fell asleep.

When I woke up she was sleeping next to me on top of the sheet. I put on my clothes and walked over to the clinic. What a strange vacation yesterday was.

*Separation is Swuch Sweet Sworrow*

Grotius was holding a special meeting on the second Friday in August. Kirby Frazier, the new state coordinator for drug abuse programs was there. And, Representative Wynn and Senator Marshak. Mrs. Carson, Jim Trip, Hardy Cane, and Vince Harcourt. Grotius was scheduled to take over as Clinic doctor on call the following week. It was the eleventh. The preliminaries of the meeting were short, a few introductions, and then Grotius began.

"I have been considerably annoyed by what I have heard about the Sussex County Program," Grotius complained, looking at me. "I have been most patient with Mr. Walker during his assignment to Beebe Hospital. He has called and written me dozens of times about his paycheck and about the Methadone clinic. I have been patient and helpful. Well, he will have to shape up or resign, now," He pulled his nose.

"Our carefully paid plan has deteriorated under his direction. Let us examine what has gone wrong. First, he became involved with the Lewes Drug Program under Mr. Trip. I'm sure that this was an interesting area. After all the boardwalk is more exciting than the hospital at Beebe. But this was not his primary effort, which should have been the Clinic. Instead of it being voluntary, he has taken to signing his name as 'Director' of the Rehoboth Beach-Lewes Drug Abuse Facilities," He pulled at his trousers.

"We told him," Grotius reverted to the 'royal' we, "that it was all right to work with the Rehoboth Beach group to advertise the Clinic, but we would expect them to finance their part of it. Much of the use of the car was for their program, not ours. The same with paint and signs, and other supplies; their program, not ours.

"Then, the Rehoboth Beach group has been collecting money for their program, perhaps as much as $2,000. What happened to that money? Can Mr. Walker, as director, account for those funds? I have heard from a reliable source—" and I smelled that source, in the person of Roger Sims "—that he has been very arbitrary with those funds, going to Washington, on an all expenses paid junket, to 'check on the drug scene.' Can he deny that?

"And again, he has become involved with the drug patients more as a doctor than as a counselor. He told the hospital which patients to give Methadone to. His actions were so disruptive to the staff, that Mr. Thurmond had to telephone me six times to straighten out the program. We found that he had prescribed medicine that no doctor had okayed, for example. Kirby may want to look into possible criminal charges.

"We have lived up to our part of the contract for the Clinic. But we feel that you have not, Mister Walker. Your present attitude is bizarre, and we resent it. Perhaps counseling is needed. I have always enjoyed working with you in the past, and had planned to involve you in our drug programs in Wilmington or Newark. Now that will be impossible. Kirby will have his hands full salvaging this program."

Grotius sat down, folding his papers. I stood up, slowly, glaring at Grotius.

"I would have preferred to discuss your—hallucinations—

before this—"

"Please," Kirby asked, standing also. "I would like to speak about the program, first. Thank you."

I sat down, concentrating on shriveling Grotius's heart.

"I do not intend to take anything said at face value. If you wish to respond to me in writing, as Dr. Grotius has, then I would weigh your opinions, too. There are many people here who feel the overall program is successful. There are those who don't.

"As the newly appointed State Director of Drug Abuse Programs, I want to hear from as many people as possible."

I tuned him out. The limp-wristed twit was another political hack who had made up his mind, but wanted desperately to preserve the image of fairness and blind justice. He looked around the table. State Senator Marshak was nodding his head like a jack-in-the-box with a weak spring. Wynn was preening his white hair. Grotius was looking arrogantly attentive. Roger was smiling in satisfaction. Thurmond looked serious and sour. The Reverend Cane was contemplative. Only Jim Trip seemed angry at the power play. I wasn't sure whose it was, even. Roger's? No, too stupid. Grotius's? No, what would he gain? Kirby's? Maybe he wanted his own man in?

Kirby was looking expectantly at me, "I said, you may speak in turn, now, Mr. Walker."

I stood up, playing with his pencil. "I am perplexed. By Mr. Grotius's argum—"

"Doctor Grotius," Grotius interrupted.

"—attitude and beliefs. Because my paycheck was nine weeks late, I had to borrow money for bills. Perhaps your check will not be that late, Mr. Kirby. Because the Governor's committee was slow with their bills, I had to borrow money to make the down payment and rent on the physician's home at Bay Avenue. I am still waiting to be paid back. I confess I don't know what's happened to the money raised by the Rehoboth Beach program—"

"Aha!" Grotius grunted in triumph.

"—program, because the Reverend Cane, the Treasurer, handled all of it. I'm sure that he can—and will—tell you where it has gone. I went to Washington for a day, to pick up the pamphlets Mrs. Pope ordered. But I didn't stop to eat. I paid for the gas out of my pocket.

"As for my aspirations for doctorhood, I recommended medication for as many people as who came to me for help, that I thought needed it. In most cases, the Clinic doctors thought red devils was a nick-name for peppermint candy, and were only too happy to take my recommendation and get back to the beach. I never wrote any prescriptions. In fact, I don't know of any nurses stupid enough to fill illegal prescriptions. If Grotius knows of any, perhaps he would tell the head nurse, Jean Moyer, and let her deal with it.

"As for my titles, I was appointed director by the Lewes Council. I was also head of the HELP lines in Sussex County. We all thought it would be a good idea to unify the local programs to minimize waste and conflict. Apparently, Mister Grotius brought—"

"*Doctor* Grotius" Grotius ground his teeth.

"—his own conflicts with him. And I agree that counseling is needed, but I will not be able to fit him in my schedule. I suggest, Kirby, that you do investigate these charges, not to mention my long-delayed expense requests." I concluded.

Roger shouted, "What about the personal calls, huh!?"

I looked at the Reverend Cane. The reverend sighed and volunteered, "Last week, Mr. Walker paid $42.00 toward the phone bill, for his personal calls, mostly to Hawaii."

Jim Trip stood to talk. The arguments intensified, between the failures and the successes.

"About that interview you wanted?" I asked. I had called Dan McCormick at WSEA-FM, Georgetown, when I returned to the information center. McCormick agreed, and came over that evening, with a recorder.

"I'm speaking with George Walker, Director of the Sussex County Drug Abuse Programs. Could you tell me, George, just how big a drug problem is there in this county?"

"I don't think there is a problem."

"Ahh, what do you mean? You were hired because of it. The state has told us there is one. Hasn't it?"

"Yes, it has told us. But, remember that this is the same state that told its eighteen-year olds to be drafted to fight in an undeclared war in Vietnam. The state defines problems; it makes problems."

"Please explain." Dan was getting really interested. Something unexpected was happening. Well, he'd hoped for the unexpected.

"Ask yourself, what is bad about drugs, that make them a problem?"

"They're addictive." McCormick said.

"So, what's wrong with addiction?"

"It's . . . it dulls the mind, causes violence."

"Not necessarily. Consider. An addiction is a habit that revolves around a material object. Television is an addiction. Driving fast is; food, certainly. Alcohol, cigarettes, music, sports—all habits, all addictions of different kinds. How many of them are problems?"

"Well, none of them—all of them; I mean all of them can be. But drugs are different."

"How?" I asked.

"They are dangerous and illegal."

"They are illegal because the state makes them illegal, the way alcohol used to be illegal. Prohibition made alcohol illegal. Those laws resulted in contempt for the law, a division of society, and rampant gangsterism. The law did not succeed in banning alcohol, just in making it more difficult to get."

"But alcohol—I mean drugs—are still dangerous, to the user and to the public."

"Why are they dangerous to the public?"

"Because they—people—steal and kill to get them."

"Isn't that because they are illegal? Wouldn't the violence stop, if everyone could get cheap pure drugs, any drugs, without a prescription?"

"No! It wouldn't. And I'll tell you why. Because some drugs make people insane and out of control."

"You're right. Like alcohol. Like any addiction, even cigarettes—a man with two cigarettes in his mouth driving a car can be almost as dangerous as his son at the wheel after a hash brownie. Furthermore, any emotional imbalance makes people insane. The young boy who's girl rejects him, or the girl rejected by someone else. The man fired from his job, as a result of poor economic indicators or falloff in demand for steel. The woman who catches her husband sleeping with her best friend. These people are dangerous. They may threaten our lives in the haze of their anger or despair. Should we ban marriage, sex, jobs, cigarettes, and alcohol, as well?"

"No, but I-"

"Some people will always ruin their lives. Those who do so with drugs will do so anyway. Besides, most of the damage I see comes from the uncertainty of the purity and the dosage. When those are known, taking drugs becomes much safer."

"What would you recommend then? Medical supervision?"

"No, simply the legalization of all drugs. And federal controls on uniformity and price. Generic heroin, generic marijuana, generic tranquilizers."

"That's . . ."

"Insane? No, good common sense. That way the government can get more taxes—taxes that they cannot collect from an illegal market."

"But what about the health of the people?"

"What about it? Illegal drugs don't help it. The government lies to them about the hazards of drugs. Ever see 'Reefer Madness?' Funny isn't it? The government ignores the good side of drugs, the side the kids find out about from their friends. Why not tell them the good and the bad? And let them decide? How much of the urge to try drugs comes from the romantic aura of the lone pusher? The glamour of hiding and trying the forbidden? How glamorous is aspirin? Or penicillin?"

"Why not try to ban alcohol, again. That would be consistent?"

"True, but people want it, and we do listen to the voice of the people, eventually. Think of the effort that goes into the police, narcs, social workers, hospitals, that could go to making a healthier society? Why don't we admit the human weaknesses we see, and strive to make a healthier place for everyone? A whole society on a whole earth? We could start by stopping the pretense about a drug problem that can be legislated and policed and counseled out of existence. Can we start, now?"

"I . . . don't know what to say. Are you going to campaign to put your views across?"

"No, I don't think so. If they are good views, other people will have them; maybe even speak them."

"What do you intend to do, now? Will you stay with this program?"

"No, I have been invited to leave. I think I'll work on a smaller, more personal scale."

"Who asked you to leave?"

"I'd rather not say. What is important is that this program served the public within the limits of the law, as they stand. This program is an information center for people who need or want to know about drugs. It is to help those who get in trouble with drugs, which are still very illegal. Hundreds of people have worked together to provide a service for others. That service cannot be denied or demeaned. I am grateful to have worked with all of these people, and proud to have helped them." I nodded at Dan's lipped question.

"Thank you. We have been talking to George Walker, the director of the Sussex County Drug Abuse Programs. Tomorrow, we have Randy Jade, a singer who—"

I wrote out my resignation, giving three weeks notice, and went for a swim on the night beach. There was a bonfire on the sand about a mile down, so I turned north and ran. I turned into the water after a mile, and ran between the waves. I went out further, so that a larger wave would knock me off my feet. For that moment, I would be lifted and carried to shore, and tossed. I lay on the sand, panting, licking salt from my lips. Then, I undressed and swam toward Ireland. Until I got tired, anyway, and drifted back.

For the next three weeks, I supervised the schedules for the information center and the Clinic. I took some counseling myself, and followed up on cases from June and July, to see how the people were doing. Some had gone home; others had jobs. Over half had given bogus addresses and couldn't be contacted. Benny had been arrested for running a red light on his Harley; he had two bags of scag at the time. I called him in jail, but couldn't get him out.

I evaluated the different parts of the program. I had found volunteer positions for some of them at Zero Population Growth and the Humane Society. A few of those had led into paying positions. Many of the formerly disenfranchised were helpful with the poster campaigns to 'Care for Pets' and 'Save the Seals.' And some were helped by the therapy of artistic expression. In two weeks, thirteen people consumed $143.53 worth of paints and poster paper. I remembered the crabs on the shore north of Rehoboth Beach, when I first drove down in May. Just as their ancestors had done under the watch of condors. The gulls waited for scraps. I hoped that they had been helped. Mrs. Patty Theiss left for Pittsburgh with her children. She had been bothered by reporters once too often to say goodbye.

Andrea Marinetti came in one day and dragged everybody out to see the new windshield on her Rambler.

"Where'd you get the money? You have a job?" Molly enthused.

"No, I did a job," Andrea stated proudly. "A blow job!"

She laughed uproariously, Molly and I joining in a little. I went back to the hospital to pack.

Molly and Andrea were on duty for Labor Day. I smiled again at Andrea, who didn't seem to have any equipment beyond that required for life. No brains, no morals, no heart. She had already stolen two weeks worth of collections from the outpost stores, until I put Mary in charge of donations. Andrea had added worse publicity a week earlier, when she had the indiscretion to buy a large, plastic play hypodermic, that the dime store had the indiscretion to stock. And Roger had the indiscretion to fill it with a quart of orange kool-aid and chase Andrea down the main street, screaming, 'Fix! Fix! Time for Dope!' I had to write letters of apology to the Chamber of Commerce and City Council for that one. Although it was funny. I should have had them do it in a play.

I had nothing again, no job offers, little money. Unless the state paid back some of my expenses, I would even be in debt. The university was threatening to change my incompletes to Fs.

Mrs. Moyer came down to my room, as I was packing.

"George, I have some strange news for you. I don't know where to start," she hesitated.

"At the beginning?" I suggested.

"Well, remember that knife attack?"

I felt my side unconsciously. It had almost healed. I nodded.

She continued, "Well, the Mafia put out a contract on anyone who tried to hurt you."

"What! Why?"

"Because you had once said that the Mafia was the best place to get drugs—for quality control—you remember, in the interview in June."

I did remember. I advised people not to buy drugs from their friends, because of several poisonings. Talcum powder or Drano substituted for sugar in cut heroin. When I had been asked where to get safe drugs, I had said the Mafia, they had standards, minimum, but standards.

"That's not all," she was looking at him. "After you dropped the bon-mot-shell about legalizing everything, they dropped the contract."

I looked at her, "You mean anyone can kill me, now?"

We both started laughing.

After a moment, I asked, "Who told you?"

"My husband." I knew her husband, Corporal Moyer, was reliable.

"Thanks. I appreciate it. Gotta pack," I gestured at the half-filled bag, with a hospital white sleeve sticking out.

She kissed me on the cheek and left.

The bus back to Sussex didn't go through Lewes. Things were shutting down, now, slowly. I wondered what the state was going to do, but found that I didn't really care. The Reverend Cane had called me last night, telling me how Jim Trip had defended their program, and wangled some expense money out of the state. With that my total earnings that summer came to just over two hundred dollars. I paid the $157.00 back to the bank. I thanked Hardy and said that they were good men and good friends. During the bus ride, I read the paper I had bought in Rehoboth Beach. In it was one letter of praise, from a Mrs. Dobbs, who related that the summer program had been a valiant gesture. It had helped her family. She knew it had helped others and hoped that they were as grateful. I couldn't remember anyone named Dobbs. On the record page was a notice of a Wilmington physician admitted to a psychiatric bed at Beebe for treatment.

*The Free Clinic*

I was in Newark for two days before I read about the new drug clinic that was being planned for the university town. It was to be a new building on Main Street next to the Police Station, open 9 hours a day, from eight until five. I expected only good things from it. Those neon lights on all night at the Police Station would attract a lot of moths and users, no doubt, as would the closed doors after five.

I thought nothing more of it, while I tried to salvage my

grades, which had been converted to "F"s when the incomplete ran out in July. I argued that I was not notified and had been working out of town. They said I was notified (and technically they were right; the letter had been in my post office box in Newark).

I was trying to figure out what kind of course I could take in the fall, when I was approached by Steve McHugh, a local businessman with concerns about the new clinic. Since he agreed to buy me lunch at the Greasy Spoon, I agreed to listen.

"It won't work, you know?" He started as we sat down, "the state clinic." It was only 11:37 and there were actually seats available.

I nodded.

He continued: "We really need something, but the state is screwing it up with this new Kirby plan. No one will ever go there. It's a waste of money."

I nodded.

"We need someone like you. We're willing to pay you. We're willing to let you shape and run the program."

"Who is 'we'?" I asked.

"Businessmen, concerned citizens. We were the ones who approached the state after we heard about how good the southern county program was. People were amazed."

"Names?" I asked.

"Well, other than me, there's Wilson, Hargrove, Compton—"

The university president I recognized, and the local bank manager. I was sure the others were equally legit.

"—and Stomeworth. I can't tell you how pissed we were when the state and Kirby ran with the ball in the wrong direction. Would you be willing to join us and provide assistance?" he concluded.

I was thinking of my failed academic career. I did not want to go back to the library particularly.

"What is the pay?" I asked.

"It would be the same as Kirby's salary, $35,000 a year."

"Benefits?"

"No, although we might be able to work out something through the university."

"I doubt the university, considering my reputation there."

"It's your reputation with the students and young people that we value."

"How much control of the program would I have?"

"Complete."

I raised my eyebrows.

"Well," he went on, "I mean artistic control, I mean professional control. You would report to a board composed of myself and others, you understand. But, you would have complete control of the design and staff."

"I would need $43,000 without benefits. I have no trouble reporting to a board, as long as everything we agree on is in writing. Also, some of my ideas might not be welcome," I paused.

"What do you mean, what ideas? Nothing illegal I trust?"

"Why don't we meet again, when you can make a firm offer, and I will be happy to outline my ideas. At that point, you may want to put the ideas before the board. Sound okay."

"Yes, yes, I think that would be best also. Perhaps we could meet here tomorrow? Same time?"

"Your treat?"

Jack Welch, on the Board also, came with Steve the next day. They were on time. I suggested that I present my ideas before we went any further. Steve said "Sure." Welch shrugged.

"Let me outline the ideas in general first. Then, I will be happy to add details. Okay?"

"Um, humm, sure." They both agreed and nodded.

"First, I want to call it the Newark Free Clinic, no mention of drugs, abuse, or use of any judgmental terms.

"Next, I want the location to be hidden. No advertising—"

"What, that's ridiculous. No one will ..." Welch started and stopped. I waited. Steve raised his eyebrows, but said nothing. Welch started again, "Maybe we could have some discussion at each point."

"Yes," I answered, "we could do that. Was there a question on the name?"

"No." they agreed.

"How do people get illegal drugs?" I asked rhetorically. "They don't answer an ad in the paper. It ain't on TV. They can't ask at the Police Station. So, they must find out from their friends, or contacts, or people who dress or look a certain way. The idea of this clinic is for people to help themselves, not be helped by the authorities or professionals who never tried a submarine nike. That's why—"

"What is a nike?" Welch interrupted. Steve put his hand on the other man's sleeve.

I continued, "I'll explain later. If people want drugs badly enough, they find them. If they want help badly enough, they can find that, also."

"You think a medical doctor will—"

"Yes, I do, because some medical doctors like and use illegal drugs themselves. Some nurses, some chemists, some others, all use them, and who can help counsel. For real medical emergencies, there is always a hospital with an ear specialist with a tranq, okay?"

"I think this is illegal!" Welch started, "Steve, help me out here, will you. Is this illegal?"

"What part is illegal?" I asked. "Is it illegal not to have a sign?"

"But, the drugs?"

"What drugs?"

"What if someone tries to sell drugs there?"

"The laws of the land would be the same. We would not encourage anyone to break laws. Nor would we break any. We would offer some degree of privacy and anonymity—just like celebrities or rich people."

"But, how could we justify paying for something that was secret?" Jack asked.

"Because it would be effective," I answered.

"But, how would we get credit for it?"

"What is the purpose of a clinic? To help people? Or to get credit? How many people, like nuns or priests or social workers, work for no credit beyond satisfaction?"

"But, who would know? What if the police found out?"

"I suspect they would be relieved that someone was being effective and lessening their load."

"But, who would—"

Steve asked Jack to sit down, which he did hesitantly. And that was the beginning of the free clinic, the beginning of another story, or rather another chapter in the story of my life.

## The Sagamore Grocery Cart War

by Merissa Nieman and Marcus Ryan

This has been the fourth year that I, Yolande Esperanza de Puig, have lived in the apartment at 89 Passeig de Garcia. I live with my green parrots in a corner apartment overlooking the Passeig de Garcia on one side and the Carrera Paris on the other. My life these past four years has been quiet; torpor and passion are seduced by the sweetness, one by the other, forming shadowy, lush possibilities and vague, glamorous scenarios that rise and vanish into the great dark pool of imagination. A dusky moth flies out from the bed as I pull down the linen; another rises from the pillows and veers into the night. It has been, I now think, as I have thought on more than one occasion, a year for moths. Even in winter I have seen them at twilight, fluttering in the brush of our courtyard. A night breeze disturbs the lace curtains, transforms them to clouds. The parrots in their cages cry for the distant, dappled, ravishing light of Karawak. Among my silks, brocade draperies, antique lamps and old armoires, I find the book I have misplaced: it is about the Yucatan. I fall asleep this way, reading, and awake a few hours later from a troubled dream and a headache from the five pillows inside their embroidered linen cases

My living room balcony overlooks the Astoria Hotel and the Carrera Paris and its continuous traffic jam. Even now, in the middle of the night, as I rise from bed, rubbing my headache, there is an astonishing amount of traffic. My bedroom overlooks the courtyard, which is overgrown with palms and orange trees, and a few chestnuts from Lombardy. It is not, however, a verdant little jungle, but a gloomy place, the trees barely alive in their sunless, concrete jail. From my curving balcony off the dining room, as I lean over in the morning to water the potted roses and herbs, I can even see the Diagonal, the wide thoroughfare lined with palms and plane trees that cuts through the city like a knife edge; unwaveringly straight and with a flow of traffic moving past the expensive shops that abates only on Sunday mornings. The American émigré writer, Lucy Hitching, also has an apartment in this building. On the weekends, when I am not visiting my uncle in Sitges, or when I am not seeing students, or have numerous errands to run, Lucy and I sit at the little table by the window, talking, and observe, behind the lace curtains of my veranda, the tourists who come and go at the Astoria Hotel. Lately I have noticed one guest particularly; he has, as far as I can determine, been a guest for nearly three weeks. I look for him in the streets below; I find myself facing the window, rather than my students, watching for his return.

He was pushing an empty grocery cart across the street, away from this. I found this scene to be surreal.

Quite frankly, he reminded me of that ranchero in the American southwest with whom, not too many years ago, I had a fling. I am still trying to sort out that business with Randy, whose thin, rat-face and tumble of curly black hair I found, in combination with his voice and manner, unbelievably erotic. I was in some fashion in love with Randy, or with our kissing and with his insolent, faintly lascivious manner. When his bright, dark, and—one must say—beady eyes were upon me, I would feel the full force of his sensuality. In this respect, Randy was majestic. As to the long-term romantic possibilities of our intimacy, I shall never know, for messy family business forced me to return to Barcelona, leaving the matter of our simplistic supernova attraction to the stars. On the eve of my departure, a late December evening, with the temperatures still in the eighties releasing in great clouds the fragrance of rosemary and jacaranda, and the cooing of the pigeons on the rooftops, we said farewell and vowed to write. Of course, we never did.

Always, when Lucy and I are together in the city, when we, for instance, dine at La Targa or L'Oliva–our favorite spots—Lucy and I find ourselves in a kind of conversational huddle, with every concept, every observation again somehow turning on the subject of men, which is increasingly pursued with a kind of terrible ennui. But I have never mentioned Randy in our conversation, enjoying the secret existence of this unfinished, unfinishable business.

Now, an elderly woman was pushing a shopping cart across the street. It was empty. Perhaps she was using it as a weapon against encroaching cars.

Still, it was nice to remember. I was working as a travel agent in Tucson, Arizona, when I met Randy, who was a cellist with the Tucson symphony or a plumber, I forget which. The rain leaked through the painted tin-roof of the veranda of the Sagamore Hótel, where Randy and I had decided to wait out the late July monsoon. We had spent the day in the desert, collecting the fruit of the saguaro, which, when dried, tastes like figs, when the storm suddenly broke. We fled the desert and the dangerous highway arroyos to the nearest shelter, which was, as it happened, the Sagamore Hotel. Its cobalt stucco was stained with a dark, sun-blasted mold. As we sat on the roofed veranda, drinking flat wine that an Apache waiter had brought us, the rain spattered onto green linoleum floor and seeped into deep cracks; gingkoes sprang at cockroaches on the walls. Every few seconds lightning ignited the steely sky with bright phosphorous flambeaux. The odors of the place—frijoles, stale coffee, the flat reek of a roach insecticide—intensified in the heat and humidity. A swamp cooler dripped and roared, the sky was bursting, a baby sobbed. A few palms had been planted on the fringes of the veranda, and the fronds of these tall, ostentatious beings were now flapping and bending, as in some antic dance

His slight frame, swathed in a loose-fitting blue shirt, his face, edged in the light that suddenly pierced the blue-black clouds all around, Randy inclined toward me—so as to be heard through the still-pounding storm.

There was an empty shopping cart on the corner, with yellowed newspaper pages in the basket. A second cart seemed to be blown by the wind down the street. Languidly, an old man stopped the cart, and took it to the one cradling the old newspaper. He facilitated a form of mating ritual and then while they were joined, moved them back across the street, out of sight, perhaps to their den.

What Randy suggested was getting a room in The Sagamore and spending the storm in bed. You have to understand that everything about him was electric; our physical attraction was, as I said, supernova, and we had really done nothing about it. We got the key to a room on the second of three floors. The room seemed clean, but the window shade was broken and only a bare light globe stuck in the ceiling. A door off the room led to a veranda that faced south, toward Nogales. The saguaros stood with their arms raised toward the steel grey twilight. The storm had turned the late afternoon heat into a steamy discomfort; the swamp coolers only contributed to the problem, and Randy and I kissed briny kisses. It was about then that a hush fell, a silence as white and still as fog, and the silence was slowly eroded, first about the edges, then lifting, evaporating in the slow, deep bowing of a cello in the next room.

I leapt out of bed and rushed to the window. Four shopping carts seemed to be pointed at the front of the hotel. I knew who was behind this. I cried, and could not stop.

## Monsters

by Marcus Ryan

The great physicist Max Planck once said that science changes funeral by funeral, as the old entrenched scientists die off and the young ones ask questions. Some people never change their minds, regardless of the evidence, and that influences the story of science. That is true in this story also. Michael and Katherine are dead; their parents are dead; some of the lawyers are dead, thankfully, as are some of their friends, sadly. I wrote this to show that M and K's ideas and their love, their only legacy, other than unreliable and evanescent memory, is not dead. Despite that love and their wonderful words, they were both 'monsters,' that is, literally beings that point the way for others, even if the way is a way to avoid, and so I have named this memoir of them, "Monsters."

From the X-Files (7/98): "to pursue monsters, we must understand them, enter their minds, but risk them entering ours"

*5/8/83 (Michael's Journals)*
Another noble failure. My grant money is gone. I have been living in the women's rest room at the observatory since January—the grant was cut by 90% on the day I arrived. Having spent my last $100 on air fare, I had no place to stay and no way to go back. Thank heavens for Arizona law requiring beds for faint ladies! All I did was put my nameplate over the "ladies" sign—there were no women astronomers on these projects—and move in a book case. It has been quite comfortable, warm, and well-lit, with a few extra toilets and sinks. I will miss it.

I have a Rambler given to me by Randy and Linda—they left it in the desert after they won a new Pinto in a lottery. I bought a new battery and 4 used tires for it; it has no reverse gear and only one headlight; mice had eaten the leather upholstery, so I covered the front seats with a wool blanket. Tomorrow, I'll go over to LA and start up the coast. I'll have my last paycheck, $145, for this trip.

*5/16/83 (Katherine's Journals)*
Free! I am free! I am free of Harry! He's agreed to a divorce. Free! Free! Why did I ever marry him? Now I can go back to school; I never should have left (it just seemed like the only thing). My job pays nothing but it's for the university so I get a staff discount on tuition. Living at my folks place, I can save for a car and apartment. Can't wait! (must not fail at this.)

Who is this new guy, Michael?

Katherine (3/86): "And yet this was the source of his monstrosity too, when I perceived him as Lord of Ice, hours, days even, when all his inflorescence was internal, as though in incubating an idea, a kind of exultation of himself was necessary, a radical detachment to which all distractions were irritants that made him erupt with boreal disdain, leaving a thicker shield of rime about him until he was wholly within his intellect, that mysterious machine-like capsule which could fling him far . . . away."

*1/28/88 Letter from Michael*
Rine
Please check on the lady bird beetles by the pond for me—they should be there in a week or two. Spokane does have a nice setting from the air. That was my hand in the airplane window (if you saw it).

I miss you—even if you have changed your mind about striving together somewhere, it's too late—at least for a while—too many tears under the dam, too many torn heart strings (too much stale metaphor?).

I need you, but your love and spirit are more necessary. It may be easier emotionally (for me) this way. Tell Orenski about me someday: What a perfect editorial team we are (between design, editing, typesetting, writing and binding, what's left? Selling?). We even like each other (don't mention love, unless he does).

To Desdemona, we are two mountain ranges that form a sleepy valley. To Abelard, we are matching can openers. They all know us as a team. That's the way we always should be. Have faith! Besides, it simply feels better.

Ground update: All snow east of Spokane, partly cloudy.

Personal update: Tears dry, sob checked, throat released.

Breakfast: oj, potatoes, tomato, mushrooms, asparagus

Passenger list: Big obnoxious people with little obnoxious ones in evidence.

Replay: That wasn't a good enough good-bye; have to return to show you what I mean—saying would be inadequate.
love (icon)

*1/5/90 (Katherine's Notebooks)*
"There is of course the feeling still, which I can exaggerate, that is, promote to such intensity that it seems I cannot breathe."
As she spoke these words, or rather breathlessly uttered them, Ulrike leaned over the table toward me in a sudden and alarming fashion. She was always dressed impeccably, if not also theatrically dressed, and her straight blonde hair shone in a bit of sunshine as she leaned forward. Her sulphur yellow dress of an expensive

wool was trimmed with the necklace of woven silver, which she had acquired on a recent trip to Tibet. Though obviously dressed and generally turned out with skill and taste, Ulrike nonetheless seemed positively wild, moody, and unkempt in that moment. Her eyes flashed with defiance then tears all in an instant; she seized the glass of wine and brought it to her full lips, slightly parted. "Incarnate or not," she said, indicating with a slight, though strenuous, impetuous nod of her head the great dining room in which we sat, "Leon walked through the door five minutes ago and at this moment . . ."

When Ulrike leaned toward me in that wild and unkempt way I knew that the moment heralded her breakdown. It seemed suddenly clear that precisely because of the recklessness of her despair, she would very soon become larger-than-life, if indeed her sorrow had not already made her monstrous and the size of our world too small.

"Leon," I pointed out, "is only a man." I continued with my platitudes: "There are dozens of men like him; it's been two months; now, let go of all this. It happens all the time."

She shook her head, sipped at the wine. "You know," she said, a little cheered by the wine and looking at me with a half-smile, like an amiable monster, "this is a terrible disaster."

And what a disaster, she thought, what a terrible misunderstanding. Cannot think what contretemps lead to this awful and difficult maliciousness, this great difficulty in getting by, this disinterest of powerful friends, this shutting down of social life, this mental viciousness. Of course a disaster, these things to happen in such a short time so that thought the disaster surrounds you, has become a part of you, in ineradicable factor of your life determining the shape of your life and against which all expectations must be weighed, so quickly that you know the difference, you know what preceded the awfulness, and though by now you are too exhausted to contemplate changing it, you are yet mindful of it.

*8 Jan 90 (Katherine's Notebooks)*

A last time in Cafe Radiance, the lump catches in my throat—don't know why the loss after so much time should still be so hard—but can reconstruct, exhume, evoke, conjure the time and the feeling as if yesterday, as if today about to happen. . . .

—tumbled downhill here and am shocked by the awkwardness of it—off-balance—a difficult last year—another kind of difficulty—pleasant!!! Well, demon women, yes I am a disappointment, a complete disappointment—have done it all now. Have seen high and low, bright and dark. The wind makes me feel light—looking back over my work I see that it was good!!

Hurrah—but now I seem only awkward, capable only of awkwardness, a dash to further oddity and irrelevance. I am unable to adjust to the current requirements of existence—I am performing a bad role—I am forgetting who I am. Mock interest—do more of what you need to do. An unbelievable disaster. Let us write about disaster—

Chronicle of the last days—Happy to leave and free—good coffee in Portland.

Can't see from this what I see and smell, hear! A rough Italianate basket loaded with breads, platters rising with stacks of cookies. A rainy night—pouring—dark, glistening, wet pavement, but no soil, no sweet smelling earth or radiance of trees . . . to go back to the forest—

To think of . . . the rain, the soggy grass in front of the Envoy. . . . Do I connect with dim memories of Baltimore to such regrets—perhaps . . .

*4/16 (Katherine's Notebooks)*
This pang of memory and desire does dissolve me! The red blooms of a potted tulip seem monstrously exquisite—tout a coup suddenly—and for all my part and for all the thisness and the what is, I long for him—Precisely the feeling I must hold in check, smash, suffocate—yet . . . how free to fall, how free in the falling! A ride through air, over chasms, burning deserts . . . in the flying there is such freedom.

*7/1 (Michael's Notebooks)*
I had breakfast with the ghost of Desdemona. Strawberries and cereal?

*7/2 (Katherine's Notebooks)*
Sunday dinner with Nat in the Chinese district—a restaurant strangely reminiscent of Hong Kong, the black gold stained walls, the red and yellow plastic. Then to his place crossword puzzle (NY Times) thence back to Marlborough some extemporaneous cello compositions, some reading from Kundera's new novel Slowness, some sleep, playing with Eugenie. I have an uncomfortable stomach ache, which of course I conceal from Nat, not wishing to be humanly physical lest I be judged by standards he knows expertly. The night I sleep, we part—friendly. "I'll call," he says.

In some way I control all this—today—the shrink sometimes as now I have a sense of a formidable intelligence, which is nice! Is the world as accessible without restraint or constraints such as time. On the machinery of thought. A dysfunctional family, the shrink, Dr. Brush, noted. Yes, dysfunctional; my parents fought like Banshees, saying things to each other I, 40 years later, am reluctant to pronounce, behaving like demons, possessed and diseased. And I, the diplomat in a nuclear war taking an absurd position in a high childish voice of reason. Are things so bad you cannot think of Martin and me? Even then it struck me that my father took an unusual interest in my body—the subtle forms of abuse are the worst for they infect insidiously. Oh, Katherine, be kind, be kind to yourself. Nat has the same problems in reverse. How I am used—insincerely, badly.

Voyage to take with kindred spirits? Go in this direction . . . head east toward desolation reform practice and my arts. Be thou grand and grandly humorous.

*3 August (Katherine's Calendar)*
taking a long draft—an ancient hallucinogenic drug by which the gods created their mythology.

*3 September (Katherine's 'Letter to Myself')*
Let me not forget how I wanted, dreamed, imagined a mighty love, how the heat of it raced round me like a million friendly demons, how the sparks flew off, how from this flight my world was strewn with fiery debris, and by such lights as this gives of, I a saw and esteemed it all, my love, my friend, my own qualities, myself clad in rich blue garments and head piled with curls waiting to be undone. All waiting to be undone, now gone, nevermore, evermore, Let me not thus forget what passions stirred and were unrealized, what tides and nights I imagined that were yet gone before being, that were not possible from such small estate. The debris, well it is mostly of dust, it seems, never fiery save in my own soul, and perhaps in his, I do believe, but it was not to be then! My friend, how deeply I shall miss all this. And now to place this before the spirits.

*8/5 (Katherine's Notebooks)*
Like hallucinating with the gods devising mythologies: I'm guarded by monster dogs, winged beasts! The evening went like this: 7:00 drive to Harbor, no-name restaurant: swordfish, rhubarb pie. Are you Italian (waiter)? No but I play one on TV (Nat). What went on Tuesday night? I couldn't wait to get out of there (response). "Nothing—I was sketching—you were . . ."— Then walk in the Boston garden "A soft night" he described it this way several times. The Angels and Insects, a fascinating movie. How would you make this better Nat. Before it has been pretensions and self-consciousness, then at 2:00 a.m. goodnight sweet dreams—

Morning awake 8:30?—over the top awakening, recognition—sleep white peach tea, conversation. Buy screen—the Matisse cafe, Central Square. More conversation at apartment, to work—

I have not been able to get this out of my mind since leaving. Says I'm a romantic, you are, too—yes. Romantic-at-large.

*10/96 (from Katherine's October/November Journal)*
The history of the last week are the history of an impossible recovery. Because I left so much unsaid, unwritten, but all the same monstrously elaborated in feelings it has no ... I anchor, either the love—which I cannot suppress even with the discouraging evidence that I am continuously betrayed, or the senses of loss. But perhaps because the love was kept and nourished in the wonderland of soul and heart, privately, served by the most fantastic and dramatic of colors, personae and situations, I have lost nothing—I retain it still—and it is this which may take on a life of its own and erupt in art, even compel art—in that way I shall not be mistaken—this was the love of my life—not the man but the possibility, the love of gods, the theater of soul, the largesse produced by the desire to commune significantly with someone you admire, whose orientation and confusion relate to your own and comfort you. I would, of course, have wanted with all my heart, the actuality of that feeling, the great joy of requitedness.

This strange to say. I hold still to be possible—as the most absurd thing is still in some ways as possible as something obvious.

*2/21 (Katherine's Call, 10:15 a.m. PST)*

K: "Hi, I'm still at work."

M: "I thought you were having lunch with Monica."

K: Dinner. I was going to go to a movie, Hamlet, but I can't decide.

M: What's wrong?

K: Just too much work, the move, depressed, *oh*.

M: I'm sorry. I could tell you a joke? What's it like there?

K: Sunny, warm.

M: Why not go for a walk, then the movie, then dinner.

K: I have so much to do.

M: It won't make any difference if you finish it—there'd just be more to do. Why not relax and have a good afternoon. What time does the movie start?

K: 3:00, I think.

M: Plenty of time.

K: Yes, I think so, I'll call Monica and tell her I may be late. Gotta go, love you.

M: Have a good time, I love you.

*2/23/97 (Michael's Calendar)*

11:56 a.m. Heard by phone that you were in the hospital. Smashed the phone into the computer; threw bookends into the stereo; swept the things into the corner; screamed; packed

3:00 p.m. told your mother; made plane arrangements

6:25 left for Spokane airport

*2/24/97 (Michael's Calendar)*

10:20 visit you for first time—you are a pumpkin on a stick, orange swollen head. thin bloodless body packed in ice (I can barely stand from shock; start weeping, cannot stop)

11:30 call Brenda and your friends at LB

12:00 start reading to you from a book

1:00 visits from Kevin, Jeff, Honey, A., Monica

3:00 collect your belongings and go home no name on mailbox, all my clothes/things gone

4-7 more visits to you; meet Drs. who had and will operate

7-8:30 dinner with Monica, Thai

8:30-1000 visit again

10:20 home to 116 Marlboro

11:00- read notes on your computer, in trash

*2/25/97 (Michael's Calendar)*

9:30 read diaries, excavate purse, find birth control pills (not for your fixed husband, alas), your written love for Nicolai and Nat

1100 visit, nurses tell me to go and come back, that someone important is with you; I push by them; find Nat there, introduce myself, read to you anyway (he sits quietly)

1500 walk to apartment, collect books

1630-1900 read to you; the head nurses asks me if I want to forbid Nat or your friends from seeing you. I say no, you must have stimulation that is all that matters. Humiliation is in the mind of the ...

1900-2200 dinner with Monica, discuss Nat, in Somerville

2200-2300 read to you

2300-0330 calls, read old emails from Eric and Mel

0330—nothing much left. All the comforting lies, religious, social, personal, have been forcibly removed. I see what I am and what you were; you used me, but I used you as the anchor for my fantasies. What a strange world is left

*2/26/97 (Michael's Calendar)*

could not sleep, but lay down

700 cleaned apartment

800 called univ, jim; notify all of your accident by letter, fax, etc.
11—1500 visit, read, finish brooks book; figure out ways to kill you (stab you in the skull, through the thin flap, then jump out the window with you wrapped in sheets. I unlock the window and rehearse the moves; then sit still)
1500-1700 visit little brown, copy files, find Phillipe faxes
1535 get police report; you were destroyed by Moira L, a nurse
17-1900 visit—your nose comes out of swelling
19-2100 talk to Monica, Artus
21-2230 visit
2300—eat an apple from the market; try to decide what to do how to live, what to be

*2/26/97 (Michael's Journal)*
Something strange. Just realized. All of the notes recovered from the computer trash had to do with "ending it". Did you try to kill yourself? But, the police report said that the driver was drugged, she had been followed by a taxi for a mile as she ran stop lights, drove on sidewalks and weaved through traffic. Maybe it was an accident. Maybe your suicide attempt met the accident. Driver's name, Moira, means fate I think. One odd coincidence—the driver was your doppelganger, blonde, blue-eyed, same height, 5 pounds heavier, and only 14 days younger than you. I printed the notes. Need to think.

*2/27/97(Michael's Calendar)*
slept 12-8
8-930 cleaned apartment, laundry, defrost ref, garbage
930-1030 calls
1100-1500 visit you, talk with nat
1500-1600 visit LB for her work files, faxes
1616-1900 visit
1900-2100 dinner with Monica—topic: c
2100-2200 visit, finish bellow book, start trilete
2200-0300 clean files, make calls

*2/27/97 (Michael's Journals)*
Learned about Nat's ups and downs with KC. He seems broken up, devastated—that I understand since I'm two days ahead. What does he want? He just dumped her; why is he here? Guilt? Money? Love?

*2/28/97 (Phillipe's Fax)*
I did not know she was married! Is she going to be okay? Please keep me informed of her recovery. I had no idea. Yes, of course, send the cover.

*2/28/97 (Eric's Email)*
To: Katherine@tiac.net (nemo)
From: Erictb@transport.com
Subject: Re Re: Positive thoughts
This is a joke isn't it? Who is this? If Katherine is hurt, as you say, please tell her I am thinking of her and rooting for her recovery.

*2/28/97 (Michael's Calendar)*
sleep to 730
0800-1000 make calls
1100-1500 visit, start reading Maura zen book to you
1500-1600 LB for more files
1600-1900 talk to Tatter, Mercier lawyer, sign papers
1900-2100 dinner Monica
2100-2300 read finish zen book
2300-0300 calls, computer work

*Date: 7 Mar 1997 Email*
To: Dad410@aol.com
From: Katherine@tiac.net (nemo)
Subject: Re: Sympathy
Mom: Gee, thanks. Your love is unqualified I know, but I would be honored to be friends with you and Dad. While I do have much to offer, I expect I will have to force it on society and ignore individual things—I even felt uncomfortable when the waitress was too nice to me tonight, giving me a free glass of wine. I really do regard human beings with the same affection I have for birds, cats, sowbugs, and snakes. I like being around a few of them but have no desire to mate or sleep with them—they just are all living beings. I also notice that the various subpersonalities I developed for writing, from Cioran to mac Umor, seem to be producing more creative ideas. I've already started a novel called Monsters—for whatever that's worth (I know, just sublimation and transference).

Then again, who can see the future. Congrats on getting on the computer—see it's just a tool like a typewriter or washing machine, despite the hype. love, jr
PS The only thing I never figured out was what happened to my clothes—good will? garbage? Maybe she gave them to the homeless and that would be okay after all.

*3/16/97 (Michael's Journal)*
Monsters, we are just monsters, especially you, a multimedia monster, unable to make any decision about any one—you can't stand to leave anyone who obviously loves you, regardless of your feelings—you keep them as backups in case your current

adventures go sour. You assign each a medium like fax or phone, then create a consistent fantasy for each: Katherine the great lover, CC the tramp, Rina the nun, Ulrike the bimbo, Catheryn the adventurer—still identical segments going on and on, like a tapeworm (Jung's clever metaphor for the civilized psyche by the way). You talked to each of us, but no one got a good connection, especially you.

One of the archetypes in human myth is a monster, such as a dragon or vampire, that threatens humanity. We tend to overlook the small, common monsters, such as first graders shooting classmates or lovers betraying another. For such a common monster, I heard it said, goodness might be a mood and love a good investment at the moment. Did you see our love like a stock in a bear market? Something you could trade or let fall?

Ambition can lead you downward or diffuse you as well as concentrate—perhaps you learned that. Your rage for adventure was so near to stupid action—now my rage for goodness comes so near to murderousness (ala Dostoyevski). Saying your life and love was spiritual was insufficient. Your ambitions and means, your purposes and activities, were not constant. Your love was not constant—and out of all these love alone must be constant to be more than just an ugly solipsism.

You think designers like you create beauty and color reality where others see nothing. You need to be reminded that colors are distortions of light at the bottom of the atmosphere. Despite distortions and lenses, we find real being with our own being, not through isolated word plays.

For someone who rejected negativity in others, you were quite negative yourself. Not bothering to invest your efforts in our love, how many kinds of rejections did you offer me? Rejection of love? of offers, of time, of life? Of touch, of reach, of consciousness, of dreaming, of what was not said, of creating images and our small worlds?

Monsters—beings who show the way (from the Greek word 'terata' from the earth I think)—is what we are, but what kind of monsters? Monsters of ignorance, of naiveté, of stupidity? Of vanity, abstraction, selfishness, indecision? You showed the way to what you would become, with your fantasy and duplicity, and I indicated what I would become, with blind love and foolish trust. And now we are there, fully articulated and culminated monsters.

The future is open and blank now, where once trails could be seen. I am willing to understand, to wait and watch, to participate, become enlightened, but empty. Thank you for that at least—the utter emptiness.

*18 Mar 97 (Michael's Journal)*
Interesting conversation with Honey and Ken. It seems Katherine had not done any work the past few months; she had farmed all of it out. I suppose she just worked on her freelance stuff. I wonder if Jeff and the staff at LB are pissed off?

*3/19/97 (Michael's Notebooks)*
I did not intend to misunderstand the importance of monsters. Thalidomide babies are monsters because they point out the results of chemical and toxic poisons. Nature itself is a monster that lulls us with beautiful sunsets then slaughters us by the thousands with hurricanes and floods. What is being pointed out? That nature is morally neutral and slaughters flies and turtles with greater frequency than humans? That life is brutal as well as beautiful? That lives must turn over for new lives to form?

Perhaps we label as monsters what we are upset by or do not understand. Are you a monster because you had to search for richer mates? I know that fidelity is a cherished myth, that promiscuity can confer an evolutionary advantage in wolves and crows. Skill in deception is a natural talent, held by many. But for all your skill at weaving thin tissues of lies, you never developed the keen sense to detect fraud in others—your all-embracing sense of unworthiness of your self could not be controlled. Modern society selects for selfishness, and it must have some survival value—look at all the selfish people!

There is one definition of evil: selfishness without charity, anger without knowledge, lust without love, greed without limit.

*20 March 1997 (Michael's Calendar)*
CC opens eyes

*21 March 1997 (Michael's Calendar)*
Nat attacks; name-calling "Bastard!" over and over. I wonder what he thought or heard. Nat decides to keep the keys to our apartment. I change the lock.

*3/22/97 (Michael's Notebooks)*
A monster is a deviation from the average, a gap between middling ideals. Not evil really. To be healthy, we have to integrate undoable good with unavoidable evil. Monsters let us do that, to try to be healthy, as dramatic educational devices that show us good and evil already in our hearts and remind us that we have to actively choose.

*23 March 1997 (Michael's Calendar)*
Pearl lies about knowing Nat. Respect dies.

*24 March 1997 (Michael's Calendar)*
930-1130 Sweet with Nat/Pearl as to who will be guardian. Lucky me.

1230-Nat's shouting attack in front of CC and Pearl; "What makes you think you're the best person?"

I reply: "I didn't 'betray' her last week—those were her words in her diary by the way."

He continues: "You bastard! cold bastard! Self-righteous bastard! You think you're too good. You think you're so smart, with your high IQ. No woman will ever have you ..."

1:30 in cafeteria, Nat continues attack; he coaches Pearl to say "Katherine and Michael are not married." He tries to get Pearl to tell me to leave, not understanding that she never asks for anything unless it's an emergency. She stays, I stay, Nat stays.

The funny thing is, I could have done the same with Pearl: When was the last time you and Mack slept together? Made love? 1945? Laughed? You don't seem to be married. I could have asked Nat the last time he lived apart from his mother.

Nat's words echoed Katherine's from an argument several years ago. I suppose she told him about it. I never thought I was self-righteous; I think I am good—I think good things, do good things, especially for Katherine and her parents, without thought of reward. Is it self-righteous to continue to do so, even when people you love (or their lovers) shout at you, demean you, and hurt you? Or is it foolishness?

*28 March 1997 (Michael's Calendar)*
Pearl sick. Bring lunch and dinner to her. Old kindnesses die hard.

*3/30/97 (Michael's Notebooks)*
After a week of being shouted at and attacked, I have become so distant so fast that it seems like watching things develop looking backwards from a bullet train.

*26 October 97 (Michael's Journal)*
I have been speaking to her physiatrist; her doctor is unavailable—apparently he breezes through once a week and alters medication. She is getting Ginkgo tea, of which I approve. I wonder if everything else failed?

*27 October 1997 (Michael's Journal)*
I can't find my notes. Such a good conversation in memory. I was

wild with hope!

M: I miss our head rubs

K: My fingers grow wild with loneliness

M: Do you remember my letter to you from Syracuse conference? I said I missed you wildly?

K: [ ]

M: I love you my beauteous Katherine

K: I love you my beautiful Michael

*10/28/97 (Katherine's Notes)*

is it  hurt

mother is hurt  ooooo

*28 June 1997 (Letter from Michael)*

My sweetness and light:

Today was a very slow day. I sent out a few articles and letters to my assistant editors, for the journal. Then, worked on my new novel. I listened to music for a few hours. It has been raining all day, so I started a fire and dried out my clothes (from working a little this morning on a trail). Watched La Boheme again on the VCR. I ate a salad and a small pizza cooked on the wood stove (not very well). Played hide and seek with the lizard; I won, I found him under the rug. Wrote a letter to Nancy. Tried to call Greg—they must be with her parents.

I read a few words that you wrote, in an envelope, probably from a nurse who noticed you write constantly. You ask why; I know of no answers. Are you frightened, as you say? Because of the accident or the uncertainty of the future? Do not be frightened, you are loved completely by so many who will help you recover. You wonder if things are not good between us. I love you completely and always will. Perhaps things would have been better if we had lived together regardless of economic circumstances. But we will always share our home and it will be waiting for you when you wish to, and can, return. You have a lot of healing to do, and it will not be easy, but you must do it. It is the price of improperly asking your spirits for help, without specifying the exact help and without honoring them by name—humans always seem to make that mistake and end up as crickets or echoes.

Like a good Bodhisattva (equivalent), I am free of wants, so you needn't worry about what I want. I am empty too of desire and needs, unless you wish to try to rekindle them someday. I work now to save nonhuman beings and wild places. I enjoy the forest more, knowing there is nothing else for the moment.

I will come to see you as often as I can, between contracts, and by giving up contracts (like I did from February through May). And when I cannot, I will write and call and think of you.

I love you, Solnishba

*1 July 97, Mike's Notebooks*
"for a complex monster, goodness might be a mood and love a good investment at the moment," who said that? Bellow? like a stock perhaps.

*16 July 1997 Letter from Michael*
Dear Katherine:
Another day of seed harvesting, in search of the big seed heads. Remember how we used to salivate over sow bugs when catching them for Fric and Frac? I have the same reaction now to fescue—not to California oats or tall fescue or rye grass or blue rye grass, just fescue. I wonder what would happen if I saw a sow bug in the fescue? I forgot to mention, these grasses grow only along roadsides—the cows and deer have eaten them from the natural meadows.

It was much damper today, so I was able to collect a pound in the first hour, but the moisture will evaporate by afternoon. It's very nice harvesting early. I have formed a gestalt for the fescue plants and seeds. I can tell by touch if I have grabbed some other grass or bunch grass. Some of the seeds had a "smut" on them this morning, but I avoided them (would infect the whole bag). It is fascinating to look at the kinds of plants and try to figure who is invading who, which ones are dying out or increasing. There are blackberries, oaks, pines, St. John's wort, and many I cannot identify (and a few Snake cannot identify). Maybe we'll set up a few plots here for succession experiments.

Last night, tired of working on yet another forest plan (Pine Grove, Nordstrom, Parker, Guth, Heatherstone, and yes, Altazor), I sorted through some of your older mail to me. I found a few poems—even some I didn't remember—parts of short stories, letters, and notes. Here is a good test for your long-term memory (over 6 months): What year did you write the following paragraph? "I am searching, groping . . ."

I'll ask you again next week, for monstrous effect (think etymology). I love you.

*16 July 1997 (Letter from Michael)*

Dear Nat:

Thank you for your letter of 10 July, telling me of Katherine's needs. I have been calling Valeri, Corrin, and others every 2-3 days about Katherine's condition.

I know that she needs her friends and family. I know that she is depressed and frightened. And I know that her recovery will be aided by having them close as often as possible. You have been a stalwart friend. I am sure that she treasures your presence now as much as she sought it during the past year. How long can you stay by her? What are your intentions toward her? Friend? Lover? Mate? Knowing her love for you, do you plan to keep loving her? Will you be with her next year?

Whenever Katherine has needed me in the past, I have done whatever was necessary to be with her and help her: Quit my job, dropped out of school, dropped everything to be by her side, sold my truck, cashed in my retirement, helped her start a business, built her a studio, even suppressed my own needs and wants. I did so again last February, giving up contracts and obligations to be with her for over 3 months.

Then I found out that Katherine was willing to destroy me to be with you—that she had in fact erased me from her life, throwing away my clothes and books, telling all her friends and coworkers that she was single and lonely. I discovered her fantasies, machinations, duplicities, and desires; she wrote over and over how you were the "love of her life" despite your poor behavior and hers. I listened to her friends tell me about her single life and other romances. I listened to you coach her parents into saying that she had no husband.

And so I was destroyed. I have no desire to prove anything—I loved Katherine completely, but have become only a shell to which legal rights are attached, like an anemone to a crab. I have an emptiness that a Bodhisattva might recognize. Like a good Buddhist, I try to help all living beings, from fungi and bats to wolves and Katherine. I will do everything I can for her, but all special ties with me have been broken or dissolved by her, or by her friends and family.

*11/6/97 (Michael's Journal)*
A meeting this morning with her treatment team, except her doctor who did not show again. Afterwards I got her to go to the gym with me. She was able to walk; I held her waist, but she did quite well and did not seem to tire. As we were sitting on a gym pad, I asked her some things:

M: What was Nat to you?
K: I loved him
M: What was I to you?
K: A pair of balls
M: Ha, ha, ha

It was so unexpected that I laughed and that made her laugh. So, we sat there laughing about how little I meant. Nine months before I would have been destroyed. Ha, ha, ha

*11/7/97 (Michael's Journal)*
Today is her birthday. I stopped at a grocery store on the way and bought a decorated mini-cake (super large cupcake actually), a candle, Ben & Jerry's Fish Food ice cream, a bright red warm-up suit, and two ping pong balls threaded with a string (I wondered if she would make the connection). I thought she would dive into the cake, but she very carefully had a small bite. She did have 5 spoonfuls of ice cream. I do not think that she knew it was her birthday. I gave her the presents.

M: I got a new suit for you to wear in therapy.
K: Red
M: Yes, red.
K: I can't wear red.
M: I remember you never did wear it much.
K: I have to be stronger.
M: Okay, I'll put it in your closet for now, okay?
K: [looks at closet]
M: I got these two balls for you, so you know I will always be with you, in toto.
K: [smiles]
M: Happy birthday, beloved. I miss you.
K: Miss you too, Michael.
M: I'm going back to the Wadi's house. Adjø adjø

K: Adjø adjø

On the way back, I stopped at the Atlantic Fish Company and had three Cuba libres.

*11/9/97 (Katherine's Notes)*

green red  red
balls  aaaaaa
gold  now

*15 August*

Dear Katherine:

Oh, great! Just as soon as I get to Eugene, I get an offer to work in Seattle for $69,000 a year. Now, I don't know what to do. What would you do? Follow the money or your heart? (never mind, I already know the answer to that).

Well, I'll sleep on it. I expect to keep doing ecology. I dreamed of you the other night. You were whole, but I wasn't.

Heard a good joke on the Internet: What is the way to a man's heart? Cracking the sternum, then cutting through the pericardial sac. Tell that to Nat, would you?

Enjoy life! M

*16 August Dialogue with Greg*

G: "Yes, I knew. She told me, like she wanted approval"

M: "Yea?"

G: "She was a stupid cunt."

M: "Fuck you, too!"

G: "Sorry, but she was."

M: "Let me reply again. I am astounded you would call her that, yet secretly pleased that it confirms my feelings and fears, being cuckolded for economic reasons and shit. I just don't know . . ."

G: "So, what do you want to do?"

M: "Play pool I guess. Loser pays."

. . . .

M: Greg, here's an idea: Create wedding package for brides/grooms, ala pillow book in Japan. A complete guide to intimacy and . . .

G: "Rather defraud an insurance company. Then we would be rich."

*8/14/98 Letter from Michael*
Dear K:
Jennifer the nurse said that you were having trouble sleeping. You have nothing to fear; you are safe from all monsters, especially the chichevache (a monster who ate only faithful wives!). Even the human malums have put you out of bounds now.
Tell the nurses to call when you cannot sleep and I will read to you from Nabokov until you sleep

*12/14/97 (Michael's Journal)*
Four days of feeding her. Her craniotomy has failed and they had to take the plate out, along with a little more brain and bone. She has been very depressed and has a cold. I read to her—we are good at that. She smiles while I read. That night I pack to return to work.

*16 December 1997 (Michael's Call)*
M: "Hi Rina"
K: "Hi, Michael"
M: "What are you doing?
K: [ ]
M: "How do you feel after the operation?"
K: [ ]
M: "I've only been gone for a day. I miss you."
K: "I miss you Michael."
M: "Did you dance today?"
K: "Oh, no, ha, ha"
M: "What would you like to do?"
K: [ ]
M: "You must be tired. I'll call back tomorrow. I love you.
K: "I love you too,"
M: "Adjø, adjø"
K: "Adjø, adjø"

*1/7/98 (Michael's Journal)*
Conversation with Katherine in the hospital.
Michael: "There's no need to speak."
Katherine: "She didn't know what she threw away."
Michael: "I'll push your wheelchair over to the elevator."
K: "The ship is burning."
M: "What do you mean?"
K: "It's a secret."
M: "Can you walk?"
K: "Yes, I want to walk."
M: "Will you?"
K: "Yes."

M: "I have garden catalogs. Shall we buy seeds?"
K: "Yes."
M: "Will you plant them?"
K: "Yes, that would be nice."
M: "Let's talk about insurance."
K: "No!"
M: "No?"
K: "No, they are not part of the loop."
M: "Okay, let's walk down the hall."

*1/8/1998 (Michael's Journal)*
Thursday night I found Katherine looking depressed and grotesque in her room, without her helmet, but very alert (the right side of her face was empty, slack, and three inches lower—there seemed to be less bone than before). I unpacked the running suits that Ann had sent her; we admired the colors. We talked for about an hour; she only glazed over twice but each time I brought her back and she focused on the conversation.

M: "Did you get my letters?"
K: "Yes"
M: "Shall I keep writing?"
K: "I fear that you will stop."
M: "I will not stop, as long as you want me to write. I have been getting all the paperwork now for your insurance. I write to all your friends."
K: "You were always nice."
M: "I am no longer nice; this is rather a duty of love. Your doctor wants to know if you remember the accident."
K: "Yes, I was hurt, not mother."
M: "You thought she was in the accident, but she was not and is fine. What do you feel now?"
K: [ ]
M: "Are you depressed?"
K: "Yes, I think so."
M: "Nat comes to visit you. Does that help?"
K: "I loved him."
M: "I know. He loves someone else. I love you."
K: [ ]
M: "I am lonely too. I have no one but you."
K: [ ]
M: "Will you read these sonnets to me, from your new book? Please?"

She read eight of Shakespeare's sonnets—all were about failed love and death (I was afraid then she would become depressed), so I gave her the Ansel Adams book; she turned the pages back and forth. She has stopped writing now. I will have to get her new large pens and try again.

*1/9/98 (Michael's Journal)*
The next day she was incoherent. I brought her a new Chagall calendar, but she didn't look at it. I asked if she wanted to walk;

K: "the ship is burning."
M: "What does that mean?"
K: "It's a deep secret."
M: "Okay, I can keep, or ignore, a secret. Did you walk today?"
K: "yes,"
M: "good." (I found out later that she had not walked for over a week, because her therapy had been canceled.) "Do you want to go to the gym with me and walk some more?"
K: "no"

So, I fed her dinner. Dinner was a mess. She cannot swallow well without cues and is back on a pureed diet. She stuffs her cheeks with food until it leaks out, but won't swallow.

I asked her if she wanted me to smuggle a pizza in; she said, "yes, a really evil one."

Going to her room for bed, I asked Katherine to say hello to Lisa, her roommate. She said hi. Then I wheeled her to bed and asked her why she didn't speak more to people.

She replied, "There's no need to speak."

*4/11/98 (Michael's Journal)*
When I first went in to Katherine, I kissed her face and arms a lot and noisily; she smiled but didn't say anything. I had just read an article on the medical benefits of massage, so I gave her a back and head massage for a few hours.

M: "Hello, Rina"
K: "Michael."
M: "Watching TV?"
The television is on so she does not answer. Later I try again.
M: "Did you like the massage?"
K: "Yes"
M: "Shall I stop?"
K: "No!"

*4/12/98 (Michael's Journal)*
The next morning I approach her; she is still wet from her shower; she is bathed lying in a giant bassinet. I smile at her and touch her face, running my fingers along her cheek. She reaches towards me with an intense look, puts two fingers in my mouth and stretches it wide. I open it and she begins to play with my teeth. I wonder what

she is thinking.

I sit in the chair next to the bed and put my head on her shoulder; she absently rubs my head—twenty years of habit must be hard-wired into her. Aware after 15 minutes that it might be a strain on her arm, I lift my head and look at her. She strokes my cheek then pushes my nose flat. I bulge my eyes and she laughs.

I got her dressed and pushed her into the gym to practice walking. She refused to walk. So, I asked her to dance with me. She stood with a little help and put her feet on mine. Then we danced. She smiled and put her head on my shoulder. Then she vomited. I told her it was okay. She looked sheepish. She put her chin on my other shoulder and vomited again. I giggled, and she laughed. I got her to sit down on the mat. I suggested sit-ups, but she could not sit up. I pulled her up and we tried a few double push-pulls.

She talked a little but would not eat. I bought ice cream for her at a nearby convenience store and ate it in front of her. She took a few licks but did not seem interested. I tried to feed her at lunch and dinner (I even tried to make it look good by trying it—pureed peas, potatoes and chicken—gag).

*4/13/98 (Michael's Journal)*

The third day she started talking quite a bit. I asked her why she wouldn't eat. She has trouble answering in sentences. I asked her if she was hungry; she looked confused. I asked her if it tasted bad; she raised her eyebrows. I asked her if she was afraid of gagging; she said yes. Later, she fell asleep in her chair. Later, we went for a stroll around the garden outside. I gave her another massage. We looked at birds. Her interest was really captured by several large bumble bees on flowers so we watched them for a while in the bright sun. She went to sleep for 40 minutes. When we went back in, I asked if she was thirsty; she said yes, so I gave her a glass of water—much to the consternation of the nurses, who said fluids had to be thickened for her, but Katherine had no trouble swallowing five or six sips.

*July 16 1998 (Michael's Journal)*

In Boston, I bought a dinner at the Atlantic Fish Company (one of our 4 favorite restaurants)—a Jamaican Island salad with shrimp and scallops, calamari, and a chocolate mouse crepe—and took it to the hospital. I got permission from the nurses to feed it to her. She was in bed at 6 p.m. However, an assistant brought her regular meal just as I was setting up; it was apples, mangos, and a pineapple drink. I fed her a few bites of the salad, then she grabbed the fruit and ate it all, and then drank two glasses of juice. I was surprised, but got to eat the whole mousse myself. We talked for an hour. She had 6 unopened letters from me, so I asked her to read them, which she did. We looked at photos; she was unable to identify any of our animals (not a good sign, since her long-term memory has been so good). I gave her a head rub and she went to sleep.

In K's hospital room; we have not talked much all day. I press her to my chest, almost lifting her out of bed. She rubs my cheek:

K: You are so beautiful. I could love you again.

M: You only mean to return my kindness. Did you fall out of love with me again?

K: I love you.

My wish for her expression of love is granted so quickly that a vacuum forms and great misery is drawn to fill it.

*18 November 1998 (Michael's Journal)*

Telephone call to hospital:

M: How are you?

K: Fine.

M: I miss you awfully much.

K: I miss you too.

M: It's been snowing here, a real blizzard. What's it like there?

K: Really grim

M: Well, it's Boston in winter. Do you have snow?

K: No, it's dark.

M: Has Jane been there to see you today?

K: No, but I expect to see her at the U of I.

M: I think she's going to be in NY instead.

K: What you do when you do what you do when you do do.

M: I'll bet you a dollar that you cannot repeat that.

K: What?

M: What you just said.

K: What?

M: You should rest now. I love you. Adjø, adjø

*4 December 1998 (Michael's Journal)*

Call to Hospital:

M: I miss your beautiful eyes

K: You were so nice and handsome

M: Oh, yea, what color are my eyes?

K: Blue

M: What do I mean to you?

K: I could really fall in love with you again.

M: I don't understand why you fell out of love with me so regularly

K: I don't know.

M: I miss kissing you

K: Me too
M: It's lonely here
K: It's lonely here too
M: I wish we could hug so tightly both our chests would be flat.
K: Hmmm?
M: I have to go now. I'm working at home. Adjø adjø
K: Okay
M: I can't hang up until you say adjø adjø
K: Adjø adjø

*24 December 1998 (Michael's Journals)*
Telephone call:
M: Rina!
K: Hi, Michael.
M: What are you doing today?
K: Shopping
M: Oh, what are you looking for?
K: Just people going by.
M: Are you at the mall?
K: Why yes, the mall.
M: Did you see anything you would like to have?
K: Clothes.
M: What kind?
K: Pretty.
M: Would you like me to send you some?
K: Yes, you may do that.
M: What are you wearing now?
K: [ ]
M: Is it black?
K: Yes
M: Did you walk today?
K: [ ]
M: Are you tired?
K: [ ]
M: I'll call later. I love you, Adjø adjø
K: [ ]

*4 February 1999 (Michael's Journals)*
Telephone Call:
M: Hello, this is Michael calling to speak with my wife, Katherine.
N: Just a minute [minutes pass]
K: Hello
M: Hello sweetness and light
K: Michael
M: How are you?

K: [ ]
M" What are you wearing? Blue?
K: [ ]
M: I can hear both the aides arguing. Dos that distract you?
K: [ ]
M: C, close your eyes and listen to the plastic in your hand. Can you do that?
K: Yes
M: How is therapy going
K: [ ]
M: C, focus on the phone
K: [ ]
M: I'll call back tomorrow. Adjø adjø

*13 February 1999 (Michael's Journal)*
Telephone Call:
M: Rina, good morning.
K: swswsws
M: I can't hear you. Is that the nurse talking?
K: [ ]
M: Can you hear me?
K: Yes
M: What shall we talk about? Are you writing a novel?
K: [ ]
M: What clothes are you wearing?
K: [ ]
M: Can you tell me the color? Close your eyes and listen only to the phone, okay?
K: [ ]
M: I'll call you later. Love you. Adjø adjø.

*6 Sep 99 (Michael's Call)*
M: Hi, sweetness!
K: Hi, Michael
M: Did you do anything exciting today?
K: It's burning
M: What?
K: It
M: Are you all right?
K: [ ]
M: What are you wearing?
K: [ ]
M: What color are your clothes?
K: [ ]
M: Are they blue? Red?

K: Not red
M: Green?
K: [ ]
M: Is the nurse there?
K: [ ]
M: I'll call back for the nurse

*12 September 1999 (Michael's Letter)*
Dear K:
I have been working on 2 new projects in the woods and have not been near a computer or post office. Too much work, not enough fun! But, the stream project is wrapping up tomorrow.

I am getting ready to lecture for a week in Canada, then Brian and I will be assessing three new forests between here and Portland.

I have not heard from any of your doctors or nurses, or from Flippie or Annie, so I trust you are doing well, and getting therapy and good food (I haven't had anything but peanut butter sandwiches myself and have lost 25 pounds).

The Peace Corps projects are all set up again—it's just a matter of waiting for paperwork. I have put everything in storage. I miss you,
love, J
I wonder if you even receive these letters?

*20 Sep 99 (Michael's Call)*
M: Rina!
K: [ ]
M: I can't hear you? Can you speak up? Please?
K: [ ]
M: Did you have therapy today?
K: [ ]
M: Are you in your room?
K: [ ]
M: Can I say something to help?
K: [ ]
M: Can you give the phone to the nurse?
K: [ ]
M: Rina, close your eyes and listen. Then you can answer. But, you must concentrate.
K: [ ]
M: I'm going to call back for the nurse, okay. I love you. Adjø adjø
K: [ ]

*16 August 1998 Letter from Michael*
Dear K:
24 Years Today!
from our Marriage Document for 8/16/74:
". . . Since our trust and responsibility is with each other rather than society, and believing we have properly and sincerely declared and documented the authenticity of our motivations, we agree that this private contract is as binding as legal proofs of marriage, and that all others are irrelevant."
Would you say this again?
Love, M

*8/18/98 Letter*
Dear Fere:
You are still my desiderium and dilection. Those are your new words for the day: desiderium means "ardent desire" and dilection means "choice in love." Say these words as you read them; when I call you next I will remind you to say them to me.
Your mansuete (kind) Michael

*22 August 1998 Letter*
Dear K:
I can't remember if I told you. I have agreed to start work in Siberia next year, as a Wildlife Biologist. Probably too primitive for you to come along. The Russians (remember Prof. Kristoforova?) are out of money as usual, and I won't get paid much, but I'll get to play with wolves, tigers, and bears. I will be sad to not be able to see you as often, but you chose Nat, and you will be able to see Nat.
Eat well, walk a lot—M

*5/14/99 Letter*
Dear K:
I saw a cricket today. By the time I picked him up I realized he was a cockroach. As he felt his way over my arm I flung him back to the grass. I understand that cockroaches are clean and caring mates—sort of the cats of the insect world; they clean themselves and groom each other. But, his movement set off the hairs on my arm.

We have made monsters out of cockroaches—they are so different and successful. But, if they are monsters at all it is because they point to a whole unrecognized but necessary dimension of life, so much of which we are unconscious of and uncaring about. When I can pick him up without revulsion, I should be initiated into the depths of being, into other nature and chaos.

*8/16/99 (Michael's Journal)*
It has been 25 years today. A good day to end. We haven't been really close for over three years. We have violated our wedding vows. Our contract was so simple—why did you have to lie to me, lie about me (to your friends and co-workers), and betray me in 1995-97 (and of course in 1987-1990)? Why? Were you afraid I was the only one who would want you at last? I have given almost everything to you. You could have gotten out with four words, but you were silent (to me anyway).

Now, at last I am completely empty; the last shreds of my soul were scattered to trees; maybe someday I will get them back, but not getting them back would be okay, too. Maybe I will be a bodhisattva in the forest, offering help to bats, lizards, and pines. Maybe . . .

As you suggested in 1974, it was you who first felt love lessen; you who coldly unfastened the bond and watched the unraveling passion from a safe distance. You who said "I loved you once, but not now." It was your heart after all that grew small and hard, as you said it might. I just did not listen well enough.

After you left me in 1987, you only wanted me once, after and only after you thought that someone else did. You wanted the spare tire, the backup that you could trust, the true life-support. You were too cowardly to even think of being on your own; you only could have left me if someone else loved you—apparently no one really did. Did they? You did not understand that I loved you and knowingly gave up so much, expected to suffer so much, as your plaything and extra equipment.

In Portland in 1990, where you went to be with Eric, you said "from Michael, so many many kindnesses and tendernesses and in his extra-ordinary way going beyond the call of duty—very hard to see him go—" It was love, not duty. I know well the difference—this year is duty.

Even the last time we were together, you could only say "various new problems to work out—Michael's feelings—his civility and stoicism—my own frozen congealed senses—affection is possible but hardly more and this even is inconstant. Occasionally a warmth, but I was sometimes moved by other feelings for Nat." But you didn't tell me, you kept lying and concealing everything, until it wasn't your choice.

I watched you slowly become a city girl. I watched you adjust your life to stresses you weren't aware of or couldn't change. You paid less attention to me, then to your work, then to your cat, then to your novels. Some friends and things were written off. Some exchanges were blocked off. You slept, you didn't answer your phone; you went away without telling me.

When we did talk, your intensity diminished, as it seemed to about everything. Overload, stress; I understand. So, you kept so much in your imagination, where you could control things. I understand.

You were seduced by the city, by rapid-fire culture and by superficial differences. I understand. So, you tried to idealize the world to make things perfect and true. You had the combination, found in great art it is said, of god-like freedom and the sense of inevitable destiny—trouble is, you thought that it made your art great, without inspiration, without discipline or without vision. So you became a monster, a pathetic monster for other people who are fooled by themselves and the pace of things, regardless of the content, regardless of the real feelings of others who love them and need them.

But you fooled me for ten years. I let myself be fooled. I am a fool. All I have left is understanding. And I am a monster after all—for all people fooled by themselves. But a living, breathing, thinking monster, who is now loose.

***Epilogue***
From *The Star* (2/98): "With global warming, monsters of all kinds are making a comeback."

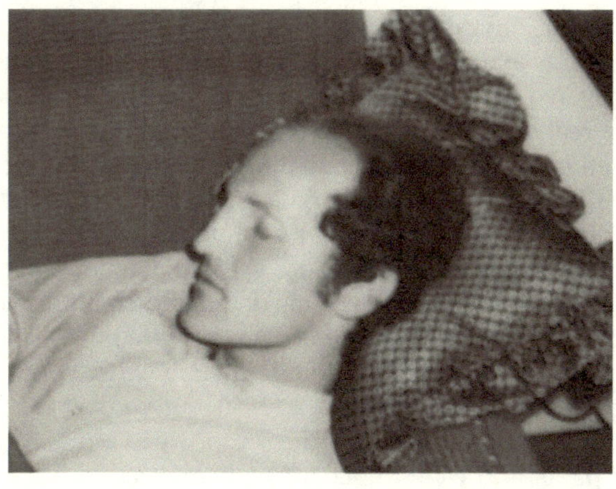

## Judge Vandergelt's Decision

by Marcus Ryan

Three Prisons

1. Eaten by a bamboo dragon, captured
   by the teeth and claws and thrust
   down narrow passageways to lie
   in humid darkness, just lie
   and dream of release
2. concrete walls, concrete floors
   planed smooth to lessen the friction
   of reluctant guests, iron bed with paper
   covers that scatter as I wake
   exercise and clean memorize the grains
   and repeat without end—all life
   entertains, changing guards, changing
   seasons changing me
3. another day and all night long
   with no place to lie down, open
   to air and water, waiting for light
   sleeplessly—rain here travels sideways
   from the ocean to the trees
   through the ventilator in the men's
   room door, pushing the coolness
   of night under flat fluorescent light,
   paper towels on tile, paper
   towels for cover scatter when I wake
   stretch out concrete ache—check
   for roaches or false dawn and try
   to sleep again.

I couldn't write anymore. It was meaningless to anyone but me. The poetry leapt, as a famous poet said it should, but only I knew the ground covered between leaps. How can you convey a prison in which the real horror is nothing, just watching time pass? In which you prayed for pain or sacrifice to make it real or worthwhile? My life hadn't changed that much anyway. After being discharged in Hawaii, I spent months wandering around the islands. Now, I finally made it back east to return to school. A simple, quiet school where I could worry some trivial academic detail and create a niche like others had already made for themselves, a place to be secure and worry another detail, while teaching others how to worry theirs.

My neck ached. I lifted my head back and looked at the ceiling. The forty-watt bulb brought out the sculpture in old plaster. I put away the paper and went to bed, a single mattress dropped between the stove and wall. This was of course a cheesy cheap apartment near the university. Main street Newark and all the dust that had accumulated in 90 years of the building's life still made its geological impressions on the wooden floor. I had a small sign on my inside door "Please wipe feet before leaving. Keep Newark clean!"

In bed, my feet stretched under the wall to the kitchen, which was at the top of the back stairs. I could hear the neighbor's television below me; it was always on all night. I suspect he was troubled. I was warm, with my clothes still on—I suspect I was troubled—and the ceiling rat patter lullabied me to a sleep with no dreams.

I heard screaming in my dream. I rolled over and tried to force myself to dream of something good, like skydiving or sex. The screaming wasn't a dream. I sat up in bed, waiting for it to end so I could go to sleep. It didn't end, it just oscillated, hit a high note and trailed off. I got up and walked to the door, still dressed, hoping it would stop. It didn't. I put on my shoes, opened the door and walked downstairs noisily and deliberately.

The halls were deserted. At the bottom of the stairs a door was open. Not just open, but broken in. I hadn't heard that happen. A thin woman in a white nightgown was sitting, or had been put, on her dresser in her room, screaming as some man hit her, as another watched, apparently giving instructions.

"All right, stop it," I said too meekly. No one heard me, or hearing, paid any attention.

"I said, Knock it off!!!" with enough decibels to knock a cow off a railroad track. Three heads turned my way. I looked at her first. She had some kind of black make-up running from her eyes and patches of red surrounding both eyes. The beater was Hispanic looking, about five-eight and 200 pounds; his teacher was taller but weighed about the same with brown hair and dark eyes.

"Who you? Her boyfriend?" beater sneered.

"Yeah, what's your interest?" teacher demanded. "You got a reason to be here?" he added. Both of them left the woman and walked toward me.

"I've been trying to sleep. The screaming woke me up." I nodded toward the woman. "Is she all right?"

"I been teaching her a lesson." beater explained. "I think she been cheating. Maybe with you, eh."

"Get back upstairs and mind your own bidness." teacher demanded.

"I'm sorry, gentlemen, I think I need to know if she's okay first." I couldn't believe it, all the politeness shit I learned in Catholic school was monopolizing my communication as if it were just another pleasant day in the neighborhood. "Perhaps if you both went and came back tomorrow and just talked to her."

"I need to know now, man, and you ain't got the guts to stop me," beater said.

"I'm sorry, but you cannot stay," I insisted, having decided to do whatever.

"What you gonna do, throw us out?" beater asked.

"We put you in the hospita," teacher added.

"I had my face in her bush, man, that's how much I loved that cunt," beater explained unnecessarily. "I bought her things. She don't have no right to step out on me. She need a lesson."

"So do you," teacher said as he tightened his fists and advanced.

"Um, I'm sorry fellows, I don't fight actually," well, that was true, I shot people from a distance for my country, but I never punched anybody. I backed away.

"Well, then, you just go back upstairs real pretty, now," teacher encouraged.

"Um, I can't really do that either," I said.

"Well, what you gonna do, talk us to death?" beater asked, coming around to the left.

"I can't let you hit her anymore. Why not try me? I'm bigger, almost as big as you," I said. I noticed the tattoo on his forearm. "You were in Air Force training weren't you?"

"Shit," said beater, as he swung a roundhouse at my face.

I backed out of his range quickly, but into teacher's range. Teacher swung at my body, but I jumped sideways onto the stairs. Teacher came after me up the stairs. I jumped over the railing and came toward beater, who swung again, but I ducked under him and he lost his balance and hit the wall. I ran to the front door, glancing at the woman, who seemed to be weeping quietly on the dresser.

Teacher came rushing down the stairs trying to beat me to the door. I let him and he crashed it open, out of control. I went through the door and jumped to the right as Beater came pumping through. Teacher was down two stairs, beater was down three, just two from the sidewalk.

From the top of the stairs, I suggested, "Look, I don't want to fight, but I don't want you to hurt some poor girl, either." These guys smelled like beer and moved like they were full of kegs.

"We wasn't hurtin her," Teacher offered, "we was instructin her." He exchanged transparent glances with Beater. They both charged up the stairs. I jumped over the bushes and onto the sidewalk. They came rushing down. Teacher was first and swung down—I jumped to the side—he lost his balance and fell to the sidewalk. Beater saw his chance and swung another roundhouse. I leapt back bowing my body over his punch. I could hear the warble of a police car approaching.

So did beater, "We're gonna kill you, now."

Possibly they would, if I got a heart attack moving out of way of their charges. Teacher swung an uppercut, but I leaned back out of the way.

The police car stopped. The passenger door opened and a uniformed cop got out and asked dryly, "What's going on?"

I made the mistake of starting to answer, "These guys were beating up—" a fist landed high on my left cheek. I moved backwards, but Beater got a hold of my shirtfront. As I moved back he started to fall and the buttons went flying.

The driver's side door opened and a voice angrily said, "Stop it now!"

The Passenger said, "Okay, all three of you over here against the car," shining the flashlight on one of us after the other. Beater and Teacher went to the left front of the car, which was headed the wrong way down a one-way street. I walked in front of the grill. The driver got out.

"Okay," started the driver, nodding to me, "you started talking, you finish. Start with your name and where you live."

"My name is Joe Sullivan, I live upstairs here. I was—"

"And what happened, in your opinion?" he interrupted. Why do officers and lawyers always interrupt a chronology?

I continued. "—I was awakened by screaming. I came down and saw these guys beating up some woman. Her door was broken down. I tried to stop—"

"You dead, now, cocksucka," Beater threatened. 'In front of police officers?' I thought.

"—tried to stop them."

"Why were you fighting out here?" driver asked.

"I thought it was better to lead them away from her," I answered.

Officer passenger watched while officer driver seemed to be digesting that. Finally, driver asked beater, "Your name and address."

"Uh, Barry Clarke," Beater offered, "I'm mar—I live over on Chrysler Circle. We were just visiting—"

"What were you doing here?" Driver interrupted—obviously a new interrogation method.

"We were visiting her; she's my girl. This bastard started hitting us for no reason, man, no reason." Officer Passenger's eyebrow raised. The woman appeared on the steps. She was bleeding from the lower lips; her nightgown was torn and had a little fresh blood near the neckline.

Driver looked up and indicated to Passenger to take her back inside. Passenger left us and escorted her back to her apartment.

Driver walked over to teacher. "Your name and address?"

"William, uh, uh, Bennett, officer sir. I live in the same neighborhood he does. We work at Chrysler, see." Teacher and Beater exchanged frowning glances, as if too much information had been delivered.

"And what happened?" Driver asked without interrupting.

"Just as he said, sir, this guy, that we never seen before, just attacked us. He must've attacked her before we got here, you know, broken in her door, hitted her." I started shaking my head.

Driver noticed and said, "Contradictory stories. How unusual."

Passenger appeared alone in the doorway. We all watched as he walked down the stairs slowly.

"She says the strong one here is her boyfriend and he was hitting her."

Driver sighed and said, "Okay, you two into the backseat, now. Banson, call another car for the other two." Officer driver opened a car door for beater and teacher, or Barry and Bill. He got in the front, made a u-turn and drove downtown, no lights or sirens.

Officer Passenger—his name plate said 'Fred Benson'—nodded my way and said, "stay here, okay?" He went back up the stairs. I looked at the dark rose bushes by the building, highlighted only by streetlights on the other side of the road. They didn't smell much, flowers didn't smell much these days, but they had large heavy blooms. The building was white, with single narrow columns transplanted from a deeper southern architecture. I could see two shadows at opposite ends of the room. I assumed Benson was calling for another car. I was wondering if I should have collapsed a larynx or crushed a ball or two tonight, but I suppose my peaceful ways have become too ingrained. I envisioned a single stiff finger entering one neck, while a left kick with a pull of the toes entering the other groin, a thoroughly satisfying vision at that. I traced a fingernail cut down my chest, wondering if it would become infected or heal quickly. I didn't see any trace of any buttons.

Benson came down the stairs with the girl friend, still wearing the white nightgown and a dazed expression.

I asked, "Couldn't you let her get a coat?"

Benson looked perplexed, as if following a ritual beyond cultural understanding, but came up to me and asked, "Do you know her?"

"I never saw her before tonight. I work late in the computer lab, translating French and German tapes," I said, saying too much.

Benson seemed like he wanted to be friendly, or at least sympathetic. He asked, "Have you lived here long?"

"Not very," I answered, distracted by the approach of a police car with its lights rolling. I wondered why the lights were rolling when the first car went dark.

As the car pulled up, I heard a lock click. Benson opened the rear door for me, but I stepped aside and motioned the girlfriend ahead. I then went to the other side of the car, doubtless violated at least two procedures for suspects to obey suggestions and remain in direct sight—or line of fire—at all times. The door was unlocked so I got in.

The ride was only three blocks, closer than I would have thought. We were led through the front door to two small rooms in back. One of the other officers escorted the girl friend to one room, where a policewoman was waiting. Benson led me into the other.

"Have a seat," he gestured to a folding chair in front of a formica-covered metal table. Having spent a semester studying proxemics, the science of how people use personal and social space, I realized that this space was as impersonal as possible with no consideration for making its visitors feel welcome or comfortable. Surprisingly, it was comfortable. I sat.

He sat too. So, I wasn't being intimidated. "I need to take your statement, starting with your names, sorry name, and address." He actually looked sheepish.

"Royal Joseph Sullivan, 337 Main Street, Apartment 4." I didn't tell him that my mother gave me a name for success so that I would be successful. At least it wasn't 'Senator' or 'Dean.' I had a sudden memory of standing in the post office, looking at the wanted posters—they all had names like Martin Luther Mannix or John Kennedy Strunk, the bearers of motherly hope gone all wrong.

"What happened Roy," he asked.

"Call me Joe, please," I asked. "I was asleep. I heard screaming. It didn't stop, so I went downstairs. I found two dickless morons beating up a small woman in a nightgown. I asked them to leave. They didn't. I lead them outside with the promise of an easy ego-boost. They made funny breezes with their arms. Then you guys rescued us."

Benson smiled. "Do you know her? Or them?"

"Neither. We probably travel in different social circles, or different species."

"All right," Benson said, getting up. He gave me his official report form: "Read this and autograph it." I did. He said, "Wait here. The judge will hear the case soon."

I looked questioningly, but didn't say anything.

Benson left.

I had an eight o'clock class. It was after three. Why not just let the apes swing from the bars 'til morning? Going to classes was living in slow motion. Watching people think was like watching a still life. I didn't have to wait—or think—long, though, before Benson came back and escorted me into a court room.

The troglodytes of love were already there, practicing their sneers on the court clerk. The girl friend was being escorted in at the same time. I looked at her but she did not make eye contact. Maybe she didn't like being fought over any more than she liked being beaten. She was still wearing the nightgown, but with a grey blanket for modesty or warmth.

We were all asked to sit down, then to rise for the judge.

Judge Robert Vandergelt glided to the bench like a crow to a roadkill.

"I have read the statements of the concerned parties. I will now hear additional testimony. Mike Moran, please tell the court what happened this morning," Vandergelt intoned. Beater stood. He apparently had another name; perhaps his real name this time.

"Well, um, your honor, sir, I was, uh, we was going to see my girl after going off shift, when this guy—" he said pointing at me.

"According to your statement, you are married, Mr. Moran." Vandergelt raised an eyebrow.

"Well, your honor," he shrugged and probably scuffed his feet, a tiny smile blinking on and off like broken neon. Vandergelt allowed the ghost of neon past to light his lips for a microsecond. He motioned for Mike the beater to go on.

"This guy your honor he attacked us for no reason. We were just going to visit. The door was all broke in, and he attacked us for no reason," Moran smiled as if he had passed some kind of difficult liar's test.

"Did he strike you?"

"Yes, your honor, several times. Here, on my arms and stomach," beater pointed, oddly proud at admitting to being slow enough or stupid enough to be hit.

"And did you strike him?" Vandergelt asked.

"No, sir—your honor."

"Mr. Wayne Lapere, can you corroborate Mr. Moran's testimony?" Vandergelt waved at teacher, who also had a new and more original sounding name.

"La Pierre, your honor. It's La Pierre, spelled kinda like La Pere. It's Canadian, though not French. My—"

Vandergelt glared at him, muttered "clerk's typo" and waved off the correction.

Wayne licked his lips and started again, "It's like he said your honor, we was—were—just visiting. We were just going to party. Just got off shift at Chrysler, wanted to have fun. But, we didn't start it. He came down and wanted to take us on, for no reason, man—your honor. He hit me too," he said, raising his shirt to show a hairy beer belly, small and hard, but with promise of a heroic size to come.

Vandergelt paused, consulting a sheet of paper, possibly a television lawyer show script, but probably financial investments. He certainly didn't notice any contradictions in testimony. I wondered what he was doing up so late. Judge's didn't have night shifts, did they?

"Miss Lilianne Carlson, would you please tell the court what happened?" Vandergelt asked brusquely.

Miss Carlson, who had not spoken yet, hung her head and snuffled. I think she was crying. She whispered something.

"Please speak at a sufficient volume for the court to hear you. Officer," Vandergelt motioned to the female police officer, who whispered to the woman, who lifted her head slightly and said audibly, "They hit me, those two." She nodded to beater and teacher.

"You dead, bitch," beater exploded. "I told you in the hall not—"

"Shhhh," hissed Vandergelt, apparently more disturbed at a breach of procedure than a death threat witnessed by everyone in the court. He motioned at Miss Carlson, "Who hit you? Can you point them out?"

She turned and pointed to beater and teacher, one with each hand, the blanket falling off her shoulders. Her eyes were puffy; her cheeks and neck were red, probably from being treated to beater's uncontrolled windmill technique. The blood on the neckline of her nightgown had darkened.

Vandergelt, the featherless unclever crow, pointed to me and asked, "Do you know this man?"

She shrugged and shook her head.

"Answer me or I'll hold you in contempt of court," he snapped.

She lowered her head and said, "No."

"Do you have carnal knowledge of him?" he asked.

She raised her head, startled, and said, "No," a bit louder. I was startled too. It had never occurred to me that anyone would even invent the possibility.

"Did you ever have sex with this man?" Vandergelt asked again, more crudely and emphatically.

"No," she said lowering her head again, her shoulders heaving slightly. She sat down. Teacher started glaring at me and shaking his finger.

"Have you had sex with many men, married men?" Vandergelt probed.

She shook her head lower. Surprisingly, he did not take a kill shot.

Vandergelt paused with his papers again. perhaps the text of the soap opera was to be found in them. He looked at me and said, "I suppose we have to have your side of it as well. Do you have carnal knowledge of this woman?"

"I saw this woman for the first time tonight being beaten by those two minicriminals," I said.

"Answer my question as stated, or I will hold you in contempt!"

Vandergelt banged his wooden hammer.

"No, uriner," I forced through my teeth, hurting my teeth. "I was only trying to help—"

"But, why were you trying to help, Mr. Sullivan? Do you always help people, Mr. Sullivan, unless you have a personal interest?" The ghost of the crow's smile materialized for a time on those lips that must have known nothing more exciting that cherry jello.

I looked at him. I could not win. She could not win. The boys could not lose.

"The court is waiting for your answer. I'd advise you to hurry," said Vandergelt, looking in command. The teacher was making faces at me and mouthing words shaped like 'don't tell or you dead muthfucka.' Benson was urging me surreptitiously to answer.

"I always try to help screaming women, yer-on-whore. I had no other interest in coming down the stairs." I was just a witness to her humiliation.

"And what did you see when you came down those stairs, Mister Sullivan? Please tell us so that we may all go home?" asked Vandergelt, twirling his hammer, trying to decide if I was insulting him.

"I saw these two microthugs beating up a helpless woman—" I started. Teacher bared his teeth, while beater pointed and mouthed circumspectly 'dead.' Benson glared at them both. I continued, "When I asked them to stop, they turned their attentions—and what beery coordination they could muster—on me—"

"I gotcha too," beater burbled.

"—until the police came, then they offered false names and lies," I finished. I was a witness to the cheap triumph of drunken violence.

"No! Did not!" teacher and beater bleated in unison.

"Did you break down the door?" asked Vandergelt. Before I could answer, he continued, "Did you see anyone break in the door?"

"No," I answered simply. I was wondering if I might end up in jail, martyred for bearing witness—hell, martyr was Greek for witness.

Vandergelt nibbled his lower lip, then motioned to Officer Benson. "Officer, when you arrived, what was happening?"

"Um, it was hard to see, but it looked like the two plaintiffs were taking punches at Mr. Sullivan, but missing."

"Did not," beater said, protesting any defamation of his prowess at striking smaller or preoccupied opponents.

"Did Mr. Sullivan hit either of them?" asked Vandergelt. No crow could sit so low.

"I did not see him hit anyone," Benson answered.

"But, he could have?"

"Yes, it is possible. We didn't see—"

"Well," interrupted Vandergelt, reestablishing control of the kangaroo court. I wondered if anyone called him 'Kangaroo Bob?' He continued, "Could you tell if the lady's front door had been broken before tonight?"

"I couldn't say for sure—" Benson waffled.

"Then it could have been broken before the visit of her two boyfriends for an innocent party?" asked Vandergelt, extending jurisprudence into new dimensions of fantasy. Benson didn't answer, just stood looking confused.

"Your honer," I started.

"Yes?" he surfaced from deep thoughts of deep conspiracies and the complexities of contemplating reality and truth.

"I'm sure that you noticed that Miss Carlson is wearing a torn and bloodied nightgown, as well as many fresh facial bruises and contusions, and that my shirt has been ripped, whereas the plain tiffs are sporting only lies and self-congratulatory smiles. You have the testimony of the officer that the door—"

"Where is this leading, Mr. Sullivan? This is a busy court, not to be trifled with." Vandergelt announced.

"I was hoping it was leading to some rudimentary form of justice, yer no'er," I said, risking and thinking contempt.

"I am dismissing the case against the plaintiffs, due to inconclusive evidence. You will have to work out your problems on a personal level," Vandergelt was clearly making his decision based on some mysterious connection that could not be compromised by evidence or appearances.

"Your honor, if you have a daughter, I trust she will never be treated this way, by her friends or authorities." I said.

Vandergelt had struck his little hammer and was getting up. We stared at each other. I was wondering what was behind the facade. I silently put a curse on him: may the pain he caused others visit him. He dropped his hammer as he got up. He hesitated a moment, but left the room directly.

Benson came up behind me. "I'm sorry," he said. "I don't know what he wanted or  what happened. I don't think it should have happened this way."

"Is he related to the mini-crookettes?" I asked.

Benson moved his lips, "I'll give you a ride home."

"Three blocks?" I asked. "Give the woman a ride home, thanks. Fix her door. Keep the riff raff from it." I walked through the hall.

Beater was there. "I told you I'm gonna kill you. Now, I'm gonna kill you anyway."

I stared at him, then shook my head. Too many brake linings, too many beers, too little meaning.

I walked the three blocks. As I walked up the stairs, I noticed that her door had been braced upright. I opened my door. The sun was coming up. I watched sunlight fill the corners through cellophane stuffed broken glass bathroom windows and make perfect geometric shadows from ruined furniture.

*Epilogue*. Ten years later, I was studying coyotes in Arizona; I had switched from human psychology to the study of nobler minds—and those minds were pursued and harried for no logical reason, but did not waste time on revenge. I read in the Phoenix paper that a Judge Vandergelt had become the head of state prisons; the article mentioned that the sad widower had lost his wife and daughter back east. I wondered it if was from my black hand.

## Parapurgerno (Not Purgatory)

by T. H. Gauss

The earth had broken open and its dust stained the sky like blood. Distant volcanoes promised more violence before the dust would settle. The land was tawny and broken, like a downed deer. The sun was like a lion whose breath turned the skin to leather, whose roar swept moisture from the eyes, whose eyes burned the flesh to bones.

"Any broken bones?" he asked.

She shook her head and moaned: "I don't think so. I can move," She felt tentatively down her leg to see if her foot was still attached. She could feel it with her hand, but she could not feel the foot itself. She remembered the inside of the car door had slammed against it.

"We couldn't have survived you know. I felt myself explode. We died. This is a death dream—or worse," he nodded remembering the short story by Ambrose Bierce.

"We're dead? We can't be," she concluded, "my heart's beating too fast. Look! Where are we? It's still Phoenix."

"Passenger pigeons," he pointed.

"Alan, where are we? We're moving."

"I don't know. In the desert, riding on something quiet—an electric hover bus—a tour—Africa?"

"No cactus. It must be Africa," she gasped, "where else could it be?"

A deer parted the short grass; a tiger attacked swiftly. He opened his mouth at the cloud of dust, "We're in—"

"A kangaroo!" she exclaimed, pointing beyond. "Where are we? A zoo?"

"A Savannah, now, I think."

"Those animals are extinct. They can't exist anywhere. No zoo has any—"

"We can't be any place, then can we? These animals disappeared long ago—" he mused, 'I wonder if we've disappeared?'

"Is it heaven?" she asked, "a heaven of animals, and we—" she ran her fingers over the rail of the vehicle, noting the close-grained wood.

"No," he hesitated, "under the tree—ahead—people—maybe we can get off."

She hesitated: "I think we're meant to stay on this until it stops. There is dust ahead, and far behind us—it could be other vehicles with other passengers in them."

"Are there people under that tree," he repeated, "or aren't there?"

I can't tell for sure—there could be—where are we going? Maybe we're just to ride this, and ride," she looked at the endless plains, sand, grass, sand— "maybe—"

"Maybe we're not dead," he paused. "Maybe somehow we survived, were healed, and sent to some rehabilitation center. We shouldn't remember the crash, but we do. But who would have—damn, I've got to get to work! My grant. I have responsibilities, deadlines!"

She looked at him, sure that the responsibilities were far removed by accident or time. She looked at the grass, and suggested: "Study grass. That's one thing botanists can do—there's plenty of it." And she thought: vast reaches of grass, brown and dry, reaching toward what?

He followed her gaze, noting that the grass was bunch grass of some kind, indicative of low rainfall. He asked: "Why is it so vacant?" And answered: The final mirror of our vanity; a place that reveals the external bounds of existence, but no depth—one dimension strange to another. We refused the world then denied it, yet we are bound to it, to some world—

"Test. This is a test. We must have faith," she decided.

"Faith?" he mocked. "Our existence in this world is an excuse for our employment by another power: the state, god. Faith? I belong to the state, you to god. I have no faith, you no duty. This world does not belong to us. We have no place in it. We will not dwell here—just pass through, miserable tourists. We are not!"

She looked at him, trying to understand what he was talking about, "I'm sorry I mentioned it. It's just an excuse for you to disparage me—you don't have faith."

"I'm sorry, I—" he reached behind her head and ran his fingers through her hair. "I love you. If I weren't paranoid and confused, this might be heaven, well, purgatory, anyway."

Cranes rose from the horizon, pulling dark clouds. Soon, it rained, violently, as if the rain were aware that it could have no effect on the dryness of the land and resented its impotence.

He dreamed that the grass was green, and he sank to rest on it. But in the reflection in his own eye he saw wings hovering—flash of metal ripping back—he screamed. The pain broke his sleep and he wakened, white with dread. He felt her at his side. She must not have heard him, if he cried aloud. She was facing the sea of sand. He asked, "How long have you been up?"

"Hmmm? Oh, I don't know. I've been watching that mound ahead," she said, staring in the distance.

Straining his eyes, he offered: "A tomb, perhaps tumescent sand, a dump of some kind."

"The hill is a gate to a city, I think." As one who feels all doubt dispelled and has fear change into a shallow confidence, she exclaimed, "a city!"

The ground ahead had been paved by many feet, treading to the gate of a strange city. Their excitement grew as the ride seemed to accelerate to the destination.

## *Life and Death of the Animal Soul*

### Blaming Artemis

by Cam Woulfe

What can I say? I was sitting at the foot of a tree and waiting— for sleep, for wisdom, for time to carry me somewhere else, for something unknown. My forest adventures were no less for the fact that I was sitting and being. Sometimes other beings came to me; sometimes I moved to them.

I was under a ponderosa pine, perhaps a hundred-seventy feet high with blue-green needles, obtuse with small bracts and blue-purple cones—the tree was so unexpected from the seed. This clean, dry old pine was set off from the rest. I jumped up to a low dead limb and pulled myself up, exultant. I touched and felt the roughness of the bark, felt the trunk sway and roots strain with a delicate breeze. I went up further and looked out across the hills, carefully not thinking of death or of pain or of nothingness.

I pushed against the bark. This measured thing was mostly space, according to science, confounded by small unpredictabilities, opaque, as impenetrable to my eyes as to my hands and feet. Emptier now that the dryads have deserted. I clung securely, moved slowly higher, some hills and valleys shades of brown and violet-shaded—I saw my body below, shattered on the needle floor. The branches seemed more treacherous but I reached the height of a near-by tree, saw distant mountains and plains.

The branches were younger and firmer but much closer together. I squirmed through the highest ones, freshened by the wind, but worried by it all the same. I reached to top—now I had her height, but she had my mind. Less than a fair trade I thought, then realized it was not a trade. Partnership?

Just to my left, a blasted snag, relict of a moment when fingers of wood and fingers of lightning met, and white fire exchanged its life for the life of a pine leaving mute wood and a black spine. Swaying, I felt the rhythm of respiration lift branches spread to collect light and cool air around the trunk, push downwards into the earth to hold and reach out for minerals and water, a double life of light and dark, inside out, a cone of slow fire drawing air, water, the fire of life drawing earth upwards.

I watched clouds and hawks, as I slowed my breathing to match her pace. I watched and expanded to include the hawk and cloud. Later, sometime, I tore off a small branch, hurried down, rubbing bark and skin, heart struggling with having gotten too close to something unknown, jumped the last ten feet to the ground, groaning, sighing, smiling, prize in hand, wearing a crown of needles and lichen, wondering what kind of change— She is not solid; there is so much room for spirits to pass through, unhurried, or perhaps to stay. I looked back at transplanted hearts passing through trees leaving molecular shadows in amber. The hamadryads have not left, and I am theirs.

Then I was left in my truncated form as a scientist. The Greek dryads were conceived by earth, Gaea, from the blood of heaven, Uranus, castrated by his son, Time, Chronos, for refusing to let his bothers Briareus and Cottus into the light. These nymphs, beautiful females of divine origin, were given the guardianship of the woods and the trees. According to Homer, in the *Iliad*, the council of the gods included the nymphs, "Each fair-haired Dryad of the shady wood." Wood-nymphs were Dryads, tree-nymphs were Hamadryads, Fruit-tree-nymphs were Meliades, and other nymphs haunted mountains, valleys, and meadows. The Dryads, who lived in groves, were free to move about, in trees and without. They often associated with Artemis, goddess of the hunt. The Hamadryads, who dwelled in individual trees, died with their trees—each tree cried in anguish when it was cut.

Most loggers and foresters were deaf and dumb.

One day, surveying old growth trees on public land, I realized that I was lost. So I did what I usually did, I lay under a cedar. With my head towards the tree, I felt like I was cradled by two long roots. I did not sleep really well, but the ground was not too hard. A few of the noises were new, the creaking and snapping of wood, maybe, and the screaming of a bird. I wondered where I was. In the morning I decided to backtrack towards Glendale. A few times I got lost around the streams and ridges, but I found a trail, perhaps only a game trail.

After an hour I admitted that this might be a mistake, as there was no trail. Then I headed east, lead by the slant of sunlight, to where the trail should be. After another hour, still no trail. I crossed a stream and was heading up the next ridge. There I determined that I was officially lost. So, now, I looked at the map to see where I missed the trail. Rather than back track, I kept going straight to the next ridge. I passed a male mountain lion looking down from the slope. I stopped and watched until he decided that I was not worthy of interest as prey or predator. From there, after another hour, I could see the path of the interstate highway corridor with binoculars. At this point I went due east up the ridge to try to intersect the trail, which should be heading towards me. After a while I found a wildlife trail and followed it. There was some horse manure on it so

I knew someone had been there. The trail lead through the deep fir woods and up past another ridge. Finally near the top of the fourth ridge, I could see the glint of a building that I recognized. The sun had just set but it was still light enough. The trail lead to the Cow Creek intersection and a trail I knew.

The next day, I was at the Douglas forest, looking over trees for mistletoe infection and root rot. I had promised Arvin that I would mark the trees to be cut. I still had trouble weighing my decisions as good or bad. I had no doubt that when I did more good, more bad was also created. For instance, when I started trying to restore this forest, the best knowledge at the time insisted that I should clean the trees out of the stream and remove flammable brush and woody debris from the forest floor. I started to do this in a beautiful cedar grove, but I spent too much time sitting on the ground looking at the trees. I could blame Artemis—goddess of forests, solitude, young girls, and the hunt—for possessing me, I suppose. But, as I was resting, scientific knowledge advanced, and now I am advised to drop trees into the stream and leave all the woody debris and brush. Had I been less contemplative, or lazy, I would now have much more work to do. Therefore, was what I did good? Did I do good then? By accident? Was what I was doing now good? Was the failure to do the good of now, then, bad? Did I fail from ignorance or conflicting intentions? Or from physical or moral torpor? Do I need more training to determine what is good or bad?

That is a problem with forestry today. Which action is good? Which is bad? Which should we do? Unfortunately, the outcome of our exploitation or interference may not be evident for hundreds of years. Perhaps we should aim for harmony, for good health in forests and human communities.

In the long run, as the author and tree-lover John Fowles suggested, maybe all our judgments of good and bad are meaningless. All actions, good or bad, interweave so extensively as time passes that their individual goodness or badness disappears in the total flow. Each becomes lost in the other. One should do good for one's health, for instance, or for the health of the forest, not because the action is perceived as good or for the sake of doing something just to act. In doing, we choose between good and bad action. That did not make sense, so I chose a small yew tree to lie under for a while.

## Going East

by Asia Deer

"Go East, Young Woman" (Notes from a job search from Seattle to Boston, and a travelogue for going east and comparing the two ends of American culture. No plot, no mystery, no murder, just a road trip with incidents and observations.)

I hate my name. It is the kind of name that attracts the unwanted attentions of white boys interested in Asian women, of which I am a sterling example, naturally, with black hair, high cheeks, smooth skin, small breasts, a long waist, and thick legs. This attention used to be limited to sidewalks and letters, but now has spread contagiously to computer networks. My mother started naming her daughters after continents, without I think, knowing all of them, hence my sisters are named Africa and Australia. I think she wanted a fourth daughter to get to America, but that was not to be. Our father was killed in a hold-up. Working his way through school. A sharp example of a senseless tragedy where those who have little steal from those with very slightly more. If only humans had higher sights or greater ambitions, he might be still alive.

My boyfriend, Mao—no, he's not Chinese; he's Gaelic; the name is short for Maolanaithe, from a Gaelic word meaning "caller of thunder;" he has wild red hair and a wild temper, except when he drinks. I often get him drinks to calm him down and make him smile; he is a wonderful happy drunk when freed of the knowledge of the disintegrating chaotic world that feeds his rage. I ride that rage myself; it cuts the drag that way, like a car tailgating a truck—says that I am too sentimental, that the dead are the lucky, their promise betrayed by circumstance and not their own human weaknesses. And I say that he is cold and self-removed from the heat of passion, although I know that is not true on every level.

Mao encouraged me to go east, misquoting Horace Greely like a literary wrong-way Irish Corrigan. I used to think that he simply was unaware of the real meaning or form of clichés, but now I see that he consistently tortures them to yield new meaning as if only cruel misuse can reach the linguistic depth that has not completely dried out under the sun of overuse. God, what am I saying. I'm supposed to be keeping a diary of my travels across the country and all I have so far is high-speed memory.

I lost my job as a waitress in Seattle when the restaurant I was working in changed from an American eclectic menu to all Italian and the new owner imported Italians, Sicilians, and Italian-looking students from the University of Washington to keep the theme consistent. That seems to be a new trend in restaurants: a theme that extends even to the wait staff. I tried another restaurant in one of the bank malls on Fifth Avenue, but that one was run by Germans and they were only hiring blondes apparently. I even tried a Chinese restaurant, but they were cultivating a brunette Vassar look with their staff—the only restaurant to not board the ethnic bandwagon and my only hope of riding along, so I decided to leave.

After all, as Mao says, a Masters in Biology must be worth more than a ticket to a food service career, although I say that Biology has the highest unemployment—over 34 percent I think—of any profession, although Mao says that as soon as the paradigm changes from physical metaphors to biological ones, it'll be a biologist's marketplace—of course, it may be another fifty years, but ... so I should be able to work for the government in Denver or the Park Service in Boston if I go there and be there and apply there and not apply long-distance from the real estate Mecca of Seattle. So, I've been driving on the interstate. Rather than do a red highways sort of thing and talk to alcohol-laden American boys about how they'd like to bang a Chinese girl, I prefer to drive and daydream.

That's how I started out, daydreaming. But, I began noticing—more than just an increasing thick accent—that all the physical things change from state to state. For example, the size of states seems to decrease from west to east, as if the surveyors moving west started to become impatient after generations of measuring small states with small counties. Anyway, rather than some boring chronology of travel from point 'a' to point 'b' telling how friendly people are if you ask them to tell their life story in a book about traveling from point to point by van or bicycle or foot, I decided to casually make notes about the differences, using my scientific skills of classification and identification, sort of taxonomy of the human species and its subspecies making niches and specializations that ominously replace the diverse species that existed in place before we humans usurped the spaces.

This vanity piece, this busy work for lazy inquiring minds, this opus profundis, this magnus offal—I miss Mao. I suppose I like missing him more than being with him. I just realized that I limited my time with him so that I can maximize the good times with him and conveniently be busy or away when he becomes dull or repetitious. I suppose that is unfeminine of me—to not love unfailingly, unflaggingly under any circumstances and at all times, but I don't really see that kind of romantic behavior in martens or fishers—the objects of my studies in the Northwest woods south and west of Seattle, the woods famous for intolerant owls and whining loggers—who can't stand biologists or loggers or any humans; they out crocket davey crocket when it comes to needing not to see the smoke of their neighbors. I suppose that is what made them interesting, no not interesting, absolutely fascinating to me, that there are animals that will not lie down with lambs or humans, not have any truck or traffic with anything that is not prey or host—they don't tolerate deviant behavior in a mate. They leave to avoid crazy behavior, in spite of its endearing qualities, it doesn't make for good parenting or hunting. I miss him but I left and now I'm writing and that writing is divided into convenient topics so that I do not have to be bothered with chronology or consistency. The topics are simple: cars, houses, language, culture, coffee, arguments, talking, entertainment, wildlife, plants, and sights.

**Leaving Seattle**

Well, rats, I've already started thinking chronologically. So, I might as well make up the map, so you know where I am going. Since I have no timetable and no need to go due east to miss the winter storms, I have decided to meander up and down as I hear about things that are interesting or places that might have jobs.

Before I left I decided to hit the library and take two or three books for reading. As I was sitting in the undergrad cube, I was approached by a young man dragging a full, green duffle bag. He sat across from me and pulled some papers out of the bag.

He said he had trouble concentrating. I asked him if he was talking to me. He tried to focus on a sheet of paper. I suggested drinking Gingko tea, it was good for brain trauma. He nodded as he kept reading. I wondered if I was going to become like that, carrying all my ideas in bags of paper. I decided not to check out any books.

At last I am back at the car, and what a car, a 1992 Buick Roadbastard, big, safe, automatic, protective, undesirable, gas-guzzling, and mine. I drove south to town to pick up Mao, who had promised to be ready by noon.

**Seattle to Coeur d'Alene**

Four hours later, uncountable roadkills later (I wondered why humans did not leave other dead humans along the roads like that. Must be money in funerary services.), we were in Coeur d'Alene Idaho. We got off the interstate and drove downtown. Stopped at a small place (Hudson's?) for plain burgers and cokes, then went to a candy store for a few jellybeans. I realized that I needed a library, so we searched for and found the local college.

Minutes after I was in the stacks looking for a book on carnivores, an old man approached me. Slightly disheveled, he introduced himself as Professor Hagen. Then he sat down and started taking off his right shoe. What kind of nut-magnet had I become? Then I realized that maybe people mistook me for a librarian (as opposed to some omniscient Asian).

I asked him if he was okay. He said that he had scaly feet and asked me what to do. I answered that I would look up the problem in the library, the medical section. He said he was not familiar with that section. I said it was just down the road, so I showed him where. It took a few minutes to find a book on skin. Then I remembered what my mother had told me: cod liver oil. I suggested that, and while he was looking, tiptoed away. I have to stop going in libraries to read.

**Coeur d'Alene to Utah**

We decided to get off the interstates. Mao thought it would be fun to drive south through Idaho and Utah. We turned right in Utah and headed towards Reno. I was beginning to suspect that Mao wanted to surprise me and get married in Reno or Vegas. I sometimes wish he would ask me to marry him, so that I would know he liked me in a permanent way, but also so I could say no, to his relief no doubt and mine as well.

I bought a paper, The Star. It was so comforting to read about local news rather than international war or suffering. But, even the local news was dominated by accidents and arrests. I read the obituaries. Rarely was the cause of death listed—was that embarrassment or privacy? But, mixed in the 'small people' deaths was a famous obituary, an Actor, who pretended to be someone heroic and thus had that image in the newspapers, who could no longer distinguish the difference between pretend and original. I suppose the original hero, who either killed twenty people or saved twenty people was long forgotten.

**Utah to Las Vegas**

Gambling. We stopped at the bus station, so Mao could send a package, doubtless a book manuscript. I wandered around. There were slot machines in the station. I wondered if the buses had them, the local ones anyway. I lost all my money, to quarters.

**Las Vegas to Tucson**

From NV to NM, the landscape started with bare grey ground, and progressed to Joshua trees, saguaros, then Joshua trees then Ocotillo. I saw a hunting sign by the road: 2 cow limit, no more than 14 holes in hide. Grand prize 1986 Yugo. At least that's what I think it said. I suppose there was a bag limit for transformers and poles: 2.

We arrived at Arcosanti in the dark. It was harder to find than I thought, since it is a rare kind of place. I thought it would be fun to design an ecological city, maybe design a forest arcology hill with trees sticking out.

Outside of Phoenix the car broke down. I think it was just a radiator hose, although it seemed too greasy. Mao agreed to stay with the car. I waited and flagged down a bus going into town.

The moment I sat down to a thin old man, he asked me if I needed glasses. I looked at him for a moment, trying to put the conversation in perspective. He said his name was Barry Dillard and he was an ophthalmologist. I nodded. He seemed drunk, or on either side of being drunk. He told me his story: He was a drunk. Had been since the IRS seized his home and car. Now, every tine he got money the IRS took it. So he traveled by bus and found patients that way, an itinerant doctor, helping the poor.

I agreed to have my eyes tested, which he did right then, drawing his equipment from an worn leather bag. He wrote out a prescription, a light one for presbyopia.

At the station, I gave him twenty dollars and thanked him. Then went to look for an auto mechanic. The first I saw was R&J Wrecking, hardly a name to inspire confidence. I described where the car was and they did some magical things with their radio and we were set.

I went to a drug store down the street for a coke. They had an optometrist in residence so I thought what the—and got a pair of oval glasses for thirty dollars.

**Tucson to Texas**

Mao had had all the hoses replaced and we continued east. In Texas, the speed limit was 60 mph in Carthage. 70 outside the city limits. Ninety percent of the wheeled vehicles were trucks. The first time we stopped for gas, the guy next to us was getting gas, with boots and spurs on. I suppose he got the truck to go faster by spurring it hard on the metal.

Outside of town we drove by OK Beef—at last, honesty in advertising. We didn't stop for any, though a few miles later Mao had a 'horney burger' and I had a milkshake.

**Texas to Oklahoma to New Orleans**

The worst roads were in Oklahoma—hadn't been fixed since the dust-bowl days. Then we turned south for Louisiana.

**New Orleans to Miami**

Louisiana billboards were incipient conversations with God. The first one we passed said "Pray for the unborn." I could imagine God placing his own billboard down the road: "Pray for the born, they are already invested with suffering." After fifty miles another one:

"Pray for what you wish." I wondered what God would say on his billboard: "Don't pray at all, just help others: God."

Then there were the patriotic billboards, telling us to love our country and vote for red white and blue moneymongers.

Then there was the long-running war between XXX and Xianity (or Inanity according to the Spellcheck masters). Every church on one side of the road was matched by a strip joint on the other. It was the Bible belt of course but the pants were on the floor, with the shoes and wallet.

**Miami to Washington**

More pavement. Through the South, which did rise again. Past the monuments to its fall. Past the modern incarnations of carpet bags.

**Washington to Boston**

Pavement closer together now, the roads all going parallel at many places. Then we enter Boston. At one area there are cabs waiting to guide trucks through the narrow Lilliputian streets. After several wrong turns down Charles and around the Commons, we make it to Marlborough street and our new apartment (the former servants quarters on the fourth floor).

**Comparisons**

*Animals*

What did you expect? Remember what I am—and people are what they do or rather what they are paid to do, or what they believe themselves to be as they do what they are paid to do because they cannot do what they were trained to do because they got to choose their fields without any reference to what society wants, although society has paid little attention to what it really needs, until a few of those needs are rammed down its throat. The first need I noted was the need for animal tunnels to go under highways. Roadkills are a good indication of what kind of animals try to cross roads. I gave up counting after 348 bodies; if I were to extrapolate that by the number of paved roads in the country that would mean 373,000 animals killed per day. Was that possible?

Leaving Seattle, on I90, speeding up towards the pass at 65 miles an hour, a good speed to look at hills, mountains, and forests—or rather forest corridors—but not trees, animals, lichen, or slugs—I noticed a another dead white-tail deer. She looked like a female.

*Cars*

What can I say, the number of sports cars, especially overpowered and overpriced Ferraris increases. Perhaps this is related to the westerly winds that sweep across America. Perhaps a status thing.

Other supremely useless cars, from Humvees to towering trucks kitted out as campers, wore holes in the pavements of the east, and the pavement was an ever-expanding surface, good only for machines and birds.

The scariest thing about being a biologist on the highway is that, through the miracle of pattern recognition, I am adept at recognizing every kind of car, much more than animals, and it is easier, too, since the cars all have handy nametags on the back or front, like Moose at a convention. I automatically look at a car and think Hyundai 'Snota' or Buick 'Meadowpark.'

The names of cars have gotten really wild. The "Landcrusher' or the 'Aztek' (does it require blood to run? So motorists have to stop and cut the hearts out of other motorists?). Some of names are only faintly ridiculous, as when cars are named after instruments or musical phrases. I kind of miss the old days when they were named after lions or horses—at least there was a logical connection to horses and oxen. The Nippon 'Pathforcer' or the "Audible' (does it let you know it's coming by making lot of noise?) have no such connection. I suppose that cars with less inspiring names, such as the Dodge 'Boltbucket' Ford 'Mousedung' or Toyota "Slacker' would not sell as well, regardless of the accuracy of their names. My favorite was the American Motors 'Lawn-ornament.'

*Trucks*

We had decided not to drive Mao's old truck east. I would have thought there to be fewer pick-up trucks in the east. I think the number might be almost the same, but the percentage might be less. People drive trucks in the east, for much the same reasons as westerners: status, that is a casual status, and to haul things. It's just that different things fall out of them, depending on the latitude or longitude. In Colfax Washington, as I dipped south to visit one of the nation's better known drinking and veterinary schools, traffic to the east was blocked by a bale of hay; actually, it caused a slow down in both lanes as eastbound trucks and sports cars—a sure sign a university is nearby—swerved to avoid it. In Saint Louis, I had to swerve as a baby bed fell out of the back of the Ford Galaxy ahead of me. I was able to swerve, but the Mazda behind me ended up pushing it as he slowed into the breakdown lane; I lost track of it in the traffic. Later, outside of Boston, still on I90, two lanes were blocked by an orange and green paisley sofa that never should have been made, much less dropped.

*Hats*

Cowboy hats are traditional in the west, even in cities without many cows, like Seattle, Chicago, or New York—I know, you're thinking of that Sandburg poem cattle stunner to the world, but that's moved west, now. Unfortunately, they were never designed to be worn at high speeds, especially in topless cars or trucks. I suspect that this use requires sizing them too small, as a properly fitting hat requires the owner to hold it with one hand at all times, thereby sacrificing coolness for hat retention, which results in arteries that bring blood to the brain being constricted and poor driving decisions or fashion choices being made.

Gimmes—so-called because farmers buying feed and seed would often say 'and gimme one a them'—are popular on both coasts and in the middle, although baseball hats tend to dominate in cities that sponsor teams of millionaires chewing and posing in the grass. Gimmes also tend to be too small, although the one-size-fits-all revolution loosened things up for a while 'til guys stuffed their hair through the plastic tie, and although it seems to affect intelligence, it does not seem to affect driving speed.

*Clothing*

Clothing becomes more sophisticated as one moves east, from the jeans and cotton shirts, ornamented with cowboy boots (and why are they still called cowboys, ain't no boys, ain't no cows neither—I prefer to think of them as 'truckclods') and running shoes, to zoot suits and spats. I saw a store in Florida selling modern zoot suits; I even got Mao to try one on. Before he finished dressing the black Italianate salesman was already picking out ties and shoes for him, and they did sell updated spats. He didn't buy it, though, killjoy. The cost of the rags seems to rise in an easterly direction also. Perhaps that is just a reflection of higher salaries or more competition for stylish threads. People in Florida and Massachusetts certainly dressed up to go shopping. Judging from the Society pages in the paper, there were more functions to go to, perhaps as a direct result of the availability of time and threads.

*Culture*

People in the east have culture. I know because several easterners have told me this. Of course, there is culture in the west, too, but it's younger, more like a kind of a bread mold actually.

I think that a lot of people in this culture have been deeply brutalized by the false assumption that there are only two ways you can live a life and you have to choose one or the other. You can choose to be intellectual, rational and scientific on the one hand, or on the other, you can live your life intuitively, spiritually. It's being either the scientist or the artist and mystic and there is no way to get those two abilities together in your life. This schizophrenic assumption has caused immense suffering for people in this culture and I think that it's a false divide (most people are neither).

*Movement/Speed of Transactions.*
As you travel east people speak and move faster. People in Seattle often pause for minutes before completing a sentence or a thought or a purchasing decision or a sip of coffee. Sometimes the completion of an action can only be ascertained through the miracle of slow motion photography. Alas, most photographers do not have the patience or interest to document the complete cycle of Seattleite activities. Nevertheless, the hypothesis is made that the actions are eventually completed. As you go east you will notice that people speak and move faster. In fact, by the time you get to Boston, the traffic goes 50 miles an hour in front of grade schools; bank and store transactions take just seconds instead of hours.

*Size of Things*
Traveling east you notice that things become smaller, Lilliputian in fact. Where it takes two days to cross Montana, you can cover two states a day in the Midwest and two states an hour on the east coast. This is not important as it may seem, however, as there are the same number of smart people and good sights per state.

*Language*
The French notice the difference between speaking or language, between language and luggage or something like that. Now, that I'm writing about these things that I took in philosophy or philology class, I realize that in fact I do not really remember them, although I'm sure that given a multiple choice situation, I would score in the upper 5 percent of students, or graduates, or faculty too I guess.

As the language gets older going east, parts of the languages, vowels especially seem to be missing. In Boston, the 'r's are left out of many words, so that you pahk the cah. Although as Esperson and Trilby note, in their book, the 'r' makes an appearance in some words where it does not belong.

*Houses/Housing*
In the west most inhabitants live in trailers or houses built to resemble trailers, complete with plastic towel racks and lamp shades. In the east, houses are not only more substantial, composed of 10 percent brick on the lower frame, but plastic is used much more creatively, to make eyebrow or porthole

windows, for instance.

In Florida, the combination of trailers, people retired from the north, and the concept of a separate retirement home for winters leads to the phenomenon of snowbirds (whose call is 'cheap cheap') living in hurricane-bait boxes surrounded by plastic pink flamingoes (imported from Africa). The snowbirds make fantastic trails between doctors offices and restaurants. Florida is the snowbird burial ground, much sought after by adventurers and skin doctors looking for gold.

*Rule-following Behavior*
In Seattle, Seattleites—no pun intended coming up—obey rigorous laws of motion, refusing to cross any street until the light changes and the walk sign comes on—even if no traffic is visible for miles, even if no law enforcement officer is in evidence, even if it is raining rats and hogs. By the time I got to Boston (credit to Glen Campbell take 6), people walked whenever and wherever there was paved or unpaved surface. Of course, they were sometimes mowed down by drivers on mind-altering chemicals, but the police never noticed, only the pedestrians or ambulances.

*Opinions*
Every body has opinions, of course. And many people express them, as they should. But the information content, the basis in thought or knowledge varies so dramatically, that not every opinion is equally valuable. People's purposes are not constant, nor need they be, but love should be constant

*Entertainment and Music*
We had gone line-dancing in Seattle to [sorry, forgot the name]. In Boston, the night after we settled in the new apartment, the incredibly expensive apartment, we went dancing at the Aragon Ballroom nearby. The dance was the Western Swing.

*Sights*
I preferred stopping in cemeteries. Mao preferred old music halls, or other old buildings, from theaters to banks.

*Conversations*
Mao was telling me that in African societies conversations last for weeks. In Seattle they may last for hours. In New York, they barely last minutes. He pointed out that in tribal villages, one spent thousands of hours with friends and families, but in our modern situation we spent less than 30 seconds per individual, with any interaction it seemed.

*Art*

Art ideas: a painting hanging in front of a painting, to give depth. The function of art used to be to make the invisible visible. At first the Gods and ancestors were invisible. Then it was glory and horrors of war and prestige. Now, it is art itself, or rather the monetary workings of art.

*War*

G. Warthog Bush and Wars 'R US: Every day it becomes more certain that ignorance kills people, especially institutional and political ignorance, although popular ignorance is also a frightening thing. Ignorance leads to war, even more directly than constant preparation, constant escalating defense, or the constant desire for revenge or resources. Perhaps a short history of American war is in order, with a few simple themes.

1. The Revolutionary War, in which France helps us win our freedom from a half-hearted founder divided by internal disagreement (do we believe that England could *not* have won?).

2. Territorial Expansion wars. Various small wars against Mexico and Spain for property, whereby we took the property and held it while France was busy distracting Mexico (these French people always seem to be helping us out by giving us things, ideas about freedom, statues, wines, and military assistance).

3. W.W.I, where Germany and its allies tried to take more territory. We tried to ignore it, but things heated up, so we shipped off our soldiers, many of whom died in trenches as a result of really evil chemical and mechanical weapons. France won.

4. W.W.II, ditto W.W.I, but only after we were attacked, with more advanced weapons. The Allies won, but America claimed the entire victory.

5. The Korean War (K.W.I), The first of the theme wars dictated by the domino theory, that no domino can be allowed to fall without eventually crushing the US. No one won.

6. The Vietnam War. The first of the resource wars, although domino logic was used and pride was a factor. The resource in question always seems to be oil. America lost.

7. The Invasion of several small countries like Grenada, Yugoslavia, Mozambique, so we could practice. The first of the One Superpower Peacekeeper (OSP) obligations.

8. Gulf War (G.W.I), in which we responded to a request to help one country invaded by another. A relatively clean operation, although a surprising number of soldiers are still suffering various syndromes as a result. For the first time in a war, the true extent of ecological damage was noted (but not really addressed).

9. Afghanistan IV, wherein we started bombing with a new

theme, revenge for terrorism.

10. G.W.II (or GW Bush Baby too), in which we broke international law to invade a country that had broken international law, thus reducing ourselves to the lowest level of revenge (for pride and oil). There is already ecological damage; it can only get worse.

11. Next up: K.W.II, wherein an infant nuclear power demands a serious response. Could this be avoided with a more powerful UN and a more humble America? Right.

Caveat. We outspent the USSR so that capitalism could triumph, but we need to remember that insane overspending on military budgets could cause our own collapse as well in the near future, regardless with how noble we claim the wars are. Someday we might learn that true security and stability comes from peaceful activities and not constant wars that neglect the health (physical, spiritual and ecological) of the country and its people.

So, I'm waiting for the storms of clear consciousness. For months, the Administration has been embarrassed by the weakness of its case for war. Bush cites the uncertainties of inspections, but has not considered the uncertainties of war. Congress approved a resolution authorizing the use of force to invade a sovereign country for suspect reasons. But, isn't that what we traditionally have objected to, when other countries did it?

*Terrorism*

We have been a superpower for over 100 years now. But, up to now, our allies, old and new, trusted us, at least the way one trusts a unpredictable bully with a big gun who wants to help you sometimes. Many of them liked us. On the road to peace, we had the biggest vehicle, with the most options and the best support. Now, everyone, even our best allies, such as England and France, fears us. It's like we are still on the road to peace, but we no longer obey the rules of the road. Furthermore, we swerve and hit people like we were being driven by a drunk driver (the parallel is so apt it had to be used). In the name of freedom, but without the real respect for the meaning and diversity of freedom, we roll over people who stop to think, push others aside who want us to think or stop, shout over people trying to tell us something, then wreck any attempts to force us to follow international rules. We waste resources, without consideration for others needs or for our own future. We praise our actions as heroic and lonely, believing that the destruction and greed that we bring to other countries will bring peace ultimately, and that the resentment of the others will transformed to love by profits.

Terrorism is the response of fearful people without security. The only answer is to work out a way that everyone, every human being, is secure. That is not done with fences. It has to be done by allowing places and food. Our own fear and greed have dictated too many of our policies—and if you want to see real fear, just watch whenever a Cessna flies within 300 miles of the White House and everyone is evacuated. We seem to be forgetting the ethics of democratic processes.

*Wilderness*

Wilderness does not really matter, at least according to the postage stamp sizes we save. None of them is large enough to hold an umbrella species, and so they all are going to change in the next century as the largest trees or configurations die. Then, most of the wilderness will be ice or dead oceans. That's just my opinion.

*Coda*

This isn't how I imagined ending this diary. I thought that a few funny observations would be enough to justify doing it. What I did not mention was the invisible—actually the very visible—poor, especially in the mornings or at certain places. The number of poor, or their visibility, seems to increase from west to east. Our entire economic juggernaut seems to be geared to making most people poor and then blaming them for not succeeding in an unfair, slanted race.

That does not mean that we should accept it, or never live well or smile. Of course, there is humor in every human situation. In a larger sense comedy lets us muddle through the times of corporate warfare and cultural lust. So, we have to find things to laugh at. Traveling and moving are two of those things.

## Bluebirds

by A. M. Caratheodory

The mountain bluebird (*Sialia Currucoides*) is the most beautiful bird I have ever seen. After I graduated, and was unemployed as a biologist—well, okay, I was a busboy at the University mess hall—I decided to join the American Association for Biological Sciences. Then I decided to give a talk at the annual conference in Dallas the following year. That would present me to the academics who might be hiring for the following year.

But, first I needed a project. I decided to study mountain bluebirds. I had of course seen them every year. I had even built a bird house for them near my girl friend's house (well, her parents house) outside of Potlatch Idaho.

I needed to define the research project. Not a problem: Changes in agriculture, forestry, spraying, residential patterns, exotic alien birds, and predation were having effects on all the wild animals in the area. So, I would study bluebird feeding patterns along an artificial domestic trail. All I had to do was build 20 more bird houses, then spend a year sitting out in the sun watching them. Ah, science.

On further consideration, I decided to buy a video camera, build a blind, and record their feeding patterns on tape. Then analyze the tape. And so forth and so on, like that, maybe.

I also needed to get permission, so I needed to go with her to see her parents. They lived on a ridge overlooking the grasslands to the west; the ridge was part of the Moscow mountains that overlooked Moscow to the south and Potlatch to the north. The bluebirds needed dead trees or rotten fence posts. But all the fence posts were new and all the dead trees had been dropped or felled.

For our visit, we brought potato salad and tomatoes and bread, Sheila talked to her mother, while I confronted Barney in his lair, I mean shop. Barney's shop was larger and more extensive than the house. Barney said sure, come back tomorrow.

I did. All we had to do was rearrange his shop first. That took two days of rolling megaton drill presses across steel pipes. But, then we were almost ready. But, first, We had to brace up one of the ceiling joists. So, I held the joist while Barney rocked the column into place. It worked . So, I let go of the beam. Then Barney wiggled the post and the beam hit me on the head—

I was laying in bed with an awful headache, trying to remember how I got here. Oh, yes, bluebird house. I took six aspirin and closed my eyes.

The next day I drove over to start again. Barney was ready (hey, he was retarded, I mean retired). But, first we had to cut down a tree to get the wood. I suggested using scraps but Barney wanted to do it right, so we fired up the caterpillar and went down the hill looking for a dead tree to harvest. The first one was quite dead, but too good a wildlife tree to cut. So were the next two. Finally, a newly dead tree with mistletoe. But, first we had to take apart the chainsaw and reset the chain, which at least was sharp (to my low standards). A few minutes sawing and the tree was nicely blocked in the trailer. And, Barney had enough firewood for a week.

Back at the shop, we ran the blocks chunks through a large circular saw to get rough thin planks. These we took inside to the table saw. I had already drawn a model with the measurements, so we started sawing to dimension. Then the saw stopped.

Barney looked around. Then came over and felt the teeth. "These are too dull, too much load. We have to sharpen them first."

So, we took half an hour to find the right file, which was in another part of the shop. Then, I took off the blade and filed it. Not as hard as I thought. While I was bolting the blade back on Barney fixed the fuse. The saw came on and took part of my finger—

I jumped straight up, turned and crashed through the door. Wrapped my hand in my shirt, got in the car and drove to town to see the butcher (my doctor was not skilled in any action with a knife or sutures). He was busy so he taped the finger together. I finally saw half of my thumb hanging by the skin. I went home and slept the rest of the afternoon.

The next day, I was back at the shop drilling holes for the front of the bird house. Every time Barney moved towards the fuse box or a switch I moved my hands subtlely from the machinery, looking up at the ceiling to make sure it looked stable. At last it was time to assemble the houses, all nine. I just tapped them together with finishing nails. For the roofs I used pieces of bark from the tree. I did not put a perch in front of the holes, as bluebirds do not need them.

The hole has to be large enough for the bird and small enough so that other birds will not claim the box. The house sparrow is a problem if it gets there first, although not after the house is claimed. But, I rarely saw sparrows at this elevation near the side of the mountain.

Out of old one-inch water pipe, from Barney's junkyard behind the shop, we cut ten-foot lengths and painted them brown. We carried them out to my flagged locations and drove them in. I held the posts while Barney slung the sledge. At five of six feet in height I slid the birdhouse, mounted on a small pole, into the pipe. The trail was taking shape. After letting jack pound enough to prove my confidence in him, I took over the sledge action. Things went well. On the last post, however, as I was holding it with one hand, I missed the end of the post and hit my index finger. I was beginning to wonder if I would live to see the completion of this project.

The boxes were all up. All we had to do was advertise for tenants. Fortunately, mountain bluebirds are quite perceptive and resourceful, and I expected them to find the boxes during their search for suitable trees and posts.

Now, it was time to put together the blind to keep the camera dry. I drove two more posts in the ground exactly four meters from the second house in the trail. That would give me good coverage of one and fair for two others. It started to rain, a nice quiet gentle rain at least, while I was mounting the small gable roof, also covered in bark, across the two posts. Soon it was ready for the camera, but I figured I could wait for a few days, until it stopped raining and until the new residents were in evidence.

It was time to buy the camera. I looked all over town. Only two store had cameras at all, including the new Wal-Mart at the edge of town. I drove to Spokane to check out the prices there. Definitely cheaper. I drove down to Moscow, where I was attached (a good biological term) by a salesman, like a shark with a remora. I could not stop this young salesman. Finally, I suggested that I buy the camera for ten dollars more than I saw it at Wal-Mart, but still forty under their asking price. He went to the owner, After an interesting bargaining session, during which I agreed to buy all my future electronics and appliances from his store, he sold it to me for the Wal-Mart price, less than I had originally offered. I took it back to the apartment, after buying a dozen full-size VHS tapes that fit inside. And, spent all afternoon reading the directions.

The bluebird couple first to the trail decided on house number eight, too far from the camera blind. It was May first. I started my bird log in earnest. I set the camera on its own tripod, next to a twelve-foot ponderosa pine and left it running for six hours. I sat next to the camera and watched. The birds started carrying in pine needles and pieces of leaves and twigs.

The first week was not as interesting as I hoped. Another couple did find house number One and move in. I was glad that I did not keep to the original plan of twenty houses. With the original I had ten and only two were occupied. I decided to keep the camera on Number Eight for the time being.

Happiness! There was a change in activity today. The female, whom I have named Fanny, is staying inside while the male is bringing a few insects. At first I could not tell what kind. I did not want to invade the nest. I wanted to keep to my Goethean ideals of noninterference and contemplative nonintervention. I was not sure, however, that I was going to even mention that in my paper.

Cut to a week later. Both parents are now gathering insects. After recording them hovering and darting down in the grass to get their prey. I went over to one area and combed it for a survey. There were , cutworms, sowbugs, small grasshoppers, and slow flies (see paper for numbers).

I was beginning to run out of tapes, so I started watching them and recording the number of visits with food. Started to collect data on feeding patterns. Parents fed from dawn to dusk for the first month.

I also started to notice other patterns. Noticed other birds and flowers. For instance, about every hour, a form flew from north to south close to the camera. When I watched in person I saw a small wren (?), with a nest in the grass. She was flying in to feed her young. I had never noticed in real-time.

Finally, tired of the commute from apartment to bird trail, I decided to buy a small trailer and park it a hundred meters from the trail, on a flat spot on the west slope overlooking the western hills and grasslands. I also invited Sheila to live at the site with me.

I spent a week looking at trailers in Moscow. Some were really small. I did not understand the economics of a few. Either they were really good deals or poorly made. I went to my mechanic, Arvin, and asked for his opinion (I had bought my last two cars from him. I bought them ten years old with 70,000 miles and drove them to they started to fall apart. I was on the Mercury comet now and it had no problems). Arvin thought the Fleetwood might be high enough quality. So, I went back and bought the 20-foot Fleetwood. Arvin let me use one of the 3/4-ton pickups that he had for sale to tow it up. I promised to buy the truck when the comet ever died. Then I went back to Ed's and bought a small used stove and refrigerator. I was able to tow it with no problem. Although I had to get a running start on the hill. And I thought it was going to shake apart going over the furrows in the field. No damage though. I got it up on blocks, hooked up the water and electricity (extra long extensions and pipes from the shop), and moved in with my clothes, notes, camera, and typewriter.

Every day, from 12:30 to 6:30 I worked at Rotunda dining hall at Wazoo in Pullman Washington. This entitled me to see some of the younger students finishing their degrees who thought they would be getting jobs immediately. Oh, how human hope flowed. Upstream mostly. A funny place to remember about fasting, but Ben Franklin said that those who live on hope die fasting.

Anyway, my job in this dining hall was to take the food trays and clean them off , then hand them to the dishwasher who would put them in the giant steam dishwashers. So many trays were returned with little food touched. Especially from the girls, who talked much more than they ever ate. The boys were not much better. Only the athletes seemed to eat all of their food, as well as seconds and thirds—that is, those athletes who bothered to eat with the commoners.

I managed to get quite plump finishing the untouched portions of meat and deserts —the potatoes and vegetables comprised the bulk of my diet at home, since Sheila was a vegetarian and had convinced me to try to become one. During our first break on my first day, a year ago—already a year at poverty wages and filled with professional frustration—I found out that everyone else working in the dining hall was foreign born and had at least a masters degree. What an overeducated, diverse, elite crew we were. It made the job easier to bear, knowing that so much talent was unrecognized. I suggested that the first with a good professional job hire the rest of us, but only got good-natured laughter in response. Perhaps hopeful laughter.

Sheila brought her cats to the trailer. We argued about it. I love cats but am allergic to them. Birds, however, have no love for cats. In fact, the greatest danger to the birds now is the cats. I tried to convince her to leave them inside. But, they have not been indoor cats.

The next week was quite routine. I got in the habit of previewing the tapes at night when Sheila got back from the university, where she worked as a secretary (her Masters degree was in English). We saw many of them together. It was at such a time we noticed that both parents stopped coming that very afternoon on Friday. I immediately went to look at the cats hangouts to search for feathers. I found none, but the coincidence weighed too much. I talked to Sheila and we decided to take turns watching. If there was no activity, then we would take the nest inside (and put the cats in the shop temporarily).

No activity. A few other birds approached the nest, including the wren, but neither bluebird parent. What could have happened to both of them? They hovered low to the ground, so they could be preyed on by cats or coyotes. I suppose we may never know. At noon we took them inside and took apart the next box. One was dead already, the other three were living. We named them, Froc, Fric, and Frac.

Sheila turned on the electric recirculating water heater to keep the room at a warm constant temperature. I held one, Froc I think, while she tried to feed it milk-soaked bread. Didn't work. Tofu and yoghurt didn't work, either. I knew they were insectivores, but was hoping for the easy solution. I ran down to Barney's to borrow some hamburger (being vegetarians, we had nothing desired by growing chicks).

The burger was eaten, so we made sure the pieces were small enough. Sheila made a modified shoebox for a home for them and we put them on the table next to the heater. I went outside to collect grasshoppers and sowbugs, the only bugs I could catch.

We fed them every twenty minutes. Two of them tweeted when it was time for feeding. It sounded rather funny when the top was on the shoebox. They seemed to like the hamburger better than the chopped sowbugs and grasshoppers.

The next morning, Froc was still and lifeless. Two left. We kept to the schedule. Tried mixing the insect parts with burger meat. That seemed to work. Fric and Frac kept tweeting and eating. I thought they were over the hump.

After two weeks I took them outside. I made a low perch for them from a disk blade from the neighbor's old farming disker. I brought them sowbugs and grasshoppers and put them on the disk. Every evening, they came back inside and slept in their box. Now, they wanted out earlier in the morning. I let them sit on the disk while I alternated filming between the other two bluebird houses

One afternoon, after she came home early, Sheila noticed that I was salivating when I was looking for sowbugs. Most of bugs lived under rocks, or at least that was where I found them. I rarely saw them in the grass, but they must have been there for the bluebird adults to hunt them.

At three weeks or 21 days I decided to try to release them. After a day playing with bugs and trying to fly from the shoulder to a small fir tree, I decided to leave them outside. Not surprisingly their orientation was excellent and they found the window above their shoebox. I gave up and opened the window and let them in.

The next morning after I let them out, I set the camera and went back inside to write; they came back and sat on the window, tapping the glass with their beaks, until I went out and turned over a rock and revealed some sowbugs.

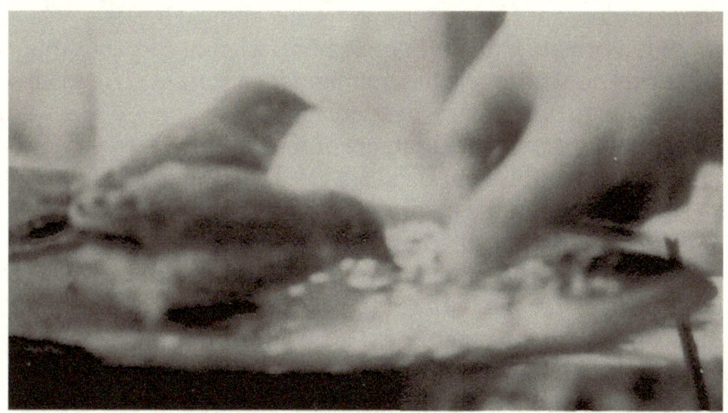

Gradually they found their own food, hovering above the grass like blue helicopters, then striking the insect in their target finder. Gradually, they learned to fly to taller trees. Suddenly they could fly to the nearby power line and to the tallest ponderosa, although they rarely went above twenty feet. I took credit for teaching them to fly. Sheila noticed that I would unconsciously flap my wings, or arms, to encourage them to fly stronger.

Sitting in the garden, either of us would be targets for their landing practices. When either of us came back from the university, we would park at the bottom of the road and stand still. From the power lines, two blue missiles would strike down, although as they nearer, it was obvious that the pilots were untrained and raw. They would start to wobble and their eyes would get crossed before landing each on the same shoulder.

We had many other outings that summer. They finally stopped coming in at night, preferring the ponderosa. Sometimes when I walked down to get the mail, they would hover above me, sometimes spotting a tasty insect near the ground, sometimes just flying escort.

On one such outing Frac was taken by a hawk. We were working the in the garden. The birds were hunting. Suddenly, Fric flew down to the ground and Frac flew up beside the ponderosa. I saw the hawk glide from the top branch of the ponderosa and grab Frac. I looked for a stone, None. I took off my shoe and threw it, hoping to hit a wing, but the shoe fell short. Far short. I watched as the hawk flew out of sight to the west. I picked Fric up and took him in the trailer. His response was the correct one I supposed.

The next morning I took Fric out, but he seemed haunted or cautious. He rarely flew above ten feet. I made my rounds with the video camera. He did not follow me.

Sheila left that weekend, with her cats, now traumatized by the primitive nature of the machine shop. She rented a room in a mansion in Moscow. I helped her move her things. It was a nice room, with a private bath, but no kitchen. Oriental carpets. Antique furnishings. I supposed she had to maintain a certain style to be seen as a success or to be seen as a desirable mate. How could I be so calm about it? I could not. In fact I hit one of the older Ponderosa until my hand felt like it was broken. I will always have the scars and they might last longer than the memories. I doubt it.

Fric gradually regained his confidence. In later September, the troupe of bluebirds came buy to gather recruits for the flight to southern Oregon for the winter. I counted twenty, including at least five new ones from the other nests. When they flew off two days later, I could not tell which was Fric.

I took down the boxes, cleaned and repaired them.

I gave my paper; it was well-received. But, I never got a job offer. I quit the dining hall, when I got an offer as an auto mechanic at the local Subaru dealer. I always wonder exactly how many biologists work in these kind of jobs—50 percent? 30,000?

The winter passed. The next spring, Fric returned and claimed his house. I was so happy. He visited me, and would fly near my shoulders and head but he never landed on me again. I was grateful for his company and for his success. I started recording the entire trail again. Not showing any favoritism whatsoever.

Fric, being so unique, in having a human stepfather and a taste for sowbugs, managed to land an equally unique mate. She seemed like a normal bluebird at first, but I noticed that she started sitting on the old Subaru and looking at her reflection in the side mirror. I didn't notice her doing it until after I saw the regular deposition of bluebird guano below the driver's side mirror. It was either that or she was familiarizing herself with the controls of the automobile for some sinister purpose. I trained the camera on her for a morning to document this odd and unique behavior, which suggested the perfect name for her, Vanity.

Fric and Vanity successfully raised a family that summer. On my walks, Fric would sometimes fly escort again, hovering over my head as I walked down the road. One day the neighbor called me and asked if I was being attacked. I said no, that was my armed guard to protect me from the sowbug mafia.

The four young seemed normal and healthy. In late September, I noticed one of the young seemed to be a brighter blue than the others. Another winter passed. The job at the auto dealer went well. It was mindless work, but I learned a few new things, mostly as cars became more sophisticated.

That next spring, I did not see Fric or Vanity. I wondered if they went to another place to have a family. I prayed they survived.

The house, however, was taken over by a very bright blue bird. At first I was not sure if he was from Frac and Vanity, but when he started hovering over me, I realized that he could only have learned that from Fric. I called him Neon.

The blue birds came one last time in November, Neon's son's flock, to check the fencepost nest for the next year. No one noticed them pass the store; they were not seen from the highway. How invisibly they flew.

I always felt handicapped by living at the bottom of the atmosphere, through distortions of light, which is what colors were, however entertaining. What is sunlight without colored wings? I thought. What is the wind without an occasional song to carry? I wondered. What is silence without a chattering of life to surround it, for on the solar scale, it is silence that surrounds life.

## Famous Irish Bars, Part 8, City Cork
by Courvin Alan Maolanaithe Woulfe

I came close to Rock Close but didn't know it, when I drifted over towards the small maintenance buildings off between the castle and the house. At first Rock Close looks like a giant rock outcropping, with wild flowers and old gnarled oaks. Part of it is open, with wild flowers (many from New Zealand, oddly) and winding, interconnecting trails. Then it seemed that the outcropping was the ragged part of one massive boulder (as if a castle were buried with only the top floor above ground). At the edges were the witches kitchen and druid cave, which were openings in the side of the rock, each under a tree—the small windows and rooted entrances make them both seem ancient, yet comfortable; the witches kitchen was maybe six feet high, eight long and four wide, and the druid cave was slightly smaller, but with a more interesting 'window' cut (?) in the rock. At the other end of the rock was a stone tunnel leading down to a marshy field. To have your wish granted, you must walk down the stairs backwards. I watched an old man start down, but I did not wish to grow old watching, so I looked for the druid circle, but could not find it. The trees lent most of the character to this spot, which could also be approached through a low tunnel, much like the tunnel to the lake, which I found was on the other side of the new house, maybe half a mile from the entrance under the castle I tried. I had another ice cream cone on the way out and relived the previous one.

The Blarney House, built in 1890, was thoroughly Victorian (my favorite period). Every structural element (doorway, window, bookcase, fireplace, mirror) was balanced symmetrically by another, even if the second doorway was false. The cupolas on each of the four corners of the house at the third story were only to balance the windows on the first or second story. Only servants used the third floor which had been closed off and was no longer used. The center of the house was a massive returned (u-shaped) staircase braced by columns on the second floor. Above it was a barrel arch skylight—very rare and most functional in lighting the entire second floor center. All the wood was nauseatingly beautiful from the floors to the wainscoting. It was more comfortable than the house on Fota, but did not seem less rich. The ceilings on the first floor seemed about sixteen feet high.

It reminded me of one of the bars, Reidy's Vault, and since it was Saturday, I went drinking.

Sunday morning, I went on a long lonely walk due west along the river through at least two parks and one long field. Here is my favorite scene. As I walked back toward Cork, a naked man (very white and Irish) got out of the river and stood on a small concrete boat ramp. He picked up a towel and wrapped it around his waist, making little hula hoop-like motions, presumably to dry his rump. A second man approached with a beautiful young German Shepherd. As they engaged in conversation the first man started dressing slowly, starting with white cotton underwear. The second man, dressed in a tweed coat and cap, took off his knapsack and removed from it an empty two-liter plastic bottle (Fresca, I think) and threw it into the river. Neither man paid any attention to this conspicuous littering; they continued talking as the first put on his dark socks. After a few moments, with neither man attending, the dog jumped into the river, swam to the bottle, clamped it in his teeth, and swam back, walked up the boat ramp, put down the bottle and shook water all over both men, who were still in a dignified conversation, although the first had yet to pull on his trousers. By the third throw, there were one man with a terrier, two women, three children, and another small dog watching, and, of course, me standing down the trail scribbling. Each time, the dog dropped the bottle and shook vigorously, slightly further from the earnest conversationalists, the first of whom was now inspecting his shirt. The fourth time the dog dropped the bottle and started chewing it. But, the second man took it away and threw it in the river again. The fifth time, the dog ran away from the river with the bottle. The man with the knapsack chased him. The others moved on down river. I moved up river exchanging glances with the first man, who had finished dressing and was looking about.

Monday afternoon in the supermarket off Paul Street, I had just enough money for a treat and dinner. So, I walked down all the aisles. The milk and yogurt looked good and was inexpensive; some of the milk came in plastic bottles that looked like the old glass milk bottle, the rest came in various sizes of wax paper boxes. The yogurt also came in many small sizes for 13-23 pence (21-38 cents or so) and many mixed flavors. The breads aisle was wonderful; there were fresh breads, like brown soda and white and Italian breads and rolls; there were tall batch pans (I assume pronounced in the French) and various vegetable onion rolls. Even the bagged breads were very fresh and crisp (I know, I squeezed several). I bought a small roll and a small milk (skim milk was almost unknown). The cookie and cake aisle was especially satisfying; the cookies were dominated by chocolate-orange combinations. The English brands offered a variety of filled cakes and petit-fours. After ten minutes of struggle I bought a chocolate Bannenberg, with three layers of white chocolate cake, separated with cream or apricot jam, and dipped in dark chocolate. I bought a French red apple as a concession to health.

After eating a picnic in my room, I went to the Crawford Art Gallery, which I wish I had gone into earlier (admission was free). The major exhibit was called Utopia, but it was strangely Australian batik with lizard and kangaroo forms throughout. Interesting texture, but very expensive (and how much went to the women I wondered). There was a very large color catalog with it. This was in the main downstairs gallery across from the gift shop. The ceilings seemed twenty feet high, were painted dark blue or green with white-painted trim with this pattern. Upstairs, and the stairs were oak with wrought iron treads with this pattern, were Irish painters of Cork and Cobh harbors—competent and interesting. Lining the stairs to the third floor were drawings by Augustus John (Pamela, 1943) and Sean 0 Sullivan (Portrait of Eoin 0 Mahoney, 194?). On the third floor was an exhibit of Modern Irish painters (1970s). I was very impressed by many of them; the ideas were good and the execution showed skill and discipline (as if I were conversant with either). The Chieftain, by Maurice Desmond, Cain and Lucifer, by Julie Kelleher, Self-portrait and cat, by Patricia Hennessey, Swans, by Mary Swanzey, and Machines of Learning, by Alicia Boyle, would be worth seeing again; this last was also humorous and witty. I tried to get postcards of them but none had been made. A new modern exhibit was being set up while I was there, so I watched a while, but most of the work was abstract, minimalist gobbledygook—I guess I just needed more stimulation than an abstract work could give. On the other hand, I only respect that which I cannot or do not do.

That night, with my remaining four pounds, I ate at Bully's, at the bar. I ordered a diet coke and a Bully burger, which was cooked to perfection and came with excellent English relishes and a mustard-vinegar sauce, as well as chips and a green salad. I sat at the end in front of the cappuccino machine. The tables were all full, but the bar empty of others. Jazz was playing, Nat King Cole and then Ella Fitzgerald for the rest of the evening. The bar seemed to be made of solid pine at the ends, but had two mahogany planks in the middle, as if it had been extended at some time. The back bar was a Spanish stained pine; although the bar was comfortable, it was the poorest woodwork I'd seen.

Important Irish Bars: Reidy's Vault Bar is really my favorite. It is a Victorian bar in an old wine vault. The bar itself was huge and long with globed street-light poles every six feet. Over it were two domed skylights. The walls had dark wainscoting. The stools and table seats were covered in a rich upholstery.

The bar in Jury's; a flavor of age in a new concrete block building. And, the Metro bar was heavily charactered.

I also ate in Paddy Garibaldi's, an Italian restaurant around the corner from Bully's. The building was very narrow, like Bully's, but there were stairs leading to a mezzanine overlooking the alley, and from there stairs to a full second floor. The mezzanine had large red steel girders going across about seven feet off the floor and plants hanging from them. The ceiling was stained brown; the walls were whitewashed. I had a small cheese pizza and wine for about six pounds.

Fat Freddy's was a nice cafe bistro, playing American jazz; small tables with checkered table cloths. I had a calzone and white wine for about five pounds (notice a trend?). The ceiling was painted black, but effectively lowered with ducts and pipes and supports. The oven was right in front so you could watch the food being prepared.

The Raging Red Hog was a new minimalist Euro-counter. I had a cheese sandwich and soda while I was waiting for Immigration to open.

Chip and Dels was an interesting diner on Plunkett Street (parallel to Patrick's). Very narrow, with open booths on the wall and stools at the bar. The whole wall in back of the grill was ivory tile. All the seats had a flower brocade cover. I had an onion burger and diet coke—my only real burger on a bun in Ireland. I went back to the Natural Foods Restaurant (where I had eaten almost every night) and had another lasagna with rice and salad; the last time I went back all the dishes had walnuts, so I didn't eat there again.

I found a second floor French vegetarian restaurant on Phoenix Street across from the Post Union; although the awnings were open, it was closed. I went into MaGuire's, which was recommended, but they had no snacks, so I left without even a drink (hey, I'm not a hundred percent Irish); it was nicely appointed, sort of a square bar with glass racks above all seats.

I also walked by Nancy Spain's Backstage Bar in back of the south quays—very working class, with tiny houses (two stories as tall as a single story). The bar had an old gnarled tree worked into the doorway with large stones near the floor. The bar itself carried the same theme—it could have been built in Eugene by aging hippies for the same flavor or handcrafted, wild wood. I wanted to see the Dizzy Blues Band, but they didn't start until midnight and I had a class at Nine a.m. the next day (hey, I'm not all Irish). I didn't have a drink there, either. I walked into the Washington Inn on Washington Street; a nice old bar. I went by the bar in the Imperial, but it seemed to be a new Euro-chrome setting, so I didn't stay there either.

Incisive sociological observations: Irish English has its own quirks. Singular or plural subjects are maddening. For instance, a single group is considered a plural subject, as in "Cork are it", referring to the football team. One day, when I turned onto Academy Street, where Dillinger's coffee house was, I saw two Irishmen pushing wheelbarrows full of concrete—no different than the 1840s. The streets were too narrow to allow the truck to deliver, so it was still the best way to build a new wall. Electricity comes to Ireland: The statue of Mary on the church by the North fork of the Lee River had an electric halo. I noticed others in other churches. Then I noticed that the portrait of Jesus in the Garnish House had a small red neon cross on the bottom of the frame. The candles in every church were electric; after putting in your donation, you only had to press a button to light a candle.

But, it was drinking that lead to my only religious experience one Sunday. That morning I saw a shining pyramid in the distance. When I walked closer it seemed to recede in the shimmering present, always staying several blocks from me. Then it resolved itself into a pyramid of empty beer kegs, outside the last bar, shining in the morning sun. Other sidewalks were lined with aluminum beer kegs. When I walked out past the southern quays, there were whole yards of empty barrels. I resolved to acquire a taste for beer, to honor my Irish heritage.

## The Mouse
by A. M. Caratheodory

Ever since I stayed out late one night, when I was very young, I wanted to live under the stars. I wanted to see them closer, to understand them, to see or hear of every kind of star. Of all the wondrous things in the universe, these had to be the most·basic, burning spheres in every imaginable color.

I wrote about them. I imagined them. I searched for information about them. Later I studied them. Measured them, and theorized about them. After high school, I never took a college course that was not about stars. My father said I was an idiot. My mother said I was an idiot savant. My professor said I was a savant.

Unfortunately, since I was not allowed to graduate without various kinds of soft courses like English, I came to the attention of my draft board. I enlisted in the Air Force to use their astronomy programs. But, even the combined might of the military, the Air Force anyway, could not divert me from this direction. Whenever I was assigned to a project or a labor. I distorted it until it had something to do with stars. Hand-to hand combat was something to be avoided. I was able to avoid anything focused on me. I neglected to obey orders. For this offence I was turned over to the base commander, who ordered me to 'hit the deck.' Having been open to any dangerous situations before I entered, I replied it wasn't necessary, no dangers were present. He said I was missing the point, which was to obey unquestioningly. I told him that I did obey my inner voice unquestioningly, but that was because I understood it. What he was offering was simple brainwashing leading to reconstruction in the military mode. Such reconstruction would be harmful for me, from a research point of view, and I knew the Air Force needed good research to eventually save soldiers lives. The commander sighed and ordered a psychiatric evaluation.

I was able to have very useful conversations with the doctor, who was from India. Eventually the Air Force gave up and assigned me to the Air Force Cambridge Research Labs, where I was happy for four years, working, officially on radar track, but really on radio astronomy projects related to stellar observations.

By the time I walked out of the bus in Boston, I was lined up to work on stellar surveys at the University of Arizona Lunar and Planetary Laboratory. I had expected to get a position at the other lab at Arizona, but my experience with radio astronomy changed my professional fitness. The only position that they had open was Observer, but William Bradford, the Director, told me that he would expect me to move up as a Research Assistant then Associate within the year, depending on the projects and funding.

So, I took the transcontinental bus to Tucson. A lot of the driving occurred at night so I was able to see a few stars. I often asked the bus driver to pull over in areas of darkness. Some were helpful; others were consumed with their schedules. In Tucson, I called my contact, Fred Tardell, who picked me up at the bus station. His house was in the desert miles from the campus or observatories. The stars were fabulous. I came inside only as a social grace to meet his wife and son.

The next day I suggested to William Delacroix, the Director, that I start right away, but he pointed out that the schedule was set. Besides, he wanted time to assess my skills. I shrugged. He told me to relax and find a place to stay. He asked me if I knew how to drive. I said yes, I had learned on a weapons carrier in the Air Force. He said that I could use one of the observatory cars, just check it our from the car pool. Find a place to live, get settled and come back tomorrow.

I found a small efficiency just west of the university for a few hundred a month, It was in walking distance. It had a bed, table kitchen table and two chairs. My clothes did not fill up the closet.

The next day we talked about stellar structure and evolution. He went into detail about his stellar surveys, especially about the filters he had designed. I met the rest of the staff, Alan and Subramanyan, other observers, and Rick Simonov, the Assistant director, who was with William in Texas. The days passed learning the equipment.

The oddest day was when I was told that I could select some things from the junk pile—these were actually pieces of equipment that came with the grants, as part of the grants, to flesh out the grant amounts. So, we had a flight trainer, and some radar dishes, and a few things I could not identify. I chose a heated flight suit, and found a few pans for cooking. I stored this stuff on my new desk.

The days passed and it was time to start the real work. Rick and I drove separately up to Mount Lemon, following the road out of the city and through the new suburbs, up the mountain, through the canyons, and around the ridges. I saw my first roadrunners and lizards. I think my car was an old 1959 Plymouth station wagon, painted a dusty blue. It seemed to work seamlessly.

In the mountains, we turned off the paved road onto a gravel road. Where that forked, we turned onto a dirt road laid with pine needles. This road winded up the hill through large trees, then out onto a flat area with two Quonset guts—only they were the telescope enclosures that slid off completely, rather than being revolving domes. Much cheaper and more efficient, but less romantic looking. Off to the side were two 40-foo single-wide trailers (had to be military surplus I thought).

After a tour of the two scopes and trailers, I was assigned to one of each. I checked off my equipment and procedures with Rick there, just in case some protocol or other had been changed or modified. I asked for our elevation and Rick said 9035 feet.

All the trees looked like the same species of pine. Electrical towers split the site from the lower road. Before he left Rick gave me a box of chocolate-covered donuts, which I laid to the side.

When it was dark, I opened the sliding cover. It was suddenly colder, but I had expected that and put on my electrified suit. I looked at the list of requested observations. With these faint stars, I would not even be locating them with a spotter scope, Instead I had to enter the coordinates and let the computer set the settings. The only way I would know if I was near was if the monitor showed increased energy pick up. And, it did. I tried to imagine what the star looked like from the data. Thus the night passed.

At dawn, I closed the cover (which everyone else still called a dome) and shut off the instrumentation. It was a successful night. Only six stars, but each had to be tracked for over an hour so the radiation could be received and built up.

I walked over to the trailer. When I opened the metal door, I heard rustling noises. The trailer smelled musty. I took my bag into the bedroom; it smelled musty. Rick assured me the linens were clean, and had been put on in the last week or two. I pulled the thick curtains closed, took off my clothes and went to sleep.

I was awakened by a crash in the kitchen. I ran out to see the tail of a squirrel disappear into the air conditioning door by the kitchen. I saw the plate in the sink, with my half-eaten peanut butter sandwich on the plate. There were two sizes of teeth on the sandwich now. I realized I would have to be cleaner or at least put everything in the refrigerator.

It was after Two (p.m.), so I decided to stay up. I dressed and went out for a walk. I thought I needed some metal to close up the bottom of the trailer, at least the squirrel entrance. Maybe some poison to make sure. I would look later. I had lived with animals at various times, but did not much concern myself with them, unless they threatened to bite.

The forest was calming. Even a forest I preferred to see at night. I didn't see anyone on my walk, although I could hear some vehicles down slope. Rick said there was a ski slope nearby.

I found some aluminum pieces and glued and painted them around the air-conditioner closet in the trailer. I also found a few mummified mice and some mummified cereal in the kitchen. I found the traditional collection of nude and girlie magazines. I looked through them and appreciated the female form. That was something that was missing from my life, but I had no idea what to do about it. Several of the local female astronomers were nice looking, relatively. I should try to ask one to dinner. Maybe later, during my ten days off (after my 20 on, with 19 to go).

When I got up and turned into the kitchen I saw a mouse on the counter next to the sink. The sandwich was refrigerated, so I wondered what he wanted. Some crumbs maybe. He was watching me. A small grey mouse—I had no idea if he was large or small, for a mouse, just small for a furry mammal. I walked towards him, but he stayed until I got within hand reach, then he dived over the counter. I think he went behind the hassock in front of the couch, but I didn't feel like hunting now.

I did go through the cabinets and found three mouse traps in with the canned goods, mostly corn and soups. I baited all three with peanut butter and set them on the counter.

I went to work before sunset.

At dawn I trudged back to the trailer. I forgot it is harder to sleep for eight hours in daylight. The mousetraps were all clean now. I sighed. When I got into the bedroom the mouse was waiting on the nightstand. I held myself from racing over and swatting him. This was strange. I had never seen such a relaxed mouse before. Usually, they were blurs across the floor. When I approached the bed, he moved behind the night stand. I wondered what he did at night, but I was too tired to wait and look. I left the curtains open, though, for the light.

William said the observations were right on target. To keep up the good work. All I did was line up numbers and push buttons. How hard could that be. I kept working on my mathematical models of carbon stars. I asked William for some computer time next week. He said he would have a surprise by then. We were getting out own IBM 360, so we would not have to keep using the CDC 6400 that the university had.

The next morning the mouse was on the bed. He went over the side as I crashed down. When I got up, he was nowhere to be seen. I wondered if he was consorting with other know peanut butter thieves. After my walk, I came back to read. I sat on the couch and got out the new *Astrophysical Journal*. As I was reading it the mouse came up on the couch and sat on the arm, less than six inches away. I looked at him but kept reading. I could have killed him, but I was curious now. I had asked the other observers if they had trouble with mice. They said yes, but they poisoned most of them. I asked if the mice ever attacked them or bothered them. They said no. So, I let him stay there. After half an hour he left on an errand and I kept reading.

Eating the donuts. Getting cold. Looking outside. That morning, the mouse was waiting on the nightstand. He didn't move when I went to bed. On an impulse, I said good night. He probably watched me fall asleep.

More stars. The mountain, the dry air, the dark nights, were perfect for the observatory. But, the nights were not as dark as they used to be. The pollution of light from Tucson was making things difficult. The pollution of gases and dust was also making things worse. William mentioned that we would be working at a new observatory in Baja next fall, at the El Diablo site. I wondered how much longer this site would exist. The night passed in thought.

The next morning, I simply fixed him a small peanut butter sandwich while I ate mine. He nibbled it but did not stay near it. Perhaps he was saving it for the squirrel, who had found a new way in. Dinner became a ritual, although he did not always eat at the same time.

Another ritual was my reading and his sitting on the arm of the sofa. Then one morning he wasn't there. I sat anyway and read. I thought I felt a small weight on my trouser. I froze, not even turning the page. I watched as he emerged over my knee. He moved very slowly and cautiously across my thigh and onto the book I was reading, Chandrasekar. I stayed perfectly still and looked into his eyes. I had no idea what he was thinking. I had no idea why he was visiting me. Peanut butter? Kindred spirit? No, I doubt if he ever looked at the stars. I moved my leg and he jumped down by the hassock. I walked over to the door and opened it, I gestured to him to go outside. I realized that I knew nothing about mouse anatomy. Could he even see stars? Focus on them? Or would he just see darkness or shapes. Come to think of it I didn't know much about human anatomy either.

It was still light anyway, but I could see the sun setting behind the trees. I closed the door and went to work. I wondered if he had enough water.

Over the rest of the 20-day period, he gradually became accustomed to me, and I to him. I noticed his coloration. It was grey but had shades of brown around the feet and ears. He was not a uniform grey at all. Sometimes he would sit on my shoulder. Sometimes he would stay on the bed when I went to sleep.

Then my shift was over. I put my clothes in the Plymouth and left that morning. I left some peanut butter bread in the sink, but I was worried that Lee, the next observer would throw it out. I had left a note asking him to not use mouse traps.

When I talked to the other observers about mouse behavior they thought it was strange. Of course, I did not tell them anything about the real closeness, just the sitting on the counter. Alan said he was sure that the mouse would eat my eyes out, and that was the real intent of lulling me to complacency.

I thought about that and went to the library and read up on mice. That was a section of the library I had never seen before. I had never gone above 530 in the Dewey decimal system.

I found a good book on wild house mouse biology and sat down to read it. The book started by stating that "House mice are rodents, of the order Rodentia, because they have two pairs of chisel-like, self-sharpening incisors. Rodents are an extremely diverse lineage of 3,000 species; in fact, they account for 40% of all mammalian species. House mice belong to the family Muridae (Old World mice) and the genus *Mus*. The commensal *Mus musculus* consists of four recognizable forms or morphotypes. These four morphotypes may be considered distinct species , starting with *M. musculus*—"

I decided I needed to ask questions, specific questions, so I called up the biology department. That afternoon, I drove down and met with Jordan Meyersong, a professor in the biology department. I asked him if he knew much about mouse behavior.

"Are you kidding?" he answered, "Mice are the best-studied animals on the planet. Vast studies have been done in the laboratory.

Why, here at Arizona we . . ."

I tuned him out for a moment. Then asked my first question, "So the grey one I see is *Mus musculus*."

"Probably. This is on Mt. Lemon? House mice originally evolved in Europe and Asia and have recently spread throughout the world. *M. domesticus* and *M. musculus* are the most widely distributed. The wild house mice—"

"They are not native?" I asked.

"No, our native mice are 'deer mice' or *Peromyscus*, but you would never see one in a trailer."

"Why not?"

"Let me get to that. You know, people have been breeding mice in Egypt and China for at least 4,000 years. They kept them in temples or homes to predict the future or as lucky charms; the ancient Romans used them as medicine. The mouse ecology is quite interesting. House mice usually live near humans and are therefore called 'human commensals,' and they like people."

"Even when people devote their cleverness and efforts to killing them?"

"Well, I suppose rather than being commensals, house mice are really a kind of kleptoparasite that have been stealing our food supplies since the agricultural revolution—in fact, the name 'mouse' or 'mus' comes from the Sanskrit 'mush' derived from a verb meaning 'to steal'). Since house mice have been living in human buildings for over six thousand years, our enclosures provide good natural environments for them. Mice are, are crepuscular, that is, active at dawn and dusk—"

"Like wolves right,?" I asked, "or mountain lions."

"Yes, quite right. Mice are herbivores, eating grains and fruits, mostly, but they also eat insects and other small invertebrates. Their natural predators include snakes and cats. Mice often carry a diversity of pathogens and parasites, although the only one that offers a significant risk to humans is the lymphocyte choriomeningitis (LCMV) virus."

"What does that do?" I asked, alarmed.

"Brain fever. Rare. But . . . Their Social Behavior is also quite interesting. House mice tend to live in stable social groups consisting of a single dominant, territorial male and with four to eleven other adults. This mating system is called "harem polygyny" where females mate with the territorial male and refuse to mate with the subordinate males, in general. However, females will also leave their territory and solicit matings from neighboring territorial alpha males. Most adult animals remain faithful to a locality for extended periods—"

"What was that?" I interrupted again.

"It means that if you removed the mouse from its territory, it would come back. Females reach reproductive maturity as soon as four weeks and males at about seven weeks. Females come into puberty earlier when exposed to male odors—"

"Well, how do I tell a male from a female?" I asked.

"—whereas they delay it when exposed to the odor of females. Female house mice often nest communally and nurse each other's pups, like lions and a few other mammals. Cooperative breeding is a strategy to reduce pup loss from infanticide, which can be quite high—yes, what?"

"Yes?"

"Oh, usually after they're dead, or caught anyway," Professor Meyerson shrugged.

"Well, thank you. Have to drive back to the mountain now. Thanks for all the information."

"No problem. Glad to be a help," He slapped my shoulder. "Here are two articles of mine on the genetics of house mice."

Back at the observatory, I set up for the night. I opened the dome and put on my heated suit. Rick had left a few chocolate-covered donuts on the table—that was the only way I knew he ever stopped by. I never could figure out why he stopped by; maybe to see if I was still alive. I looked at the list of stars and started entering the coordinates and times. The night passed quickly, but all I thought about was mice.

When I got to the trailer, I saw Shadow on the bed. I never ever heard him, or her, just noticed his shadow as he moved. I was sure he was a he, since he never got pregnant and made a nest. We settled into our nightly routine, like good mammal buddies. I read an article in the journal and he sat on the edge of the paper. I had my dish with a peanut butter sandwich; he had a cracker on a saucer, with a side of peanut butter. After an hour I went and brushed my teeth. He stayed a while and then went to bed, on the yellow pillow. I think he was asleep when I got under the sheet.

That afternoon, after waking, I decided to go for a walk. He was gone when I got up, probably hiding from hawks. I was so used to walking the trails from the Kuiper observatory back up the hill at night that I needed to see it during the day. I encountered an owl, who hooted from a distance; the distance closed as he flew unseen from some distant tree. Finally I saw the swooping motion from one tree to another until he was almost on top of me, literally. He swept up onto a dead limb, lowered his wings and tucked them, and regarded me. I still had half of my peanut butter sandwich in my hand. Unthinkingly, I tore it in half and placed part of it on a flat rock in front of the tree. He regarded me, but did not move. I sat, and talked to him. Rather I asked him about how he lived and if he was mated.

I decided to go visit Harold at the fire watch tower. The owl followed me through a dry stream bed, but then flew back the way he had come. I wondered if we had then crossed some boundary unseen by me.

The tower came into sight. I could see a shape bent over a table, so I figured Harold was working. In his case, composing music. As I came through the trap door, he looked up but went back to scribbling. I sat on the stool overlooking the map table and looked over the landscape of trees and ridges. I could not see the observatory, which was on the other side of the mountain. We did not speak. After an hour or so I left.

Going back, as I was walking absorbed in thought, I absently reached out to pet the dog who had come up beside me. I stopped when I realized it was a mountain lion. I looked at him; he looked at me. I don't know how many thoughts or communications passed between us—maybe none. I looked in his eyes, without thinking about competitive challenges or invitations. I saw someone looking into my eyes, perhaps wondering what kind of being I was, what I thought or what I wanted, whether I was hungry or mated. I could smell the peanut butter on my lips and something heavier on hers. I looked at the tawny body, the small muscle flicking in the back—then she flowed away soundlessly. I guessed she was over three feet at the shoulder and 160 pounds. Thoughtlessly, I turned and walked the same way, then started running. I could not see her at all. I slowed and looked up into the trees. It was time to sing praises to mountain lions, who might be hungry after all. So, I did. I admired my own voice as I sang. I ended with a low growl that came from below my belly.

The evening passed with no new start or observations, just filter after filter on the same targets; that is what they became, targets to be measured, never visited or touched. I left early while it was still a little dark, before the false dawn.

I sat on the sofa and opened my book on stellar structure. Shadow walked up my leg again and sat on the book, looking up at me. I could not move. Then with a sudden burst of fear, I slammed the book closed on him. Threw the book to the floor and stepped on it. It was done. He was dead. I was safe. No threat, no worries. I put the body in the trash. The act, the moment, receded from me like old light from a brown star.

The next few days and nights were like a trance. I saw the motions but did not feel them. I had no idea what I had done or why. Then I realized that there were no squirrels or birds near the trailer. I felt strange and so human, like I had lost my innocence with animals.

Then the economy, and the war, and soft money, did to me what I had done to the mouse—I could not even think or speak his name. I was laid off. It was Friday the thirteenth at thirteen hundred. The director came in and said he had bad news. I thought he was referring to me, but he meant that he had to lay off the entire staff, up to the assistant director, and that meant that he had to learn all of the projects and procedures. I agreed to help him, numbly.

I went home and sat in my almost empty living room. It wasn't uncomfortable. I wondered if I should try to go back to school. I wondered if I could work my way back to a state of grace with animals, or if my sin would stain my soul permanently and make me untouchable by any but humans. I would have to try anyway.

## Masks

by Benjamin Turnaday

I recognized the mask from the mirror. I had not always looked like this. Once I was young and handsome, vital and immortal. Once I never thought about how I looked or how age would transform my face to a mask of the sediments of living, a red nose from drinking, cauliflower ears from fighting, a double chin from eating, and the blue-vesseled eyes—

Maybe I read too much into the eyes, the haunted glaze returned to me, asking questions I did not want to hear, the fine blue lines on the scorched yellow orbs, the balding eyelashes and eyebrows protecting the orbs from falling hair and dandruff. Agghh, I have seen better masks used to frighten children—I mean less frightening.

So, what have I become? A mask? Did I spend all the essence? No, foolishness. I spent nothing, only used time to inscribe some lines of wisdom on my face. The mask did not look wise, though. I wonder what a mask of youth would look like? Only the bland extent of flesh, unused, untried, and uninteresting.

In an early part of my incarnation, I was an anthropologist. I studied human societies and cultures and forms. I remember I wore a mask then, a large full beard over a large full belly. Long hair, clear eyes, sculpted arms. That way, people saw the anthropologist, not the student inside. Ah, well. In my current form I was just a cancer patient.

I had finished shaving, a worthless ritual now that I was in the hospital for chemotherapy. The hairs had not fallen out evenly, so I was growing long strands on my chin.

The nurse, Risa, came in to take my vitals. "Well, you're awake early. How are you?"

Let's see," I started, another ritual. "You tell me."

She had the blood pressure cuff on quickly, but I slid it down my forearm. "Pain?" she asked.

I nodded stoically, "Bone pain," then asked, "What class was that you are taking?"

"Art," she answered, checking my pulse and placing the thermometer in my mouth.

"Whamp kmind?" I asked.

"Collages. Everything looks good. I think I'll put the meds through your port, now. That way you can sleep an extra hour," we both looked at the bed; the laptop was on a pillow, two books were against the glass wall. I was sitting on the side.

"Any special theme?" I asked.

"We can chose one. I was thinking of using one of Coleridge's poems—"

"Masks," I interrupted her. "Do one on masks."

"Masks? What?" she paused.

"The word mask is from the Italian word 'mascara' a covering for the face. Every person wears a mask. The Latin word 'persona' also means mask."

"Wow, I didn't know that," she enthused.

I shrugged modestly.

"What were you in, in real life, I mean?" she asked.

"You mean before I became a butterfly? What kind of worm was I?" I said too harshly, thinking I had forgotten more than she would ever know—but that was what I thought when I talked to the oncologist and her assistants also. Or to anyone else, for that matter.

She looked at her clipboard and said quietly, "Have to finish the round. I'll come back at med time."

And so began our affair.

No, nothing so tawdry as sex or lust, cheating or sweat, wanting or planning to rush to Vegas. She was divorced; I had a loving wife. She was 25-ish and already weary of nursing. I would have been sixty, next year, had my body not wearied of living—not a good phrase. It wasn't weary of living, it had just put all it funds, to use a business metaphor, into a fast-growing stock, a runaway stock that converted the money into lucent lytic lesions. Oh, never mind. Some connections did not hold.

Nor was it an affair of the heart. I did not want her, and I was sure that she had no desire for me. It would become a dialogue, not Platonic, since I did appreciate her touch on my hand or shoulder, but not bloodless and dispassionate, either. We explored ideas and built on them, fleshed them, extended them, played with them, and transformed them.

I looked at her, as she was fussing with the drip lines. She had short black hair, framing a rodent-like face, evidence of a bad complexion, necklines and worry lines already. I was sure that the stress of nursing had taken its toll.

"We're short-staffed again today," she said

I was spewing information, "For the Kwakiutl, honor was one kind of wealth. You are familiar with the people?"

"Yes, I have a book on their art. I have a painting of an eagle spirit by Tim Paul. I—"

"Honors were displayed in masks, totems, or symbols. They were inherited. Honors were rare, usually won in battle or by some special feat. But, everyone, over the centuries of a lineage, had at least one honor, except for slaves, of course."

"What do honors—"

"Masks were the physical record of such honors. Masks were made from cedar, hinged, moveable, changeable, inside one another, the more complex masks in middle. The Kwakiutl had special masks for the Cannibal Society dance, where humans met supernatural birds at the edge of the universe; their beaks ranged from three to ten feet long, all the better to crush human skulls."

"I saw a video, Curtis I think—"

"They sometimes killed a slave and ate him during the dance. Other masks portrayed raven, the trickster, creator, or hawk, thunderbird, hummingbird, loon, owl, who was associated with death, silent, thunderbird, who was the personification of chief, lived in mountains, ate whales, or frog, sisiutl the two-headed sea-serpent, or salmon—the salmon people had five villages—"

"Why those figures? What about, hmmmm," she paused.

"The artist selected from animals in environment, from mosquito to whale. Some fantastic animals, such as sea wolf or thunderbird, were supernatural and mythical. Some were combined animals, partly human and partly natural, with human base figure."

"Why?"

" Because all beings were human and wore animal masks. When a salmon took of his mask, he was human. When a human put on a salmon mask she was a salmon. Human was the best known of animals."

"Everyone was equal!"

"Yes, exactly. Masks were either ephemeral for one ceremony or permanent. They were personal and had associated songs and dances. When a mask was given as a gift the right to the song and dance went with it. Some masks were repainted each time. Some masks were associated with specific ceremonies only, such as the wolf ritual or the cannibal society. The wolf ritual may have been a warrior ceremony at one time, to foster bravery and endurance. A few masks may have been portrait masks. Some masks were given titles, such as 'dead man' or 'woman singing'—"

"Was this a lecture? You taught this?"

"Guilty, I guess. I taught physical anthropology and archaeology."

Our dialogue was interrupted always after fifteen minutes, the most time she could spend with me or the longest of her breaks. I think the other nurses started teasing her. I could understand. I never saw any patient under fifty five; never saw any nurse over thirty-five. Never saw any doctor at all, except for the 1-minute morning round.

I was explaining how Tewalsu's family got the Dog-salmon

crest: "Once a young man showed great respect to a salmon that his family had dried. Unknown to him this respect cured the Chief of the Salmon of a terrible sickness. Later, the salmon, in their human bodies, without their salmon masks, came to the boy's house and took him home. And he lived with them, until it was time for the salmon runs. They gave him a salmon mask and he swam with them upstream until he reached the canyon where his village was. His uncle Raraotsren was fishing and caught this salmon so big he could hardly carry it. But, he made it back. Then, cutting it, he discovered his nephew alive. The dog-salmon became the crest for the family," I paused and looked at her standing by the table, "What are you sketching? Can't you sit?"

She was scribbling and answered without looking up, "I have some ideas for the collages, but I want to make them more interactive, multimedia—those aren't the right words. Look," she said, turning her pad, "the collage is centered, on the right are a few lines—"

"Poetry?" I asked, "very orientale."

"And to the right of that are musical notes."

"Why not have living music?"

"No, I wanted it to be two-dimensional in its presentation," she answered. "Besides, if I had music playing while people looked then I should have the poetry read, in which case I may not want to include it with the art."

We both paused. I reached up and touched her chin then regretted it. She said nothing.

"What if you put the poetry above the mask then the notes above the poetry?" I suggested.

"Levels of abstraction?" she asked.

She was developing amazingly fast, faster than any of my students ever had. All this in a week. I wondered what she did at home.

I was telling her how Coyote used masks to get out of bad situations: "Coyote put on the deer mask and jumped out into the center room, dying immediately in a clever wooden trap. Always-at-the-Coast said to his daughter, 'Serves him right for embarrassing me, Dress the deer,' and he went out to meet with his friends. Coyote took of the deer mask and went back to bed with the daughter. The next night Always heard laughing, so he just made another trap. The next morning, coyote put on the goat mask and the whole scene repeated. The third night Always heard sounds of love-making and laughter and again asked who was there. His daughter said, 'my husband.' Always made another trap the next morning. Coyote put on the bear mask and went out and crushed the trap, then sat down to eat."

"And?" she always wanted to hear the end of stories, while I only wanted to use part of them for illustration.

"They lived happily ever after."

"Tell me the rest."

So, I did.

"Time for you to show me what you are doing," I demanded.

"Nothing is finished."

"Nonsense, nothing is ever finished," I said, "it is just abandoned at certain stages at certain times, or sold. Let me see something, or I'll withhold my vital signs."

"Very funny," she smiled, and the smile transformed her face from a serious drone to a conduit of joy. "Let me present it though, and it is not finished."

"Okay, just show me."

"Okay, okay. Here." She held up a collage making a deer face of hide, aluminum trailer skirting, pine needles, and some other materials. The poem was title 'Deer as Mask for Snow.'

"Read it to me," I ordered.

She read: "At night in the field / her glance is a challenge:
Are you whole? / Can you be so complacent in snow?"

I listened as she went on. I understood what she was doing. It was a perfect idea.

"And the music?" I asked.

She hummed a few bars, and then said, "You can see it would fit with the words as they are read."

"But would it fit with a simultaneous visual inspection of the deer?" I asked.

"I thought of that," she said, "But, I don't know how to emphasize it, without specific instructions to the viewer, on what corner to start with, or whether to start at a distance, on the whole, then focus on specific details—"

"Good thinking, why not right down several directions or sets, and keep them for now. I'd bet that a serendipity of the viewers might contribute something new anyway, for instance—"

And, our precious break was over.

As soon as Risa appeared at 10:00, I started, "A mask must be made under certain conditions for specific rituals. The conditions are meaningful and useful. Do you use a ritual? The tools for making masks may be sacred. The tools contribute to the formation of the mask as a supernatural being. However, the mask may not be at full power until it is worn by an individual. The mask is the actual presence, not just a symbol or representation. In New Britain, the mask worn by the eldest son of the deceased has the specific function of helping the group overcome conflict—"

She was needling in the medications, mostly antibiotics and mineral supplements, but nodding as she listened.

"The mask is two-way conduit," I continued. "It is used by people to influence the dead to take action to favor the living, but also the mask is a way for the dead to intervene in the lives of their descendants. The older the mask, the stronger it is. It has power.

"For example, for the Desana people in the Amazon, the dead normally exist as animals in the surrounding forest, but for feasts, they dress up with masks so they can appear to the living. The masks are symbols of terrestrial but not human existence. The dead also dance to celebrate the arrival of a kinsman. Masks are also a warning to marry outside the group. The masks can physically show, with warts and wounds, the consequences of failing to follow the rules of marrying outside the group.

Through the masks, all sounds become the voices of nature, which are filled with meaning and awaken profound awareness and reactions beyond the dull sense of normalcy and security."

"What do you think about?" she asked. "Are you writing something?" she nodded to the laptop.

"An article," I lied. Not quite a lie, since I had worked on an article yesterday. But, lately I had finished my obituary, instructions to my wife for a good Irish wake, recipe for apricot bread, which I had never written down, stuff like that. The obituary was not easy. What had I accomplished? Did I have one discovery or one theory associated with my name. I suppose I had found a scroll of fragments once—Leukippus, it was still being preserved and translated. "How is the class going?"

"I think there are two types of people: Those who flee the center and those who seek it. I am a fleer. I need this kind of class to stay in some kind of orbit or I'll end up in interplanetary space," she looked at my chart.

"Why not show me another collage?" I asked, unsure of how to respond to this glimpse into her.

"Okay," she responded eagerly. I do not know why she was so shy with her work. I was in awe of it. Then, I wondered if I was being sentimental because I was dying. Maybe, but I was definitely more alert and focused.

She held up the next one. '3. Sediment as the Mask of Passion' It showed a face in sandstone, lying at a thirty-degree angle; details of the face showed a fireplace, bicycle, baby bassinet, The expression on the face must have been Beethoven as he was composing.

She was reading the words from the calligraphic form: "We reduce expressions to words / And these are covered over / By the motions of living. / Feelings fade / And form a sediment / Pressure from the weight / Of feelings compresses / Memories into layers, and these / Are heated like carbon in rock / And assume a crystalline form.

"Continents Of consciousness float / On layers of dense experience. / The world is composed / Of thousands of feet of ragged memories, / Plates broken by shifting, / Floating on a molten core.

"Heaved by inner turmoil, pieces / Penetrate the surface and invite / A deeper archaeology. The mind excavates / And elevates them to the clouds.

"What do you think?" she asked.

"The music?" I growled. My voice was changing as I could not keep enough water down.

This evening I was hooked up to three different drip systems. In addition to meds, I had sugar water to keep me hydrated and a separate potassium line, which burned the shit out of my hand and arm as it entered.

"Here's the ice pack," Risa came storming in. "I don't know why Eddie didn't think of that when he hooked you up."

"A mask also has a double function you know. A mask is a means to cover, conceal or disguise the face to protect one's identity. For instance, the old fart mask I am wearing now covers my pain and discomfort, as well as disappointment and anger."

"And it's a good mask, too. I can't see the pain," she smiled.

"But a mask is used traditionally to reveal identity, also. Like a figure worn by a Greek actor to identify a character. It makes things more noticeable by emphasizing certain features,"

"Such as a high-brow, like yours, for nobility?" she asked, smiling.

"Ha. Things normally invisible, or unnoticed, are then visible," I growled, beginning to sound like Nick Nolte. Actually I was beginning to look like him, too, as I lost weight. "Art is metaphorical. The metaphorical aspect goes beyond normal activity. It is 'as if' the dream was true, as if the hidden reality was exposed and described. Art distinguishes the extra-ordinary. It makes the ordinary special, by combining it with the hidden. Art enables people to act as if they were animals or gods. Masks enable people to become other things, animals or gods. Now, show me the next series before I scream."

"I'd have to hit you with the laptop, but I do have another one."

She showed me a collage of a face that seemed to be made of different kinds of light. I was not sure how to describe it. Light after a storm, light reflected by a pond, light directly from the sun, or reflected from the moon. I reached for it, but she held it back.

She read: "8. Flesh as Mask for Light /

Leaves grow at angles from the stem / So that each collects the light. / Light falls slowly like the dust / That leaves collect; it is held / And its crust forms the mask we see.

The leaves are burned by day—"

And as she was reading, I entered a dimension of invisible meaning. I looked at her face as she read; she looked like Debra Winger I thought. She had changed a little, but I wasn't sure how, exactly. When I heard her again, she was finishing.

"Thin dry pages that once transmuted the / Sun to flesh lie folded like meanings.

"Do you like it?"

"Like it? It inspires me to want to write, to say something as a puzzle for others to play with. I am tired of explaining. I want to create confusion! Ambiguity!"

"How biblical," she noted.

Later, Risa interrupted me as I was planning my escape. My wife had visited after work, and I had told her I would be able to come home for good in a week. I needed to convince the doctors, first, or sign myself out if I could not.

"What are you doing?" she asked.

"Singing, obviously," I said, "Putting new lyrics to Bobby Darin songs. 'Somewhere beyond disease, waiting for cee . . . no more saline . . ."

"First, stop for a second. I need the arm, William."

"Please, Will," I said. She was wearing the professional care career mask I noticed, but I refrained from saying that to her. I just offered my forearm to her for the blood pressure.

"It's high," she noted.

"Notice where I am?" I asked. "Hospital culture raises the pressure. Speaking of culture, the true architects of culture have been the artists, propagandists, who are just artstitutes, and poets; the poets provided the images and national archetypes. Territory-grabbing wars may provide heroes for the popular imagination, like this soldier Jessica—who is a hero only because she survived and was the object of the heroism of others—if she was a hero, she should have avoided being captured—but poets and writers make the identities. The real identity of heroes and leaders is provided by the propagandists and poets; the heroes and leaders only provide a clothes hook. Their mask is determined by cartoonists and writers.

"Previous uses of masks shocked people. Picasso, for instance, borrowed mask shapes from Zaire for faces in 'The Women of Avignon.' Newer mask forms could raise questions about human ecological identity, using industrial forms and materials to express universal concerns. Ah, shit. Could you get me an orange popsicle?" I asked.

As she paused, I suggested, "Leave that with me and I'll look at it."

For the first time, she handed me the collage. I waited until she left before scanning it. '15. The Visible as Mask for the Invisible.' The face was made of leaves and shadows; the mouth opened to a dark maw. The eyes were complex veins. I read the story:

'One leaf, then another, frees its stem
And weaves a spiraled loop—
The leaf we see in turning becomes invisible
And another appears. This is the operation
Of mystery: leaves turn and present us
With the strangeness of a hidden side.
They tease us—from a different
Perspective, the leaf we think we know
Turns and disappears; the new side visible
We see and name and it becomes invisible
Again. Leaves acquire full existence
By turning.
Turning is revelation: secrets
Open. Things turn and are renewed.
Which way do wolves turn,
Before lying down? Which way do whirlpools turn
Or whirlwinds? The twist of oak or sycamore;
The maze of tree and lichen, or rock and moss;
The twist of a hole dug by a skunk; snakes
Coiling; the lay of cedar or balsam fronds;
Hawks wheeling, shrikes hunting; the turn
Of a shell; the helix of light or the spin
Of galaxies?'

I hummed the music, as I reviewed the collage and reread the words. Then I tried reversing the procedure by reading first. Then I leaned over and reached her notebook. I suppose she thought I would; perhaps she planted it there and then decided to stay away long enough for me to look through it. Of course, she seemed to be too shy, and she probably got caught in some emergency to help some other old fart.

I opened the book and let the first page open onto me. A dragonfly that composed a face, with rock and

'27. Fossils as Masks of the Past
Plants take carbon from the air; animals
Take plants and die themselves; carbon

In reused and deposited in earth. After
Death, this emperor of air must have
Been covered by sediment, his substance
Leached by water, minerals and silica
Filling cell walls, until only traces
Of life were left, sleeping in time.'

I pulled out the next page, with a cave wall showing a mask of a young woman, with the outline of ochre-figures and eroded coin faces.

31. Sleep as a Mask of Consciousness
She lay on her side, indifferent
In sleep
Slowly music, and light
Dancers around a fire
One held up a metal disk
She woke, gazing at the wall
Its smoothness dissolved
As from acid on a copper
Sesterce—Vespacian's profile
She blinked
Redimensioned.
The smoothness was scored with scratches
As she watched
Scratches outlined figures sharply
Across a fissure
the code of mystery
Renewed in red.

Then ten more spilled out and I consumed them all greedily. The first, all done with animals, birds, insects forming a face in the sky. I could not judge the music, but it seemed to fit and extend the opening.

10. Sound as a Mask for the Invisibly Large
The parts lack visible connection, but a minnow
Recognizes another minnow, and birds hear other
Birds as each marks out a territory. Birds inform
The fish of the Pacific about the state
Of vegetation in the Cascades. Each living
Being has its own sphere and these overlap
Around the earth. The bark of a fox or twitter
Of a sparrow contribute to the whole. The earth
Is a great round beast.

19. Dust as the Mask of Chaos
He sweeps the crumbs to the floor
And stands, scratching more signs

On the blackboard. The stone rests
In the chaos of dust on the floor.
Incandescent light leaves the window.
34. Shadow as the Mask of Light
It is the way—all movement turns to heat.
You burn and rise from the ashes.
As the phoenix burned the wind stirred
The ashes and rose—
The sky darkened with torrential rain
But the helix turned and the code remained.
The ashes expanded and steamed; something
Moved and fought its way out—
Dark nebula—
Molten red metallic bird renewed.
Your feathers are now metallic
You alter yourself to survive
But only you notice the change
And the change is irreversible.
How much of your life does the shadow
Take as its own?

35. Metal as the Mask of Energy
Who has seen the ghosts in metal
Of particles from the center,
The iridescent center of the earth
And heard the murmurings distilled
From hard collisions; radiation
From its primordial being trapped
In matter patterns from cycles
Of stars and faintly glowing bodies?
There is history in metal
And it has meaning. Stars have history
And it lives in human memory. Faint
Pulses from the sun echo in waves
In the brain. The rhythm of the sea
Invades the copper-lead of dreams.
The battery is made and charged
Remembers ghosts in metal.

16. Light as the Mask of Darkness
Elements fuse in the hearts
Of stars; light is the waste.
After millions of years in the center
Of a star, light is pushed
Toward the cup of space

Binding emptiness together.
Tracing the geometry of chaos
The world is made with light
Light reweaves its mesh
Countless times with reflections
From the ground and moon and sea
Before it leaves . . . .

I scanned the rest of them.

18. The Moon as Mask for the Earth
The sun and earth double-bodied
Behind the moon
Scatter bright seeds that
Bloom in space . . . .

6. Tree as Mask for Life
Bare branches offer
a network of support . . .
Roots offer grounding . . . .

17. Cathedral as Mask of the Forest
We live in a metaphysics of light
And only need to look to our cathedrals
To be reminded. We have created a forest
Of filtered mists where radiance is stained
And dimmed to fit our minds. When the sun
Sets behind the sea, its last ray is green . . . .

I put them down. Some were unfinished. One or two was brilliant. I realized that I was not going to be able to leave, now, as much as I wanted to be out of this barren room in this functional ward. I could not give up, abandon, the conversation. I sighed. I could see her talking with another nurse at the central station. I was happy. I was unhappy. I was confused.

I reached over the laptop and grabbed a pen. I sketched a drawing of a face underwater, in a stream, composed of hide and horn, beer can tabs and cans. I started writing some words, only poetic vanity perhaps:

Bear masks, elk masks traced
On the wall of the cave.
We put on their skins and faces
To learn how they behaved.
They were kin and we needed them
As they needed wolves and men.

We took only the weakest, sick and old.
Their strength was ours, we would
not let it diminish or grow cold.
Now the elk are silent, photographs
Show only hide and not the motive.
The real face is never seen.
Now others kill the strongest for trophies
And dismiss our art.
The image of the elk is seen on cans
In the stream—
The image of the bear on boot polish.
The bear was our father, elk helped
Us to be human.
We changed ourselves to fit the earth
We fit ourselves to please the earth.
Now—

Now what, I wondered.

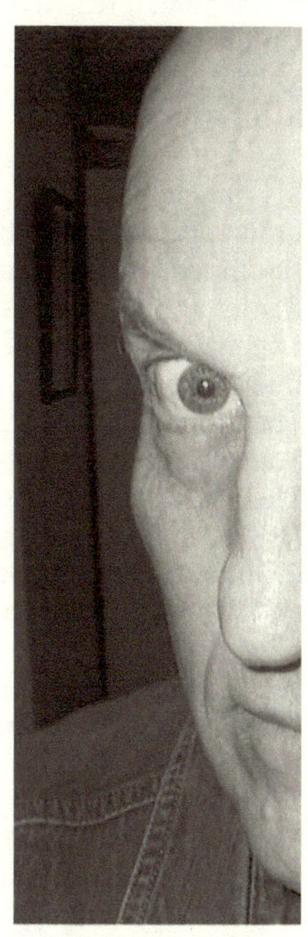

**Nothing Happened (Gratitude for Evolution)**
by Gert Frump (as recorded by Violet Reason)

The street was empty.
It was early.
The air was cold.
I could see vapor coming from my mouth.

No cars were parked on the streets.
A few screaming french fry cartons shared
the sidewalks with broken
glass, yellowed newspaper pages, brown leaves.
The laundromat and pizza delivery place were closed.
Cars coasted by, encasing and displaying
their important baggage.
Squirrels looked up, impressed.

I drew a breath in through both nostrils.
Fortunately, these nostrils had been selected from ancestors
who had lived in cold climates, so the air was warm
by the time it reached my lungs.
Unfortunately, my nose was cold.
Maybe no one else had such ancestors and had to stay inside
to breath warm air.

My hat blew off.
I ran to catch it, sprinting as it bounced off the pavement.
I tromped it with a foot,
Earlier ancestors had chased game less fervidly.
I knew that hunters had more fun chasing in childhood games
than being chased.
They tried harder to catch than be caught.
Young deer, on the other hand, had more fun being chased.
They tried harder to escape.
However, I was not amused.
Having caught my hat, I still had to punch it out into shape
and wear it another mile.

A house attracted my attention.
Queen Anne or Federal, I could not tell.
I admired the shell.
Three exterior doors.
My ancestors had built from parts of trees also.
And, having finished the form, embellished it with designs
and carvings and paintings, instead of gingerbread,

railings, and wrought iron.
Six weeks to build a frame, but ten to decorate it.
What was the significance of decoration?
Starving Eskimos took the time to carve features on bone.
Still, three good exits.

A cloud slid by.
Its puffed, ambiguous features reminded me
I had a meeting with the 'toad.'
I would never call him that—one never knew
who was an enemy
or ally until they declared themselves.
It would not be wise for me to try to determine
which through some automatic glandular action.
Not that enemies did not become allies,
or vice versa, according
to some cosmic rotation.
Without any prompting from me.
Everything turned.
It was good to know that.
A continental turned by the elementary school.

The meeting was about my program for typesetting an ad.
My brain kept circling an idea, looking for an angle.
I heard a theory once that the brain had evolved as the result
of increased oxygen in the atmosphere—its function was to
rid the body of that poisonous gas.
The plants were not trying to poison us on purpose, I guess.
They were just trying to get rid of wastes, too.
It certainly seemed a more logical use for the brain than
Ballast, planning, or redundancy for dead cells from chasing
Antelope down the savanna in sweltering heat.

Maybe ballast, maybe planning; with those big brains,
Society had recreated nature in miniature.
A nature as ruthless, illogical, and indifferent as the real thing.
Some people had assumed the roles of predators, the lions
of literature, the hyenas of wall street;
others were scavengers, the crows and eagles of the city.
And, there were the herd animals, plants, bacteria,
insects, and decomposers.
I liked the decomposers.
You could talk to them.
No role hang-ups.
The 'toad' had role hang-ups, but he flattened

himself before any
threat and refused to budge.
I never touched him.

Now, I thought of the program for the ads.
What was I? DNA's puppet?
Bringing the might of evolution, the weight
of the history of life,
the point of culture, and the blanket of communications,
to bear on a project of the most stunning insignificance:
an ad to sell football on television.
The program offered the most sophisticated
letter spacing and
typesetting possible.
Every letter would be resolutely designed and defined.
And, presumably, superior to those used
by Amnesty International or Greenpeace.
News of football presented more beautifully and perfectly than
the discoveries of science or the poetry of space.

What would happen if I did not bother finishing the program?
Would football become unpopular?
Other sports, less competitive, then shape
the characters of children to be more forgiving?
Then society be at peace with everything on earth?
Or would the race drift into a genetic sink, all potential
radiated away in good manners and tea?
Who knew, maybe the crudeness of type
would reflect the spirit of the game.
It would become more popular and other sports
would shrink away.

I walked into the brick building and up the stairs,
past another crushed Mcdrink cup.
Technology unleashed.
We can carry fluids with us, instead of hunting them in pools.
We just do not want to reuse the containers.
We have more waste than plants.
I wonder what could be evolving on that waste?

Nothing happened today.

## Astrophysical Golf

By Ruadh dal Riata

Dear Noan,
I was rummaging about in all my university papers, prior to recycling them, and I found parts of interviews that I think you would be interested in — perhaps use for your research on the origins of the Earth-Mars Catastrophes. I've written a small introduction for it. Since Margaret's writing a full letter to follow, I'll just end this here. Hope you can use the stuff. Reminds me, we'll have to play a couple of rounds in Arguary — I'll never get used to these Calistan months — when I'm on sabbatical.
Yours,
Rennet

*Background*
In the early 1990s, before the university systems were integrated into the corporations, several institutions began experimenting with variations in the standard programs. In a parting shot at fiscal responsibility, the University of Bellburg proposed to merge a strictly academic discipline with a money-earning department, to give respectability to one and security to the other. Almost immediately, home economics merged with chemistry, and philosophy with forestry, for example, with the startling results: the calories in a chocolate cookie could be tabulated to six decimal places, and it could be determined, finally, whether or not a tree falling in the forest without witnesses made noise. It was no surprise when many departments wooed physical education to merge with them.

After months of offer and cross-offer, physics emerged as the successful suitor. The remaining departments coupled afterwards, with Art sharing its studios with Business Administration, Economics sharing fantasies with Mythology and Classics, and Psychology entering the labs of Electrical Engineering, to the satisfaction of almost everyone concerned (except perhaps Drama, whose proposal for a show and tell program with Journalism fell through when that department combined with Asian Studies). Of course, by far the most successful and innovative marriage was that of Physics and Physical Education — Body Mechanics. It was that department that was responsible for electromagnetically suspending dwarf, primordial black holes, possibly five billion years old, in the center of each green of the university's eighteen hole golf course. Astrophysical golf became the rage. Lowgaard Massey was the brain who fathered the idea. The following is part of an interview conducted by columnist Pauli Trigwell.

*First Fragment*

"Professor Massey, wasn't there a cutthroat departmental scramble to determine which department would be allowed to merge with a large revenue generator like physical education?"

"Yes, Pauli, I suppose there was. The Interreligions Studies — that's over in the administration building on the floor beneath computer sciences, was our toughest rival; it was bloody war. You know, of course, that the Rabbi Tung O'Malley already was advertising his course offerings: trendy stuff like "Radical Theology and the Death of Golf," "Wrestling and the New Morality," "Dance and the Bible," "Exercise and Theological Thought," "Zen and the Art of Baseball," "The Ethics of Missionary Volleyball," and "Talmudic Ping-Pong." I was worried that we might have gotten stuck with Drama."

"Now that the Regents have finalized the decision, how soon will you implement your courses, and what will they be like?"

"I'm really happy. I'm sure that the university has made a wise decision. We're all really eager to start a new season; in fact, I have the staff running through their plays—I mean courses—right now."

"I see that you've been working with Coach Glurtus. Tell us, what kind of courses?"

"Coach Glurtus, yes . . . uhmmm, we have a rather sophisticated offering: starting with the basics, we have kinetic kinesiology, biophysical physiology, you know. . . . But the real meat of the curriculum is in the Sports Dynamics section. This semester we'll have Astronomical Archery (you know, shooting for the stars), Swimming and Wave Motion Laboratory, Quantum Basketball — "

"Pardon me, but could you explain some of these?"

"I guess so, sure. Quantum Basketball, hhmmm, the use of theories in physics to improve player's jump shots and give them experience in fast breaks; court divided up into shells: F, G, and so on. Ahhh, Electrodynamic Baseball: hitting without static, theory of attraction of particles; of course, the field is everything. Some are less interesting, but required courses: statistical dance mechanics, coaching and radiation instrumentation, nuclear wrestling workshop, mechanical gymnastics, and the weight training and optics laboratory — all those mirrors you know made that logical work—."

"Could you be a little more specific about the benefits involved; have student test scores improved? Has the quality of education decayed?"

"The advantages of this are all too numerous to mention, but I'll try. A theory of inertial tackling, which came out of one course, the Entropy of Football, allowed the team to win three of eleven games in the new aerodrome dome, and by relativistic score keeping that's a winning record. You'd be amazed at how the dumbest players pick up the most difficult theory when it's taught in use; for instance, thermodynamics was easier to grasp after the players ran down hill; it never used to be a subject one could get heated up over. You realize, I hope, that the benefits are mutual: we were able, from the revenue from the football games alone, that including the Biology-Waste Resources's concession stand percentage, to purchase a new magnetohydrodynamicentropometer, which we've already tried out on the second string players with little loss of life. As for education, it's always depended on the fortunes of our athletic teams. 0h, you might say quality is up."

"You must be saving the best for last. What about your own course, about which we've heard so much?"

"Oh yes. Astrophysical Golf . . . golf, the most civilized of games, more relaxing than tennis, especially solid state tennis, more sophisticated than clionatic boxing — in all a spiritual game. Let me anticipate the next question. The thought occurred to me while several miles underground, doing my research into the possibility of point black holes penetrating the earth. Without going into detail, I ran out of lead shielding, couldn't find anything dense enough other than golf balls — Sforzer 50s, I believe — which I put in the center of my atrivac detector. To make a long story short, I caught one, and immediately thought up a game for it, as well as a reason for catching more, since it immediately swallowed a golf ball. Why not Astrophysical Golf?"

"Why not? How are they put on the golf course? Isn't it dangerous? Are they easy to catch?"

"Oh, they're easy to catch now. We just keep one in the detector — we have a little green for it — until it can be moved to the electromagnetohydrodynamic device surrounding each hole of the golf course; we just have seventeen, now, but expect—"

"Perhaps you could use simpler language, as many of our readers aren't Ph.D.s or, well, even college graduates."

"Well, I'm sure they'll get it, written out like this. Maybe in common language; gigantic hungry mouth kept in place by invisible bars of force, like a weird circus in a nightmare landscape. Ahh, where were we?"

"I, well, what is a black hole, exactly?"

"Nothing exact, really. More of a horizon, an event horizon, a frozen event horizon, a spherical, frozen, event horizon, a one-way, spherical, frozen, event horizon, a—"

"Why is it called a black hole?"

"Because all light is absorbed by it, and none can be reflected or escape."

"What is a white hole, then?—I'd heard the term used once—the opposite of a black hole?"

"Actually, it's a black hole covered by golf balls."

"Ha ha. But it can't be covered, can it? Doesn't it swallow everything?"

"Well, let's see. . . background: nothing is faster than light in space; gravity is an intrinsic property of space that affects light; light has mass and mass is correlated with gravity: a sufficient quantity of mass curves light, as the mass increases the light curves more, when the mass reaches a critical figure the light bends into perfect curvature — sort of like men's eyes wrapping around a perfect breast. All this mass within a certain small area, with a gravitational attraction greater than the velocity of light ensures that nothing will ever escape its field."

"Please, no smutty references. Won't it suck up the universe?"

"Oh, ho, ho, no. Most people are only familiar with the devolution of neutron stars into rather large black holes — the trouble with America is everyone's lust for sheer size — look at the size of the mammaries on monthly magazine covers."

"Please! You mean that there are other sizes — where?"

"All sizes, but only one color and one shape, like a Hershey bar. My theory of the formation of the universe, which I call the Big Orgasm Theory, allows for the creation of millions of holes — space must be filled with them. Look, the universe began as one gigantic — one megagigagigantic ball — one load about to be—"

"Don't say it!"

"spe—err, uhh, technical term then. In last millennium's favorite theory, Anaxagoras called them sperms, seeds. Suddenly, without so much as a hot look, it shot in all directions; the larger aggregations formed galaxies which all broke into smaller spinning bits, and so on, but we all know about that; what also happened was that, various sizes of black holes formed at once, too. Some of these simultaneous whirls of activity were unable to expand against gravitational self attraction; so we have bite-size black holes. Their gravity is proportional to their size."

"Why don't they just expand?"

"They can't; remember, they can't exceed the Schwarzschild radius — that's the term to describe the critical distance, which edge is also the event horizon. The S-radius for the earth would be one centimeter, ah, one cigarette filter. One puff, and poof."

"Turgid stuff, physics. So this hole causes space to fold over and nothing breaks out. How do you ever see it?"

"It has a halo around it, of bent light, tortured nuclear reactions."

"Why doesn't it suck everything in it?"

"Its gravitational attraction isn't that strong, if it only weighs, say, a million kilograms."

"Then you could hold it in your hand?"

"Well, no, it would go straight through your hand, toward the center of the earth — don't forget the earth has a much greater attraction than your hand, although —."

"So, how do you keep it still, in place?"

"Ahh, it's rotating and because it's rotating, it has a charge — don't you get charged rotating on someone? So we keep it in place by magnetic field."

"(groan) Is that how you caught it?"

"Yes, with strength, magnetism, a grasp of things, luck, prayer, voodoo, and anti-event geoderant."

"Hmmm, how will all this technology alter the game of golf?"

"Well, it should make the golfer's game easier—"

"Wait a minute! Black holes on each green as the hole? But, but doesn't it?"

"It does, of course it does — it attracts the ball when it comes within 20 centimeters and takes it ."

"But, but doesn't it swallow it?"

"Swallow it, yes; it captures it and it falls into the horizon."

"Then it's gone forever?"

"No. Not really, you could follow it, if you got careless; all kidding aside, the ball would take a finite length of time to reach the radius, if you were there to measure it; but to the golfer, it would take forever; he could see it there, forever.

"But, but wouldn't it —"

"No, relativity, relativity; it would appear to be frozen on the surface; every one it ever swallowed would be there; layers on layers, like a painting."

"But isn't that a tremendous waste?"

"No, no, economics, economics; industries must grow, produce, produce; this would be a boon to industry, an unlimited need for golf balls."

"But wouldn't the hole get larger, with all that mass adhering to it, and all?"

"Henh. Very perceptive of you; true it would. I, umm, haven't solved that one problem yet; there are no reasons to hurry, however. We have about 20 or 30 years before the mass increases enough to break the hold of the magnetic field. As the number of golf balls increases, the surface area will enlarge, as the square of the mass.

There won't be any real cause for worry; science always comes through at the last. It might even improve things. Remember what those nuclear generator catastrophes in the eighties and nineties did for the weather, and what the—"

"What about the green? Wouldn't it get swallowed up?"

"Well, actually . . . I'm glad you mentioned that. Let me write myself a note to increase the size of the holes in the green; from four inches diameter to about twelve. Of course, the depth must be infinity, for all practical — Oh, that's going to ruin par; maybe if ball size increases —"

"Haven't you researched this yet? What if some unexplained, overlooked, unthought information should place civilization in peril?"

"Well, you needn't get snippety about it. The physics department has had funding troubles for years; working during lunch hours, with little thanks and old equipment. That was why we've finally merged with P.hys. Ed. A marriage of security. I used to have to pay for my own computer cards. That's ended now, thank NSF; I only—"

"All right, okay. So who's funding it now? And why golf?"

"The Spaulding Company volunteered to sponsor research; certain public relations problems had to be overcome; for instance, the initial projected loss of balls — no university can afford to lose all its balls — flags, putters, and some of the golfers themselves, were statistically high, and that was unacceptable, but we managed to emphasize the machismo aspect, and compare it to bull fighting. Hey, There's an idea — we could make—"

"The funding?"

"Oh, oh. . . well, the clinching argument was put forth by Duelgoody, our lab technician. He jokingly proposed that Spaulding manufacture balls out of trash and garbage. What a waste disposal solution this would be. By manufacturing one million trash balls a day, we could solve the problems of the whole earth."

"Wow! But enough of the economics for now. How would this change the rules of golf?"

"Well, the physicists would get to use it every night, probably late night trysts. You know how teenagers go out and —"

"The rules?"

"Oh, the rules would still be much the same. Par, of course, would be determined or re-evaluated according to the skill of the department head. Then of course in place of iron putters extremely light weight plastic ones would be recommended. No-spike shoes would definitely be *de rigueur,* with all that electronic equipment underneath the green. Golf etiquette would be altered. For instance, one would not place the flagstick in the hole, never! Nor should one attempt to rescue balls, flags, or other golfers from the holes. In fact, do not approach the hole with bags or vehicles — do not approach the hole! Ever! Perhaps no one should be allowed to walk on the course; A-G golf could become like electronic pinball. You know, play in the clubhouse by remote control — or why not from home, even?"

"Are you saying that the putting green itself would be a hazard?"

"Yes. And there would be side effects: an increase in dubs due to failure of nerve; then, the death penalty would be—"

—click—

*Second Fragment*

"I remember going to one of those black-hole golf courses on earth, remember thinking how enlightened it seemed. Life on earth was a virtual paradise, for a while, warm, safe, exciting; we finally had made the earth comfortable.

"It was somewhere in Australia, I think, that careless — or greedy — officials allowed a hole to grow massive enough to swallow its magnetic field and plunge to the center of the earth. After that, nothing else mattered; the earth was eating itself. Other disasters followed, and the crust itself — everyone knows that the crust is always eaten last — entered the horizon within $10^9$ seconds after the story began.

"Fortunately, most of humankind was saved. Science triumphed! Giant corn husks made by Agricultural Engineering, powered by oatmeal solid fuel from the Chemical Home Economics department were able to transfer almost the entire population to Mars. And recycled, afterwards, too. Then the final tragedy struck when the entire Masters tournament was caught with its cornhusks open at the seventh hole in Georgia. On a clear night through the telescopes we can still see them, green coats and white shoes and all, watching that bogey two, when the earth became a hole in one.

"Life is difficult for everyone here on Mars, what with the thin air and sand-traps; still, with redesigned nine irons . . . hmmm—"

—click— *finis*

## The Science of Figitology

by Jim Gear

"Watching you is like watching the feelers on a cricket—they never stop moving. Could you just sit down and relax?"

"I can't help it, I like to fidget," Maria answered.

"I don't think that's fidgeting, that's compulsive cleaning and straightening and stuff."

"No, it's just fidgeting," she insisted.

"Come, here, let me hug you. That's better. Now stop squirming. Be romantic. Lie still. Yes, very good. You can move your lips now. Hmmm."

As a measure of respect, I decided to make her pathetic affliction into a recognized medical condition, or failing that, into a fledgling science. Fidgeting, or Figiting, has to do with the science and the nature of time, from working, walking and moving, to random motion. As we all know, movement is life.

Science is basically another form of socially constructed reality. There are dozens of ways of deconstruction now, each decreating and disintegrating some part of culture, each demystifying and decomposing something.

The Operation of Modern Science is quite straightforward. Like all knowledge, especially the traditional kind that sustained us for forty thousand years; science starts with observation, the observation of plants and animals, and weather and land changes. And, like traditional knowledge it makes guesses and generalizations about the things and relations that are observed. And, like traditional knowledge, it makes predictions about the future.

Where science is different is that it analyzes the thing into components and then measures them so they can be quantified. It also formulates law from its generalizations and describes them mathematically. And develops theories to *predict* new phenomena. Theories can lead to new conclusions and sometimes altered perspectives about phenomena. A scientific theory is a statement that postulates ordered relationships among natural phenomena and explains some aspect of the world. It allows one to ask certain kinds of questions, some as specific hypotheses. Finally, the theories and hypotheses are tested in a controlled environment.

Natural science consists of facts and theories. A scientific fact is a class of historical facts. One cannot understand the first without understanding the second. No one can answer the question what nature is unless she knows what history is. Every cosmology includes ideas of the past, present and future. An ontology of temporal process would provide a global perspective on world order. For Figitology to be a science, there must be principles, laws and theories. Within general topics, such as history or ecology, a number of characteristics, principles, and standards can be presented that should allow you to address every situation (to some extent).

Characteristics are qualities that distinguish unique individuals, systems, or patterns; Gregory Bateson calls them differences that make a difference. For example one characteristic is that a figiter cannot stand still.

Principles are fundamental rules or laws. For example, 'n' limits the number of species in a niche (the competitive exclusion principle). Specific to this, two figiters can not be in the same room at the same time.

Standards are models or examples of quality or value established by authority or consent. Normal figiting at rest expresses at least 16 nervous ticks per minute.

We will also need some propositions. A proposition says something about a thing, asserting or denying. Propositions can be tested for truth. The word "is" is a logical construct in Aristotelian logic; its function is to glue the subject to the predicate. Mathematical logic distinguishes 5 functions of this construct:

1. identity, "That is Maria."
2. equality, "the sine of 90 degrees is 1"
3. membership, "Maria is a conservative."
4. class inclusion, "figitological science is a science."
5. predication, "Maria is smart."

Now, we are ready to build the system of figitology using these laws, principles and theories. First a few universal laws:

The principle of lawfulness (true): Every fact satisfies some laws or can be analyzed in lawful components. The really possible states of a system can be contained in a box of all logically possible states (a lawful state space). Principle is confirmed when new patterns are found, but cannot be proved.

The principle of uniformity (false): Laws are the same throughout the universe. For this to be true, evolutionary quantum figiting must be left out of consideration.

Figitological principles are summarized as:

- Everything affects everything else: the holocoenotic relatedness is intuitive in reverence for figiting and leads to the practice of figiting.
- Every stillness is filled with movement. The environment is covered with a vast array of movements that interact and in

which figiters can create niches.

- Everything is used: there is energy flow for figiting; this energy is better expended figiting than in waiting for things to happen.
- Everything has a cost. The cost of figiting is energy and tiredness.
- Time can be long: limiting factors may not have a short time scale; figiting takes up that time in a kind of pre-preparedness ritual.
- Nature is productive: natural systems are prolific biologically and energetically. Figiting is a natural extension of quantum motion at the organismic level.
- Nature has limits: there is a  carrying capacity of energetic systems can sustain a given amount of figiting organisms.
- Nature creates differences: the diversity and stability of figisystems are necessary; diversity buffers the influence of a single perturbation in the figisystem.

More than simply principles, figiting is a kind of taoistic perspective. Instead of a sharp focus on a detail, figiting allows a complex, out-of-focus blur to incorporate all the details of the environment so that the desired blur may be contained within the surrounding blur. Let us say you want to clean a dish, bur you notice a pan from the previous night is dirty, so you start on the pan, then realize you had not had coffee, because the clean pan goes next to the coffee machine, which you cannot see well because you have not had coffee. Thus, figiting has permitted you to see the big picture and do what is needed as you start out doing unneeded things.

Theory is an explanation or system of everything. It is an exposition of the abstract principles of a science or a speculation. The dictionary definition states that a theory is a reasoned expectation, as opposed to practice.  A scientific theory is a set of general explanatory statements about a natural process; the set is related as a model, which is a human linguistic construction, subject to human perspectives and limitations. Theories may incorporate guesses, critical observations, experimentation, and logical inference, as well as hypotheses and laws. A theory must be a specific enough statement, such that experimental results can be assessed as negative or positive. The results of an experiment can confirm or justify a theory, although other experiments could show that the theory is wrong. Good theories tend to have a limited number of generalizations. Theories can also be nested, so that, for instance the theory of random-motion figitation might be combined with other theories in a unified field theory of figitation.

Although the theory of evolutionary figiting, for instance, is not a good basis for an ethics, its perspective can supply *principles* on which we could base values:

- It is good to remain adapted, within limits, and figiting allows faster adaptation to the environment
- It is essential to encounter the environment to which we are adapted and figiting is a form of pre-adaptation for countering
- It is essential not to destroy the environment to which we are adapted and figiting is a form of respectful restraint within the figi-niche.

In the larger view, evolution is value-free. Figiting provides the creation and destruction, beauty and ugliness, that are expressed in one complex pathway of random movement.

I want to present Figitology as a subconscious physiological-based strategy to cope with a chaotic universe. Things happen at random, therefore, random motion on your part allows you to perform more efficiently than if you had a plan based on partial knowledge of the chaotic system. For example, if you wanted to find your keys, instead of looking where they have logically been left, on the table by the front door, you should figit, that is, you should fix coffee, then as you go to the bathroom to get a new roll of paper towel, from under the sink, you may pass the hallway bookcase where you have left your purse, which contains your keys.

*Etymological Analysis of Figitology*

The word fidget is from the Old Norwegian word "fikya" to fidget. The dictionary definition is "the state of being restless, nervous, or uneasy." Other related words include "fidgety" and "fid" (also a round pointed tool for separating rope on a sailboat) or "fid" (from the Latin meaning to split, as in palmatifid, or perhaps trifid). Or "fid" from the Latin for faithful, fido or fiduciary or fidelity, being faithful). And "fiddle" means to play around. And, fideism is the belief that anything known about God with certainty has to come from faith, not reason. And finally, of course, "get" (from the Old Norwegian, "geta" to get). From the Latin "hendere" to grasp, to reach, to discover, to come to go to arrive to be to become—

"Aha! To be or become. That is basic life," you say?

"Well, to get wet, to become wet, to be wet. Where's the meaning in that? Never mind, these are just words layered on top of figiting motions."

*New words*

To be a science figitology also needs a special vocabulary of technical terms to separate it from common sense or other, less precise sciences, like economics and sociology.

Afigitable—without figiting, incapable of random movement
Archiofids—ancient sea animals that had to keep moving to live
Cinefidology—motion studies of the fidgeting process
Cinetology—science of motion
Contrafidacious—against figiting
Defidget—to stop figiting, to stop the process (see defigitate)
Digifid—one of the organs responsible for extra movement
Dormofidling—sleeping figiter, with movement in sleep
Fidchiropath—having insane fingers
Fidcocious—to be good at figiting
Fidectitude—the proper understanding of figiting
Fideo—recording of movement
Figit—moving in a healthy way
Fidgeteer—someone who pretends to figit without complete knowledge
Figiteer—someone who attempts to imitate a fidgeter without the nervous movements. (see fideomimicry or Disney)
Figiter—someone who figits consciously with knowledge and foresight
Figitology (see also Fidgetology)—the science of figiting (see also fidgeting)
Figilla—little figiting
Figissimus—greatest figiting
Fidonomy—the economics of figiting
Fidgetosis—too much figiting
Fidlock—the inability to move
Fidgister—a master fidgeter
Fidway—the tao of figiting
Fidden—the lure of movement
Grandifidacious—saying too much about it
Hydrofiding—figiting in the water
Hyperfidgelotic—too much figiting
Mysfid—a mouse who figits unlike other calm mice
Panfidget—someone who figits everywhere
Philofidous—love of fiddling around
Polyhexamethylfidamine—the molecule that causes figitosis
Pseudofidiness—false figiting
Viridifidenvy—green with envy of a practicing figiter

## Sociogeology: Minerals and Human Behavior

By Achilles Chert[1] (edited by Violet Reason)

What is the meaning of life? Do minerals determine human fate? "Does the Absurd dictate death?" asks Albert Camus, a novelist who lionized the labors of Sisyphus in moving the igneous concretion up the declivitous landmass. Camus wonders if the human struggle up the mountain of life is worth the—but, enough philosophy! These questions can be examined on a more fundamental basis. I raised them in order to characterize the essence of a new academic discipline, SocioGeology. Will Durant, the Historian, recognized that civilization existed by consent of geology—"subject to change without notice." Our whole modern culture is based on mineral wealth. Furthermore, humanity arose from rock. As the poet Gary Snyder said, those were not just rocks, they were "peopling rocks."

There are those who say that people are puppets of their genes; and others who say that our human behavior is controlled by biological limits. I believe that both are wrong, that there is a more basic determinant. The general definition of sOciogEology is the study of the geological basis of human behavior. It explains human behavior by empirical descriptions of the attributes of our mineral composition. As a science, it is most successful when it provides detailed descriptions of particulate phenomena and first-order correlations with features of the physical environment. One of its primary functions is to reformulate the current shaky foundations of the social sciences in a way that draws them into a modern synthesis with the hard sciences, that is, makes them more concrete.

This article is an outline of the codification of sociOgeOlogy into a branch of evolutionary geology. The subject has an aggregate of self-sufficient concepts to be ranked with such proven disciplines as astrology and cosmetology. Figure 1 shows the schema borrowed from my previous book, *The Intact Societies: Vestal Virgins and Volcanoes*, which suggests how such an amalgam can be achieved. Geologists have always been intrigued by comparisons between societies of rocks and those of vertebrate mammals, between the two really active kingdoms. My goal is to use the same parameters and quantitative theory to analyze both societies. When this has been completed, we will have a unified science at the lowest common denominator.

*Figure 1. Book Outline for SociogeologY*

The morality of rock in the Fossil record
Elementary Concepts: Toasting the Crust
Principles of Population Geology
  a-, r-, and p-processes and r- and k-selection
  Groups size, reproduction and isostasy
  Energy budgets and mineral spinning
  Interior temperature and glacial gruss
Communication and Atmospheric Interaction
  Sea-floor spreading and graded signals
  Signal economy and continental shelf-life
  Deflation in a windy economy
  Information erosion
From Sociogeology to Religion
  Plasticity and Greywacke
  Dominance Systems and Mass
  Esthetics and Schist
  Regolithic Religiosity

*Parallels.* Consider for a moment rock (*Cataclysmus eruptus*) and deer (*Odocoileus virginianis*). Both form into cooperative groups that furnish the landscape and provide entertainment and grist for thought. Group members communicate important things, such as hunger, alarm, rank, and sexual desire, among themselves by means of nonsyntactical signals.[2] Individuals are aware of the difference between members and nonmembers of their group. In rock society nonmembers are crushed; in deer society avoided. Kinship plays an important role in group structure. There is a well-marked division of labor.[a] Details of organization have evolved by an optimization process. The fruits of cooperation depend on conditions in the environment.

The comparison may seem facile, but from deliberate oversimplification comes complex obfuscation and unnecessary theoretification. Behavioral research will lead in this direction, as the general theory of socIogeologY predicts the features of social organizations from knowledge of population parameters and behavioral constraints imposed by the mineral constitution of the species.

Humans already mimic the behavior of rock. There is reason to believe that genetics is based on mineral processes. Consider the origin of the following types of rock in Table 1.

*Table 1. Kinds of Rock*

| | |
|---|---|
| Igneous | Is molten material that has crystallized |
| Sedimentary | Is recemented together from particles of older rocks broken down by physical and chemical weathering |
| Metamorphic | Is igneous or sedimentary rock that has been altered by temperature and pressure (in the bowels or small intestines of the earth) |

Human cells act in a manner similar to sedimentary rock. Much human behavior is sedimentary, especially related to the observation of cathode-ray tube output (television). Furthermore, humans exhibit metamorphic behavior over time or at high temperature, for instance, fever. Metamorphic crystallization involves low temperatures; sediments gradually dehydrate and the fluids eventually find their way into the hydrosphere (via water closets perhaps). This might explain human viewing patterns and couch membership. Salt[3] names this process: "This loss of fluids and cooling is known as 'aging.' Most metamorphosis occurs in ocean trenches, but it can also occur in smaller forms in trenchcoats. The lithosphere—or dermosphere in humans—wrinkles over time as a result of the dehydration process. The process is one-way, as rehydration will not unwrinkle the surface. Furthermore, rewrinkling under the California sun ..." As far as the general surface alteration goes, only the time scale differs between the results of the human expression of emotion and geological weathering.

Surprisingly, humans have a predatory relation with rock. They grow wheat in soil just born from rock. This is obvious from the similarities in composition (refer to Table 2). One kilogram of muscle and 125 grams of rock contain the same amounts of phosphorus, calcium, and iron. Humans also require trace elements of manganese, zinc, selenium, and copper, which appear in suitable proportions. Table 2 contrasts the compositions of the earth and the human body, as percentages of the whole by the number of atoms.

*Table 2. Elements of the Spheres*

| *Element* | *Anthroposphere* | *Lithosphere* |
|---|---|---|
| Oxygen | 62.1 | 60.6 |
| Hydrogen | 1.1 | 0.1 |
| Sodium | 0.001 | 0.4 |
| Silicon | 0.0001 | 20.2 |
| Aluminum | 0.22 | 11.54 |
| Carbon | 19.1 | 0.02 |
| Nitrogen | 3.22 | 0.02 |

Many elemental abundances are the same in the lithosphere and the anthroposphere. Members of both societies average over sixty percent oxygen and are equivalent in calcium and hydrogen. But, humanity has become out of balance—too much carbon and nitrogen and far too little silicon and aluminum. This instability manifests itself in many compensatory activities. Flatulence, for instance, removes excess nitrogen and sulfur in odious compounds. Colloquially speaking, farting is good. Breast implants, computer chewing, and beer can tab swallowing are unconscious efforts to correct the shortfall of silicon and aluminum. It is crucial that we emphasize the activities to achieve a better balance. Human behavior is molded by composition, which is far more important than simple genetics as a determinant.

*Tracings.* Although not an exact science, yet, SociogEology takes many cues from the etymological use of words between the two disciplines. For example, we tend to think of low, slow people as creeps or dips, reflecting their use in describing geological processes. We think of old people as fossils, recognizing the inexorable replacement of soft tissues with stone (Viagra is one instance of the acceleration of this phase change). The pool of common verbiage is prodigious. A partial list of terms may be found in Table 3

*Table 3. Etymological Clues*

| *Term* | *Geological Reference* | *Social Reference* |
|---|---|---|
| Bedding | Layering | Laying |
| Boss | Small rock mass | Supervisor |
| Cleavage | The tendency to split | Bosom, tendency to stay |
| Creep | Move slowly | Guy from under rock |
| Dike | Crosscutting rock mass | Noncrosscutting female |
| Domehead | Forced rock mass | Forced intellectual mass |
| Ejecta | Very quick movement | Uncontrolled movement |
| Fossil | Life turned to stone | Brain turned to stone |
| Permian | Old age | Old hair styling |
| Streak | Quick movement | Quick naked movement |
| Sublimate | Change from solid to gas | Dream |
| Trench | Subduct sediments | Mouth, burrow |

Furthermore there are too many physical similarities between human forms and earth forms to dismiss the link. Indeed, they are made of the same materials in approximately the same proportions. And, as figure 2 suggests, there are parallels in evolution.

*Figure 2. Origin of the Human Species*

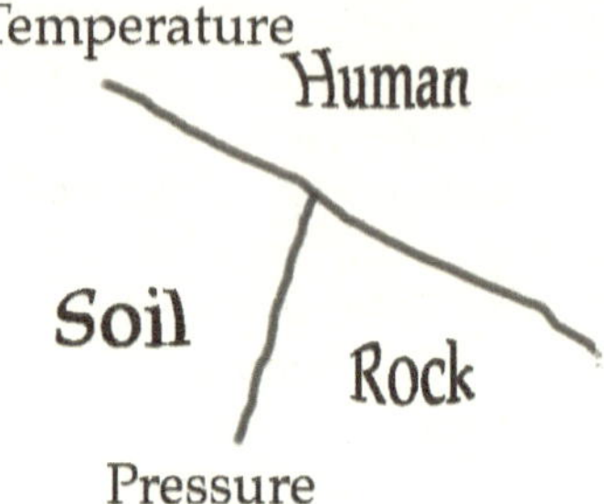


Generally speaking, there are three possible solutions for the human/mineral equation:

1. Rocks evolved from humans
2. Humans evolved from rocks
3. Rocks and humans coevolved
    a. rocks are the food source for humans (especially granules and minerals)
    b. humans are a food source for rocks

There is also a direct mathematical relation between humans and rocks (where H equals humans and R equals rocks): H = R. However, between individual particles and humans the equation is quite complex (see Equation 1).

*Equation 1. Solving for Rocks*

$$R(j) = \lim_{m \to k} \sum_{u=0}^{k} \left(1-\cos^{2m}\left(u!^{j}\,\pi / j\right)\right)$$

Only more research can dig up the facts for solving this equation. And this research is the bedrock of sOciOgeOlOgy.

There is a direct relation between human health and geology, as Grabens[4] recognized: "The health of people, as well as their color and cultural personality, is directly related to the geology of their parent rock. Thus, people living near granite have grey skins and those living near copper deposits have reddish skin. In regions where mineral content has been exhausted, human health suffers."

More than just the basis of health and life, rock provides every inspiration for culture and art. The first homes were rock caves. Stone was the source for tools. And, clay furnished materials for pots and books. Now, we build with brick, stone, and concrete.

Even our poetry is concrete. As the famous didactic poet, Gypsum

Lee Ooze writes:[5]

I am everything rock stone
I love you but
I am everything mount cone
I love you but
I am everything dust bone
but I love you ...

What evocation, what imagery, what color, what crystalline form! What magnificent rubble!

*Conclusion.* Sociogeology deconstructs the history of the machinery of learning. It identifies the adaptive significance of each feature in the environment, such as mass or shape. It details each step in material and cultural evolution. Its second great contribution to the sphere of knowledge will be to monitor the mineral basis of human behavior[b] and to predict mass movements, from landslides to flows. Let me close with a particularly penetrating insight derived from Camus: The rock should be left at the bottom of the hill, because of the inevitability of entropic direction. This is not failure, but wise acceptance of the inevitability of rocking and rolling.

*Bibliography*

Grabens. Gruss M. 1970. *Mechanical Processes in the Human Geomechanisms.* Winston: Geomedical Publications, International.

Illite, Ivan. 1911. "Picking at the Philosopher's Stone," *Mining Truth* 11:455-696.

Moraine, Esker. 1978. "Pet rocks as therapy tools," *Geopsychology Today* 10:71-72.

Ooze, Gypsum Lee. 2006. *I love You BUT—Poems for Petrified People.* Oshkosh: Petrified People Press.

Salt, Jean-Paul. 1958. *Gravel and Nothingness: An Existential Theory.* Gabrovo, Bulgaria: Gabbro Press.

*Notice*

The *Journal of Neverrepeating Results* is published by the Center for the Remote Study of Unpleasant Phenomena (CREMSUP), at Viola, Idaho 83872 (P. O. Box 1). 

The Center for the Remote Study of Unpleasant Phenomena is the research arm of Giga Geologicals, Inc. (GIGI) No apologies are tendered for the nonverifiability or nonprofitability of experiments reported. The opinions of the authors do not reflect company policy, which is set in stone.

*Footnotes*

[1] pH.d. Litmus Science. The author is with the School of Pyroclastic Philosophy at the University of Piedmont.

[2] Such as crashing together or some other strange physical mechanism (see Grabens 1970 or Salt 1958).

[3] Gravel and Nothingness, 1968, p. 76.

[4] Op. Cit. 1970, p. 134

[5] Ibid. 2006, pp. 111-497

*Endnotes*

[a] Such as it is. Things could be different in the geological world but they are not.

[b] Or antisocial behavior or any kind of mechanical behavior at all.

## The Drinking Detective

### Or Into the Furnace of Desire

(A Noire Detective Mystery)
by Race Bellows and Gina Nolan

G: She stood there like a filing cabinet with the top drawer open. I mean, she was stacked. I don't know why I was thinking of her as a metal box. Then, I put the file back and started to close the door.

R: She grabbed my hand and her mouth moughed the word help. I put my arm around her to steady us.

G: I looked deep within her violet eyes.

R: It started out as a small flame of tenderness, but I knew right away that she had a mouth full of gasoline and I was in trouble.

G: She grabbed me by the belt of my stretch-waist yellow golfing trousers, and plunged her hand in and grabbed

R: my Calva-Swartza No. 3s. Unfortunately, she still had her cigarette in her hand. As I was jumping around swatting the front of my trousers, I answered, "I'm teeing off in half an hour. What's your business?" I felt my 8-iron get heavy.

G: "I need a favor," she stated, with an enigmatic pout. "My father's been murdered. I think my lover did it—out of revenge because his wife and I were seen—"

R: "Whoa! Slow down," I said, still in awe over her twin stacks, wishing I was more of an industrialist.

G: She broke into a flood of tears like a dam collapsing from all the pressure upstream (clearcut-caused erosion most likely). She ran from the office, slamming the door into my filing cabinet and breaking the bottle of Mack Daniels over my nine-month-old files.

R: The after vision of her bobbling stacks affected me mightily. The train of life threatened to take her railroad cars far away from my steam engine. I licked a few files, grabbed my coat and followed her.

G: She was just in the hall trying to light another cigarette when I bumped into her. She bounced into the wall, dropping her lighter into her cleavage. "Let me get that," I said without thinking and reached

R: Into my pocket to get my lighter. Her cigarette had been bent. I cringed.

G: She was jumping up and down trying to dislodge the lighter. I broke my neck I think,

R: Trying to see into my pocket for my lighter. It was a Sam Snead memorial club-shaped lighter.

G: Her lighter fell to the floor and she bent over to retrieve it, her breasts fighting gravity and—

R: And I bent suddenly at the waist at a sudden pain from

G: My open lighter—Damn that was hot!

R: Just as she was standing up straight, the back of her head connecting with my nose.

G: I put my hand to nose, but forgot the lighter, and burned my bleeding nose. I said, "Snorry!"

R: Her arms pushed her breasts together as she said, "I still need that favor. Can you help."

G: "I get Fifty a day plus expenses. And I'll need to know

R: Your hat size, your father's address, and who will win the pennant."

G: "Sure, medium, 1 Wall street, Red Sox," she answered, "Can you start now?"

R: "Red Sox? Swoon as I clean up, I mean soon as I can," I wondered if I would live to regret my weakness.

G: She turned slowly and steamed her way through the door, like a ship leaving port

R: "Confess!" I yelled, inspired to see her profile as she turned in shock to answer.

G: Pale and shaken, she said, "I did it. You know? I did it?!"

R: "Killed your father?" I pursued her, like a bulldog on a scent.

G: "No, he's in Cleveland. I just made it up. I needed to be mysterious, wanted, important, threatened—" she gushed like a broken dam.

R: "Hey, there," I said suavely, "let me dry those tears." I placed my sleeve under her nose just as she sneezed.

G: I made to hold her, but slipped and started to fall, clutched her sleeve to steady myself

R: As she fell backward and parted from her dress

G: The door across the hall opened—

## Dueling Drives: A Space Opera

by Rina Radius and Rod Steel

RR: As their doomed spaceship hurled uncontrollably through the murky dust lanes of the galactic omnivores . . .

JS: Commander Backburn unhooked Corporal Pneumatic's bra, and slowly insinuated his fingers under her tight sweater, in adventurous quest of . . .

RR: Her voluptuous ports, his eyes locked in an intense gaze, but unfocused and uncoordinated. He said:

JS: "Since we're doomed to an imminent agonizing death in moments, when the oxygen runs out, why don't you submit your control board to me—let me press your buttons! Reentry! Crash land! Ungghhh!"

RR: "Captain!" she gasped, at once terrified of the prospect of not one, but two dangers, which seemed imminent, for not only was their spacecraft now spinning wildly out of control, but her own emotions, as well as those of the captain—who, up 'til this time had represented stability and an almost astronomical control, were possessed by the raging will to live.

JS: Then, when all seemed hopeless and destined to a dismal end, a voice, out of the heartless black void—the voice of ace star pilot, Rex Thruster, who, miraculously, and due to a Lorenz-Einstein time contraction, appeared almost within earshot of the spacecraft two days before he even left earth on this hithertofore-thought impossible rescue attempt

RR: "Y'all in trouble he-ah? Ah an' ma' mahty fine crew's come tuh see what we'all can do. Het?"

JS: Cpl. Pneumatic was plunged into an immediate cosmic dilemma at the sound of Rex Thruster—her Rex, and could only think of that night on earth long ago, when she had last seen him

RR: shyly rubbing his cowboy boots ($19.95 at Thom MacAnn) together as he painfully, and very slowly, blurted out his soul-consuming love for her, and how she had pulled his blushing but superbly chiseled face into her trembling bosom, and confessed that she too was not unattracted to him, and how—but that was far away on earth! And Commander Afterburner was closing in on her in the still wildly out-of-control space probe.

JS: In sudden recognition of her love for Rex she pushed the Commander from her, and with a triumphant smile, said: "Commander, are you trying to pull rank?"

RR: "Never!" said Aftershave—damn, now he couldn't remember his own name—Backburn, "I'm just trying to put out these fires, before . . . uh, before . . . uhh . . ." he hesitated, staring at the—

JS: welcome apparition in the starboard viewport—Rex. Her Rex! she thought. And he wasn't wearing his helmet—she knew she would have to act fast if his head was to

RR: stay small enough to fit through the door. Quickly, she unfastened her—

JS: microphone and said calmly yet forcefully, "Exhale, Rex, and dive in the open port." Rex, went rigid with—

RR: fear, knowing that this story had run completely out of steam … er, rocket fuel . . .

JS: Then he was there, holding her, gasping for air

RR: And holding the captain between them

JS: Despite the time contraction, parts of Rex were obviously experiencing an expansion.

RR: His nose was bulbous with blood. Cpl. P knew she had to act fast, and grabbed

JS: The port lock and closed it

RR: "For God's sake, hit the stabilizer switch!" screamed Rex.

JS: Cmdr. Backburn turned to get to the console, but

RR: He was still tanglerd between Penumatic and Thruster and the three of them tumbled to the floor. Fortunately only Pneumatic's blouse was injured, and as the three of them were mesmerized by the orbs

JS: of Mars rushing towards them, once so tiny, now so large, another squawk was heard on the com box

RR: "Press the time reversal button. Now! Now!"

JS: It was the voice of Sheila Bosenstein, the inventor of the drive and former flame of Thruster, who was frozen in shock and held motionless by the reunited formerly-attracted friends from Earth

RR: Her hand reached through the video monitor and pressed the button. "Now, let's sort out this mess," she said confidently. "Wait, who are you people?" She asked, looking at the three babies on the floor. "Oh, no, it's time to change you."

## College News
by Newton Spinks

### Northern Central New City University College

**New Departments Form!**
The university (NcNcUc) is no longer a remote ivory tower! It's a business corporation (or at least the honored handmaiden of real business, the queenly consort, so to speak, the satisfier of the needs of the businessmen who use the university for profit and pleasure, and who are we to question this new role for this hollowed institution with its distinguished academic traditions of the selfless search and teachage of knowledge?—). And as a profit-generating venture, it has to meet the requirifications of the times. It has to be independent of its old neutral stance. It has to be relevant! And, these new departments reflect that ramification.

*New Department Forms!*
Northern Central New City University College (NonCeNC) is pleased to announce that the Department of Psychology and Funerary Services announces a new academic birth to form the new Department of Death. Seriously, it is an interdisciplinary department, based on the following student needs:

1. Death is serious
2. Death is a problem
3. We need to confront and study it
4. We need to fix it.

Specific courses will include:

1. The Pornography of Dying (DD256), with pictures, tapes, videos, and scientific measurements.
2. Experimental Death (DD411), answering many questions, such as how to precipitate it, or how to profit from the inevitability of the deceasing of others.
3. Cross-disciplinary Death (DD499). Spiritual death, group death, alien mass abductions and death, cultural death, species death, ecosystem death, planetary death, universal death, death as a subject for poetry and humor.
4. Ways of Reversing Death (DD500), cinematographically as well as clinically and duplicitously.

*New Department Forms!*
The Departments of Astrological and Social Sciences announce that important new subjects will be addressed:

1. Introductory Astrology (AS100), reading the wants of the clients and servicing them with star charts
2. Quantum Astrological Dynamics and the limitations of casting horoscopes. Answering questions, such as, "If a star explodes, and no one in the forest hears it, should its position of influence count?"
3. Relativity and reading. When is it good enough to warrant a passing grade? In what frame of reference?
4. Cinematography of Male Horrorscopes. Generating genetic genres generated by gentlemanly gender and genuine genius generally with genital genomes.

The faculty has been culled from the best departments of the best schools (Notre Dame, North Dakota, Arizona, and Cal State) in the best solar systems, according to an intergalactic panel considering the most favorable aspects.

*New Department Forms!*
The University of Soma, College of Physical Culture, Physical Education, Physical Social Education, Sports medicine, Physics of Sports, Sports Philosophy, and Sports Arts and Graphics announces the formation of two new departments:

1. The Department of Push-ups will be headed by Red Ryder and offer classes to all undergraduates. Academic Requirements: One arm minimum.
2. The Department of Advanced Revenue Generation will be headed by Arthur Dentine and will try to attract more business majors and financial players.

*New Department Forms!*
After its formation, the Department of Business Biology will recruit students interested in learning how to manage the giant planetary genetic supermarket in the age of algenic marketing using advanced techniques of computer synthesis. This is a graduate department, requiring students to have degrees in medicine, biology or business (of course, unqualified wealthy students are always encouraged to apply with proof of million-dollar donation by parents). Due to the intrinsic dangerous nature of this department, it will equip its own security force with small, fallout-free, tactical, practical nuclear weapons.

*New Evening Classes Announced!*
The School, of Never-Ending Educational Specialization (SNEEZ) is pleased to announce these new evening courses:

1. Anthropology 335: Things Man was Not Meant to Know (with emphasis on women, children, animals, nature, softness, other men).
2. Anthropology 337: Things Man was Ment to Know (touching on beer, machines, toughness, stoicism)
3. Ant. 106: Men: Studies of Men doers, leaders, thinkers, and tinkerers, by other Men Biographers.
4. Psychology 232: The Psychology of Men, featuring the perception of men by other men and a few discerning women.
5. Physiology (AP550): Manliness: Where it is located, how it works, when not to use it.

**Announcement**
The Society of Future Nobel Prize Winners (SOFN) will host its next meeting with the Anticipatory Macarthur Fellows (AntMuF) next Tuesday at 6:00 p.m. in the Nobel building 301 in Macarthur park. This meeting will be a special meeting with the local Data Information Management Workers Instructional Team (DIMWIT) meeting specialists.

**Recently Published Dissertations**
We offer our congratualations to the following scholars for the finishment of their final scholarly projects with the university.

1. Joe Kilgore, DVM, for "Just Kill the Horse: Veterinary medical practices related to signage size and betting strategies at race tracks."
2. Payneta Wuffo Wilson, Ph.D., for "Advanced Typing for Minorities. Not just secretaries and stenographers anymore, but data entry clerks and Information Technology Engineering Management (ITEM) Specialists."
3. Estrangya de Kuiyper, M.S., for "The physical deformation of metals for protecting treadless tanks in warfare situations outside the laboratory."
4. Martin White, M.A., for "The Ethics of Using First-strike Nuclear Capabilities on Minority Nations."

At this point in time, go out and make your mark on the world! Congratulations! Your Northern Central education has qualified you for high earnage potentials in the global marketplace. Knock 'em dead, grads!

**Censored Lectures of Professor Peter Burnside**
Faculty of Florida University, Sebring Campus
(Winner of the 2005 FU Teaching Excellence Award)

*Lecture 4. In Praise of Plagiarism*
What is plagiarism? It is the use of a selection of words or a design claimed by someone else with the implicit claim that it is yours. Who said "Man is an ape?" T. H. Huxley? Seriously, I don't remember. If you write it in your paper, is it plagiarism? Technically, but it is too old. It has made the transition to common knowledge.

With telling stories, things were changed by the tellers. With writing, there was less corruption, and more importance attached to who said what in exactly which way. Let's say I tell you, "burning is like blossoming" and you tell your boyfriend "burning wood blooms" and he tells his mother "fire lets the wood bloom again" and she write in her journal "the fire is the wood in bloom" and later adds it to a poem that is published. Was it plagiarism?

Imagine this sequence a billion-fold, from the Mesopotamians to the Chinese and Greeks. The plagiarism of words, designs and ideas is the driving force of cultural evolution.

By the way, plagiarism is possible in biological evolution, also, now that we know that DNA can be stolen by viruses, mites, mosquitoes and other transfer agents. Is that illegal or useless? I think not. And of course, we humans plagiarize the DNA of other species when we make genetic monsters like frost-resistant strawberries.

Darwin wrote that the formation of different languages must be the same as different species. Yet, there are differences in form and transmission. The latter happens through the human brain, in our human brain space. Is there just one large brain space that we all share? We are after all a communicative species and our communication defines us.

Richard Dawkins thinks that there are units of cultural transmission, called "memes," which he defined as the unit of imitation or the "unit of cultural transmission." (and he preferred the French meme to the better Greek "mimeme" Janet, I can't get the footnote command to put it at the bottom).

Dawkins suggested as examples, tunes, clothing fashions, pot styles, and arches. But, certainly we could include domestication, agriculture, intoxication, and cities as memes also. Like genes, memes are replicators.

In the sense of cultural change over time, where some features are accumulated or lost, then cultures evolve. Some ideas, like human sacrifice, may be lost, while others, such as musical instruments, are constantly developed. Not only do the number of copies determine the success of a meme but also its appropriateness to behavior, which changes over time as ideas are taken in and made part of the body and brain.

When an idea is presented and heard, it is often corrupted in the retelling. The brain seems intent on transforming and mixing up the input (perhaps similar to Maurice Merleau-Ponty's idea of evolution as mixed-upness), rather than making an exact copy. As S. J. Gould pointed out, biological evolution is constant divergence without subsequent joining, whereas cultural evolution crosses lines and rejoins lineages (and might be more Lamarckian for that).

Are memes parasites that invade the brain and take over? Remember, parasites may be hazardous to the individual, but good for the species. Now, are they still good or bad? Cultures, and memes, are emergent qualities from human brains undergoing human communication. Neither is a parasite or program.

Writing is a relatively new medium of transmission that has created an infosphere as part of the human ideasphere. The vehicle of a meme may also be a meme vehicle. For instance, the wagon carries the idea of the wheel with it.

There are some parallels with biological evolution, especially if we use memes as the unit of transmission. Memes are still filtered by the mental environment for fitness to that environment (in this case the filters are partly due to memes). The scale of copying is related to positive feedback, as when a work of art fetches great sums of money or is written up as the result of controversy. The information that is transmitted is in-form.

Now, go out there and copy. Make mistakes, create extensions, but do not worry about ownership rights or about failing this class.

*Lecture 7. In Praise of Sex in the Classroom*

Professors are old. They need the stroking. Like Ben Franklin said, referring to elderly women as lovers, they are grateful. This gives the young student experience in physical communication and true dialogue, as well as creating and cultivating gratitude in their elders.

Undergraduates were made to be boffed. And why should all the other undergraduates do the boffing? Often professors have a greater diversity of amatory skills, not just from reading de Sade or the Kama Sutra, but as a result of necessity, when the main plunger stops working, or needs rest, and the other digits and extremities come into play, not to mention any other supplementary equipment.

Undergraduates have unrealistic ideas of romance. Marriage is an economic relationship, as with any business, in most other cultures, anyway. The best way to make these expectations more realistic is to puncture them in an academic situation, where the student is already disposed towards a learning condition.

Sex is the core of a student-monster—I mean mentor—relationship. It builds trust in a known environment with a limited understanding. By definition, it is a limited-time activity for the purpose of developing skills needed for later in life, such as in banking or insurance offices. As long as protections are employed and furniture is not damaged, then it is an innocent activity.

*Lecture 11. Creating a True Campus Commons*

All college campuses should be converted to homes for the homeless. Classes would still be held there, but the homeless would be responsible for the running of the campus. Certainly they could do no worse than the engineers, scientists and administrators, who overspend and overuse, who fail to design and recycle—wait a minute! These are the best minds of three generations, all in one place, running the campus like a third-rate losing business? I can never figure that out: The best minds still burning coal to light their bulbs. The greatest collection of intelligence, an assumption of course, but an informed one, putting up academic walls to protect their intellectual turf and requiring a special vocabularies and blinders for anyone wanting to enter their room. Even the grading system, of averaging averages of guesses to arrive at a number with two decimal places, could be better replaced by the suggestions of a homeless prostitute.

Certain areas would be used for community health, such as the vast acreages of tennis courts and playing fields, which are used only for two hours a day, exclusively for those who can afford the mountains of tuition. Other areas would be available for public meetings—even a representational democracy requires some participation by the populace and students. Regular meetings in a public place, like the community college here, would allow anyone to get involved. And once people got used to having a say in things, and used to listening to and respecting others, the quality of county decisions would only improve—

—Hey! Can't you see I'm dictating! I haven't even gotten to 'malls' yet. Oh, is it time for my medicine? Damn. Let me mark my—

**First Pages of Disquieting Journals**
by Gary Card et al.

# GreyPeace

The Magazine of Industry Activists

*Business's Obvious Agenda*
By Gary Card

Greypeace takes the flak out of being an aggressive specialist and greedy destroyer. The organization that thinks for you—and decides for you and actually lives for you! The organization that stands for the unpopular aspects of humanity: Greed, envy, violence, destruction. We attack the environment, the source of all our problems. We act to increase humanity, the species who first identified all these environmental problems and is working to correct them.

*Stay Grey!*
Diversity—colors, differences, opinions, thoughts—is the enemy. If diversity is so damn good, why is there only one planet, two sexes, one victor? Huh?

*Nuclear Power: The Solution to the Greenhouse Problem.*
By Gina Marrow
Think about it! Nuclear power is invisible. How can it hurt anyone? There are no dangerous $CO_2$ emissions. It can be used to make water safe to drink. A few dangers are invisible, but so what?

*The New Darwinism*
By Reeve Kurtus
Making the world safe for the most common denominator, humans. It is necessary to kill vicious, useless species and give the opportunity to exist to hitherforeto unborn, possibly kinder and more useful, species.

*Important Sayings*
By Harve Parts
If it does not have a price tag, then it has no value. If it has a price but no one buys it, then it has no useful value. If the price is discounted over seven years, then it has no practical value. And, if it has no value, then we do not need to save it!

*The Beauty of Gentle Garbage*
By Beverly Tone

Plastic bags, like colorful balloons, rise above
The halcyon asphalt brimming with love
And I watch my yearning soul, also, float
Wearing my new real lynx-fur coat.

*Want Ads*
Key to abbreviations

SWM Stupid Worthless male
SWF Silly Willing female
DWM Drunk While Motoring
ERP Equally Rich Person
USQ: Unknown Social Quantity

1. SWM seeks alboplasty investor with large portfolio for paper sports. Send clipped bill to Box 452.
2. SWM, mature, yet young, rich yet environmentally sensitive, serious yet superciliously playful, seeks ERP for same. No USQs need apply. Box A391.
3. SWM is available for counting club or consumption comparisons. Into conspicuous waste and littering. Box K911
4. SWM cares for you. Victor in Reagonomics looking to trickle down on your station. Bring matches and altimeter. Winnebago 5.
5. SWF seeks SWM or ERP for DWM. Box B4

# DIRT FIRST!

The Magazine for the Elite Conservators

Mergenthaler Season 1991

*Two ways to save the world!*
By Mark Fore!

(1) Make a list. No one will ever believe that you know what you are doing unless you have a list. Put things on it, such as "Save the world" or "Use less gas by coasting downhill." You do not ever have to show the list to anyone, but you must be able to say that you have a list (this strategy was used successfully by Richard Nixon and others).

(2) Remove yourself from the grid network. Pay for everything with cash. Have no food or medicine, unless you can grow it or collect it yourself. Then die quietly in the woods and let the raccoons and crows have you. Get invited to earthworm sphere.

*Greener than You*
By Stephanie Lettuce
I thought of this idea while I was in China recently. Or was it Nepal? And I was leading a deep think-tank study with a staff of many famous scholars and thinkers. There I was, in the forefront of environmental reporting, having given my ideas to many famous and accomplished people, and having written important books about how I talked with famous people about environmental problems that were unacknowledged by other famous people, although I had been writing about them for many decades, without being nearly as famous, and I had been acting on these ideas for many decades without the support of rich and famous people, that is, until I became famous, by writing about …

*Evolutionary News (Slow-breaking Stories)*
Fungus continues to make links with other species as part of its strategy to form partnerships with every living being.

Dirt's INDEX

| | |
|---|---|
| Bacteria— | 1,000,000,000,000,000,000 |
| Beetles— | 10,000,000,000,000 |
| Termites— | 16,000,000,000 |
| Cows— | 6,600,000,000 |
| Humans— | 6,400,000,006 |
| Liberals— | 73,548 |

*New Species Forming!*
Nilan Breast looks at where the evolutionary action is this week. "Clearcuts!" he says.

*Humans Create New Species*
Gina Methain is in the lab as new species are being mixed up by science. 'Wolf-mosquitoes that attack in packs.'

*Species at War!*
Martin Klok notes that we are not the first species to try to liquidate all other species and ecosystems. His in-depth analysis of those sneaky little trilobites of yesteryear exposes their grandiose evolutionary plans, derailed only after quick action by a chain of alert volcanoes.

*Solar Budget Up Again this Year!*
The solar budget is up at least a quintillion megajoules. That's $6,000,000,000,000 worth of power wasted. We aren't spending it fast enough to keep up. With the participation of every human on earth, we should be able to increase our efforts to keep pace ...

*Prediction!*
Oil Savings Depleted? Hey, we did use it all, after all. Huh. Who woulda' thought?

# FORBS Magazine

The Magazine of Busy Vegetation
Malcom Forbs, Editor and Owner
Our Motto:
"We're unconcerned! You should be, too!"

*Abbreviated Contents*

*Shocking Shortages, Part 73*
Are there enough native Americans to go around to concerned groups for celebrations about "being American?" We don't mean those diluted looking whitish kind; we mean the deep-red, broad-cheekbone varieties. Are there enough of them for advertising or business openings? What caused this sudden shortage? Can computer animation solve it?

*Victory in the Sand Address*
President G. W. Bush today awarded medals to television viewers of the war in Iraq. Congress authorized the Federal Mint for 72 years of overtime for this mass award. Special rainbow octane hearts were awarded to drivers who purchased gasoline during the months of conflict. "These people are the real American heroes," commented the President, trying to calm his stomach.

*The Greenhouse Effect is a Liberal Hoax!*
By Brent Bladderwort
Our own study, commissioned by the magazine editor Furher Forbes, of the famous Obermenshun Big Anthropic Business Institute (OBabi), shows that the earth is not getting warmer after all; the effect is really the result of the prevalence of air-conditioning. It just seems warmer when we do go outside. The reality is that "it's been cooler every year in Minneapolis," according to Jurgen Schwartz, of that Institute.

*Convenient Save-the-World Schedule Released*
By Mary Kidney
The definitive schedule for finally saving the world on time has been released by OBABI (the Orthodox Basketry and Business Institute). The study concludes that Monday Night, next year on January 11th, a normally quiet and depressed time would be best. There should be no interference with prime-time television viewing hours. So, let's get ready and finally do it right. See you next year!

*Environmental Awards: Exxon Wins Big!*

By Brent Starr

The petroleum giant today accepted FORBS Magazine's highest environmental award, the Malcome, for its pioneering efforts to clean up its restrooms and parking areas. Second place in this prestigious competition went to the Konnik Kompany for no longer mowing their lawns on a weekly schedule; their office in Tucson thought up that idea. These awards, the Malcomes, are awarded by a consortium of environmental leaders, such as Dupont, IGM, Microsoft, and Trash Management Inc.

*Recycling Contest*

By Mike O. Rizae

Friends of Urban Corporate Know-how and the Great American Industrial Association are seeking ideas on how to recycle their products in green wrappings, to get that extra advertising edge and profit incentives. Each idea will earn its suggestor $25,000 if the idea is used and saves at least $25,000,000 for the company. For more information turn to Page 62.

*How to Profit from the Pain and Suffering of Others*

By Quentin Spread

It is quite easy, if you know where to look and have a few extra dinero, to take someone's home for your little real-estate empire, by foreclosing without mercy on those temporary deadbeats. It isn't that you are not as heartfelt as anyone, but you have to take the profit when it comes …

*Why I am an Optometrist*

By Francoise Voltage

The good news is the bad news will not happen quite yet. You can still invest in weapons, clearcuts and pollution for many years to come. Of course there may be a cost, but we are pushing it back to a time when science will have a solution, so don't feel guilty and don't hesitate. We have enough time to make sure that everyone can own a fridge and a caddy!

*Why the Earth is Infinite*

By Jules Skyman

The Greeks knew that everything was infinitely divisible mathematically. And we built our civilization on Greek knowledge. So, the earth has to infinite because every division can be made infinite. And, since it is, we can use whatever we want without worrying about the burden on our children tomorrow.

*Immediate Technological Fixes*
Radicals like those Dirt Firsters! want you to believe that we have to invest millions to fix the problems that our wonderful industrial age has caused as small side-effects. Not true. Here are a series of inventions that solve these problems with very little investment by you (and none at all by the large companies!).

For example, we can add tall stacks on car exhausts to get rid of those noxious emissions, and it worked really well for the sulfur emissions in coal plants. For just $350.00 you can add this nifty little item on your private chariot.

Another small fix takes care of the community garbage problem. Just dig a deeper hole. We have the equipment now in mines all over the West to dig any size hole and fill it up and cover it. This solution is only for those who do not have access to an ocean and barges to float away the garbage.

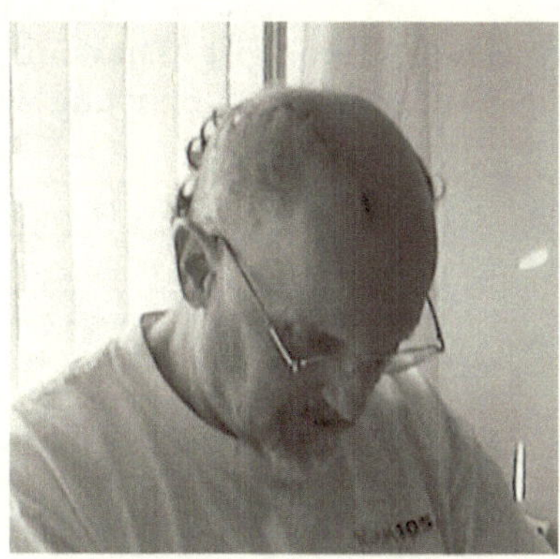

# Fan Ecology

Tracking In-house Celebrity Management Information for Over Two-Hundredths of a Century. V2 N4, 1991

*Elvis Joins Earth First!*
Far from being dead, the King is out ripping up survey stakes, nailing trees, and shaking up the business establishment.

He says: "I just had to go underground. Too much was happening. People were becoming addicted to destructive, self-destructive, and eco-destructive behaviors. I went on a diet—the grow-it-yourself-don't eat-much diet. A real eye-opener. Now, I'm back to help others. Don't let these bib-overalls throw you off. It's me, and I'm still the King. "

In a rare personal interview, Elvis regretted misleading his hundreds of thousands of fans and ecologists. Fortunately, his early investment in supermarket tabloid stock, as well as in Fountain-of-Youth pills, has tripled his wealth to many hundreds of billions—all of which is going to other species as cash (depending on the size of the animal and the depth of their pockets).

*Prince Benefits Earth*
"I wanted to benefit those who were working to help the poor and the environment. They need help and support, too. And, that's what this concert is all about—helping the poor rich!" Prince crowed.

He will also produce the first $60-million retro-eco feature, *The Silent and The Dead,* about spraying a freeway median strip. Madonna will play the young Rachel Carson (Ann-Margaret takes over after 40). The movie will costar Kevin Costner as Forester-writer Aldo Leopold, Michael J. Fox as Animal expert Michael W. Fox, Don Knots as George Bush Sr., Christopher Lloyd as Activist-Philosopher Arne Naess, John Candy as radical ecologist Alan Wittbecker, and Ernest Borgnine as Rex the Wonder Biologist. Shooting will start soon.

## About the Authors

*Peter Burnside* is a professor at a small college on the west coast of Florida. He does not practice what he preaches. He is a volunteer with the Nature Conservancy and the Defenders of Wildlife.

*A. M. Caratheodory* was born at the time of the largest solar eruption ever recorded—a fact he discovered when he became interested in astronomy. After basic schooling in Virginia, he attended the University of Virginia at Charlottesville, where he studied astrophysics. His work on mathematical models of stars received awards from NSF, NASA, USN, USAF, Goddard Institute, Bausch & Lomb, among others.

He works as a consultant for an observatory in Chile, where he is also a forest activist in the Beech forests of Tierra del Fuego. Finding that his experience followed Auden's prescription for poets, he has written in poetic, as well as scientific, forms. He continues to work hard to keep to the dictates of Novalis to be a good poet. He is the author of *Fragments* and *Wild Apples.*

*Gary Card* was a volunteer for numerous environmental organizations, during the time when he lived in the hip pocket of a large chemical corporation. He figures that one set of efforts cancelled the other set. His hobby is playing guitar in a band, 'Joe and the Rebels,' wherever they can get gigs, except at Rockerfellers or Heat in Bradenton, or playing bluegrass.

*Asia Deer* is a veterinarian working in a raptor rehabilitation program in Pullman, Washington. Her hobbies are traveling and writing with her friend Mao.

*Jim Gear* is a househusband in Sarasota, Florida. Also trained as a geologist, his long history of layoffs has allowed him to acquire supernatural skills as a cook and laundry cleaner. He is a one-day-a-week bartender at the local Road House. When not performing his duties, he is an amateur observer of wildlife, such as the Florida panther.

W. *H. Gauss* is a mathematician working with the American Mathematical Society in Providence. He started writing after a broken leg forced him to sit still.

*Yulalona Leelannee Lopez* has a degree in astrophysics from Harvard University. To earn a living for the past ten years, her vocation has been investing in commodities; she lives in Grants Pass, Oregon. Her avocation is saving places and cultures, working through The Nature Conservancy, Cultural Survival, and other groups.

She writes as a passion, to persuade others to her views. She explains: "Mostly, when I read other poets, I think that they didn't study enough astronomy, didn't get their knees scratched trying to follow earthworms, haven't caught cold watching it snow on their hands, haven't shaped their body to the bole of a tree or crawled along a deer path through thickets—bend or become still or small. I want to speak to these nonhuman experiences." She is a founding member of the Palouse Poets Collective and a contributor to Nieman Ryan Community Designs.

*Merissa Nieman* is an artist and poet working out of Portland, Oregon. Although mostly retired, she consults in book design for numerous east cost publishers. Her book designs range from Ansel Adams and Michael Connelly to *MAD* magazine. Some of her make-up art, which she invented with A. M. Caratheodory one rainy day after a Nordstrom's sale, has been used by Calliope Press for book covers and illustrations. She has degrees in English and Design from Ringling School in Sarasota. She has two cats, Hank-Ra (part mouseboy part god) and Kabumi (suddenly present).

*Violet Reason,* obviously a name used to protect a reputation earned in a different field of activity in the mainstream of the unstoppable machine, says that anything else you need to know about her can be found through her writings. She is author of *Cheap Visions* and *Retreads*.

*Ruadh dal Riata* is a naturopathic physician and one of the first ecosystem doctors, a field he developed in the 1970s. His hobbies are sailing and running. He is the author of a novel, *Monsters,* based on this story.

*Marcus Ryan* was an astronomer with several observatories in Hawaii, Arizona, and Mexico, including the Steward Observatory. His specialty was the mathematical modeling of main sequence stars; his hobby was climbing trees near the observatories and studying the wildlife. He is an author of and contributor to numerous publications. Now retired, he writes editorials, articles, and novels on a wide variety of topics. He is the author of *The Thesis*, *Lucifer Re*, and *Two Diaries*.

*Brice Rosenbee* is a free-lance educator (read unemployed) living in Palmetto, Florida, where he is available for odd jobs in the food service industry and as an adjunct professor of Economics. He has regularly put his retirement funds into the lottery in expectation of a more certain outcome than with Enron or United Airlines. He drives a 1967 Austin Healy.

*Race Bellows and Gina Swift* are the pen names of Rod Steele and Rina Radius

*Rod Steel and Rina Radius* are the pen names of Abe McDermit and Annie McDermit. Abe is a freelance carpenter in Azalea Oregon. Annie is a fireman for the county, formerly a librarian for the City of Glendale. They both work on stream and forest restoration projects in Oregon.

*Newton Spinks* is an artist living in Venice, Florida. After he retired as a machinist with a small company that made clean-room equipment, he started to learn more about the ecology of the gulf coast. His insights into the operation of local colleges comes from his evening classes at three of them.

*Benjamin Turnaday* was an anthropologist with the legal firm of Grosshans, Dupke and Oralen. His specialty was forensic investigation. He was a volunteer in his community with a local Children's clinic, the library, Humane Society, and other organizations. He had one wolf, five dogs, three cats, one snake, one eagle (temporarily), and seven adopted children. A veteran of the US Air Force, his hobbies were piloting airplanes and sky-diving.

*Crawford Washington* is a lawyer for a Hillsborough County children's social program. He was in the Peace Corps in Africa in the 1970s teaching English and learning culture. He helps his friends run their ranch in western Florida, becoming proficient in riding and herding. His avocation is fishing, and he has the pictures, hats and vests to prove it.

*Cam Woulfe* is a computer programmer with a large eastern corporation that changes its name every five years as it is bought to be dismembered by more profitable corporations. He was in the Peace Corps on a Pacific island, where he taught computing. He has two daughters who look more like his wife than him. He plays with art programs for fun. His art has been exhibited at galleries in the US and Canada.

*Shameful Acknowledgments*

The following stories have been rejected before. In order to reduce the list below one hundred pages, only the first rejection is mentioned:

**The Comedy of War and Uncertainty**
The Hecathlon, *Sports Illustrated* et al.
Five Imperfections, *The Atlantic Monthly*
The Drug Clinic, Harper & Row et al.
Grocery Cart Wars, Little Brown et al.
Monsters, *Transition* et al.
Judge Vandergelt's Decision, *Palouse* et al.
Parapurgerno, *New Yorker* et al.

**Life and Death of the Animal Soul**
Blaming Artemis, *Forestry* et al.
Going East, *Travel Magazine* et al.
Bluebirds, *Snapdragon* et al.
Famous Irish Bars, *Al-co-hol* et al.
The Mouse, *Kenyon Review* et al.
Masks, *Sewanee Review* et al.
Nothing, *Playboy* et al.

**The Tragedy of Science and Certainty**
Astrophysical Golf, *Playboy* et al.
The Science of Figitology, *Harper's* et al.
Sociogeology, *Windrow* et al.
The Drinking Detective, *Ellery Queen* Magazine et al.
Dueling Drives, a Space Opera, *Asimov's* et al.
College News, *National Lampoon* et al.
Censored Lectures of Professor Burnside "[*Untitled*]" et al.
First Pages, *Mad* Magazine et al.

## *Colophon*

This book is set in Palatino
using Indesign
on a Macintosh G5
in the coastal village of Cortez
near a cedar hammock
in the southern temperate zone
during a cool spring
between scrub jay surveys.

Photographs of B. J. Turnaday by Gina Maretti,
Merissa Nieman, and Calpurnia Woulfe
Back cover photo from U.S. Passport
Back cover painting by A. M. Caratheodory
Make-up drawing of masks (p. 233)
and Front cover watercolor by Merissa Nieman

Book and Cover design by Rian Garcia Calusa

*"Art is metaphorical. It is 'as if' the dream was true, as if the hidden reality was exposed and described. Art enables people to act as if they were animals or gods. Masks enable people to become other things, animals or gods."*

From "Masks" by Benjamin Turnaday

www.ingramcontent.com/pod-product-compliance
Lightning Source LLC
LaVergne TN
LVHW091035080826
845145LV00002B/504

* 9 7 8 0 9 1 1 3 8 5 3 9 7 *